"I didn't reenlist. I'm li... now."

"You shouldn't have done it for me," he said.

She stiffened and took a step back. "I did it for *me*."

"I'm sorry. I didn't mean to make assumptions. It's just that..." He paused, trying to backpedal and not having much luck. "Then why are you here?"

She flinched as if he'd struck her.

Damn, he should have handled that better. "I didn't mean to be a jerk. I guess my mood is only slightly better than it was the last time you saw me."

"You can say that again." She arched a brow then slowly shook her head.

"I owe you an apology for that day, too. But keep in mind that I'd just gotten the worst news of my life."

"You were also loaded down with pain medication, which can really take a toll on your thought process." Her down-turned lips slowly curled into a pretty smile. "So you're forgiven."

As she took the place beside him, she said, "I came to tell you something."

"What's that?"

She bit down on her bottom lip and paused for the longest time.

Finally, she said, "I'm pregnant."

A Texas Soldier's Ready-Made Family

USA TODAY BESTSELLING AUTHOR

JUDY DUARTE

NEW YORK TIMES BESTSELLING AUTHOR

TINA LEONARD

Previously published as *The Soldier's Twin Surprise*
and *The Cowboy SEAL's Triplets*

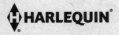 **HARLEQUIN**®

Recycling programs for this product may not exist in your area.

ISBN-13: 978-1-335-97692-5

A Texas Soldier's Ready-Made Family
Copyright © 2020 by Harlequin Books S.A.

The Soldier's Twin Surprise
First published in 2018. This edition published in 2020.
Copyright © 2018 by Judy Duarte

The Cowboy SEAL's Triplets
First published in 2015. This edition published in 2020.
Copyright © 2015 by Tina Leonard

This edition published by arrangement with Harlequin Books S.A.

For questions and comments about the quality of this book, please contact us at CustomerService@Harlequin.com.

Harlequin Enterprises ULC
22 Adelaide St. West, 40th Floor
Toronto, Ontario M5H 4E3, Canada
www.Harlequin.com

Printed in U.S.A.

CONTENTS

Since 2002, *USA TODAY* bestselling author **Judy Duarte** has written over forty books for Harlequin Special Edition, earned two RITA® Award nominations, won two Maggie Awards and received a National Readers' Choice Award. When she's not cooped up in her writing cave, she enjoys traveling with her husband and spending quality time with her grandchildren. You can learn more about Judy and her books on her website, judyduarte.com, or at Facebook.com/judyduartenovelist.

Books by Judy Duarte

Harlequin Special Edition

Rocking Chair Rodeo

Roping in the Cowgirl
The Bronc Rider's Baby
A Cowboy Family Christmas
The Soldier's Twin Surprise
The Lawman's Convenient Family

The Fortunes of Texas: All Fortune's Children

Wed by Fortune

The Fortunes of Texas: The Secret Fortunes

From Fortune to Family Man

The Fortunes of Texas: The Rulebreakers

No Ordinary Fortune

Visit the Author Profile page at
Harlequin.com for more titles.

The Soldier's Twin Surprise

JUDY DUARTE

To my son, Jeremy Colwell, who serves as a medic in the United States Army. I'm so proud of you and all you've accomplished. You make this mom army proud.

Chapter One

If Captain Clay Masters hadn't been so focused on the sexy brunette wearing a red bikini, he might not have been nailed in the head by a spiraling football.

Damn. He glanced at his old high school buddies, both of whom were laughing like hell, and then he retrieved the ball.

Over the last thirteen years, he'd stayed in touch with Duck and Poncho via email, texts and occasional phone calls, but they hadn't spent any real time together since they'd all gone off to college. But you'd never know that. The moment they got together last Saturday in the baggage claim area of the Honolulu airport, it seemed as if they'd never gone their separate ways.

Now here they were, spending their well-earned vacation time on Oahu's North Shore. The surf season had ended weeks ago, so the beach was secluded and nearly empty, other than the three friends and the petite brunette stretched out on a towel on the sand.

Poncho nudged Clay's arm and nodded toward her. "She sure is rocking that red bikini."

He had that right. Clay hadn't been able to keep his eyes off her ever since she set out her towel on the sand. And when she'd applied her sunblock? He'd been tempted to ask if she wanted his help.

But he hadn't come here to hit on the first woman he saw. He wanted quality time with his buddies. Once they arrived, he'd traded in his flight suit for board shorts and flip-flops. He hadn't even bothered shaving the past two mornings, which gave him a shadow of a beard. And instead of answering to sir or Captain, he'd reverted to the nickname he'd earned as a star quarterback at Wexler High—Bullet.

"Remember what I told you when I picked you up at the airport," Clay told his buddies. "This week, I'm just a good ol' boy from Texas, soaking up the sun and enjoying the surf."

"We heard you," Poncho said. "But hell, Bullet, maybe you should reconsider and proclaim your military status. Just look at her."

Clay *had* been looking. She was stunning, with long brown hair and a body shaped to feminine perfection.

But ever since he'd gone to West Point, he'd been assigned to a military installation. And it hadn't mattered where he was stationed, there were always plenty of local women who wanted to latch on to a military man, particularly an officer, for the bragging rights. And the benefits package wasn't bad, either.

That didn't mean Clay hadn't had his share of romantic flings, but whenever he left the base, he usually kept his Army status under wraps.

"She looks lonely." Poncho nodded toward her. "I'm going to talk to her. Maybe she'd like to join us for a cold beer."

Duck laughed. "Just leave it to me, y'all. I've had more luck with the ladies than either of you."

"Maybe so, but she doesn't strike me as being your type." Clay stole another glance at the bikini-clad brunette. "She doesn't look like a buckle bunny or a rodeo queen."

At that, Poncho gave Duck a nudge. "Don't get carried away, man. She's got her eye on Bullet. I've seen her stealing peeks at him every so often."

Clay had noticed that, too, which was more than a little tempting. But he wasn't about to desert his friends, no matter how gorgeous a lady was. "Come on," he said. "This isn't supposed to be a week of nights on the prowl. We're here to relax and have fun—with each other. So are you going to stand around gawking at our neighbor or play ball?"

Poncho snatched the football from Clay's hands, and the game picked up right where they'd left off. But like before, Clay had a hell of a time keeping his focus on throwing passes. Or catching them.

"Hey, Bullet." Poncho slapped his hands on his hips. "You're lagging, old man."

Clay shook off his hormone-driven thoughts, realizing he'd gotten sluggish. So he threw a hard spiral to Poncho, who dropped it. "Ha! Look who's lagging now."

They continued to toss the ball, but how was Clay supposed to keep his mind on the game when he couldn't keep his eyes off the sexy brunette?

Finally, he decided to throw in the towel. So he called a time-out to his friends. "I'm ready for a cold beer." He was also ready to start the grill.

As his buddies trudged through the sand to the place where they'd left their stuff, two other young women, a blonde and a redhead, arrived at the shore and began setting out their ice chest and towels.

"What do you know," Poncho said. "Looks like we have company. And if Duck and I play our cards right, we could all get lucky tonight."

Poncho and Duck might be willing to sidle up to the newcomers, but Clay was still drawn to the olive-skinned brunette who could've modeled for the latest *Sports Illustrated* swimsuit issue. Not that she was doing anything especially sexy or alluring. Hell, she was just reading a book.

"It's clear that Clay has scoped out the brunette," Poncho said, "which is fine by me. I've always favored blondes. That is, unless Duck wants to arm wrestle me for her."

"No problem," Duck said. "I'll take the redhead."

"Okay, guys." Clay folded his arms across his chest. "What if they're not interested?"

"Oh, they're interested. They keep looking over here and giggling. But you'll have to work a little magic on the brunette." Poncho chuckled. "Something tells me you've gotten a little rusty at laying on the charm."

"I've still got the touch. There are some things a guy doesn't forget." But Clay wasn't in the mood for romantic fun and games tonight, especially if his friends struck out with the new arrivals. In fact, he had half a notion to go back to their rented beach house, open a cold one, turn on the TV and hang out inside. Alone.

"While you light the grill," Poncho told Duck, "I'll lay a little *buenos días* on the lovely twosome and invite them to our barbecue." Then he glanced at Clay. "What are you waiting for? Go offer the brunette an invite. Or would you rather I lay a little groundwork for you first?"

"I don't need your help." Clay stole another glance at the brunette. Chances were, she was on vacation, too.

Oh, what the hell. He supposed it wouldn't hurt to talk to her. Maybe she'd be interested in the cowboy type and in sharing a night they'd both remember—long after they each went their own ways.

Sergeant Erica Campbell lay on her back, her open historical romance novel held up to shield her eyes from the sun's glare while she read.

Earlier this afternoon, she'd noticed the three hotties who'd been splashing in the water and playing football on the shore. The one called Bullet had glanced her way, and when their eyes met, he tossed her a big, Texas-size grin. She meant to ignore him, but he seemed so boyish and charming that she couldn't help returning his smile.

All three of them were attractive and well built, but Bullet either spent a lot of time at the gym or had a job that required strength and vigor.

His light brown hair was short, much like his friends'. Water glistened on his broad shoulders. Six-pack abs and a taut belly drew her undivided attention like a sharp, crisp salute. Now there was a real hunk. And a drop-dead gorgeous one at that.

But the last thing she needed to do, especially this weekend, was to give someone the idea that she wanted company. So she quickly averted her gaze, reached into her small tote bag for the spray bottle of sunblock and applied it. Then she lay back down on the towel and reached for her novel.

Male laughter erupted yet again, drawing her from her story as it had several times since she'd come outside her rented beachfront bungalow to catch a few rays. As much as she'd wanted to ignore the three men who were sharing the same stretch of beach with her, she found that next to impossible. Two of them had a slight southern drawl, and she suspected they were Texas natives, just as she was. One of them also appeared to be Latino. So was she, although she couldn't speak a lick of Spanish.

Their short haircuts suggested they might be in the military. That wouldn't be unusual. There were quite a few bases located on the island.

She made it a point to avoid men stationed on Oahu, even though that wasn't easy. Men often approached her, even when she was in uniform, and tried to hit on her. So the bikini she was wearing today was a little risky, since it might draw even more attention to her.

It's not that she was stuck-up or prudish, but she'd witnessed firsthand how deployments and conflicting duty assignments could take their toll on a relationship, especially when both people were in the military.

She loved being stationed in Honolulu. She didn't much like being downtown in Waikiki, though. It was too much like other big cities. But the North Shore, as far as she was concerned, was paradise on earth.

Again, she glanced at the handsome tourists. They seemed to be in their late twenties or early thirties. And they shared a playful camaraderie she found interesting.

Listening to their conversation, she'd picked up on their nicknames. She and her sister Elena had done the same thing, calling themselves Rickie and Lainie when they were girls. She wondered if they would have continued doing that until adulthood. Probably. They'd been so close. And for the most part, they'd only had each other.

As the guys teased each other about a dirt-bike crash that resulted in Bullet getting a gash in his head and Poncho puking at the sight of blood, she realized they'd grown up together. That they'd been friends for a long time.

She wished she'd kept in contact with some of her high school friends, but when she enlisted nearly six years ago, she'd lost touch with them. Not that she hadn't made new ones. It's just that the Army had a way of shaking things up with regular deployments or reassignments.

Again, the three laughed at something that had landed them in detention, further convincing her that they were high school buddies who'd come to Hawaii on vacation. Not that it mattered. Erica wasn't here to gawk at hot guys. She was here to think, to regroup and to kick that shadow of guilt she felt as she grieved for her adoptive parents.

She'd cried when she'd gotten the news of the accident and then again at the funeral. She'd loved them. How could she not? They'd rescued her from the foster care system when she'd been in the third grade.

Still, it had taken a long time for her to bond with the couple. But that was probably due to the hospitalization and the death of her twin sister that same year. Now there was a crushing loss that had struck hard, leaving a void that would never go away.

Needless to say, the Army was Erica's family now. And in a couple of months, when her contract was up, she'd eagerly reenlist without giving it a second thought.

She'd just reached an especially steamy part of her novel when a shadow crossed her face, drawing her from the heated love scene. She assumed the sun had passed behind a cloud until a man cleared his throat.

Startled, she glanced up. When she spotted one of the guys standing over her, the hottie she'd heard them call Bullet, she slammed the book shut and set it aside with the cover facedown. Her cheeks, already warmed by the sun, as well as the words on the page, heated to the boiling point.

Talk about getting caught red-handed—or rather red faced! Had he realized she'd been in the middle of a love scene?

"I'm sorry," Bullet said. "I didn't mean to surprise you or interrupt your reading."

She sat up and combed her fingers through her hair. "You have nothing to be sorry about. That book wasn't very good anyway. I was just about to throw it into the ocean."

"I could do that for you," he said. "I've got a pretty good arm."

"So I noticed. I assume that's why they call you Bullet."

His lips quirked into a crooked grin, and he gave a little shrug.

Arrogant guys were a real turnoff. Usually. But she loved football and found this particular quarterback intriguing. But there was no way in hell she'd hand over that blasted book to him. And even though she'd claimed otherwise, it had been a great story, one she intended to finish, although that wasn't going to happen this afternoon.

Neither of them spoke, and as he studied her, she felt vulnerable. And half-dressed. If her swimsuit cover-up was handy, she'd slip it on now.

She blamed the self-consciousness on that damn love scene, but in all honesty, Bullet wasn't making it easy to forget the words she'd read. The bare chest. The heated kiss. The hand slipping into the slick, silky folds...

"You on vacation?" he asked.

She rarely shared intimate details about herself with strangers, but the guy seemed like a friendly sort. So she nodded and said, "Yes." She had to report at the base before midnight on Sunday.

"My buddies and I are checking out on Sunday morning," Bullet said.

She used her hand to shield the afternoon sun from her eyes. "I noticed your accents. Are you guys from Texas?"

"Yep. We grew up in Wexler. It's in south Texas, about two hours from Houston. Ever hear of it?"

"Actually, I have. I was born in Houston and went to high school in Jeffersville, which is about fifty miles from there."

"No kidding? Small world."

"In some ways." But it could be a great big world, too. And lonely.

Bullet swept a muscular arm toward the water. "How 'bout that ocean? Ever see anything that blue?"

"It's amazing, isn't it?" In fact, that's why she spent a lot of her free time at the beach on the North Shore.

"You here with friends?" he asked.

"Not at the moment." She glanced at the two women sitting together on a blanket in the sand. It might be nice to have someone with her today, someone to offer solace and a diversion. But she didn't.

"Just spending some alone time?" he asked.

She didn't see a need to reveal that she was staying by herself this weekend, although she was pretty damn good at defending herself—with a gun or in hand-to-hand combat. "I have two vacation days left,, so I rented that bungalow behind me."

"That makes us neighbors." Bullet nodded toward his friends, who'd stopped playing and now stood with their hands on their hips, talking to two other women who'd just arrived. "We're staying in the house next door."

She'd already come to that conclusion, but she didn't comment.

"We're going to be grilling brats and hot dogs," Bullet added. "And we've got plenty of beer on ice. Sodas, too. We even have a bottle of vodka and some OJ. You're welcome to join us."

Erica looked at his buddies, her gaze returning to Bullet, her attraction growing by leaps and bounds.

"Just so you know," he added, "my friends and I are nice guys. Trustworthy and honorable. Especially Poncho. His day job is driving a squad car down Wexler's main drag, keeping the residents safe."

One of them was a police officer? She hadn't expected that.

Erica was usually skeptical of flirtatious men, but something told her Bullet was honest. And that she'd be safe with the three Texas tourists.

So in spite of her plan to spend the rest of the day and evening alone, she agreed to join them.

"We'll be starting the grill soon," Bullet said. "How does an ice-cold beer sound?"

Every bit of common sense she'd ever had prompted her to say that she'd reconsidered, that she was going to pass on the barbecue after all. She wasn't especially fond of hot dogs. But the loneliness and grief were getting to her, so she felt compelled to say, "Sure. Why not?"

"I'll bring a beer over to you," he said. "Unless you'd

prefer a soda or mixed drink? I could make you a screw-driver."

"Actually, the beer is fine."

"You got it." Then he turned and walked away, gracing her with a view of his broad shoulders and swim trunks that rode low on narrow hips and outlined a great pair of glutes. Dang. The guy had a heart-stopping swagger.

Moments later, after she'd shoved the novel into her tote bag and brushed out her hair, he returned with two ice-cold longnecks and handed one to her. She looked at the label. It was the Longboard Island Lager, made by the Kona Brewing Company. Apparently, these guys wanted the whole Hawaii experience.

"Mind if I sit here?" he asked.

"Go ahead." She moved the ice chest, making room for him to sit beside her on the towel.

Instead, he chose the sand. She appreciated the humble move. She hated it when men tried to push boundaries. And the fact that Bullet seemed a bit shy and cordial was a bit of a turn-on.

Who was she kidding? It was more than a little al-luring.

She took a long, refreshing drink. It had taken her a while to get used to the taste of beer, but after some time in the Army, she'd come to enjoy it after a hard day in the field.

"Tell me something," she said. "Honestly. Is Poncho really a cop?"

"Yep. In fact, he was just promoted to detective."

"I suppose he looks more like an authority figure in his uniform."

Bullet laughed. "I don't blame you for being surprised. Poncho used to be the rowdy one who led me and Duck astray, but once he turned twenty-one, he shocked the entire town, if not the high school, by joining the Wexler Police Department."

"And Duck?" she asked. "Is he in law enforcement, too?"

"No, he'd rather be a lawbreaker."

"Seriously?"

Bullet chuckled. "Maybe back in our high school days, but not so much anymore. Actually, he's a rodeo cowboy. And a good one."

She tended to be skeptical by nature, especially of men she'd just met, but Duck had a soft Texas twang and a lanky, muscular build. Of course, looks could be deceiving. Yet something in Bullet's eyes suggested he wasn't giving her a line of bull.

"What about you?" she asked, more curious about Bullet than the others.

He didn't answer right away, then offered her a charming smile that dimpled his lightly bristled cheeks and made him appear both rugged and boyish at the same time. "Let's just say that I can outride, out rope and outshoot both of them."

That surprised her, although she wasn't sure why it would. And he'd admitted that he was a better cowboy than the others, which just might be true. At least he hadn't bragged about the number of silver belt buckles he'd won in the rodeo.

Erica had pretty much outgrown the type of guys she'd known as a teenager back in Jeffersville. Nevertheless, she found Bullet far more attractive than she should.

"How long will you be in Hawaii?" Bullet asked. Erica wasn't about to reveal too many personal details with a guy she'd just met, no matter how hunky he was or how trustworthy she thought he might be. But then again, she didn't see any reason not to be somewhat honest. If she kept the story simple, he wouldn't have enough information about her to find her again—if he turned out to be a jerk. He didn't need to know that she was stationed in Honolulu for the time being.

"Actually," she said, "I just flew in from Houston." It was the truth, of course. And it supported her comment about having two days left of her vacation. But she'd actually just returned from bereavement leave.

Several weeks ago, she'd gotten an early-morning call from the Texas hospital where her parents had been taken after the accident. Her father had suffered a massive coronary while driving home from church. The car had crashed through a guardrail and rolled down an embankment. He was pronounced dead on arrival, and her mom died from her injuries a few hours later.

Erica sucked in a deep breath and slowly blew it out. It had been a long month, a sad and lonely one. She'd gone to Texas to bury the parents who'd adopted her.

But the worst was past. She had two days left of her leave before she had to report to duty at Schofield Barracks, so she'd rented the bungalow through Airbnb, where she hoped the warm sun, the soft tropical breeze and the sound of waves lapping on the sand would provide a healing balm.

She and Bullet sat there awhile, both caught up in their own thoughts. Or so it seemed.

"What's your name?" he asked.

She could have told him anything at that point—Jennifer, Heather, Alexis. She'd heard that it was a game some women played. They'd create fake careers and backgrounds, too. But Erica wouldn't go that far. Instead, since he and his friends referred to each other with nicknames, she'd offer him one, too. The one her twin sister had given her years ago. "My name is Rickie."

He nodded, as if making a mental note, then took a chug of beer. Since he hadn't offered up his real name, she didn't ask. What was the point? She didn't expect to see him after she checked out and returned to base.

It was weird, though. She hadn't been called Rickie since the night Lainie had gone to the hospital for the surgery that failed. At the memory, at the thought of the final words they'd shared with each other, a pang of grief shot through her, reminding her that she'd lost her entire family. Two of them, in fact. Not many people could claim to be orphaned twice, but this time around, at twenty-five, it was a lot easier than when she and Lainie had been eight.

Under the circumstances, she probably should keep to herself tonight so she could dwell on her emotions and come up with a good game plan to face the future. Wasn't that why she'd come to North Shore this weekend?

For someone determined to keep to herself, she couldn't explain why she'd let herself be enticed by the hunky, football-playing tourists. Maybe it was some sort of coping mechanism preventing her from dealing with her own issues, her own sadness.

If she could distract herself with the antics of a trio of strangers reliving their glory days on the beach, then she wouldn't be forced to think about her recent loss.

But she'd much rather laugh than cry. And these guys were playful and entertaining. Intriguing and handsome. Especially Bullet. Besides, she didn't have to tell him that she was in the Army and actually lived nearby.

Why get so personal when, after Sunday morning, she'd never see him again?

Chapter Two

By the time the sun went down, and a couple of automatic porch lights from the nearby beach house kicked on, Clay's buddies had moved closer to the blonde and the redhead. But Clay was right where he wanted to be, sitting on the sand and enjoying a second cold beer with Rickie. Things seemed to have clicked between them, which was a little surprising.

He hadn't planned to hook up with any women this week, but he also hadn't expected Rickie to be so easy to talk to. She was a little on the quiet side, but she was bright. And her laugh, which he'd only heard a time or two, had a mesmerizing lilt.

Hey. The night was still young…

Of course, that didn't mean he wasn't being realistic. She'd be returning to her life in Texas soon, and after he drove his buddies to the airport Sunday morning, he'd head back to Wheeler Army Airfield. Still, that left them thirty-six hours. More or less.

"Are you ready for another beer?" he asked.

She looked at her nearly empty bottle. "No, I think I'll switch to soda—if you have any left."

Clay got up, headed for the ice chest and retrieved two cans—one cola and a lemon-lime. Then he took a moment to walk to the grassy area near their beach house, where Duck had set up the small grill about fifteen minutes earlier. The coals were coming along okay.

He glanced over at his buddies. Duck, who'd just said something to make the redhead laugh, glanced up and caught Clay's eye. Clay nodded at the grill, gave him the thumbs-up sign and returned to Rickie.

He offered her both cans. "Take your pick."

She chose the cola. "Thanks."

"We'll be putting those dogs on the grill soon," he said. "Are you getting hungry?"

"A little." She scanned the beach, her gaze landing on the others, who'd moved over to the grassy area, near the grill and within the perimeter of light coming from the porch. "You know, even though I said I'd join you guys tonight, I'm not really in the mood for a party."

Neither was Clay. In fact, he'd rather sit here all evening, enjoying what little time he and Rickie had left. "Why don't I bring over a couple of hot dogs for us once they're cooked?"

"That'd be nice. Thanks." She made a little hole in the sand, one big enough to hold the bottom of her can. Once she set it down, she turned to him and blessed him with a pretty smile. "So what was it like growing up in Wexler?"

"I doubt it was much different from your neck of the woods. I lived on a ranch, though. So I had a lot of chores to do each day, plus a cow to milk and a couple of chickens to feed."

"That's cool. I never had any pets."

Clay wouldn't call an old milk cow or four harpy hens pets.

"Do you still live in Wexler?" she asked.

"No, after high school I moved on." He nearly added, *to bigger and better things*, but there was no reason to share his West Point experience. And his military career was still off the table.

"Do you miss it?" she asked.

"The ranch? No, not at all." He didn't consider himself a small-town boy anymore. He was a soldier now. And Army proud.

"When I was in high school, I lived on a quiet street in Jeffersville," she said. "The houses were all two-story and pretty similar, except we were the only ones who had a pool in our backyard. Actually, I guess I still have one."

The comment struck him as a little odd. "So you live with your parents?"

"No, they both passed away recently. In a car accident. So the house belongs to me now."

"I'm sorry. That must have been tough."

She shrugged. "It was, but I'm dealing with it."

He was about to say something, but the shadow that touched her gaze passed faster than a ghost, so he let it go at that. He didn't want to stir up any sad memories for her.

Apparently, she didn't want to dwell on them, either, because, after a couple of beats, she asked, "Does your family still live on that ranch?"

"My mom does. My dad died when I was young.

When I was a teenager, she and I moved in with my paternal grandfather and my step-grandmother."

Rickie turned toward him, her knee drawn up and bent, her hands clasped around her shin. "Tell me about her."

"Who? My mom?" He hadn't seen *that* coming.

"Yes, I'm curious about her. My real mother died when I was really young, so I never had the chance to know her."

"I thought you said your parents died recently."

"They did. I was orphaned the first time when I was eight and then adopted when I was nine." She cast a glance his way. When their eyes met, she seemed to reel him into her story. Into her life. "My adoptive mother was good to me, but she wasn't very maternal. At least, not the way I imagined a mom should be. Know what I mean?"

Not really. But he nodded just the same.

"I'm not complaining. It's just that I had a super-cool foster mom once." She seemed to brighten from the memory, rebounding easily, which was a relief. Clay didn't like the sad, pensive look that had touched her expression a few moments ago.

Hoping to prolong the happier thoughts, he asked, "What was cool about her?"

"Pretty much everything." Rickie's smile deepened, her mood transformed. "Her name was Mama Kate—at least, that's what we called her. I have no idea how old she was. Probably in her sixties. She was heavyset with an easy laugh and a loving heart. She never turned down a kid needing placement, so her house was packed with children. Yet she always found special time for each of us. And she was a whiz in the kitchen. She made the best meals—healthy and tasty at the same time. And her cookie jar was always full."

Clay's mom was a good cook, too, although she didn't do much baking anymore. At least, he didn't think she did. It had been a long time since he'd seen her face-to-face. They talked on the phone, of course. Usually on Sundays. But he didn't go home too often. Just for Christmas—and only if he wasn't deployed or stationed too far away.

"How long did you get to live with Mama Kate?" he asked.

"Not long enough."

She didn't explain, but Clay sensed a sadness about her. Without a conscious thought, he reached out and placed his hand on her bent knee, offering his comfort and support. Or maybe he just wanted an opportunity to touch her.

"It sounds like Mama Kate set a good example for you," he said.

Rickie smiled, and this time, when their eyes met, something warm surged between them. If he didn't know better, he'd think they'd made some kind of emotional connection, one that might linger indefinitely. But they really hadn't. How could they? They'd just met. And they'd never see each other again.

Yet the longer they sat in the soft glow emanating from the porch lights, the more surreal the evening seemed. Sure, Rickie was just as pretty, just as sexy as ever, but there was so much more to her. And if she lived around here...

But she didn't.

Reluctantly, he removed his hand from her knee. "I grew up without a father, but my granddad tried to set a pretty good example for me. He was tough as nails, but he also had a soft side."

Again, she smiled. "So you grew up with a lot of love."

"Too much at times."

Her brow furrowed. "What do you mean?"

"My mom was one of those helicopter parents. She hovered over me, hell-bent on keeping me safe, close to home and under her wing."

At that, Rickie drew up both knees. Her smile deepened, sparking something in her pretty brown eyes. It felt pretty damn good to think that he'd done or said something that had caused her pleasure. But for some reason, he didn't want her to get the wrong idea about him or his mother.

"You might think that's cool," he said, "but you have no idea how tough it was to live with a mom like mine. Our relationship was pretty strained most of the time, which caused me to rebel every chance I got."

Rickie cocked her head to the side, causing her curls to tumble over her shoulder. He was tempted to reach out, to touch, to see if they were just as soft as they looked. But this time, he kept his hand to himself.

"In what ways did you rebel?" she asked.

He thought for a moment, wanting to choose the right example to share. For some dumb reason, he didn't want to tell her about the time he and Duck got caught drinking Granddad's Jack Daniel's behind the barn. Or when he and Poncho lit up cigars in the old lot near the ball field and set the dried grass on fire.

"When I was just a little kid," he said, "maybe four or five years old, my grandparents came to visit. It was right before Halloween, and Granddad's wife made me a purple superhero cape to go with my costume. Even days after I'd gone trick-or-treating, I wore that silly thing all the time. And whenever I'd see my mom standing at the kitchen sink and gazing out the window, I'd climb one of the nearby trees and jump out of it. I knew I couldn't really fly, but I'd pretend to. And my mom would really freak out."

"Surely you don't blame her for doing that. You could have broken your neck."

"Yeah, I know. But she used to hit the roof about a lot of things. And the older I got, the more protective she seemed to get. I can't tell you how many camping trips I missed because she couldn't go and didn't want to let me out of her sight." Clay took a sip of his cola, wishing he'd gotten another beer instead.

"I'm surprised she let you play football," Rickie said.

He laughed. "I grew up in Texas. We love high school football."

"You're damn straight," Rickie said. "*Friday Night Lights* and all of that. Did your mom go to your games?"

"Hell, she sat in the front row for every single one. And once, when I was sacked especially hard, she ran out on the field to make sure I was okay. The coach had to tell her to back off and return to the bleachers."

Again there went that pretty, heart-strumming smile that lit her honey-colored eyes. "Your poor mom."

"Maybe so. But she would have been better off having a girl." One like Rickie, who would have enjoyed baking cookies with her or sitting in a cozy chair reading story-books. A girly-girl who wouldn't mind sticking around the house all day instead of messing around with the guys and getting ready to jump on any wild-ass idea that Clay or his friends thought would be fun and exciting.

"Hey, Bullet!"

At the sound of Poncho's voice, Clay looked over his shoulder to see his buddy manning the grill. The ladies had moved over to the grassy area, too. And from the looks of it, the evening's festivities had begun.

"The hot dogs are just about ready," Poncho called out. "Come and get 'em."

"I'll bring a couple of plates back for us," Clay told Rickie.

When he returned, one plate was loaded with hot dogs. The other held a couple of paper cups filled with condiments.

"Oh my gosh." Rickie laughed. "Who do you expect to eat all of that?"

He shrugged. "I thought you'd want more than one."

"No, I'm not very hungry—or a big fan of food that comes wrapped in a bun."

He handed her the empty plate. She took it, then reached for a hot dog from the stack. When he sat beside her, this time sitting on the edge of her towel, he asked, "So what kind of food *do* you like?"

"Anything served in a tortilla."

"Tacos and burritos, huh? I like Mexican food, too." Clay reached for a hot dog, just as Duck turned up his iPod, which he'd programmed with all his favorite country-western tunes.

"Ooh," Rickie said. "I love Toby Keith."

"Me, too. Apparently we have a lot in common."

"We do?"

Clay nodded. "We both grew up in small Texas towns. And we like football, Mexican food and country-western music."

"That's true," she said.

Rickie was a girl after his own heart—at least for the

rest of the weekend. He was batting a thousand when it came to finding things to like and admire about a woman he wasn't ever going to see again.

Yet that didn't matter. Not on a night like this. Maybe it was the tropical breeze, the moonlight glistening on the water or the soft sounds of a sultry ballad that played in the background.

Hell, maybe it was her. Or just him.

Whatever it was, the air was filled with sexual promise.

A glance at his buddies proved that. They'd already formed couples.

Had Rickie noticed? Was she feeling it, too?

As another tune began to play, something alluring and suggestive, Clay cut a glance at Rickie and tried to read her mood. She was still seated, but she'd closed her eyes and was gently swaying to the music.

Clay got to his feet, and when she looked up at him, he held out his hand. "Dance with me."

Her lips parted, and for a moment, he thought she was going to decline. But she surprised him by slipping her hand in his and letting him draw her to her feet, away from the light—and the others.

Clay couldn't believe his luck. He'd wanted to get his hands on Rickie ever since he first laid eyes on her, and now he was dancing with her in the sand.

She felt so good in his arms. Their swimsuits left little to the imagination and didn't provide much of a barrier, so he held her skin to skin.

The coconut scent of her sunblock mingled with the tropical fragrance of her shampoo, something floral. It was an interesting combination. And intoxicating.

Her breasts, soft and full, pressed against his chest, and her cheek rested on his shoulder. But they weren't just swaying to the music, lulled by the beat. There was a lot more than that going on. Pheromones filled the night air, and his hormones were pumped and at the ready.

He ran his hands along her back and over the tiny bow she'd tied to hold her bikini top in place. It wouldn't take much to remove it. Just a little tug on one of the strings.

It might be a tempting thought, but it wasn't one he'd put into action. Instead, he continued to caress her sun-kissed skin until he came dangerously close to the small piece of red fabric that barely covered her lovely backside. It took all he had to refrain from moving lower, from stroking her…

Watch yourself, man. Don't ruin the moment.

He wished it would last forever, but it wouldn't. Minutes from now, the last chords of this song would fade. Then they'd return to where they'd been sitting in the sand. Or maybe Rickie would say good-night and leave him out here alone.

If that happened, he'd deal with it. Like they said, all good things must come to an end.

And then they did. All too quickly. The music that followed the love song had a lively beat, one that lent itself to a Texas two-step. Something better suited for a crowded dance floor on a rip-roaring Saturday night than a moonlit tropical beach.

Rickie was the first to draw away, breaking their embrace and dashing the romantic mood—until Clay took a close look at her face in the soft amber glow of a distant porch light.

When she looked up at him and smiled, his body

hardened with desire for her, and he damn near stopped breathing.

"What do you think?" she asked. "Should we take this inside?"

"Good idea."

Granted, she might only be suggesting that they go indoors, turn on her favorite playlist and dance in private, but right now, with his hormones raging, he'd follow her anywhere.

She took him by the hand, led him across the grass and to the front of the bungalow. After opening the door, she stepped inside and flipped on the light switch. He followed her in.

He still wasn't sure what she had in mind until she crossed the room, headed for the sliding glass door that provided a beach view and drew the shutters, securing their privacy.

Apparently, they were both on the same page. He scanned the single room that provided a sitting area, a kitchen and a double bed. It was small, but nice. Clean and cozy.

He took a moment to check out the simple island decor, the framed surf posters, a watercolor of a sailboat on the high seas, a display of conch shells on a shelf near the wall-mounted television.

"This place is pretty small," Rickie said, "but big enough for me."

She'd implied earlier that someone might join her here. He suspected she hadn't wanted him to think she was all alone. But apparently, she felt comfortable with him now.

She closed the distance between them and studied his face, his mouth. She lifted her index finger and wiggled it at him. "You have a smidge of mustard on your lip. Do you mind if I...?"

He probably ought to be embarrassed and swipe his hand across his face to remove any smears or brush off a lingering crumb, but he longed for her to touch him. "Go ahead."

She placed her finger against the side of his mouth and gave it a little rub. If he had anything there, it wasn't much.

As her hand lowered, he reached for her wrist and held it firm. "I'm not sure where this is heading, Rickie, but I know where I'd like it to go."

She gazed at him for a couple of beats before tossing him a breezy smile. "Looks like we're both in agreement."

He could have swept her into his arms right then and there, but it wasn't that easy. He released her wrist. "There's only one problem. I don't have any condoms."

She bit down on her bottom lip and furrowed her brow, apparently stymied by their dilemma.

He supposed they could walk into town and look for a drugstore. But that was going to put a big damper on the mood.

Suddenly, she brightened. "I just remembered. I have one in my overnight bag."

"Then we're in luck." And not just because of the condom. Rickie was a sexy little package, and he was glad she was prepared.

"I've had it for a while," she confessed. "I don't make a habit of inviting men home."

He believed her. And somehow that made tonight even more special. He opened his arms, and she stepped into his embrace. As she wrapped her arms around his neck and pressed their nearly naked bodies together, he cupped her jaw and drew her lips to his.

The kiss began sweet, but within a heartbeat, it deepened. She opened her mouth, allowing his tongue to mate with hers, dipping, twisting and tasting as if they were so hungry they'd never get their fill.

He let his hands slip along her neck, to her shoulders and down to her waist, where he stroked her skin and explored her curves. When he reached her breast, his thumb skimmed against the red fabric, across a taut nipple, and her breath caught. A surge of desire shot right through him. With one hand still kneading her breast, he used the other to reach around to her backside, cup her bottom and pull her close, against his erection.

She pressed back, rubbing against him and heightening his arousal until he was tempted to lift her into his arms and carry her to bed. But before he had the chance, she ended the kiss.

"I'd better go find my tote bag. We're going to need that condom." She strode across the room and to the sofa, where a blue canvas bag rested, and reached inside. Moments later, she turned to him with a smile, holding the small packet like a prize. "Got it!"

Silently thanking whatever island god was looking out for them, he took her by the hand and led her to the bed. She placed the condom on the small nightstand. Then she reached behind her back, removed her skimpy bikini top and dropped it to the floor. As she peeled off the tiny bottom piece, his gaze never left her.

If he'd thought she was gorgeous before, he found her flat-out breathtaking now, standing before him in all her naked glory. Feminine perfection at its finest. And tonight, she was his.

Following her lead, he slipped off his board shorts, then joined her on the double bed and eased toward her, determined to please her and to make sure she wouldn't have any regrets in the morning. He sure as hell wouldn't. Not when their chemistry was off the charts.

She reached for the packet and handed it to him. He tore it open. Once he'd protected them both, she reached for his erection, opened for him and guided him home.

Okay, not *home*. That sounded too permanent, too lasting. This was a temporary relationship, a fling, one that was as short-term as a beachfront vacation rental. Here today, gone tomorrow.

He shook off the stray thought as he entered her. As he thrust deep, her body responded to his. She arched up, matching the tempo, creating their own.

As she reached a peak, she cried out and let go. He shuddered, releasing with her in a sexual explosion, their very own display of fireworks. He almost wished the rush could last forever—

No, *not* forever. This was just a one-night deal—or, hopefully, two. He'd have to make a drugstore run first thing in the morning and purchase a box of condoms. They'd never have the time to use them all before they said goodbye on Sunday morning and went their own ways. But after what they'd just shared, he suspected they'd need quite a few.

Erica never slept with anyone on the first date, let alone the first *meet*. But she'd been through a lot in the past month, suffered a tragic loss. And for some crazy reason, she'd wanted to feel a connection to another human being. To be held. To be…

Well, she didn't expect to find love or anything like

that. But she'd thought it would be nice to feel liked, valued and appreciated.

And wow. She'd gotten so much better than that.

She wasn't a virgin, but neither would she consider herself to be sexually experienced. That was, until tonight. Bullet had taken her to a place she'd never been before—and one she feared she'd never go again.

She felt beautiful. Special. Adored.

Their lovemaking had turned her world on its axis—in a good way. While basking in his arms during a stunning afterglow, she'd been able to forget the funeral, the grief, the meetings with her parents' attorney, the house that needed a slew of repairs before she could sell it or find renters.

But more than that, she'd found herself reevaluating the future.

Not her decision to reenlist, of course. That wouldn't happen. She'd found strength and courage in the Army. She also had a sense of pride in herself and her accomplishments. There was no way she'd go back to Texas and to the small-town life she'd once known.

But that didn't mean she couldn't see Bullet again. Maybe visit him sometime. She might even be able to spend her next leave with him in Texas.

Of course, she had no idea how he'd feel about seeing *her* again after this weekend. Either way, a future together didn't seem likely. Not many men would want to follow their wives from base to base.

Okay, so she was putting the proverbial cart before the horse. Their heartbeats had barely slowed to normal, and they'd yet to say a word about what they'd just done, let alone discuss what might come next.

So she continued to lie with him, cuddling in bed with

their legs entwined. But she wasn't ready to move, unless it was closer to Bullet.

When he pressed a kiss on her brow, she finally spoke. "That was amazing."

"I couldn't agree more."

She'd hoped he'd say that, although she had every reason to believe he felt the same way she did.

"I could stay here forever," she said, then wished she could reel in her words. She hadn't meant to overstep or to imply something that might frighten him off. So she added a bit of a disclaimer. "I meant stay here on the North Shore. In this cute little bungalow. And if I didn't have to go back to work, I'd stay in bed with you."

He stroked her shoulder, which suggested he hadn't let her comment bother him.

What would he say if she suggested they meet up in Texas in the near future? She could take personal leave so she could find renters after the handyman had made the repairs to the house. Up until now, she'd planned to hire a property manager so she wouldn't have to do it herself.

Still, if she oversaw things on her own, she could look up Bullet. Would he be up for something like that?

He said he no longer lived on the family ranch in Wexler, but he hadn't mentioned where he lived now. So it might not work out the way she thought it would.

Actually, there was a lot she didn't know about him. It hadn't mattered earlier, but it did now. She supposed they'd have to talk about stuff like that.

She glanced at the clock on the nightstand. Did they have time for that kind of discussion now? Or should she let it go until morning? She propped herself up on her elbow and glanced over Bullet's shoulder to get a better look.

Apparently, he must have realized what she was attempting to do, because he asked, "What time is it?"

"Almost twenty-one hundred."

He stiffened. "What'd you say?"

"I'm sorry." She sighed softly. "Military time comes naturally to me."

He didn't respond right away, but the muscles in his arm seemed pretty tight.

"Were you in the military?" he asked.

"Actually, I still am." She supposed it wouldn't hurt to lay her cards on the table, to have that little talk now. "I'm going to make a career of it. Why?"

His biceps twitched. "Something tells me we just came to a place where the old don't-ask-don't-tell line would be appropriate."

Uh-oh. Now it was her turn to stiffen.

"What branch of the service are you in?" he asked.

A sense of foreboding crossed her mind, and her heart hammered in her chest as if trying to break through her rib cage. "I'm in the Army."

He inhaled deeply, then slowly blew it out. "Where are you stationed?"

"Schofield Barracks. Does that matter?"

"It might."

Oh, for Pete's sake. Surely he wasn't in the Army, too. If so, was he stationed in Texas? But wait, that's not what he'd said. Was it?

She rolled away and practically shot up in bed. Then she folded her arms across her chest and turned to him. "You lied to me. You're not a cowboy from Texas."

"I grew up on a ranch in Wexler, and I've ridden plenty of horses over the years. But I never claimed to be a cowboy."

"So you're in the Army, too?" she asked, dreading the response.

"Yeah, I am. And apparently, I wasn't the only one to withhold some details over the last few hours."

"I *am* on vacation," she said. "But only until tomorrow night, when I have to check in at the base."

Bullet sat up and scrubbed his hand over his hair. *Please don't let him be an officer.* It was against regulations to fraternize.

That sense of foreboding grew, casting a shadow over her. Over them.

"What's your rank?" he asked.

"You go first."

Bullet swore under his breath. "I'm Captain Clayton Masters. I command a Black Hawk squadron on Wheeler Army Airfield. And you're…?"

Rickie blew out a sigh, plopped back down on the mattress and placed her hands over her face. "Sergeant Erica Campbell—enlisted."

What rotten luck. Her lover wasn't a cowboy from Texas. Nor was he a tourist on vacation.

Instead, he was a Black Hawk commander. An officer in the US Army.

And they'd just fraternized.

It hadn't been intentional. And as long as they didn't do it again, she supposed it was no big deal.

"I guess we screwed up," Bullet said. "Ah, no pun intended."

She blew out a weary sigh. "Big-time. If I'd known who you were, I never would have invited you back here."

"And if I'd known who *you* were, I wouldn't have come."

"I never expected more than one night anyway,"

Rickie said, although, just moments ago, she'd begun to hope for more. To wonder how they could possibly pull that off. "So no harm, no foul. Right?"

"That's what I'm thinking." Bullet—or rather, Clay—raked a hand through his hair. A military cut, she now realized.

Damn. Should she call him *Captain*? After what they'd done, that felt awkward.

"I guess we really are neighbors," he said, as he got to his feet and reached for his discarded board shorts.

"That's about the size of it." Wheeler Airfield was just across the street from Schofield Barracks.

Rickie figured she'd better get dressed, too, and climbed out of bed. Rather than put on her swimsuit, she rummaged through her suitcase and pulled out a green T-shirt and a pair of black shorts. She wouldn't bother with a bra or panties.

"What's your MOS?" he asked, referring to her military occupation specialty.

"I'm a sixty-eight whiskey."

"So you're a medic."

"I work at a clinic unless I'm sent out for training ops." And those often began on Wheeler, especially when she and her unit had to fly out to the Big Island. Damn, what a disappointing—not to mention *awkward*—mess this was turning out to be.

She slipped into her clothes, covering herself quickly as if they could pretend none of this happened. But good luck with that. The sex had been too damn good to forget.

"I suppose that means we could run into each other."

True. So far, she hadn't been on any missions with him, although she could. The Black Hawks usually flew soldiers out to the Big Island, where a lot of training took place. And since he was the commander of a squadron, it could happen in the future.

Yep. Definitely awkward.

"You know," he said, "we can't do this again."

She wasn't stupid, although she felt like it. "I've never done this before—made love with a guy I just met. This was just…one of those things. So I wasn't expecting any more than one night."

"Neither was I."

She stole a glance at Bullet. Or rather Clay. They hadn't actually lied to each other. They'd just withheld information that would have helped them avoid doing something like this.

"Are Poncho and Duck in the military, too?" she asked.

"No, they're actually civilians visiting me. And I took a week off to stay with them. I didn't mean to trick you…"

At this point, she figured it didn't matter. But for some reason, it did. "I wasn't trying to pull the wool over your eyes, either. I flew in from Houston last night and don't have to sign in until tomorrow night. I didn't see any point in sharing my life story."

Although, to be honest, she wished they still had one more day together. But it wouldn't be right.

"Well," he said, nodding toward the door. "I'd better get out of here. Otherwise, I'd be tempted to climb back into bed."

She smiled, clinging to the admission like a compliment.

"I wish things were different," he added.

So did she. Their chemistry was off the charts. At least in bed. And before reality struck, she'd been ruing the thought of going back to her barracks and him flying back to Texas. But this was different. Worse.

So close, yet so far away.

She managed an unaffected smile. "I guess I'll see you around."

He stood in the center of the room for a couple of beats, as if he was struggling with reality and ethics and everything else. "Take care."

"You, too." Rickie watched him walk toward the door.

While it was possible they'd run into each other again, she hoped not. It would be awkward at best. Not to mention disappointing.

But an officer fraternizing with an enlisted soldier was against Army regulations, and since she wasn't about to make any changes to her career plan, their short-term affair was officially over. Wham, bam, thank you…sir.

Chapter Three

After Bullet—or rather, Captain Masters—walked out the door and told her he was returning to the beach house he and his friends had rented, Rickie felt an unexpected loss. She realized the best game plan and her only option was to avoid him like a bad case of mono sweeping through the barracks. So without waiting for the sun to rise, she packed her bags and checked out of the bungalow a day early.

When she reached her car, a twelve-year-old Honda she'd purchased when she first arrived on the island, she took one last look at the darkened beach house where Clay was staying. She didn't see any lights on inside. Apparently, she was the only one who'd lost sleep over their lovemaking, and that only served to make her feel worse and more determined to escape.

Yet even though leaving now meant she could avoid

Clay while here on the North Shore, there was a real possibility that she'd run into him in the future.

Which was why, when she got back to Schofield Barracks, she began to constantly scan her surroundings whenever she went to the PX or any other place where she might see him and tried to mentally prepare for an awkward meeting.

Oddly enough, when she didn't spot him, she'd go back to her car feeling both glad and disappointed.

While Rickie worked at the clinic each day, a steady flow of soldiers came in, each one presenting different ailments and injuries that kept her busy, and she began to think she might have put it all behind her. That was, until she finally spotted Clay two weeks later.

She was in her car, preparing to cross the street from Schofield Barracks to Wheeler Airfield, where the clinic was located. While waiting for the traffic light to turn green, she noticed him up ahead, standing near the curb and talking to several other uniformed soldiers. They all bore a similarity, but she recognized Clay instantly. There was something about him, a mesmerizing swagger, that made him stand out in a crowd.

The moment he looked up and zeroed in on her car, her breath caught, her heartbeat stalled.

He turned away from the men and studied her so intently that she realized he hadn't put that night behind him, either.

But so what? There wasn't anything either of them could do about it now. So she gripped the steering wheel tight until the light turned green. As she drove past him, she gave a slight nod and continued on her way.

Three days later, while parking in front of the clinic to start her shift, she caught sight of him again. He was jogging along the street wearing a black T-shirt, Army-issue shorts and running shoes. Apparently, he was finishing his morning PT. She expected him to keep running, but he surprised her by turning off the path he'd been following and crossing the street to approach her car.

With his light brown hair mussed and damp with perspiration, he was a vision to behold. He'd shaved this morning, which revealed a professional side to him. A military side.

She reminded herself of his rank, of the serious consequences they'd face if their one night together turned into a second and a third. The first time they'd made love had been a mistake, a misunderstanding. But there was no way they could continue to see each other.

Yet she couldn't keep her eyes off his sweat-dampened T-shirt, which clung to his muscular chest and his taut abs. As he closed the short distance between them, her pulse thundered, matching the cadence of his steps, and when he slowed to a stop, her heart rate darn near skidded to a complete halt.

"Hey," he said. "How's it going?"

"Fine." She managed to tear her gaze away from his body, but she couldn't seem to get her pulse under control. "I'm doing okay. How 'bout you?"

"I can't complain." He nodded toward the clinic entrance. "So you work here, huh?"

"Yes, I do. And I assume you live nearby."

"Yep, just a couple streets away." He glanced to his right, and then to the left, as if checking for eavesdroppers prone to gossip or tattle. When they both realized the coast was clear, he said, "I wish things could be different."

He'd made that same comment after they'd made love

and realized they'd have to go their own ways. And she'd replayed his words a hundred times over the past couple of weeks, convincing herself that he'd meant everything he'd ever told her that night. "I wish things could have played out differently, too, but that's just the way it is."

He nodded his agreement, yet rather than end the conversation and go about his business, he continued to stand there, hesitant. Gorgeous. And temporarily stripped of rank in those running shorts.

"Have you already reenlisted?" he asked.

His question struck her as odd. Was he wondering if she'd decided to opt out of the military? Was he reminding her in a roundabout way that she could change her mind?

If she did, they could continue to date. Was that what he was getting at? Maybe, but she wouldn't take that risk. The Army was her family, and if she gave it all up, hoping that something might actually come of an affair with a man she barely knew, she'd end up in worse shape than she was now. At least, emotionally.

She'd learned early on—and the hard way—that the people she cared about didn't stick around very long, so civilian life wasn't an option.

"No, I haven't reupped yet, but I plan to do it soon. They're going to give me a signing bonus." She nodded toward the Honda that had seen better days. "Then I'll be able to buy a new car."

"Good for you."

She thought so, too. Yet for some reason, as she continued to study Clay, as she remembered lying in his arms, she didn't feel all that lucky. But she couldn't let that sway her. There were more important things in life than momentary pleasure.

"I like being in the Army," she added. "And I love my job."

"That's good. Apparently, you made a wise career choice when you enlisted. Being a medic is obviously a good fit."

He was right. She'd scored at the top of her class while in school at AIT. And she'd been told many times that she was a top-notch medic. She thrived on being needed. And she appreciated the praise from Captain Nguyen, her commanding officer.

"I've wanted to work in the medical field for almost as long as I can remember," she said. "In fact, I'm going to get a nursing degree one of these days."

"That's admirable. I had a childhood dream to become a soldier, like my dad."

She smiled. "Mine started when I was a kid, too. My twin sister, Lainie, suffered from several medical problems when we were little, and I used to look after her the best I could."

"You have a twin?"

"I used to. She died when we were nine."

He frowned, compassion filling his eyes. "I'm sorry."

"Thanks." She sighed. "It was tough. She passed away during open-heart surgery. And it was about that time that I decided to be a nurse or a doctor. I wanted to do something to help people who were sick and injured."

"So why did you decide to join the military?" Clay asked. "You could have gone to nursing school as a civilian."

Again his questioning took her aback. And now it was her turn to look to the left, and then to the right, checking for eavesdroppers.

There was no one around, thank goodness. But even

if there were, so what? They were just having an innocent conversation.

"I took a health class in high school, which was really interesting, and that locked in my decision to have a
career in the medical field. I didn't want to take out any
student loans, so I decided to join the military. My father was a retired ensign in the Navy, and he hoped that
I would follow in his footsteps. But I chose the Army
instead, became a medic and ended up stationed here."

He nodded sagely, as if that answered all the questions
he had about her and about…their situation.

"Well," he said, as he glanced toward the street and
the path on which he'd been running, "I guess I'd better
let you get to work."

He was giving her an out, an excuse to end their conversation. And she really ought to take it, but it still left
her a little uneasy, not to mention disappointed. She'd
never feel Bullet's hands caress her again.

No, *not* Bullet. *Captain Masters.* She wasn't even supposed to call him Clay.

"I'll see you around," he said.

She supposed that was a given. And their future run-
ins were sure to be uncomfortable, but there wasn't much
either of them could do about that now. So she offered
him what she hoped was a casual smile. "Take care."

"Will do." Then he turned and jogged away, leaving
her to stare after him and rue all that might have been if
their circumstances had only been different.

As Clay ran along the side of the road, he had a growing compulsion to look over his shoulder and catch one
last glimpse of Rickie, but he forced himself to focus on

the path ahead. He'd known that they'd probably see each other again, and sure enough, they had.

He could have ignored her and pretended that they'd never met, but he wouldn't do that. He might avoid making commitments, but he wasn't a jerk. He was respectful to his ex-lovers.

And what a lover she'd been. She had a fiery passion that had turned him inside out, and he doubted he'd experience anything like that again. He'd never been one to rate the women he'd dated, but she'd get a gold star.

She looked a lot different this morning than she had the day he'd met her, when she'd been wearing that sexy red bikini. And later that evening, when she'd been naked, lying next to him in bed.

Of course, now that they'd been intimate, he'd find her just as beautiful dressed in battle fatigues and combat boots. He had a feeling that, each time he saw her, he was going to be tempted to do more than greet her and have a friendly little chat.

And that was the problem. In the past, he'd never had any trouble moving on when a fling was coming to an end. He'd always been able to keep his hormones in check. But he wasn't having an easy time of it now. For some weird reason, he couldn't seem to shake off his thoughts of Rickie.

There seemed to be something different about her, something that drew him to her and made him want to challenge military protocol when it came to fraternization.

He wouldn't cross any lines, though, even if he still had a dormant rebellious streak. When he'd been a footloose kid in Texas, it used to flare sky-high. He'd also thrived on the adrenaline rush—much to the chagrin of his mother, who'd been determined to keep him safe.

The poor woman had really flipped out when she learned he'd been accepted for admission at West Point. But what had she expected from a kid who'd grown up idolizing his late father, a decorated war hero who was still held in the highest esteem by everyone back home?

You'd think she would've been proud that Clay had decided to become an Army officer, but she'd cried for days, sure he'd be sent off to war and would die in battle, like his father had.

He'd told her that he understood her worries, but he felt a strong conviction to serve.

"There are lots of ways you can help people. You could be a doctor or a fireman or a teacher."

"Most mothers would be proud that their kid was accepted at West Point."

"I am, honey, but why couldn't you have gone to Texas A&M?" she'd asked. "That way, you would have been close to home. Then, after graduating with some kind of an agriculture degree, you could have helped your granddad and me on the ranch."

But Clay had never wanted to be a rancher.

Even his wild, fun-loving friends had followed his lead and turned onto a straight and narrow path. Duck was now a champion bronc rider, determined to help the Rocking Chair Rodeo promote a ranch for retired cowboys, as well as Kidville, a nearby group home for kids. And Poncho had become a cop who did his best to keep the town of Wexler safe.

Of course, considering the jobs the three buddies now had, they were still hooked on the rush when faced with danger or the unknown.

With each stride Clay took, running away from the clinic where Rickie worked, voices from the past hounded him.

Rules were meant to be broken.

When he reached the corner, about fifty yards from the clinic, he jogged in place and waited for the light to turn green. But within a couple of beats, the compulsion to look at Rickie became too strong to ignore.

He glanced over his shoulder, but she was no longer standing outside. Then again, he really hadn't expected her to be. By now, she had to be inside working. Out of sight.

Untouchable.

Off-limits.

Yet memories of their amazing night together hit him hard once more, and temptation stirred his blood. He'd give just about anything to make love with her again. But he wouldn't cross the line.

He might have been a rebel while growing up, but he played by the rules now. He had to, no matter how badly he wanted to see Rickie again.

There was also something more than military regulations holding him back, preventing him from doing something stupid that would screw up his career.

Sergeant Erica Campbell was a professional. A medic and a dedicated soldier. She loved her job, too. And she'd made it clear that she had no intention of giving it up.

And neither would he.

For the next few weeks, Rickie went about her usual duties, which kept her mind busy during the day. Nights, however, were a different story.

She'd lost count of the number of times she'd dreamed

about a romantic evening on the beach, slow dancing with a handsome cowboy, resting her cheek against his broad, muscular chest, hearing the gentle thumps of his heart and relishing his charming Texas drawl.

Then she'd wake up to reality.

She had no business dreaming about Captain Clay Masters now, let alone sleeping with him back then. Sure, it had been an easy mistake to make and one that was explainable, if they were ever questioned about it. Intellectually, she knew that. But tell that to the memory that continued to batter her heart.

She'd never believed in love at first sight, but it seemed as if she'd experienced more than a memorable orgasm that night. Apparently, there'd been an emotional connection, too. If not, then why would that evening continue to play out in her mind whether she was awake or asleep?

Heck, here she was, wrapping up the last hour of her shift at the clinic and daydreaming about the guy again. She couldn't seem to catch a break.

As she passed by the supply cabinet, her commanding officer called out, "Erica? Can you give me a hand?"

Rickie turned to Captain Veronica Nguyen, a petite brunette who was a physician's assistant—and probably the best the military had to offer. Not only was she a sharp diagnostician, but she had a great bedside manner.

"What's up?" Rickie asked.

"I have to suture a patient, and the injury is a bit complex. Will you assist?"

"Of course." Rickie appreciated having the distraction.

As they walked toward one of the exam rooms, the captain slowed her steps and pointed to the bulletin board that hung on the wall. "Oh, that reminds me. I'm taking leave on Friday. My grandmother is in the hospital and isn't doing well, so I'm going to fly back to the mainland to visit her and to check on her myself."

"That's too bad," Rickie said. "I hope it's not serious."

"Me, too." The captain pointed to the calendar. "Yesterday afternoon, I marked off the days that I'll be gone, but I didn't get a chance to tell you. Captain Schwartz is going to cover for me."

"No problem. I'm sure we'll be okay." Rickie glanced at the red line that stretched through the following week, and a troubling thought crossed her mind.

She counted backward to the day she'd met Clay on the North Shore and then to her last period.

Uh-oh. She was late. And she'd always been regular. Could she be...?

No, that wasn't possible. They'd used protection that night.

Of course, things had been pretty heated. They might have gotten a little reckless while caught up in passion. Also she'd had that condom for a long time. Had she kept it past the expiration date?

Cut it out, Rickie. You're letting your imagination take flight.

There had to be another reason for skipping a period. Nerves and stress could do a real number on a person's health and their hormones. This was probably just a fluke. Or a miscalculation of some kind. That would explain it.

Yet she couldn't deny that it was possible. She could be pregnant. And if she was, having a baby was going to be a real game changer in terms of her future plans and goals.

Oddly enough, as unsettling as that reality might be,

a quiver of excitement built. If she were to have a child, a son or daughter to love and care for, she'd have a family again.

In time, she might have handled the losses fate had dealt her fairly well, but she'd been devastated when Lainie died, and to this day it felt as if a large part of her heart and soul was missing.

Maybe that's what was going on. Rickie wanted to be part of a family so badly that her psyche was playing a trick on her and her body was going along with it. She wasn't pregnant. She just wanted to be so she could have someone to love.

But there would be plenty of time to have a baby in the future—when she was married and had a house to bring her little one home to.

So she shook off the stray thought and hurried to the exam room to assist Captain Nguyen. She even managed to get through the last hour of her day without dwelling on the possibility that she and Clay had conceived a baby.

That was, until she walked out to her car and spotted him again. He was wearing a flight suit and headed toward one of the hangars. She expected him to continue on his way, but when their eyes met, her heart flip-flopped. And when he crossed the street and walked toward her, her heart rumbled in her chest.

"How's it going?" he asked, that slight Texas twang a calming caress, soothing her like his hands once had.

Funny you should ask, she was tempted to say. *My period is late, and I might be...*

Again, she shook off the possibility, as well as the urge to even bring up the topic. "I'm fine. Same old, same old."

She glanced at his uniform—the flight suit he wore

so well. Her gaze traveled up to his face, to those daz-zling green eyes.

If they were to have a baby, would its eyes…?

Oh, for Pete's sake, Rickie. Stop it.

"Are you heading out or coming in?" she asked.

"Going out. Night training on the Big Island."

She nodded, wondering which medic would be join-ing his squadron and wishing it was her. Not tonight, of course. But…maybe someday.

"I'd like to talk to you," he said.

"About…?"

He scanned their surroundings, then lowered his voice to a near whisper. "About that night."

Under normal circumstances, she might have told him that wasn't a good idea to broach the subject. Wouldn't it be best if they forgot it all together?

Yeah, right. If there'd been any way she could do that, she would have done it already. And if her period didn't show up soon, she'd have something to talk to him about, too.

"All right," she said. "Maybe some time next week?"

He nodded his agreement. "We could meet in Waikiki."

She was tempted to suggest someplace on the North Shore, but that was a bad idea. And one that was wrong.

"Have you gotten that bonus?" he asked.

"I haven't reupped yet." And if she actually was preg-nant, she'd have to rethink that decision. She'd be a sin-gle mother, and if she were deployed, she wouldn't have anyone to take care of the baby. Talk about unexpected surprises.

As if he could read her mind, Clay blessed her with a charming grin.

What was that about? Did he sense she was facing a

dilemma of some kind? Did he think she would recon-sider an Army career so she'd be free to date him?

As contrary as that might be to her career goal, a small, girlish side of her hoped that's what he meant.

"Hey, Masters," another soldier called out from a nearby hangar.

Clay turned to him. "What's up?"

"Major Ramos is looking for you."

Clay nodded toward the hangar. "I'd better go. I'll see you later."

"All right." In the meantime, she'd have to find out if she really was expecting a baby.

It would be easy enough to have a test at the clinic, but she didn't want anyone to know her secret. Not yet. So she'd have to purchase a kit that she could use in the privacy of her bathroom.

If the test turned out positive, she'd have to tell Clay. Wouldn't she?

A child deserved to know its father, especially if he was an upright, admirable man. A leader. A protector.

She took one last look at the Black Hawk commander who was striding toward a nearby hangar. They might have thought their sexual encounter was a onetime thing, but the result of it could be a lot more lasting than that. Especially if they were going to be parents.

But first things first. She'd have to find out for sure. And if the test results were negative, she could get her mind back on an even keel.

And off the man who'd occupied her dreams ever since the night they'd met.

Chapter Four

The next morning, right after Rickie entered the clinic, Captain Nguyen met her near the supply room. Her dark hair was pulled into a tight military bun, and she was dressed in uniform, but the expression she wore was more serious than usual.

"Is something wrong?" Rickie asked.

"Not here at the clinic. It's just that…" She slowly shook her head and sighed. "I hate bad news."

Had the captain's grandmother taken a turn for the worse? Had she passed away during the night? Rickie didn't want to pry, so she awaited the explanation she hoped was coming.

"There was a flight mishap on the Big Island last night," Captain Nguyen said. "A Black Hawk went down at the Pohakuloa Training Area."

Rickie's heart dropped to the pit of her stomach. Clay had gone out on a night training. Had he been involved?

Maybe not. But he certainly would know the soldiers who were. He also might have been part of the rescue operation, which would have been tough.

Still, he could have been injured, although she prayed he wasn't. Yet fear continued to build until she couldn't keep quiet any longer.

"Was…" She cleared her throat, trying to dislodge the worry and any sign of emotional involvement. "Was anyone injured?"

"Unfortunately, yes. One of the squadron commanders got the worst of it, although he'll pull through."

An overwhelming sense of dread hung over her like rain-drenched cammies, weighing her down and chilling her to the bone. Her pulse thundered in her ears and a tsunami of curiosity flooded her thoughts.

She had a slew of questions to fire at the captain, but she bit her tongue, knowing she had to remain professional. And removed from any personal involvement.

Finally, she asked, "Do you know who was injured?"

"Captain Masters and Sergeant Clemmons, the crew chief. They were treated at the scene, then airlifted to Tripler."

Panic struck hard, balling up in Rickie's throat, making it hard to breathe, let alone speak. But then again, Captain Nguyen had said the injuries weren't life threatening, which was a relief.

"How badly was he—or rather, *they*—hurt?" Rickie asked.

Captain Nguyen eyed her intently—maybe even suspiciously. She didn't say a word, but her expression seemed to ask, *Why the special interest?*

Rickie wasn't about to admit that she'd had a one-night fling with the Black Hawk commander—albeit after a case of mistaken identity. And even though they'd agreed to go their own ways, she felt a connection to him, one that might now include a baby.

But the complexity of her weird feelings was hard enough for her to understand, let alone to put into words that would make sense. Either way, she regretted that she hadn't picked up a home pregnancy test yesterday. No matter how complicated a positive result might be, she needed to know for sure.

"It's always tough to hear about serious training injuries and flight mishaps," Captain Nguyen said. "But let's try to put it behind us. We have a full schedule today."

Rickie nodded, hoping she could do just that. But the CO had implied those injuries were serious, even if they weren't life threatening. So once her shift at the clinic ended, she was going to drive out to Tripler Army Medical Center in Honolulu and check on Clay's condition herself. Surely a hospital visit wouldn't be considered fraternization.

But right now, she didn't care if it was.

Clay had drifted in and out of consciousness all day, thanks to what the attending medic had called head trauma and the pain meds he'd been given. His leg hurt like hell and was in traction. One of his eyes was bandaged, and his vision in the other was blurred. He assumed he'd gotten a serious concussion, because his thoughts were scrambled and he wasn't entirely sure what had happened.

Now, as a physician stood at his bedside, explaining the extent of his injuries, he tried his best to focus.

"You did a real number on your knee, but it'll heal and, given time and physical therapy, you shouldn't have trouble walking. But I'm afraid that leg may never be at one hundred percent. You also have a head injury that damaged your optic nerve. You may not lose your vision in that eye, but it's likely to be impaired. That all being said, it looks like you won't be fit for duty. So you'll be getting a medical discharge."

Clay's brain had been scrambled. Maybe he hadn't heard that right. "Excuse me?"

"You're not going to be fit for duty, son. As far as the military is concerned, it's case closed. But on the bright side, you'll be able to do most of the things you're used to doing."

"Can I fly again?" he asked.

"With a vision defect, it's doubtful."

Clay closed his good eye as disappointment swirled like a Texas twister, wreaking havoc in his disjointed thoughts. Maybe he'd wake up and this would be a bad dream. A hallucination triggered by pain pills.

"Do you have any questions?" the doctor asked.

"Yeah. Are you sure about that discharge?"

The doctor nodded. "I'm afraid so, son. The military puts the needs of the aircraft and the crew above those of the individual. You must be operationally ready and fit for duty at all times."

Clay turned to him, his good eye attempting to focus on the shadowy figure before him. "You don't know me, Doc. I heal quickly. And I'll work harder than anyone else. I'll be back at one hundred percent before you know it."

"The ultimate decision is out of my hands. It's up to the MEB and the PEB."

The medical and physical evaluations boards. A bunch of upper-level doctors who decided who got to stay and who had to be medically discharged. Was this really happening?

"I'm sorry to be giving you bad news," the doctor said.

It wasn't just bad. It was devastating. Sure, Clay would recover. And he'd walk again. He could handle the pain and the extensive rehab he was facing. He was tough and determined to heal. But none of that seemed to matter when his military career was over.

The head injury, a serious concussion, was no big deal. He'd had one when he'd crashed his bike and another when he'd played football in high school. He'd suffered a multiple fracture in his leg. He could deal with that, too. But the fatal blow, the parting shot, was the damage to his eye, the effect it would have on his vision. And that meant he couldn't fly.

Everything he loved—the Army, piloting Black Hawks, commanding a squadron—was being taken away from him. And the reality sent his hope plummeting.

What in the hell did he have left?

Talk about tailspins. His entire identity lay in his military service. If not a soldier and a pilot, who was he?

A rancher? A *farmer*?

He closed his good eye once more and blew out a ragged sigh.

"You were lucky," Dr. Simmons said.

Clay didn't feel the least bit lucky. His injuries hadn't killed him, which should make him happy. But they'd put a complete halt to his military career. Hell, even if he wanted to work as a crop duster—and he damn sure didn't—he wouldn't be able to.

He tried his best to look on the bright side. He was

going home to Texas, where he still had friends and family. But that didn't lift his mood in the least.

Life as he knew it, as he'd always dreamed it would be, was over. And as far as he was concerned, nothing was going to make him feel better.

It seemed like forever before Rickie was able to leave the clinic and drive to Tripler, a huge coral-pink structure located on the slopes of Moanalua Ridge. If Clay had to be treated anywhere, this was the place. Tripler was the largest military hospital serving the Asian and Pacific Rims.

On the drive down the H-1 to the H-201, she gripped the steering wheel with clammy hands. By the time she parked, entered the hospital and learned where his room was located, her heart was pounding like thundering luau drums, and her legs felt as immobile as tree stumps. But she managed to follow the directions she'd been given.

She paused in the doorway and spotted the bed where a single male patient lay. She'd been told his injuries weren't life threatening, but they had to hurt like hell. His head was bandaged, one eye was covered in gauze and his right leg was in traction.

Her first impulse was to hurry to his bedside to soothe him, to caress his face and whisper words of comfort. She'd always been a nurturer. But then again, maybe in this case, she merely wanted to be near the man with whom she'd once been intimate.

Either way, she held her emotions in check and entered slowly, her boot steps making far more noise than she'd like.

"Hey," she said, gentling her voice as if she were approaching a stray dog with a wounded paw.

Clay turned to the door, and when he spotted her, recognition dawned in the eye that wasn't bandaged, but he didn't even offer the hint of a smile. "You shouldn't be here."

He was right, but checking in on him had been a growing compulsion she hadn't been able to squelch. "I heard you were going to be hospitalized for a while, and since I was in the neighborhood, I thought I'd stop by to see you."

He didn't respond, but she approached his bed anyway. "Captain Nguyen told me about the flight mishap. I was sorry to hear about it."

"Not as sorry as me." He turned his head away and glanced out the window.

Had it been his fault? Was he assuming responsibility for the downed helicopter? Did he feel as if he'd caused his crew chief's injury?

"Those things happen," she said.

"Not to me."

Okay, then. She'd dealt with surly patients before. In this case, she figured it was the pain he was in, the medication they'd given him.

"I could sneak you in some better food," she said. "Maybe a big juicy cheeseburger with all the fixings. Some chocolate cake…"

He slowly shook his head.

"You shouldn't be here," he said again.

She knew that. But she'd come anyway. She hadn't been able to stay away, although his tone and his obvious discomfort with her presence caused her to regret the impulse to visit.

Yet she'd wanted to see him, to learn the extent of his injuries for herself. And she wasn't about to ponder why.

She damn well knew why she was here. Something had stirred inside her that night they'd met. And right now, it was possible that a little someone was stirring in her womb. A child they'd created.

But she didn't dare voice a possibility like that. Not here. Not now.

"How's your crew chief?" she asked.

"He'll live. And he'll fly again." Something in his harsh tone, his lack of sympathy for the guy, suggested there was more to it than that.

But she knew better than to press for information he wasn't yet willing to give. So she said, "That's good."

"Yeah. For him."

Her stomach knotted, forming something cold and hard that dropped to her gut. "But not for you?"

He turned back to face her. "No. I'm going to end up with a medical discharge." He lifted a bruised hand to his bandaged eye. "And I'll most likely have a vision problem that means I'll never fly again."

"I'm sorry."

He let out a guttural sound, something raw and torn that revealed a wound deep inside, one that couldn't be seen or treated with gauze or pain medication.

She hurt for him, grieved deep in her heart. She knew the Army was his life, as it was hers. Yet, on the other hand, if he was getting out, that took the fraternization issue off the table.

"Well, I can come back to visit you, and when you're released we could keep seeing each other." She hesitated, realizing this was a fresh wound for him in more ways than one. "I mean, technically we're not crossing any forbidden lines anymore, so—"

He slowly shook his head. "Don't bother. I'll be going back to Texas as soon as I'm discharged."

Now, there was a downside she hadn't considered.

He cleared his throat. "Listen, Sergeant, I'm not feeling very good. I need to get some rest."

She could certainly understand that, but the fact that he'd called her by her rank rather than her name said a lot more than his actual words. And so did his tone. She tried to blame it on his obvious disappointment at his diagnosis, on the pain and his medication. Yet it still hurt to be dismissed.

"Sure, I'll let you get some rest. But I'll be back." She'd have to, especially if that pregnancy test revealed what she feared it might.

"Like I said, *don't*."

She nodded, then turned and walked away, accepting the news like a good soldier. But before she got two steps down the hospital corridor, tears filled her eyes and an ache settled deep in her heart.

Clay wasn't the only one whose plans had gone awry. She was facing her own dilemma. And apparently, he wasn't going to be much help to her.

Not only did Clay hurt like hell, he felt like an ass. He hadn't meant to treat Rickie that way, to be so rude, but he'd just suffered a devastating blow. He'd hardly had ten minutes to digest the doctor's diagnosis, which had been far more crippling than a bum leg or vision problems, when she'd popped up unexpectedly.

Just the sight of her had made things all the worse. Sure, he was tempted to reach out to her, to accept her concern and sympathy. But that would have only complicated the issue.

Guilt continued to niggle at him, building until it rose up and struck him like a football helmet to the chest. He glanced at the empty doorway, where she'd once stood.

He'd more or less dismissed her like a bumbling new recruit. But he couldn't deal with that now. Not when he was still struggling to wrap his mind around his new reality.

Granted, he could use a little comfort and TLC right now. But not the kind Rickie would bring. She seemed to think that, once he was discharged from the Army, they could continue seeing each other, which would never work.

Even if he were up for a relationship of some kind, he'd be damned if he'd sit back as a civilian and watch her Army career take off. Not when his had just crashed and burned.

Besides, he wasn't the kind of guy who'd settle down with one woman. A commitment like that usually led to marriage, and Clay refused to even contemplate being tied down with anyone, even Rickie.

He'd only been five when his father had deployed for Desert Storm, and he'd been six when they'd gotten word his dad had died in battle. So he'd been too young to remember or to pay any attention to his parents' interactions. His stepgrandmother and Granddad had split up right before Clay and his mom had moved to the Bar M, so they hadn't set any long-term romantic examples, either.

Poncho had grown up in foster care, and Duck had been raised by his uncle, a single cowboy who'd sworn off women after his fiancée ran off with a country-western singer bound for Nashville. And some of Clay's military friends, the few guys who were married, didn't seem to be all that happy. Maybe it had to do with added responsibilities and curfews. After all, he'd heard that old saying—happy wife, happy life.

As far as Clay was concerned, a wife or even a serious girlfriend would clip his wings—if that blasted flight mishap hadn't already torn them off.

So he wouldn't consider a relationship with Rickie. Even if she decided not to reenlist and moved back to Texas, it wouldn't work. They lived in different cities located at least fifty miles apart. Maybe more than that.

No, it was best that Clay had pretty much ended what little thing they might have had and run her off. She'd be happier that way. And so would he. In a few weeks, he'd be back home, waiting for his head to clear and his bones to mend. Then he'd work the family spread, taking some of the responsibility off his mom and Granddad. Even if he'd had other options, it was only right that he step up and take his turn.

Still, he'd never wanted to be a rancher or a cowboy. Not day in and day out, season after season. It'd make for a boring life, if you asked him. Yet now it was the only viable option he had, and he rolled his eyes at his new normal.

Yippee ki-yay.

After leaving Tripler, Rickie stopped by a pharmacy and purchased an over-the-counter pregnancy test. But instead of taking it home, she pulled into a nearby fast food restaurant and parked. She wasn't hungry, even though she'd had a light lunch and it was already past her usual dinner hour.

She was too nervous to eat, but since she wanted an excuse for going inside to use the restroom, she ordered a cheeseburger to go. While it was being prepared, she carried her small shopping bag into the ladies' room.

In the privacy of a stall, she opened the package. While holding the testing apparatus in one hand, she read the instructions. It was all pretty simple. If she was pregnant, a plus sign would form. If not, she'd see a minus. It wouldn't take long.

So she followed the directions and waited for the results. She was both excited and frightened at the prospect of being pregnant, which made no sense. She ought to be scared spitless after the way Clay had treated her, after the words he'd said. He'd made it clear that she'd be facing parenthood on her own.

She'd held her head high as she left his hospital room, but it hadn't been easy not to crumple at the way he'd treated her. It wasn't just his words and tone that had hurt her. He'd brushed off that night they'd shared on the North Shore like a stale bread crumb, when she'd considered it special. Apparently, their lovemaking meant nothing to him, which only served to gradually turn her hurt to anger.

She glanced at the test, afraid to look yet afraid not to. Talk about being mixed up and confused.

As a plus sign began as a light shade of baby blue and then darkened, she slowly shook her head. She was pregnant. With Clay's baby.

Now what?

She was both shaken and delighted—shaken because she didn't have any experience with babies, and now she was going to be a single mom. Yet at the same time, she was happy to know she was going to have someone to love, someone to love her back.

At this point, she had no idea if that little someone would be a girl or a boy. That really didn't matter.

But something else did. That son or daughter was going to need her. So how could she consider staying in the military and facing potential deployments? She didn't have any family support, so she wouldn't have anyone to keep her baby for her while she was gone, even if it was just for a weekend training. And if truth be told, even if she did find a trusted sitter, she wasn't going to leave her child in someone else's care.

She would raise her child on her own. It would be better that way. She just had to put some thought into the future and make a game plan. It would be difficult, but not impossible.

Besides, she had a lot more going for her than many single mothers did. She even had a mortgage-free home in Jeffersville. That is, if the busy handyman she'd lined up had actually found time to complete the repairs and paint the place.

The more she thought about moving back to Texas, putting her own mark on that little brick house and making it a home for herself and her baby, the more she liked the idea. It was the perfect solution.

As she tossed away the used testing apparatus, she thought of something else. She'd be living an hour or so away from Clay's hometown of Wexler. Not that it mattered, but she'd have to tell him about the baby. He might even want to…

No, he wouldn't. But he did deserve to know he was going to be a father, didn't he?

She'd have to tell him, even if it complicated his life. It might complicate hers, too.

Could she handle seeing Clay for visitations, birthday parties and school events? Would the sight of him always remind her of how that sweet baby was placed in her womb?

Surely, she'd get used to seeing him, to figuring out a way to coparent. Besides, the baby deserved to know its daddy.

There might also be a concern about genetics, family illnesses and that sort of thing.

By the time she returned to the barracks, her appetite had returned, and she'd wolfed down the cheeseburger. She'd also created a solid game plan.

She wasn't going to reenlist. Instead, she'd go home to Texas and fix up a nursery in her old bedroom. She'd also use her GI Bill benefits to pay for nursing school. In the meantime, she'd apply for a job at one of the hospitals. There was no telling when a suitable position would open up, but at least she could get her name in the system. She'd also have to find a competent and loving nanny, but she had about seven months to do that.

How hard could it be?

Chapter Five

It had been three months since the flight mishap ended Clay's military career, and he was finally back on the Bar M, trying to settle into life as a cattleman.

His knee was on the mend, although it was still giving him trouble and he had to rely on a cane whenever he walked on uneven ground. But it was coming along okay, thanks to the physical therapy department at the Brighton Valley Medical Center and Clay's determination to push through the pain.

It sucked to work so hard to be whole again, but how many times had he told his men "Embrace the suck"?

His head injury had healed, and he could see well enough. But his vision still wasn't as good as it had been. He supposed that was to be expected after the optic nerve damage. At least he wasn't blind in one eye.

In some ways, it was good to be home. Duck and Poncho stopped by regularly and did their best to cheer him up. It worked, but only while they were visiting. After that, reality set in, and he had to face the fact that he'd given up an exciting life for one that was so-so at best.

His mom and grandfather were happy to have him back on the Bar M, and while he tried to accept the fact that his life had changed, he couldn't seem to escape the dark mood that followed him after his hospital stay at Tripler.

He tried to shake it by spending most of his waking hours outdoors in the sunshine, but he still couldn't do much work yet, at least not the heavy stuff that would ease Granddad's daily load. So most of the time he sat on the front porch, just like he was doing this afternoon.

The screen door squeaked open, and his mom stepped outside. "Can I bring you something to drink? Lemonade or maybe some sweet tea?"

"No, thanks. I'm okay for now."

She continued to stand there, as if he might change his mind. She did that a lot these days, waiting on him and hanging around as if she might be able to say or do something that would set things back to right and lift his mood once and for all.

But she couldn't help. Like the physical therapist told him again today, some things just take time.

"There's some leftover German chocolate cake," she added. "I'd be happy to bring you a slice."

Clay appreciated her attempts to make things better, and while she tried her damnedest, that was something he'd have to do on his own, and so far, he hadn't had much luck.

On the other hand, she made no secret of the fact that

she was pleased to have him home—safe and sound—even if he wasn't the happy-go-lucky son she'd once had.

Clay understood that. He really did. But what she believed was a blessing and a wonderful turn of events he considered bad luck.

"I worry about you," she said, moving in closer. "You've lost weight, and you're not eating like you should. I wish you'd at least take those vitamins I got you."

"I'm fine." He stroked his bum knee, hoping to ease the ache without resorting to another dose of extra-strength ibuprofen tablets. "The doctors and my physical therapist haven't complained."

She lifted her hand to shield her eyes from the glare of the afternoon sun. The quick action reminded him of a half-ass salute and of the life he'd been forced to give up.

"All right," she said. "Then I'll try not to worry. But it's not easy being a mom."

Motherhood had never been easy for her. She still tended to hover over him, much like she did when he was a kid. He'd resented it then, enough to rebel every chance he got. And it still bothered him now—especially since he was no longer a rebellious adolescent, who could escape by sneaking out his bedroom window to meet his friends. About the only escape he got these days was the drive back and forth to the medical center for physical therapy.

His mom stepped around his bad leg, which he'd stretched out in front of him, and sat beside him. Before she could change the subject, an unfamiliar car drove into the yard.

"Looks like we have company," she said, getting to her feet. "Or else someone took a wrong turn and needs directions. I'll check on it."

Clay didn't give the vehicle a second thought until the driver's door opened and he spotted the pretty brunette getting out.

What was Rickie doing here? Had she gotten transferred to a base in Texas?

She'd traded in her Army uniform for a pair of black jeans and a pink blouse. Her hair shimmered in the afternoon sun, the curls tumbling over her shoulders. She'd always caused him to sit up and take notice, and today was no different.

He studied her as she approached the porch. She looked…different. He couldn't put his finger on it. There was a new look in her eye; a glow that had nothing to do with the afternoon sunshine. And while her curves had attracted him on the beach, she looked even sexier now. He had to admit that he was not only surprised to see her but actually glad she'd come.

"Hey," she said, as she reached the first step to the wraparound porch.

"What a surprise." Clay probably ought to stand and greet her, which was the polite thing to do, but he'd just gotten home from physical therapy, and his knee hurt like hell.

His mom, on the other hand, took up the slack on courtesy, because she quickly greeted Rickie with an outstretched hand. "I take it you're one of Clay's friends. I'm his mother, Sandra. It's nice to meet you."

"I'm Erica Campbell. But you can call me Rickie."

Mom turned to Clay, her expression quizzical and begging for details. When he'd been a kid, that look had bothered him, so he would clam up to protect his privacy. And, admittedly, to piss her off. But he couldn't really blame her for being curious today. He hadn't expected to see Rickie again, and he wondered why she'd come.

"Rickie and I met in Hawaii," Clay explained. "We were both stationed there."

His mother brightened and blessed Rickie with a warm and welcoming smile. "I'm glad you dropped by. Can I get you something to drink? I have fresh-squeezed lemonade. And I always have a pitcher of sweet tea on the counter."

"Sure," Rickie said. "I'll have whatever is easiest. Thanks."

As soon as his mother hurried into the house, leaving them alone, Rickie made her approach. "I hope you don't mind me stopping by."

"Not at all. It's been a long time. How'd you find this place?"

"It wasn't hard. I did an internet search, then used my GPS system."

He glanced at the car she'd been driving, a late-model Toyota Celica. "Is that a rental?"

"No, it belonged to my mother. It's mine now."

He scrunched his brow, a bit confused. She'd mentioned getting a different car. "Are you going to ship it back to Hawaii?"

"No, I didn't reenlist. I'm living in Jeffersville now."

Clay hadn't seen that coming. She'd been so intent on staying in the Army. Had she changed her mind, hoping they could rekindle their relationship? If so, that made him feel all the worse.

He wasn't the man he used to be, although he hoped to be close to it one day soon. And while he wasn't the least bit opposed to making love with her again, he hated to see her give up her dreams. If that's what she'd done, then she was hoping for more than a physical relationship.

"You shouldn't have done it for me," he said.

She stiffened and took a step back. "I did it for *me*."

"I'm sorry. I didn't mean to make assumptions. It's just that…" He paused, trying to backpedal and not having much luck. "Then why are you here?"

She flinched as if he'd struck her.

Damn, he should have handled that better. "I'm sorry. I didn't mean to be a jerk. I guess my mood is only slightly better than it was the last time you saw me."

"You can say that again." She arched a pretty brow then slowly shook her head.

"I owe you an apology for that day, too. But keep in mind that I'd just gotten the worst news of my life, and I was in a lot of pain."

"You were also loaded down with pain medication, which can really take a toll on your thought process." Her downturned lips slowly curled into a pretty smile. "So you're forgiven."

He nodded, then pointed to the chair his mother had vacated. "Have a seat."

She seemed a bit reluctant. Then after a couple of beats, she complied. As she took the place beside him, she said, "I came to tell you something."

"What's that?"

She bit down on her bottom lip and paused for the longest time. Finally, she said, "I'm pregnant."

Wow. He had no idea what to say. He gave her expanded waistline another look, and when she rested her hand softly on a good-size baby bump, he realized now what he should have seen the moment she climbed out of her car.

He wasn't an expert on that sort of thing, but one of the guys in his unit had a pregnant wife. She'd been about seven months along and had a bump that size. And since he and Rickie had been together about five months ago, she must have been pregnant the day they'd met.

"I'm not asking anything of you," she said. "I can handle this on my own. But I thought you ought to know."

Why did she think he ought to...? Damn. No way. He'd used a condom. "Now wait a minute. Are you saying it's *mine*?"

"That's exactly what I'm saying." She turned toward him, her eyes zeroing in on his. She must have read the disbelief in them, because her gaze morphed into a glare. "Are you doubting me?"

He hadn't meant to be an ass about it, but yeah. He had plenty of doubts. Was she trying to pull something over on him?

It wouldn't be the first time a woman tried to snag a soldier for his military benefits. And while Clay was no longer in the Army, his family did have a sizable spread that might seem appealing.

"It's just a little hard to believe," he said. "You look to be about six or seven months along."

"There's a good reason for that," Rickie said. "I'm carrying twins."

Clay wouldn't have been any more stunned if she'd doubled up her fist and bloodied his nose. *This couldn't be happening.*

Hell, if he didn't have a bum leg that ached like hell, he'd be tempted to take off at a dead run.

Before he could wrap his mind around the news or come up with any kind of response, the door squeaked open and his mother walked out, holding a tray filled with glasses of lemonade and several servings of cake.

At first, he thought she might have missed out on hearing the stunning announcement, but by the look on her face, he realized she'd heard at least part of it—the most shocking part. His mom loved babies and had mentioned a hundred times that she couldn't wait to be a grandma.

And that's when Clay realized he was in one hell of a fix.

Driving out to Wexler to visit Clay had been one of the dumbest decisions Rickie had ever made. And now he was looking at her as if she'd just set fire to his barn. She never should have come here today.

Okay, so he needed to know about the babies, but why hadn't she revealed her news the way she'd practiced? It had sounded so good when she stood in front of the bathroom mirror this morning and recited a script.

But when he asked why she was here, she figured she'd better cut to the chase. And that's when it all fell apart.

Rickie glanced at his mom. Poor Sandra gaped first at Clay, then at Rickie. This was *so* not going the way Rickie had planned.

Sandra leaned against the porch railing as if she might collapse. The tray she held was listing to the side, and if she wasn't careful, the drinks and the dessert were going to drop to the floor and make a terrible mess. Of course, that one would be a lot easier to clean up than the one Rickie had just created.

"Here," Rickie said, reaching for the tray. "Let me help you with that."

The dumbfounded woman, whose jaw had nearly

dropped to the ground, handed it over without an argument. Then, after looking at Rickie's midsection, she snatched it right back again. "Good grief, you don't need to be helping me. Let me carry that."

Whatever. Rickie wasn't an invalid, but she decided not to argue. Instead, she tried to soften the blow and segue into a productive conversation. "I realize this is a bit of a shock."

"To say the least." Clay raked his hands through his hair, which had grown longer than his prior military cut.

She liked it that way, although she'd better not study him too closely. Like she'd told him before, she didn't need anything from him.

"I don't know what to say. This is more than a little mind-boggling." His expression verified his words.

"Don't worry," she told him. "I know you're not interested in having a relationship with me. And you don't need to have one with the babies, either. I just thought it was only right to let you know."

"You're pregnant with Clay's baby?" Sandra finally set the tray down on a small patio table. "I mean, *babies*? Oh my gosh. This is wonderful. I've always wanted to be a grandmother, but Clay insisted he wasn't going to ever have kids. So I'm delighted at the news. Do you know if you'll be having boys or girls?"

"Actually, there'll be one of each." Rickie glanced at Clay, who seemed too stunned to speak. "I'll admit that I was surprised, too. This wasn't something I expected to happen, but I'm making the best of it."

At that, Clay finally chimed in. "Okay, Mom. Would you mind giving Rickie and me a little privacy? We have some things to talk over, and we don't need an audience. Or a cheering section."

"Yes, of course." Sandra smiled brightly. "I'll just slip inside the house and find something to do."

Once the door clicked shut behind her, Rickie continued to stand, realizing she'd better not get too comfortable. "I didn't realize you don't like kids."

"It's not that. I just… Never mind."

"And I assume you're going to want a paternity test, but that won't be necessary. I'm not asking for child support." Rickie blew out a sigh. "But for the record, even though I was shocked and had to revamp my career plans, I'm actually happy about it. And that's why I'm no longer in the Army."

"I'd think you'd enjoy the security."

"Not if that meant being separated from my children for any length of time." She unfolded her arms. "Besides, I recently found a life insurance policy I didn't realize my parents had. So that'll tide me over for a while." A very short while.

"I don't know what to say." Clay shook his head, then reached down and rubbed his knee. "This isn't going to be easy for you."

"I don't expect it to be, but I've got things under control. I'm taking a couple of night classes, which will lead to a nursing degree. In the meantime, I'm job hunting. I hope to land a temporary position at a hospital or clinic until I have to go out on maternity leave. And actually, I have an interview at a local hospital in an hour, so I need to go."

"Before you do, how can I get a hold of you?"

She reached into her purse, pulled out a small notepad and pen. Then she jotted down her cell number and handed it to him. "I live in Jeffersville—on Bramble Berry Lane."

"Okay. Got it." He slipped the paper in his pocket. "Good luck on the interview."

"Thanks. I need a little time to unwind so I can put my best foot forward."

"You're not going to be able to work very long."

"It's a temporary position, but at least I can get my foot in the door there."

"So you plan to go to work after the babies are born?"

"That life insurance policy will be helpful for a while, but not until they go to kindergarten. So I'll have to get a job. But a lot of single moms are able to provide a loving home for their kids." She nodded toward her mother's car. "Anyway, I have to go."

As she opened the driver's door, he asked, "What are you going to do about child care?"

"I'm going to hire a nanny." She didn't wait for him to respond. Instead, she climbed into her car and headed for that interview.

She wasn't too worried about childcare. She had a couple of months to find a loving and dependable person to care for the twins.

It's just too bad they wouldn't have a loving and dependable daddy.

As Rickie drove away, Clay raked a hand through his hair and watched until her car disappeared from sight. Her unexpected visit had shocked the heck out of him, and her news had left him completely baffled. He had no idea what to think, let alone do.

He still couldn't believe what she'd just sprung on him. She was *pregnant*, and not with just one baby, but two. Even more surprising than that—according to her claim, he was the father.

Now that was rich. What did he know about babies or parenting? Then again, did he actually need those skills? Rickie had said she didn't need him or his financial support, which ought to be a relief. But it wasn't. What kind of guy turned his back on his kids?

He tried to sort through his thoughts, but guilt and confusion clouded his brain.

Apparently, fate wasn't finished messing with him. Could his life get any more unsettling?

When the screen door creaked open and his mother walked out onto the porch, he realized things were about to get worse.

She scanned the deserted yard and driveway. "Is Rickie gone?"

"Yeah." Clay kept his response simple, hoping his mom would just pick up that tray of drinks and cake and go back inside. He wasn't up for a discussion with anyone, especially his mom. But when she plopped down in the seat next to him, he knew he was in for a maternal interrogation.

Sandra Masters had never been able to read her only child, so she usually said the wrong thing or reacted in a way that made Clay clam up, rather than share his thoughts and feelings with her. And apparently, none of that had changed while he'd served in the Army.

She blew out a long, slow sigh. "So how are you feeling about all of this?"

"I'm in a state of shock."

"I can understand that."

Could she? He doubted it. She'd never really understood him or his need to set boundaries between them. Nor had she known how important it had been for him to join the military and do something noble with his life.

You'd think she'd realize that the military was in his blood. Hell, he'd been born on an Army base in Germany. His dad had been a career soldier who'd achieved valor in Desert Storm.

Clay didn't remember much about John Masters, other than he'd died in battle. Then eight years later, Clay and his mom moved to the Bar M, where the sprawling ranch house was filled with pictures and awards that memorialized his father, particularly his patriotism and valor.

She shouldn't have been surprised that he would want to be just like his dad. You'd think she would have been proud, but she wasn't. She'd been afraid of losing Clay, too.

But she'd lost him anyway. That damned flight mishap had taken the *real* Clay away from her for good, and she'd been left with a facsimile who was broken down and miserable.

"Rickie is a pretty girl," Mom said.

She certainly was. And if truth be told, he'd been glad to see her drive up—until she told him why she was here.

"She seems nice," Mom added. "Do you think she'll make a good mother?"

He hadn't expected the conversation to take a turn like that, but in spite of being a helicopter mom, Sandra Masters meant well.

"Believe it or not," he said, "I really don't know her very well. But she was an Army medic, and from what little I do know, she seems compassionate. I'm sure she'll be a good mother."

"So what do you plan to do?" Mom asked.

Okay, then. They were back to the issue at hand.

Clay scrubbed a hand over his chin. "Hell if I know.

It sounds like she has life all figured out for herself and the kids."

I'm not asking anything of you, she'd said, more than once.

I can handle parenthood on my own.

"Maybe that was her way of trying to calm your fears and test the waters," his mom said.

That was possible, he supposed. No matter what Rickie had told him about her ability to go it alone, Clay would offer financial support.

Only trouble was, long before she'd made her announcement, he'd felt tied to the land and to civilian life. Taking on a daddy role would only serve to lock him down to the last place a guy like him wanted to be.

He might have gone to West Point and then served in the military, but there were some things that were part of a man's DNA. And Clay liked being a risk taker, liked pushing the limits and getting that adrenaline rush. And he was determined to somehow get his life back.

The doctors hadn't painted a rosy picture about him having a full recovery, but they didn't know him.

"I've been thinking," his mom said. "You should take some childbirth classes with her. And you should definitely go to one of her obstetrical appointments. Once you see those babies on an ultrasound, it'll make things real. And I have no doubt you'll fall in love with them and be an amazing father."

"Don't get carried away. This is all very new to me. Besides, Rickie and I didn't have an ongoing affair. Or a real relationship."

"Well, it looks as though the two of you will have one now. At least as parents."

And there lay the problem, considering the grump

he'd been since that damn flight mishap. Try as he might, he hadn't been able to shake that dark mood in months. What made him think that he could turn that around before the baby...before the *babies* were born?

Twins. A boy and a girl. Who would have guessed that amazing night on a tropical beach would have produced two new human beings in one fell swoop?

Then again, Rickie said she'd been a twin herself. Multiple births ran in some families.

"Do you know how to find her?" his mom asked.

Clay patted his shirt pocket. "She gave me her contact info."

"I hope you won't wait too long. Those kids are going to need a mother *and* a father."

Clay had always been able to read the subtext behind her words. "And a grandmother, too. Right? Isn't that what this is all about?"

She clamped her lips together, realizing she'd shown her hand. And that, once again, she'd met her match.

Clay wasn't about to let her think she could push him into a relationship. Nor did he want her to continue with the false assumption that he'd eventually find something to make him happy he'd moved back to the ranch. That wasn't going to happen.

He loved his mom, but he'd be damned if he'd let her talk him into something he wasn't ready for. Hell, he hardly knew Rickie at all. He did, however, know her body intimately, and his thoughts drifted back to that night they'd met and their incredible lovemaking.

But there was more to a woman than a gorgeous face and a sexy body. He should probably get to know the *real* her better. Especially if she was having his babies.

He had no idea how she and the twins would fit into his life, though. But he wouldn't turn his back on them.

Still, what if the doctors had been wrong? What if his vision wouldn't remain impaired? When they'd explained the extent of his injuries, they'd used the word *likely* and not *definitely*. His leg was coming along well, and the physical therapist claimed he was making a lot more progress than most people with similar injuries. Maybe things wouldn't be as dire as they'd seemed when he'd been stretched out on that hospital bed at Tripler.

Clay blew out a sigh. Even if he could accept his limitations and his new normal, he wasn't prepared for fatherhood. Or any further loss of freedom.

But ready or not, that's where life was headed. And he wasn't the only one who'd be facing big changes. Rickie hadn't signed on for this, either.

He could make a slew of excuses for reacting to the news the way he had. After all, she'd just dumped it on him. And he'd never been comfortable with the touchy-feely stuff. But he probably should have been a little more sensitive, a little more understanding.

She hadn't seemed upset when she left. But then again, she hadn't been happy, either.

He reached into his pocket and pulled out the slip of paper Rickie had given him, making note of her address and phone number. He wasn't going to do anything rash. He'd sleep on it, of course, and tomorrow he would drive out to Jeffersville and talk to her.

Chapter Six

Clay spent most of the night tossing and turning, thanks to random thoughts of Rickie. He'd had several flashbacks of that day on the North Shore when she'd worn that sexy red bikini and that night she'd spent in his arms. He'd also envisioned her on the base, outside the clinic, her glossy brown hair pulled into a tight military bun.

He'd felt awkward talking to her that day, but the sight of her had spiked his interest, not to mention his hormones. And then he'd remembered the time she'd visited him in the hospital, compassion glimmering in her honey-brown eyes. In spite of her shy approach and her awkward attempt to offer support, he'd shut her out. He could come up with a boatload of excuses why he'd done it, but that didn't make it right.

Yet it was the recent memory that had kept him awake,

the image of her standing on the ranch porch, her hand resting gently on her expanding womb.

He still couldn't believe what she'd told him. He was going to be a *father*. That was, if her claim was true. But could he accept her say-so as fact?

Tyrone Williams, one of Clay's pilots back at Wheeler, married a woman who'd claimed he'd gotten her pregnant. Six weeks later, after going to one of her doctor visits, he realized the baby's conception didn't match up with the time frame of their relationship, and it turned out the baby *wasn't* his.

Was Rickie trying to do the same thing to Clay? Was she trying to pin paternity on him? It didn't seem likely, but he couldn't help his skepticism.

By the time morning rolled around, Clay gave up any hope of falling back to sleep. So he climbed out of bed, showered, shaved and dressed for the day. Then he headed to the kitchen, breathing in the familiar, mouth-watering aroma of a hearty breakfast. He even caught a tantalizing whiff of sugar and spice as he followed the sounds of coffee percolating into the pot and bacon sizzling in a cast-iron skillet.

His mom, who was standing in front of the stove, must have heard his approach, because she turned to the doorway and offered him a bright smile. "Good morning, honey. I thought I'd get up early and make breakfast for you. How would you like your eggs? Scrambled? Sunny side up? I can poach them, if you want."

He'd never been comfortable with her efforts to mother him, which is why he usually fixed his own meals. "I'll just have bacon and toast."

"Are you sure? That's not going to help you regain the weight you lost."

Rather than comment, Clay glanced at the counter, where a dozen muffins rested on a cooling rack. They sure smelled good. Maybe he was hungrier than he thought.

He made his way to the kitchen table, which had been set for three. "Where's Granddad?"

"He's talking to the ranch hands and lining out their work for the day. He said he'd be back shortly."

Granddad, who'd always been tough as cowhide, loved working cattle. But he was in his late-seventies now, and Clay didn't want to see him push himself too hard. The old man should be thinking about retirement and not riding the range and supervising ranch hands. As soon as Clay was able to mount a horse and pull his own weight, he planned to take some of the load off his grandfather.

The mudroom door creaked open, and the silver-haired rancher strode into the house, his boot steps solid and steady in spite of his slight stoop.

"Well, look who's awake." Granddad winked at Clay, and his lips quirked into a smile. "It's Sleeping Beauty."

Clay wished that had been the case last night, but he wasn't going to offer a rebuttal that might require an explanation. Instead, he tossed his grandfather a wry grin. "It takes time for a body to heal, I guess. So I got a slow start this morning."

"I'm glad you're finally up. I've got a surprise for you." Granddad crossed the room to the small desk near the pantry, opened a drawer and pulled out a piece of paper. "Life gave you one hell of a kick in the butt, so you might not appreciate this now, but one day you will."

"What's that?"

"Something I hope will soften the blow." Granddad handed over the paper, which appeared to be a legal document.

Clay scanned it, realizing he held the deed to the Bar M. And it no longer bore his grandfather's name.

"The ranch is all yours now," Granddad said.

Clay had never wanted to be tied to the land, but it was a generous gift, a loving one made from the heart. "I don't know what to say. 'Thank you' doesn't seem to be enough."

"That's good enough for me," Granddad said. "I realize you can't do much until you're back to fightin' weight, so I'll just continue to run the place till you're ready to take over."

"I'd appreciate that." Clay hoped to be able to take charge in a couple of weeks. He could probably do it now, but the last thing he needed to do was to screw up his leg before it was completely healed.

Call him crazy and a die-hard soldier, but he still hoped to be able to prove the military doctors wrong. He couldn't do a damn thing about the vision in his left eye, so he'd never be able to fly again. But he might be able to join the Texas National Guard. That way, he could still run the family ranch and serve the country for one weekend each month. It wouldn't be the same, ever, but it would still fulfill his dream. Sort of.

Granddad crossed the kitchen and snatched a crisp slice of bacon from the platter near the stove. Then he nodded toward the doorway. "I'm going to wash up."

When he left the kitchen, Clay was still holding the deed and studying his name. He was grateful and appreciative, but...well, now he felt more grounded than ever.

"Have you given Rickie and her situation any thought?" his mom asked.

"She's crossed my mind." Actually, he'd given her and

her news a lot more thought than his mom would ever know. That's why he hadn't slept worth a damn.

His mother lowered the flame under the skillet and turned away from the stove to face him. "So what are you going to do?"

"I'm not sure yet." He had a good idea, though. A starting point. But he didn't want to go into any real detail until he'd thought through all the possible repercussions. "There's a lot to consider."

She nodded, as if she understood. "Can I pour you a cup of coffee?"

"That sounds good. But I'll take it to go."

At that, her brow furrowed. "Where are you going? You had physical therapy yesterday."

He might regret the revelation later, but for some reason, he decided to be more open with her than usual. "I'm going to Jeffersville. I need to talk to Rickie."

Mom's bright smile lit her blue eyes in a way he hadn't seen in a long time. "That's a good idea."

He sure hoped so. Either way, he couldn't ignore the situation. He preferred to address problems head-on, and this one would be no different, even though fatherhood would complicate his life in ways he couldn't imagine.

While his mom poured coffee into an insulated disposable cup, he glanced at the clock on the microwave. It was too early to show up unexpectedly at Rickie's house. But he wasn't about to remain on the ranch, where his mom was sure to throw in her good-hearted two cents every chance she got.

He'd figure out a way to stall for time, even if that meant he had to drive around Jeffersville and check out the town where Rickie lived and would raise the twins.

Maybe by then, he would come up with a way to get

on her good side, especially since he had a feeling she'd be offended if he insisted upon having a paternity test.

Rickie had driven away from the Bar M yesterday wishing she'd never made the trek to Wexler. Yet at the same time, she was glad she could finally put the much-needed conversation with Clay behind her.

She'd guessed the news of her pregnancy would surprise him, and she'd been right. It hadn't pleased him, either. But what had she expected? There was no way he'd feel the same way about the babies that she did. Hopefully, after he had a chance to absorb it all, he'd be more accepting. But even if that didn't turn out to be the case, she'd make out okay on her own.

When she'd told him she had to leave for a job interview, she hadn't been blowing smoke. The temp agency she was working with had set up an appointment for her to meet with Dr. Glory Davidson at a family practice clinic in Brighton Valley.

The doctor had a two-month position for a receptionist. And by the time Rickie arrived, she'd rallied her emotions so she could put her best foot forward.

And it worked. Rickie and the fortysomething physician seemed to hit it off from the get-go. The doctor led Rickie back to her office and pointed to a chair in front of her desk, indicating that Rickie should sit down. Then she took her seat. "Call me Glory," she said. "We're pretty casual around here."

That might be true, but there'd been no sign that they were lax. The clinic was clean and orderly. And Glory, who wore a white lab coat over a light blue blouse and black slacks, was dressed professionally.

"My receptionist has family living in Mexico," Glory

said, "and her father recently had a crippling stroke. So she's taking some time off to care for him and help him get settled in a rehab facility. We can get by without her for a few days to a week, but it looks like she'll be gone two months or more."

"The timing works for me," Rickie said. "My babies aren't due until late February."

Glory leaned forward and rested her forearms on her desk. "I like the fact that you were a medic. And, by the way, thank you for your service."

Rickie merely nodded. She never quite knew what to say to people who thanked her for doing the work she'd loved.

"Lorena does a great job answering the phone and scheduling appointments," Glory said, "but she doesn't have any medical training. So you'll be a nice addition to the office, especially since you can take vitals and draw blood."

"I'm a certified EMT," Rickie said. "And I'm a fast learner."

"That's good to know." Glory leaned back in her desk chair, the springs creaking. "Are you available to start work on Monday morning?"

"Yes, I can."

Glory studied her a moment, then asked, "Have you ever thought about going to nursing school?"

"Actually, that's been a dream of mine. I'm not sure how I'll pull that off once the twins get here. They'll keep me busy. Plus I'll also need a full-time job in order to support us. So school will have to wait. In the meantime, I'd love to work in the medical field, even if it's as a paramedic."

"Lorena mentioned something about retiring next

fall," Glory said. "So a permanent position here at the clinic might open up at the right time for you."

"That would be perfect," Rickie said. "And just so you know, I plan to start interviewing nannies before the twins are born. I'll find someone dependable."

"I have four kids of my own, so I know what it's like to work around the physical limitations of pregnancy. I've also had to deal with an occasional child-care issue. I'm pretty flexible, so I don't foresee any problems."

Rickie came away from the interview feeling good about the temporary job she'd landed. Glory Davidson was personable, and since she seemed to be understanding of a single mother's plight, it looked like it might be a good fit.

The only downside was the forty-five-minute commute, which would get tiring after a while. And if it turned into a permanent position, she'd be away from the babies an extra hour and a half each day.

It was too bad she couldn't find something closer. But she wasn't too worried. She'd found this position easily, so if things didn't work out, she might not have any trouble finding something else closer to the house.

The drive home from the clinic would have gone quickly, but Rickie had spotted a children's shop located near the interstate and had decided to stop. After nearly an hour spent checking out cribs, bedding and baby clothes, she finally drove back to her house. All the while, she made a mental note of everything she wanted to accomplish prior to her due date. Then before going to bed, she wrote out a long to-do list scheduling her priorities.

Over the years, she'd learned that organization and having a solid game plan were key, so she woke up the next morning energized and ready to get started. Her biggest job was to convert her father's home office into a nursery, which would take a while since she had to empty it first.

While getting dressed, she studied her image in the full-length mirror that hung on her bedroom door. She caressed her baby bump, which seemed to grow bigger every day. She wondered what it would look like four months from now.

A slow grin stole across her lips. As long as the little ones were healthy and she carried them to term, she didn't mind if she got as big as a barn.

She chose to wear a pair of stretchy workout pants and an oversize shirt for comfort and mobility. Then she pulled her hair into a messy topknot so the long, curly strands wouldn't get in her way while she worked.

She'd no more than left her bedroom and stepped into the hall when the doorbell rang. She couldn't imagine who it might be, but she wouldn't know until she answered. So she padded to the door.

The moment she spotted Clay on the stoop, wearing a sheepish grin that dimpled his cheeks, her breath caught. Talk about surprise visits.

His hair was stylishly mussed. Gone was the Army captain, she thought. His appearance alone darn near screamed cowboy—and much more than it had yesterday when he'd been at the ranch.

She took in his chambray shirt, with the sleeves rolled up to his muscular forearms, the worn denim jeans and scuffed boots, then scanned back up to his handsome face. The only sign of his injury was a scar over his left brow.

"What are you doing here?" she asked.

"I had some time to mull over what you told me yesterday, and I thought I'd better come here and talk to you in person."

She continued to stand there, unable to move, while gawking at him and wishing she'd been better prepared for his arrival.

"Aren't you going to invite me in?" he asked.

At that, she finally came to her senses. "Yes, sure. Of course. Come on in." She stepped aside, letting him enter the small living room, then closing the door.

"Nice house," he said, checking out the interior. "Did you grow up here?"

"I... No, not exactly. We moved here when I was in high school." It's not as if she had any real attachment to the house, but she was glad to have a place to raise her babies.

"I hope I didn't come too early," Clay said. "I was afraid I might wake you up."

"No, I've been up for a while."

Should she offer him something to eat or drink? That might make it easier for him to say whatever he had on his mind.

"I can make a pot of coffee," she said, "but I only have decaf. I also have orange juice."

"Thanks, but I'm fine. I had breakfast at a diner near the interstate." He shoved his thumbs in the front pockets of his jeans. "How'd your interview go yesterday?"

"Much better than I'd hoped. I start work at a clinic in Brighton Valley on Monday. It's only a temporary position, and the pay isn't much, but there's a chance I could land a permanent job there in the future."

"You don't mind the long drive to work?"

She shrugged. "I'm not happy about it. But there are other options."

"Like what?"

"I could find a rental house in Brighton Valley and rent this one out. Or I could sell this house and buy another."

He arched a brow, then nodded as if her plan made perfect sense. Did he realize a move to Brighton Valley would put her closer to his ranch?

He glanced at her expanding belly. "What about the babies?"

"I'll take it one day at a time. I've never been a single mother before."

"I'm sorry," he said.

"About what?" That she'd ended up pregnant after their lovemaking? That he'd practically shunned her when she visited him at Tripler when she'd been worried about him and had only wanted to offer her sympathy?

"About yesterday. It's just that… Well, let's just say that your pregnancy announcement knocked me off balance."

"I knew it would. I didn't expect you to be happy about it, either. In fact, I considered not telling you at all, but that wouldn't have been right."

"I'm glad you told me. To be completely honest, I wasn't happy. But after sleeping on it, I feel a little better about things now."

"I don't blame you for needing some time to think things over. I showed up unexpectedly and hit you with some pretty surprising news. Not only am I pregnant, but I'm having two babies."

"I guess twins run in your family."

"Apparently so." That was another reason she was

happy about the pregnancy. The whole idea of having twins reminded her of the sister she'd lost, the closeness they'd shared in spite of Lainie's frail health.

Neither of them spoke for a moment. Then she added, "I'm going to call the girl Elena, after my sister."

"What about the boy?"

"I haven't decided." There really wasn't anyone in her family that she'd want to honor. She'd never really liked her adoptive father's name and wouldn't want to call her son Edwin, which sounded too old. And her biological dad hadn't been the kind of man she'd want her son to emulate.

Would Clay offer up a suggestion? Did he have a friend or family member he wanted to honor?

Then again, he'd come here to apologize for his attitude yesterday. And he wasn't exactly offering to take on a paternal role, which was fine with her.

They continued to stand in the middle of the living room, both pensive and silent.

Finally, Clay said, "Just for the record, I plan to pay you child support. I'd just… Well, I don't want this to sound mean or anything, but I'd like to have a DNA test first."

The comment hurt, and she flinched ever so slightly. She understood why he'd want paternity proven, but it also questioned her honesty and integrity. But then again, he really didn't know her.

"I'm sorry," he said again. "It's not that I don't trust or believe you. It's just…a formality. And I think it will protect everyone involved."

"I understand." She had to admit that she really couldn't blame him.

"And that's another reason I'm here. Under the circumstances, I think we should get to know each other better."

Now that surprised her. And oddly enough, it pleased her, too. "What did you have in mind?"

In all honesty, Clay hadn't thought it out that far. Rickie flinched when he'd mentioned that he wanted a paternity test, which the family lawyer was going to insist upon. He had no reason to doubt her words or her determination to go it alone, but he caught something hiding in her expressive brown eyes, a secret she harbored beneath the surface.

For a brief moment, sadness and vulnerability stole across her face, mocking everything she'd just told him. And even if she could handle it on her own, she shouldn't have to.

So he'd suggested they spend some time getting to know each other to soften the blow, especially today, when she stood before him, alone and vulnerable, yet proud, wearing curve-hugging stretch pants and a blousy green top that suggested she planned to work out.

"We could start by going out to lunch," he said. "What do you think?"

His suggestion must have taken her aback, because she didn't say anything right away. When she finally spoke, she asked, "When do you want to do that?"

Not today, he supposed. It wasn't even close to noon. "What about one day next week?"

"I start work on Monday, so we'd have to find a place for a quick meal in Brighton Valley."

"Actually, that would work better for me anyway." The moment the words rolled off his tongue, he regretted them. This wasn't about *him* or his convenience.

Well, in a way, he supposed it was. If he didn't look out for his best interests, who would?

Still, all of his self-talk failed to do the trick because, when push came to shove, he believed her claim. And that meant those babies would prove to be his.

So now what? She'd invited him inside, but she hadn't asked him to have a seat. Should he sit down anyway?

He'd come to see her today, hoping to get on her good side, but so far his efforts didn't seem to be working very well. He ought to be happy that she'd agreed to meet him for lunch in Brighton Valley next week. But she'd probably only have an hour, which wouldn't give them much time to talk.

Instead of waiting for an invitation to make himself at home, he took a couple steps forward and scanned the cozy living room once more, thinking that the decor was scarce compared to his family home, a sprawling five-bedroom ranch house loaded down with colorful, handwoven rugs on the hardwood floors, southwestern artwork on the walls and tons of photographs throughout.

He spotted several cardboard boxes in a corner, next to a stack of framed pictures, and it struck him that she might be moving. Apparently she'd been serious about leasing out her house and finding a rental in Brighton Valley.

"What's going on with that stuff over there?" he asked. "Are you moving in or out?"

"A little of both." She chuckled softly, which was the first sign that they might be able to get through the initial awkwardness of his unannounced visit. "After my parents died, I packed up the house and put some of their personal things in storage. The plan was to either sell the house or rent it out furnished. And now that I'm home to stay, I've been bringing things back and putting them where they belong."

"I'd be happy to help."

"That's not necessary."

She'd told him she wasn't going to ask anything of him, and apparently she meant it. That further convinced him that she was telling the truth, that he'd fathered those babies. She also seemed determined to handle things on her own. Didn't that prove that she wasn't like Tyrone's ex-wife and that she wasn't trying to put something over on him?

He slowly shook his head and stepped forward. Using his best commanding officer's voice, he said, "You shouldn't be lifting boxes. Or reaching up to hang pictures. I'll do it for you. Just tell me where you want them."

Rickie folded her arms, resting them on top of her baby bump. "I didn't have any problem bringing them in from storage. And they can stay right where they are."

"I've got a couple of hours," he said. "You might as well put me to work."

She sucked in a deep breath, then slowly blew it out. "I planned to go through those boxes and take out what I'd like to keep in the house. The rest of the stuff can go out in the garage."

"Okay, so sorting stuff is something you'll have to do yourself. But I'm here now. What else can I do?"

She studied him for a moment, as if questioning the wisdom of allowing him into her home and into her life. Then she uncrossed her arms. "I'm clearing out the office so I can convert it into a nursery. I realize I have time to get that done, but I'd feel better if I had things ready way before the babies get here. My doctor said that twins often come early."

"Then you may as well give me a list of things to do. In a few weeks, I won't be as available as I am now."

She bit down on her bottom lip, as if pondering the

wisdom of accepting his help. Finally, she said, "I do need to move the office furniture into the garage."

"All right. And after that…?"

She scrunched her pretty face and placed her hands on her hips. "You're serious about this."

"You bet I am." He just hoped he wouldn't live to regret it.

"Do you know how to paint?" she asked.

"I've had plenty of experience painting the barn and the corrals on the ranch. Why?"

"The walls are white now and a little dingy, so I want to freshen things up and change to something more bright and cheerful." Rickie pointed toward the hallway. "Come on. I'll show it to you and tell you what I have in mind for the nursery."

Clay followed her past an open bedroom door and to the office. The room was pretty empty, other than the furniture—a desk, a wheeled chair, a small bookshelf and a metal file cabinet.

"Once this room is cleared," she said, "I'd like to paint the walls light green. And if I can remember how to use my mom's sewing machine, I'll try to make some curtains with a cute animal print. Or maybe I'll just put a valance on top of some new white blinds."

She was nesting and clearly more content with the life changes coming her way than Clay was. Not that he found anything wrong with that. Creating a home for the twins was a good thing. Kids needed a loving mother.

They needed a father, too, he supposed. Although he'd learned to live without one. Of course, Granddad had stepped into that position when Clay was a teenager, clamping down on him occasionally, but only when Clay got too rebellious. For the most part, Granddad had a boys-will-be-boys attitude, but he knew how to yell and cuss. And he knew how to set limits.

But even though Granddad might have set a good example of how to be a disciplinarian, babies needed a gentle hand. And Clay suspected he'd fall short when it came to being a nurturer.

"I'm going to put one crib against the east wall," Rickie explained. "And the other one will go near the closet. I think I can get by with a single chest of drawers. At least, for the time being."

He hadn't thought about that. She was going to need a lot of baby stuff. And two of most things. That was going to be costly. He'd have to make a financial contribution toward her purchases.

After she took him to the garage and pointed out the spot where she wanted to store the office furniture, he returned to the house and began moving things. He thought about driving back to the ranch to get a dolly, but that was going to take a while. And he hated to have her think he was wimping out on her.

The file cabinet was empty, which made it easy for one guy to move alone. And the bookshelf was fairly light. The desk, on the other hand, was going to be more challenging. But he was strong and industrious. Besides, it wasn't that big. When he'd been in high school, he'd had one about that same size in his bedroom.

"I can help you move that," she said.

"The heck you will." He shot her a you've-got-to-be-kidding-me look and rolled his eyes. "I got it."

Determined to prove himself and to show her that he wasn't an invalid, he kicked aside a large throw rug that had been sitting in front of it. Then he pulled the desk away from the wall. He stepped back, thinking he might use that rug to his advantage. The plan was to set it under the two rear legs, then slide the desk across the floor.

As he spun to the right, he tripped over the damn thing, lost his balance and dropped to the hardwood floor.

It all happened so quickly, he couldn't do a single thing to correct his fall. As he landed on his bad knee, a sharp pain sliced to the bone. "Dammit."

"Oh, no." Rickie rushed to his side and dropped to the floor. "Are you all right?"

No. He hurt like hell. And so did his pride.

"I'm okay," he said as he slowly rolled to the side, taking the weight off his knee, and sat on his butt. Then he stretched out his leg, which throbbed and ached like a son of a gun.

"I just need to take the weight off it for a while." Actually, he was more concerned about the long-term effect of his fall. He'd hate to suffer a setback in his rehab. But he didn't say a word about that. Otherwise, she'd probably run him off and try to do the heavy work on her own.

As Rickie knelt beside him, the alluring scent of her shampoo, something that smelled like tropical fruit, filled his head, offering him a temporary distraction. Then she gently probed his knee. "I was afraid something like this might happen. I'll get you an ice pack."

"That's not necessary. It feels better already." Hell, just her TLC was enough to take the edge off the pain.

Apparently she wasn't convinced, because she continued to finger his knee.

He tried to make light of the situation and tossed her a crooked grin. "I guess you can take the medic out of the Army, but you can't take the medic's heart out of the girl."

She blessed him with a pretty smile, and the soreness faded even more. Time stalled, then rolled back, taking him to a different place, one where the waves splashed on the shore, where the scent of sunblock filled the warm, tropical air.

The recollection was so real it spiked his hormones, and a blast of heat shot through his veins. Without a thought to the repercussions, he reached up and cupped her jaw.

Her lips parted at the unexpected touch, and as their eyes met, he brushed his thumb across her cheek, caressing her skin. Memories of that romantic Hawaiian night built into a tropical storm, stirring up the same sweet pheromones that first surfaced while they'd sat on the sand and watched the sun go down.

He had half a notion to...

No, that was *crazy*. He wasn't about to follow up on a sexual compulsion like that. He already knew what making love with her was like. And there was more to life than great sex.

Instead of going to bed and allowing their physical needs to be met, they ought to spend time together, talking and getting to know each other.

He removed his hand and glanced away, breaking eye contact before he completely lost his head. "I think I'd better leave that desk where it is for now. I'll come back with some tools and take it apart. That way it'll be easier to move."

"I'm sure you have other things to do," she said. "And it's a long drive back to the ranch."

"I saw a hardware store not far from here. I'll just go pick up a screwdriver and a wrench. It'll just take a few minutes."

"I appreciate this, but you really don't have to help me."

He knew that. Only trouble was, he actually wanted to.

Chapter Seven

"You had a funny look on your face when I asked if I could go with you," Rickie told Clay as they made their way to the curb in front of her house, where he'd parked his truck. "Are you sure you don't mind if I tag along?"

"No, not at all. I was just a little surprised that you want to go to a hardware store."

"I want to pick up some paint samples to take with me when I go shopping for the baby bedding and the material for curtains."

"Wow. You're really getting into the whole decorating thing."

Apparently, she'd surprised him yet again. But when she glanced his way to read his expression, he tossed her a grin. Then they both got into the truck, and he started the engine.

Ten minutes later, they arrived at Hadley's Building

Supplies on the outskirts of Jeffersville. As they walked toward the entrance, Rickie took a moment to watch Clay's gait, noting that his limp was more pronounced than when he'd first arrived at her house.

"You probably should have kept that ice pack on your leg longer," she said.

He shook his head. "Nah. I'm doing okay."

She wasn't sure if he was being truthful or macho. With some men, it was hard to say. But she decided to take him at his word.

When they'd gotten about six feet from the door, a little red-haired boy breezed by Rickie, practically cutting her off and causing her to trip and stumble.

Clay reached out to steady her, his grip on her arm firm.

"Mikey!" a woman cried out. "I did *not* give you permission to run ahead. Apologize to that lady, then come back here."

The boy, who was about four or five, was a cute kid, even with hair that stood up on one side, freckles sprinkled across his face and a smudge of dirt marring his chin. He bit down on his bottom lip, then looked at Rickie and frowned. "Sorry, lady."

"Apology accepted." Rickie offered him a smile, then glanced at the woman who'd called him back, assuming she was his mother. She was in her midthirties with shoulder-length dark hair and a baby bump that suggested she was due to deliver anytime. She also looked a bit worn and frazzled, no doubt from chasing after the energetic little boy all morning long.

If Rickie had been alone, she would have spoken to her and asked when her baby was due. She'd also ask the woman if she was having a boy or a girl, but Rickie wasn't about to let her maternal hormones run away with her while she was with Clay.

When he opened the door for her, she stepped inside, followed by Mikey and his mom.

"If you're good," the mother told her son, "I'll buy you candy to eat on the way home."

A sugar rush was the last thing that kid needed, but Rickie kept that thought to herself.

Clay pointed to the right. "There's the tool section."

Rickie followed him down the aisle.

"That poor lady has her hands full," Clay said. "And it looks like she's going to have another one to chase after before she knows it."

Rickie agreed, but she didn't comment. She was going to have her hands full soon, too. How did Clay feel about that? Would he offer to help out? Or would he steer clear of her?

She tried to read between the lines, to gauge the subtext behind his words. But she decided to take one day at a time. He was here with her now. And he'd offered to paint the nursery.

Clay stopped in front of a display of packaged household sets that included several pastel-colored tools, including a couple of screwdrivers, a small hammer and a pair of pliers. They were kind of cute and probably functional. But they looked a little too girly to her.

"My dad's tools are in storage, so it seems like a waste of money to buy new ones." Rickie would have suggested they go look for them, but she hadn't labeled the boxes, so it would take a long time to find them.

"I could drive back to the Bar M and pick up my screwdrivers, too. But I don't feel like making that trek, especially if it sets me back a few hours. So this will get the job done." He bypassed the pink set and chose one that was Tiffany blue in color. "Consider it a housewarming gift. You can keep them in the kitchen for little jobs that might come up. Besides, you're having two babies. There's no telling how often they'll break something and you'll have to fix it."

"Are you suggesting the twins will be as active and impulsive as Mikey?"

"Yep. If they grow up to be anything like the kid I used to be, you will." He winked, then tucked the tool set under his arm.

She thanked him, even though she didn't see the need to have girly tools. But a wrench by any color was still a wrench, right? And if she faced a bigger repair job, she'd call a handyman.

"Now let's go find those color samples," he said.

They continued to the paint section and stopped in front of a rack that displayed a variety of options. She immediately looked for a pale green, which would match the comforter set she'd seen while shopping yesterday. She'd liked the jungle animal print, especially the cute monkeys in the trees. She'd also spotted one with a Western theme that boasted little red barns, brown ponies and cowgirls and cowboys spinning lariats. If she ended up buying that one, she'd probably want beige walls.

She glanced at Clay, who stood patiently beside her, looking all tall and lean and cowboy. He barely resembled the handsome, bare-chested guy who'd charmed her on the beach or the skilled lover who'd made her feel like the only woman in the world. But Bullet by any other name was still Bullet. Right?

The chemistry they'd shared in bed was certainly still

there. Just minutes ago, while seated on the floor of the office—or rather, the nursery—he'd nearly kissed her.

She'd seen the heat in his eyes, just as she'd spotted it when they'd slow danced on the sand and again in that rented bungalow. She'd sympathized with him when he'd tripped and landed on his knee, but while she'd examined him, something sparked between them, and she'd been sorely tempted to instigate that kiss herself, which would have been stupid.

Like he'd said, they didn't know each other very well. And it wasn't a good idea to let lust run away with them.

She removed a sample that had several shades of light green, as well as one with several beige hues, and showed them to Clay. "What do you think?"

"Does it matter?"

For some crazy reason, it did. "I'm still trying to decide on the decor for the nursery. I'm torn between animals and cowboys."

A smile tugged at his lips. "I'm sure you'll make the right decision."

Yes, eventually she would, but it would be nice if he took more of an interest in her decorating choices.

"You mentioned green when we were in the office," he said. "So it sounds like you've already decided."

"Good point." She replaced the brown sample, then held up the other to the artificial light, as if it might help her check the color variances. But more than that, she also wanted to know which shade matched his green eyes.

That way, if he didn't come around very often, she had something in the nursery that would remind her of him. Of course, she'd also have the babies in their beds.

"Is there anything else you want to see here?" he asked.

"No, this is good for now." Painting the nursery was just the first step in preparing for the twins. She'd also have to buy two cribs and a chest of drawers.

From a couple of aisles over, a familiar voice rang out. "Mikey! Where did you run off to?"

Rickie couldn't help but smile. Obviously, Mikey had forgotten about the candy bribe his mom had promised him.

"Michael Allen Weldon," she called out again. "Did you hear me? I'm not playing games. And I'm not buying that candy. If you don't get over here right now, you're going to lose television privileges for a week."

"Sounds like she means business," Clay said.

"No," the boy cried out. *"Not* the TV. I'm comin', Mama."

"Attaboy," Clay said. "Smart kid."

Rickie stole a glance at the gorgeous man walking beside her, the father of her babies. Would he be a good one? Would he play an active paternal role?

Cut it out, Rickie. Do you really want him that involved in your life, in the decisions you make?

Maybe, she thought.

Or would that merely complicate things? What if he got too involved while coparenting? Or too opinionated?

There were some good things to be said about being a single mother, she supposed. She wouldn't have to answer to anyone but herself.

As they reached the end of the paint aisle, they turned to the right, toward the registers, and she caught a blur in her peripheral vision right before she felt a hard thud on her thigh. Mikey bounced off her leg and fell to the floor in front of her, just in time for her to trip over him.

She gasped. If Clay hadn't reached out to catch her, she might have fallen to the floor. Or worse, landed on top of the little rascal, who sat on the floor, his eyes wide at the near mishap, his legs stretched out in front of him and his cowboy boots on the wrong feet.

"Sorry," Mikey said, as he jumped up and dashed off to find his mother.

"Are you okay?" Clay asked as he slipped his arm around her waist and held her steady.

"I think so." She placed her hand protectively over her baby bump, which had become a habit lately. "I'm glad I didn't step on that little guy."

Clay's brow furrowed, and he held her tighter. "And I'm glad you didn't fall and hurt yourself."

"Me, too." She should have been paying attention to where she was walking and not focusing on the attractive cowboy she was with.

As they checked out, she opened her purse to pull out a credit card, but Clay waved her off. "I got this. Remember?"

The housewarming gift. Should she argue? Or just let it ride?

Clay Masters was an enigma, and she had no idea what to do about him. But she'd better figure out something before they got home. His visit had come out of the blue. And she had a feeling she'd better brace herself so he wouldn't knock her completely off balance, just like Mikey. Only this fall would be a lot harder.

Clay stayed at Rickie's house until four o'clock that afternoon. He'd only meant to take apart the desk, carry the pieces out to the garage and then put it back together again. But by the time he'd finished that task and reentered the kitchen, she was making sandwiches and cutting up fresh fruit.

"I made lunch for us," she'd said. "I still get a little nauseous if I go too long on an empty stomach."

So how could he say no?

After they ate, he carried a few boxes in from the car and stacked them in the dining room for her to sort through later. When he spotted her dragging out a ladder so she could replace the bulbs in the overhead lights, he'd insisted that he let him do it.

Needless to say, he stayed longer than he'd planned. After the forty-five-mile drive, he arrived home at the dinner hour. Fortunately, he'd been able to ward off the maternal interrogation until he sat down at the family table.

"So," Mom said as she passed Clay the mashed potatoes. "How did things go today?"

"All right." He spooned a large helping onto his plate, then passed the bowl to Granddad.

"You were gone a long time," she said. "Were you with Rickie all day?"

"A couple hours." Actually, it was more like seven, but if he admitted that, she'd never stop quizzing him.

"I hope she's feeling well," Mom added.

"She seems to be." Other than the nausea that still plagued her at times. At least, that's the conclusion he'd come to.

"Would someone pass the gravy?" Granddad said, offering a welcome distraction from the line of questioning. He'd often done the same thing when Clay had been in high school. Once, when Clay thanked him for running interference for him at times, his grandfather winked at him, his eyes sparkling with mirth, and said, "I ain't so old that I don't remember what it was like to be young. Just make sure you stay safe—and obey the law."

For the most part, Clay and his buddies had tried to do that.

Mom reached for the gravy bowl but never missed a beat. "Is Rickie seeing a doctor regularly?"

"I assume she is. She knows the importance of good medical care."

"That's good to know," Mom said. "There can be pregnancy complications, especially with women carrying multiples."

Clay stiffened and scrunched his brow. "What kind of complications?"

"High blood pressure, preeclampsia, premature labor…"

Damn. He hadn't considered health risks.

"Are her parents supportive?" Mom asked, clearly not able to quell her curiosity.

"They were in a car accident and passed away about six months ago."

"Oh, no. I'm sorry to hear that. Does she have a sister or friend who'll be with her during the delivery?"

Clay had no idea. Nor had he considered she might need emotional support as well as financial. But the more he thought about it, the more concerned he grew. "I'm not sure."

"I can understand your reluctance to get too involved," his mom said. "You probably should move slowly."

"Agreed."

Still, he had to admit that he'd learned a few things about Rickie today. She had an independent streak he hadn't realized, a take-charge attitude. And something told him that his kids, assuming those babies were actually his, would be in good hands.

Of course, that wouldn't absolve him from taking responsibility. He'd figure out a way to help her with those babies. Hopefully he could do that without making any kind of commitment that might suck the life out of him.

"Would you mind if I talked to her?"

Taken aback by the question, Clay's first impulse was to tell his mother to back off. But on the other hand, he didn't like the idea of Rickie facing labor and delivery alone. Women usually needed each other at times like that, especially if there were complications.

If his mother reached out to her, maybe Clay would feel better about setting up some boundaries. Because if he didn't, he'd find himself getting sucked into her world—and even more tied down than he already was.

"Sure," he said. "I'll give you her number."

Three days later, Clay wished he'd kept that information to himself. Not only had his mother called Rickie, but before *he* could set up a lunch date with Rickie, the two women had made plans to meet at Caroline's Diner in Brighton Valley on Wednesday at noon!

Which was why Clay decided to crash that luncheon before his mom became way more involved than necessary.

Rickie had been so stunned when Sandra Masters called and asked her to meet for lunch in Brighton Valley that a response knotted up in her throat. It had taken her a couple of beats to finally be able to speak.

Sandra had obviously gotten Rickie's number from Clay, which meant he was okay with it, so she'd agreed to meet on Wednesday. That gave her time to get a feel for the clinic schedule and to find out when she'd be able to take a lunch break.

She talked to Sandra again last night, and they made plans to meet in front of a place called Caroline's Diner at ten minutes past noon.

Rickie was a bit nervous, although Sandra had been so sweet on the telephone that it seemed silly to stress about it. Besides, spending some time with Clay's mother also meant she'd learn more about her children's father—and his family.

The diner was located on the shady main drag, not far from the town square and the family clinic where she worked. So she'd found it easily enough.

She'd no more than opened the front door when she spotted Sandra, who was already waiting near the old-style register.

The petite blonde in her late fifties quickly got up from her seat and greeted Rickie with a smile. "They don't take reservations, but I wanted to get here early to make sure they could seat us. This place really fills up around mealtime."

Rickie scanned the interior of the small-town eatery, noting the pale yellow walls and white café-style curtains on the front windows. "What a darling restaurant."

"Isn't it? And the food is to die for. If you like home-style cooking, you won't find a better meal than here. And Caroline makes the best desserts you've ever tasted. Check this out." Sandra pointed to a refrigerator display case that sat next to the cash register. It was chock-full of homemade goodies.

Rickie was drawn to a three-layer carrot cake, although the lemon meringue pie looked yummy, too. She usually tried to stay away from sweets, but she might have to make an exception today.

Sandra motioned to a matronly waitress who wore her graying dark hair in a topknot. "We're both here now, Margie."

The ruddy-faced waitress broke into a bright-eyed grin. "I'll have that booth ready for you in just a minute."

While waiting to be seated, Rickie glanced at a blackboard, on which someone had written What the Sheriff Ate in yellow chalk. Just underneath, it read, Baked Ham, Scalloped Potatoes, Glazed Carrots and Apple Pie à la Mode—$9.95.

"Caroline's husband is retired now," Sandra explained, "but he was once the only law enforcement officer in Brighton Valley. She and everyone else still refer to him as the sheriff. And that's how she announces her daily specials."

"What a clever idea. I like that." In fact, there was a lot Rickie liked about Brighton Valley. The diner sat along a quaint, tree-lined street that was the perfect place for a lazy walk—and some shopping.

She'd arrived a few minutes earlier than the time she and Sandra had agreed to meet, just so she could take a quick walking tour of downtown Brighton Valley. And she was glad she did. Just across the street and down a couple of doors, she'd noticed a real estate office. Not that she planned to relocate right away. She'd only worked two and a half days at the clinic, but she liked Glory. And if that permanent position opened up, she'd be tempted to sell her house and move.

"Your table's ready," Margie called out as she waved Sandra and Rickie to a corner booth at the back of the diner.

Sandra was the first to slide onto the brown vinyl seat. Before Rickie joined her, she noticed Margie giving her a once-over.

"You new in town?" Margie asked. "Or just visiting?"

"I don't actually live in Brighton Valley, but I got a temp job that started here on Monday morning."

"Oh, yeah? Who do you work for? I know just about everyone in these parts."

"Dr. Davidson."

"Good deal." Margie broke into a big grin. "Glory Davidson is the best darn doctor in the world, if you ask me. I've been going to her ever since she took over ol' Doc McCoy's practice. Are you covering for Lorena? The poor thing had to go back to Mexico to check on her daddy."

Rickie's only response was to nod as she slid into the booth next to Sandra.

"When is your baby due?" Margie asked.

"February 28."

Margie let out a whistle. "I thought you were going to say it was due around Christmas. You must be having a big baby."

"She's having twins," Sandra said, her eyes lighting up.

Margie brightened, and she clapped her hands together like a happy child. "How exciting. I always wanted to have a set of twins. That is, until I had my firstborn, Jimmy Lee. That boy was as cute as a bug, but a real pistol. By the time he hit the terrible twos, I was so grateful that I only had one of him."

Sandra laughed. "My son, Clay, was like that, too. A real handful."

Margie gave them two menus, took their drink orders, then left them to chat.

Sandra leaned forward and lowered her voice. "Margie is a sweetheart, but she's a bit nosy and prone to repeat things she's heard."

Rickie nodded, although she'd already figured that out on her own. Still, she couldn't help but like the server's friendly nature.

"Anyway," Sandra said, "thanks for meeting me today. I thought it would be nice if we got to know each other better."

Rickie offered her a smile. Clay was the one she really wanted to know better, but his twin mom seemed nice. And learning more about her and his family would be helpful.

"I know Jeffersville is a bit of a drive from Wexler, but it's closer than if you were still on an Army base in Honolulu. At least we can visit once in a while. I'd like to get to know my grandchildren. And you, too, of course."

"I would have reenlisted, but when I found out I was pregnant, I realized that if I was deployed, I wouldn't have anyone to watch the babies for me."

"Clay mentioned you lost your parents recently. I'm so sorry. Family is important."

Rickie nodded her agreement. She didn't want to get caught up in a discussion about her complicated family history with a woman she barely knew.

"I grew up in foster care," Sandra said. "I didn't have a bad experience. The people were nice, but it wasn't the same as having a loving home and parents. When I met Clay's father, my life finally came together."

It sounded as if Rickie and Sandra had something in common besides Clay, but before she could decide whether to mention their similarities, Margie returned with their drinks—diet soda for Sandra and milk for Rickie.

"So what'll you have for lunch?" Margie asked.

Rickie hadn't even looked at the menu.

"I'll have the chicken salad sandwich on a croissant," Sandra said. "And the fruit cup instead of French fries."

That sounded good. Besides, Rickie had to be back at work before one thirty and didn't want to take the time to ponder the other options. "I'll have the same thing."

When Margie bustled off to take their orders to the kitchen, Sandra continued to speak, surprising Rickie with her candor.

"I loved Clay's father. John and I had a great marriage. But since he was a career military man, we moved around a lot. I would have preferred to stay in one place, but I made a home wherever the Army stationed us—Germany, Washington, Georgia. John's deployments left me lonely, although the other wives were very supportive. We both thought it would be easier if we had children, but after several miscarriages, I brought up the idea of adopting."

Rickie hadn't seen that coming. Had Clay also been adopted? And if so, had he known?

"About the time I first approached an agency, I got pregnant with Clay. He's my miracle baby."

No wonder Sandra adored her son.

"I have to admit," Sandra added, "I doted on that precious little guy. They call women like me helicopter moms these days, but I'd gone through a lot to finally get him in my arms. And when his father died…" She took a deep breath and slowly let it out. She offered Rickie a warm smile, but a widow's grief still lurked in her eyes. "Well, I didn't want to lose Clay, too. Although that little rascal did everything he could to worry me to death.

And if I didn't color my hair, I would have been gray by the time he entered the second grade."

"How did Clay's father die?" Rickie asked.

"In battle. During Operation Desert Storm."

"I'm sorry."

"Me, too. I'll admit that the last thing I wanted Clay to do was to join the military. Sometimes I think he did it to spite me, although I'm proud of him and all he accomplished, both at West Point and in the Army."

"I'm sure you are."

"Then you can probably understand why I'm looking forward to being a grandmother."

Rickie didn't always open up and reveal her past to people, but Sandra was both sweet and kind. Besides, they also seemed to have a lot in common.

"I grew up in foster care, too," Rickie admitted. "So it's really important for me to create a loving home for my children."

Sandra reached across the table and placed her hand over Rickie's. "I have no idea how things will work out between you and my son. Either way, I'd be delighted to do whatever I can to help you create that special home for your babies."

Rickie believed her. And for the first time since she'd lost her parents, she felt as if she might have someone in her corner. "Thank you. I'd appreciate that."

Before either of them could comment, Margie returned with their sandwiches and fruit cups. "Enjoy, ladies."

Rickie had no more than picked up one half of the stuffed croissant when she heard approaching boot steps and the sound of a familiar soft Texas drawl call out, "Hey."

She glanced up to see Clay standing at their table wearing a smile that dimpled his cheeks.

"Mind if I join you?" he asked.

Sandra slid to the side, making room for him to sit in the booth.

"This is a surprise," she said. "I thought you had things to do at home."

"I forgot about my physical therapy appointment, so while I was in town, I thought I'd join you. That is…" He looked across the table at Rickie. "If you don't mind."

"No, not at all." In fact, she was glad he'd shown up. It was in the babies' best interests for her to have a solid relationship with their father and grandmother.

At least, that's what she kept telling herself. But if truth be told, she thought it might be in her best interests, too.

Chapter Eight

Under normal circumstances, Clay never would have intruded upon a private lunch, but he hadn't been able to stay away from this one. Not when he'd been so damn curious about what his mother might be saying to Rickie.

Or what Rickie might tell his mom.

"Well, look who's here!" Margie handed Clay a menu. "I'd heard you got out of the Army and came back to run the Bar M for your grandpa. How's it feel to be home?"

Margie, bless her heart, had better radar than a fighter jet. Too bad her intel wasn't very good. But she wouldn't get squat out of him. Not if she spread it around town that he wasn't happy to be home. Or to be looking at spending the rest of his life ranching.

"It feels good to be moving around without a cane," Clay said, hoping to appease her. "But I won't need that menu. I'll have what the sheriff ate."

"You got it."

As Margie walked away, his mother sat back in her seat and smiled at him. "I'm glad you'll be eating a hearty meal for a change."

"I'm really not very hungry, but ordering the special was easier than taking time to read the menu." He glanced across the table at Rickie, who looked especially pretty today with her soft brown curls tumbling over her shoulders. "How's the job going?"

"Great. At least, so far. It's nice being in a clinic again. Only this time I get to work with families instead of soldiers."

"Speaking of clinics and families," his mother said, "do you have an obstetrician?"

"Yes, I do."

"Oh, good. Is the office around here?"

"No, it's in Jeffersville."

Clay wanted to put a halt to the rapid-fire questions, but he cleared his throat instead, reminding his mother of his presence and hoping she'd take the hint. But she didn't.

"Do you have other family and friends living in Jeffersville?" his mother asked.

"No, not really. I only lived there when I was a teenager. After high school, I joined the Army. I've been away six years, and my friends have all moved for one reason or another."

"That's too bad," Mom said, unable to just leave it at that. "Not even a neighbor?"

Clay stiffened. He was tempted to answer for Rickie, but he bit his tongue. If she wanted to have a relationship with Sandra Masters, she'd have to get used to being quizzed about subjects she might not want to talk about.

"No, I'm afraid not. I had a twin sister, but she died when we were nine."

"Oh, no." His mother reached out and placed her hand around Rickie's shoulder. "I'm so sorry to hear that."

Clay sympathized, too. But unlike his mom, he usually pulled away when things took an emotional turn.

"It was hard when Lainie died," Rickie said, "but I've adjusted. Don't worry about me. I'll be just fine."

Yeah, right. Telling his mother not to worry was like telling a duck to stay out of a pond. But shouldn't someone in his family be emotionally supportive? Someone who'd actually be good at it?

He'd thought so at first, but as he studied the way his mom reached out to Rickie, the way Rickie responded, her honey-brown eyes glistening with tears, he worried that the women might be bonding. And that wasn't what he'd planned to happen today.

Of course, nothing about this situation had been a part of his life plan.

"How long is your temporary job going to last?" Mom asked.

"Two months."

"Why don't you stay with us while you work in Brighton Valley? Our ranch is only a fifteen-minute drive from here, and there's usually no traffic."

"That's really sweet of you," Rickie said. "But I don't want to impose. Besides, I'm trying to fix up the nursery on the weekends. I need a place to bring the babies home to."

Clay was about to mention that he'd promised to paint and to purchase the furniture, which would be his way of telling his mother to back off and not worry about it, but she suddenly brightened.

"I have an idea," Mom said. "Why don't you stay Monday through Thursday nights with us? We have a big house, with lots of room. And then you could drive back to Jeffersville after work on Fridays."

Rickie shot a glance at Clay, her eyes locking in on his as if she was asking his permission. But hell, what was he supposed to say, no? Not when she was looking at him like that and he knew that she didn't have a family.

"We have a guest room with a private bath," he said.

Rickie bit down on her bottom lip, as if giving the invitation a lot of thought. But a beat later, she looked up and smiled. "Sure. Why not?"

Actually, Clay could come up with quite a few reasons why it might not be wise. With Rickie staying on the ranch, it would be difficult for him to maintain his privacy while being supportive from a distance. But then again, she'd only be staying there four nights a week. He could find plenty of things to keep him busy while she was there.

But that didn't seem to be the answer. How busy did he really want to be when she was sleeping just down the hall?

Lunch at Caroline's Diner had gone much better than Rickie had expected it to. She just hoped that she didn't come to regret staying on the Bar M while she worked at the clinic.

"When can we expect you?" Sandra had asked.

Rickie hadn't wanted to rush into anything. And she needed time to pack a few things, so she said, "After I get off work on Monday."

The rest of her first week at the clinic went well, and now it was Saturday morning. She glanced at the clock on the mantel. No, make that early afternoon.

She'd planned to work on the nursery this weekend, which meant picking up everything Clay would need to paint. She wanted to have it here when he showed up, although he hadn't mentioned a time or even which day.

In the meantime, she had another chore to do. Her parents' accountant had called and requested some additional paperwork he needed to complete their last tax return. So she decided to get that out of the way first.

She wasn't entirely sure where to look, but she knew that one of the boxes in the dining room contained their wills and other important papers. So she opened it and began sorting through it. Toward the bottom, she spotted a manila envelope stuffed full. She removed it, then took a moment to straighten and stretch out the crick in her back before carrying it to the table, pulling out a chair and sitting down to go through the contents.

She found several bills that were due about the time of the accident: power, water, cable TV. How had she missed seeing them when she came home from the funeral and began to settle their estate? They'd all been paid, but only after she'd received the past-due notices. So she tossed them to the side, intending to throw them away.

Next she withdrew a white business-size envelope. She didn't think much of it until the return address caught her eye. The Lone Star Adoption Agency had sent it to Mr. and Mrs. Edwin Campbell. It was postmarked six months ago and had already been opened. She flipped open the flap and removed the contents: a handwritten note and a smaller, pink envelope addressed to the agency.

"We received this correspondence addressed to you," someone at the agency had written, "and we are forwarding it to you per our agreement."

The pink envelope they'd included had also been opened. Inside was a handwritten letter on matching stationery. It was addressed to "The Couple Who Adopted Erica Montoya."

My name is Katherine Donahue, although the many children I've fostered over the years, including the Montoya twins, call me Mama Kate. Rickie and Lainie were sweet girls, and I will always remember them fondly. Lainie was frail and in poor health, and Rickie used to look after her as if she were her own child. They had a special bond, and I became especially attached to them. In fact, I had begun the process to adopt them, but before I could do much of anything, I suffered a debilitating stroke. As a result, all the children I'd been fostering had to go to different homes.

It broke my heart to lose those kids, especially Lainie and Rickie. Not a day goes by that I don't think about them, and I continue to pray that they're both doing well. From what I understand, Lainie's surgery went better than expected. The surgeon didn't think she would live through it, but she surprised him. I'd give anything to be able to visit both girls, but I'm not able to travel. In fact, one of the nurses' aides is writing this letter for me.

Last week, a private investigator visited me here at the convalescent home and asked me if I had any information on Rickie's adoption. It wasn't until after he left that I recalled the name of the agency.

I realize you requested a closed adoption, and I respect that. Children often do better when they can make a fresh start. However, I would love to help these two young women reconnect, if you think Rickie would want to do so I would be delighted to hear from you. I have included my address and phone number. If you decide not to contact me, I understand.

Either way, please give my love to Rickie. I'll never forget how loving she was to her sister. I'm so glad she found a forever home.

Most sincerely yours,
Katherine Donahue

Rickie was stunned. Her sister was alive?

According to Mama Kate's letter, Lainie had faced a long road to recovery. So she hadn't died in surgery. And apparently, she'd hired a private investigate to find Rickie.

Why hadn't her parents mentioned anything about this to her?

Had they intended to? Had the accident happened before they'd gotten a chance to tell her?

Rickie had no idea how long she sat at the dining room table, holding the only connection she had to her sister. It wasn't until the doorbell rang that she finally managed to wrap her mind around the news.

Her brain continued to spin, weaving all kinds of scenarios, as she carried the letter with her. When she opened the door, she found Clay on the stoop.

Apparently, he spotted her rattled expression and sensed something was off.

"What's the matter?" he asked.

"I just got some surprising—and startling—news about my sister." She stepped aside so he could enter. "She didn't die during heart surgery."

"That's good news," he said.

"Yes, but I have no idea where she is. Or how to find her." Rickie led him to the sofa, where they both took a seat.

"Is there any chance she might have moved in with someone in your birth family?" he asked.

"No, our mother passed away when we were babies, and it was all downhill after that. My dad was an alcoholic and couldn't hold down a job. So money was scarce. I can remember nights when he came home late or not at all. Lainie and I had to fend for ourselves. Then, about the time we turned eight, he died in a seedy bar after a drunken brawl, and we were placed in foster care."

Clay took her hand in his and gave her fingers a gentle squeeze. "I don't know what to say. 'I'm sorry' seems so inadequate."

"Thanks, but his death turned out to be a good thing. We were much better off in foster care. At least we got to eat regularly. And that's when my sister's health problems were finally addressed." That was also when the two girls had become separated.

Rickie's adoptive parents had told her that Lainie died during surgery. According to Mama Kate, the doctors hadn't expected her to live. Had her parents lied to her? Or was that merely what they'd concluded had happened?

Now that they were both gone, she'd never know for sure. But they'd always been honest with her. She'd just have to believe they'd heard a rumor and made that assumption.

"Can you get in touch with the agency and see if they have any contact information for your sister?" Clay asked.

"I can try, but the letter doesn't say anything about Lainie being adopted, too." Rickie glanced at the letter she held, then brightened. "Maybe Mama Kate knows something."

"Who's that?"

"Our first foster mom. She's living in a nursing home now, but I have her contact info. I could call her." In fact, she wasn't going to wait another minute.

Rickie carried the letter with her to the kitchen phone, then dialed the number Mama Kate had given.

A woman answered on the second ring. "Shady Oaks Nursing Home. How can I direct your call?"

"I'd like to speak to one of your patients—or residents. Her name is Katherine Donahue."

The woman paused for a beat. "I'm sorry. Katherine passed away last week."

Rickie's soaring heart sputtered and dropped with a thud, reverberating in her ears. This couldn't be happening. If she'd found that letter when she'd first come home…if her parents had mentioned something to her the last time they'd talked…if…

"Ma'am?" the woman on the line said. "Are you still there?"

"Yes. It's just that…" Rickie blew out a sigh. "I'm so very sorry she's gone."

"I'm not sure if this helps, but she passed away peacefully. She told me many times that she was ready."

Yes, but Rickie wasn't ready. Still, she thanked the woman and said goodbye. After the call ended, she turned to find Clay standing behind her. He'd obviously heard her side of the conversation and had connected the dots.

Either that, or he'd seen the tears filling her eyes, because he eased close to her. He didn't say anything, and she was glad that he didn't. Emotion clogged her throat, and she didn't think she would have been able to speak anyway.

As if sensing what she needed, he opened his arms, and she fell into his embrace.

* * *

Clay had never been any good when anyone, especially a woman, got weepy. But the minute he'd seen the stricken look on Rickie's face and saw the tears roll down her cheeks, he'd been toast. So he offered the only thing he could think of—a shoulder to cry on.

He wasn't sure how long he held her, her growing belly pressed against him, connecting them in a way, yet holding him at a distance. Still, she clung to him and cried, dampening his shirt. But he wasn't going to complain. Instead, he stroked her back, providing what little support he could, and breathed in the soft scent of her floral shampoo.

She sniffled one last time and drew back, breaking their embrace. Her voice cracked as she said, "I'm sorry to be a crybaby. I'm actually pretty tough, but lately, my hormones do this to me."

He wasn't buying that. She was blaming her tears on her pregnancy, but he knew it was more than an increased level of estrogen at play. Moments earlier she'd believed that she might be able to reunite with the twin she'd thought had died. And that hope had been dashed.

"You don't need to apologize. I understand." And he'd do just about anything to make her feel better, to see her smile again. But at the moment, he didn't have any bright ideas.

She placed her hand on her womb, stroking the swollen mound where her babies grew, and a thought struck. She'd blamed her tears on her pregnancy hormones. Maybe if he appealed to her maternal side, those same hormones might lighten her load and lift her mood.

"I came by to paint the nursery," he reminded her. "Have you chosen the color yet?"

"Yes." She sniffled and used her fingers to wipe the moisture that lingered under her eyes. "I decided on a light green to go with that animal theme. But I haven't bought the paint yet."

"Then let's go get it now. And while we're out, we can look at baby furniture." Spending the entire afternoon with her hadn't been his original plan. In fact, he hated to go shopping, unless it was for groceries, sporting goods or tools. But he'd make an exception today, especially if it made her feel better.

"I can't," she said. "I've probably got red, puffy eyes and a splotchy face. I have no business leaving the house. Just look at me."

He *was* looking at her, and in spite of her casual dress and obvious emotional distress, there was something that appealed to him and caused his heart to swell and his pulse to go wonky. "You look cute. Besides, the redness will go down in a few minutes. And it'll do you good to get out."

"I... I don't know." She combed her fingers through her hair, the luscious locks glossy and soft. She seemed to be on the fence and waffling.

Before he could push a little harder, her eyes opened wide, her lips parted and she let out a silent gasp. Then she reached for his hand and placed it on her abdomen. One of the babies was moving, and he felt a little bump that might be a knee or maybe a butt. It was hard to say, but it was pretty cool.

A big grin stretched across his face. "I feel it."

She held his hand firm. "Wait a minute."

He wasn't going anywhere. Not now. The moment was surreal. Special.

And then it happened. A quick jab to his palm that nearly took his breath away.

* * *

Rickie had no idea if it was their son or daughter who'd given Clay a solid kick, but the moment he felt it, his eyes widened and he broke into a full-on smile. "Wow. That's cool. I've felt foals and calves rumble around in the womb, but never a baby."

"They've been moving a lot lately." She might have been crying just moments ago, but the babies made her laugh now. "It makes me wonder what they're doing in there."

"Does it hurt when they kick like that?"

"No, not at all. I love the way it feels. It makes them seem real."

She lifted her hand off the top of his, but he continued to touch her baby bump as if mesmerized by the experience. She found it pretty amazing, too.

Finally he stepped back and said, "So what do you think? Are you up for a shopping trip?"

"I suppose so."

"Good. Then we can go out to dinner to celebrate."

Her head tilted slightly. "What are we celebrating?"

"Maternal hormones and the miracle of birth." He nodded toward the front door. "Come on. Let's go."

She really wasn't in the mood to shop or to have fun. She'd much rather stay at home and brood about the fact that her sister was alive and that she had no idea how to find her. She'd lost an opportunity to visit Mama Kate, too. It would have been nice to thank the sweet lady for providing her and Lainie with a loving home, even if it had only been temporary.

But Rickie didn't want to hang out at the house alone. And she actually liked the Clay she'd begun to know. Besides, didn't her babies deserve to have a daddy in their lives?

"All right," she said. "Give me a minute to splash some water on my face and to change clothes."

"Take all the time you need."

She wouldn't take long. Spending the afternoon with the gorgeous father of her twins was beginning to sound like a good idea. It might be too much to hope for, especially when the future never turned out the way she hoped it would, but maybe...if things continued to develop between her and Clay, she'd be able to provide her kids with a loving home, complete with a mommy *and* a daddy.

Chapter Nine

Clay had expected the experience of shopping for baby things to be a real pain in his backside, but so far it hadn't been too bad. He just hoped that when the day was over, and all was said and done, the charges on his credit card were the only costs he'd face.

They first stopped at the hardware store to pick up the paint supplies for the nursery. The last time they'd been there, Rickie had studied the colors carefully, but today she didn't dawdle. She immediately reached for a green swatch and pointed to the lighter shade on the bottom. "This will work perfectly with the comforter set I plan to buy."

He was glad she'd finally chosen the paint for the nursery walls—and relieved that she'd stopped crying. He didn't like seeing her so upset.

After paying for their purchases, Rickie walked beside Clay as he pushed the shopping cart that carried the paint, brushes and other supplies out to his Dodge Ram. Once he unlocked the truck, he placed them in the back seat of the extended cab. Then he drove to a specialty store that sold baby clothes, toys and furniture.

As he followed Rickie up and down the aisles, he couldn't help wondering how much of this stuff the babies really needed. He had a feeling that a lot of the displays were just to tempt new parents into spending more money than they'd budgeted. But what did he really know?

As he'd expected, since it had taken days to choose the paint, Rickie studied the various bedding sets way longer than he thought necessary. After narrowing down the options, she turned to him and asked, "What do you think? If you were a baby, would you rather have your room decorated with jungle animals or cowboys?"

Normally, he'd be inclined to hold back his opinion and let her make the ultimate decision. But in this case, he actually had a preference. It was bad enough that he'd been forced to live a rancher's life. He wasn't about to point his kids in that same direction from the day they were born. So he said, "I like the monkeys."

"Me, too. I was afraid we might have to return the green paint for beige if you preferred the cowboy print."

He didn't mind cowboys. Or ranching, for that matter. It's just that he didn't like being tied to the land, unable to travel to exciting places or pursue his own interests. Of course, now that he was no longer in the Army or able to fly, not much interested him these days.

Rickie put the two comforter sets into the cart, and then she led him to the furniture section to pick out a chest of drawers, two cribs and mattresses.

"It's a good thing I have a truck," he said.

"Actually, I think we need to order the big items and set up a delivery date." She pointed to a couple of crib styles she liked, then looked up at him. "What do you think?"

His only thought was that her soulful brown eyes had a way of looking into the heart of a man. And Clay didn't like the idea of anyone digging that deep, but she'd asked for his opinion again.

"You choose," he said.

She bit down on her bottom lip, then blew out a soft sigh. "All right, then." She placed her hand on a white, four-in-one convertible model with an arched headboard. "I like this one, but since it's more expensive, I probably ought to go with a simpler style."

He'd brought her shopping to see her happy, so why would he encourage her to get something other than her first choice?

"I prefer that white one, too," he said. "Let's order two of them and get the matching dresser."

Her smile deepened, putting the glimmer back into her eyes, and he looked away, trying to shake the effect her happiness had on him.

"What else do you want to look at?" he asked.

"This will do for now. Once we paint and move in the furniture, that old office will look like a real nursery. Then, on the weekends, I can add other things bit by bit."

"What other things?"

"I'll eventually need a lamp, wall hangings and stuff like that."

The nursery was going to end up costing a boatload of money, and that was before Clay counted baby clothes, diapers, bottles and who knew what else. But he wouldn't complain. He'd expected to take on his share of the financial burden—if not more.

That was about it, though. When it came to babysitting or burping or changing diapers, Rickie would have to look for someone else to step up, because he didn't know squat about babies.

When the kids got old enough, he'd feel more comfortable being around them and doing things with them. He'd teach them to ride a horse, as well as a bike. And he'd take them camping and fishing. But for the first few years, he'd have to leave the entertaining and the day-to-day stuff up to Rickie.

By the time they'd ordered the furniture and set up a delivery date, then packed the comforters in the back seat, on top of the paint supplies, Clay asked Rickie if she was hungry. "If you want, we can stop someplace and get a bite to eat."

"Let's just go home. I'll whip up something for us to eat there."

The day had turned out to be a lot better and more productive than Clay had expected it to. And for some odd reason, going "home" for dinner with Rickie sounded like a nice way to end it.

While Clay prepared the nursery walls for the painting he planned to do another day, Rickie cooked ground turkey then added a jar of marinara to make spaghetti sauce. She also made a green salad. It was an easy and casual meal, but after all Clay had done for her today, she wanted to make it special. So she set the dining room table, using her mother's good china. While tempted, she decided not to light candles, which would provide a romantic vibe. She could hardly look at the hunky rancher without triggering flashbacks of the night they made love, and her memories didn't need any prompts.

While the pasta boiled, she went to the nursery to check on Clay's progress. He'd already washed down the walls and now stood at the window, putting up blue masking tape to protect the glass. He hadn't heard her approach, so she took a moment to admire his work ethic, not to mention his broad shoulders and the way his jeans fit his perfect backside.

As if sensing her presence, he turned to the door and smiled. "Something sure smells good. I'm nearly finished in here for today. I promised my granddad to go with him to purchase a couple more cutting horses tomorrow, so I'll have to come back to finish next Saturday."

"That's not a problem. I'd do it myself, but the fumes aren't good for the twins. I'm just happy to know it'll be done soon."

He placed the roll of tape on the windowsill, crossed his arms and shifted his weight to one hip. "Maybe it would be better if I came back during the week, while you're at work and staying at the ranch. That way, the room can air out and you won't have to deal with the smell."

"That would be great, but..." She couldn't expect him to do that. "It's a long drive."

"I'd have to make the trip no matter which day I paint."

True, but she liked the idea of being home when he came. Besides, once the nursery was painted, he wouldn't have too many reasons to return.

Their gazes locked for a couple of beats, and her heart fluttered the way it had the first time she'd laid eyes on him. It had only been physical attraction then, but he'd been so helpful and supportive today, not to mention incredibly generous, that… Well, she couldn't help thinking that a guy like him would make an awesome father and husband.

Whoa, girl. You're letting those pregnancy hormones run away with you.

Nesting and creating a nursery for the babies was one thing, but imagining Clay in a family scenario was another. She'd better reel in those whacky thoughts before she set herself up for a major disappointment, not to mention heartbreak. She'd already had enough of those to last a lifetime.

She tore her gaze away and nodded toward the door that opened to the hall. "Dinner is just about ready, so you might want to wash up and meet me in the dining room."

"Sounds good."

Ten minutes later, they sat across from each other at the linen-draped table.

"This spaghetti is really good," he said. "But I didn't expect you to work so hard."

"Thank you, but I didn't go to much effort. As far as meals go, this was pretty simple to make."

"Either way, I appreciate it."

She swirled the long pasta strands on her fork only to have them unwind and slide back onto her plate. Too bad she hadn't fixed something that was easier to eat. Next time she'd have to make tacos. That was, if there was a next time.

At least he'd come today. He'd also gone above and beyond, especially when he'd held her in his arms while she'd cried. How many men were that sensitive, that supportive?

Maybe she'd better let him know that she appreciated it. So she said, "I'm sorry for falling apart on you earlier today."

He stopped twirling his fork and looked up. "Don't worry about that. You were hit with both good and bad news at the same time. That's enough to make anyone cry."

Did he ever cry? Somehow she doubted it.

"Are you going to look for your sister?" he asked.

"Yes, but I really don't know where to start."

"You could hire a private investigator."

She set her fork aside and leaned back in her seat. "I think that's what my sister did. Mama Kate said in her letter that a private investigator had contacted her. So my sister might be looking for me."

"Hopefully she'll find you first. But in the meantime, I'll talk to my friend Poncho. He's a cop with the Wexler Police Department, so I'm sure he can recommend a good PI who's local. He also might have some other ideas and suggestions."

"That would be awesome. I'd give anything to see Lainie again."

"You could also try one of those home DNA kits you get online," Clay said. "People use them to learn about their ancestry, but a lot of them have found lost relatives that way."

"Good idea."

They continued to eat in silence. When they finished, Clay began to clear the table.

Rickie reached for his wrist to stop him. "What are you doing?"

"I'm going to help you clean up."

"Don't be silly. You have a long drive in front of you. Besides, I'll have the dishes washed before you leave city limits."

He offered her a warm, appreciative smile. "Thanks for your concern, but I insist. I'm not going to eat and run."

Since she'd tidied up as she prepared the meal, it didn't take long for them to load the dishwasher.

"See?" he said. "That didn't delay my drive home."

As he headed to the front door, she followed, wondering if he would kiss her good-night. She hoped so, but he'd have to make the first move.

He paused on the stoop and brushed his lips across her forehead, the warmth of his breath lingering on her skin.

"Thanks again for dinner. I'll see you back at the ranch on Monday evening." Then he turned and strode toward his truck, leaving her on the porch with a tingly brow.

She appreciated the friendly gesture, but it was hardly the kind of kiss she'd hoped for. And as he drove away, disappointment settled over her.

What was wrong with her? Clay had been amazing today. He'd shown her a sweet and kind side, and he'd been more than generous. Instead of yearning for more, she ought to be grateful for his support and friendship. Entertaining any thoughts of romance was crazy and would only lead to further disappointment.

Hadn't his mother told her that he hadn't planned to have kids? He probably wasn't marriage minded, either.

Clay might have a playful grin and a soft southern drawl she found mesmerizing, but he'd undoubtedly used it on other women before. He'd certainly charmed her that day on Hawaii's North Shore.

Only trouble was, that same charm had cropped up again today, promising to lure her in once more. And she'd have to be on guard. She couldn't risk another broken heart.

* * *

On Monday morning, Rickie packed her things for a four-night stay at the Bar M, then drove to Brighton Valley to start her second workweek. It was business as usual at the family clinic, and before she knew it, five o'clock rolled around.

After the last patient left and Glory locked up, Rickie went out to her car. But instead of driving straight to the ranch, she stopped by a fast food restaurant and picked up something to eat.

She figured Clay's mother would offer to feed her, but she didn't want to make any assumptions or to be any more trouble than necessary. So she headed back onto the highway and munched on a grilled chicken sandwich while she drove.

She'd no more than parked her car by the barn when Sandra stepped out onto the porch and waved in welcome. "Can I help you bring anything into the house?"

"Thanks for the offer, but I've got it." Rickie reached into the back seat and removed her suitcase. Then she crossed the yard and met Sandra on the porch.

"I'm glad you're here. Dinner's almost ready." Sandra opened the door for her and followed her into the house. "We normally eat around five thirty, but Clay and his grandfather went into town for supplies and haven't returned yet. You're probably hungry, so I can get you a snack or appetizer to tide you over."

"Actually, I already had dinner."

"That's too bad. From now on, I hope you'll eat with us on the nights you stay here. It'll be nice to have another woman to talk to. I'm usually stuck with a couple of men who'd rather wolf down their meals than waste their time on conversation."

Rickie laughed. "I was in the Army, remember? I've had plenty of experience with men." She paused as her words sank in. "Oops. That came out wrong. I meant I know all about male habits and mannerisms."

"I knew exactly what you meant." Sandra laughed. "Come on, I'll show you around. Then I'll take you to the guest room so you can get settled."

After a brief tour of the house, Sandra ushered Rickie into a large, tidy bedroom with a lemony scent. A floral comforter covered a queen-size bed and a green throw rug adorned the hardwood floor.

"You'll have your own bathroom," Sandra said, pointing to an open interior door. "You'll find clean linens on the cupboard. Please make yourself at home. And if there's anything you need, let me know."

"I'll be fine. Thank you."

"Once you unpack," Sandra said, "come to the table. You can have dessert with us. I made a blueberry cheesecake."

Rickie offered her a warm, appreciative smile. "I'll certainly make room for that."

When an engine sounded outside, Sandra brightened. "Clay and Roger, his grandfather, just got home."

Rickie momentarily brightened, too. And her heart skipped a couple beats. But she did her best to quell her excitement and tamp down any romantic thoughts.

"I'd better get dinner on the table," Sandra said. "I hope you'll come and sit with us, even if you're not hungry."

Rickie thanked her but remained in the bedroom even after she unpacked, trying to play it cool. About twenty minutes later, she made her way to the kitchen table, where the small family of three had just finished a meal of meat loaf, baked potatoes and green beans.

Both men stood when she entered. Clay's grandfather, a tall, gray-haired man in his seventies, reached out a big, work-roughened hand in greeting. "I'm Roger Masters. You must be Rickie."

"Yes, sir. It's nice to meet you. Thanks for allowing me to stay with you on weekday evenings. I'll try not to disrupt your routines or to be a bother."

"Nonsense," Sandra said. "We're happy to have you. And our usual routines could use a little shaking up."

Clay pulled out the chair next to his, and Rickie took a seat. While Sandra cleared the table, the men lapsed into a talk about the new horses they'd just purchased and the ranch foreman's search for another hand.

When Sandra passed out slices of cheesecake, the men quickly dug in, and their conversation stalled.

"Rickie," Sandra said, "how was your day?"

"It was good. I really enjoy working with Dr. Davidson."

"Any exciting moments?"

"Actually, two. A woman came in for a checkup, and while she was sitting on the exam table, she mentioned having an upset stomach and an ache in her jaw. It turned out that she was having a heart attack. We'd no more than sent her off in an ambulance to the hospital when a mother brought in a kid who'd sliced a deep cut in his knee while trying to saw into a watermelon with a bread knife."

"How in the hell did he do that?" Roger asked.

Rickie'd wondered the same thing when she'd first talked with him and his mom. "Apparently, he was sitting on the floor and holding the melon in his lap."

The elderly rancher chuckled and shook his gray head. "That boy's lucky he only sliced into his knee."

At that, Rickie laughed.

"When is your next doctor's appointment?" Sandra asked.

"It's on Friday afternoon." Rickie glanced at Clay. "A lot of fathers go to those appointments. Let me know if that's ever something you might like to do. You'd be able to see the babies on the ultrasound."

She'd expected him to decline, but he surprised her when he said, "Sure. Why not? I'll pick you up at the clinic. That way we won't end up with two cars in Jeffersville."

Stunned by his response, Rickie was still reeling when Sandra said, "I'd like to go, too."

Before Rickie could tell her she was more than welcome, she caught a frown on Clay's face and bit her tongue. Didn't he want his mom to go with them?

Clay's mother was getting way too involved. Fortunately, when he cut her a stern glance, she took the hint.

"I didn't mean to suggest that I tag along to that appointment," she said. "But I'd love to go to another one with you someday."

"Of course," Rickie said. "I'm going to schedule my appointments as late in the afternoon as possible so I don't have to miss too much work."

"Maybe we can make an evening of it," Mom said, apparently forgetting Clay's silent admonishment. "The men can call out for pizza or something, and we can have dinner in Jeffersville. We can even go shopping. You're going to need a lot of baby things, and the twins will be here before you know it."

"Clay already bought the major stuff," Rickie said. "So I have the cribs, mattresses and bedding."

"That still leaves plenty of other things to buy. And I'd love to shop for baby clothes with you." Suddenly his mother brightened. "I have an idea. I can plan a shower. I have a lot of friends from church and the Wexler Women's Club who'd come."

Clay didn't doubt it. Sandra Masters was the friendly type with a big heart and a generous nature. So women seemed to gravitate to her. She was also easy for them to talk to, so they often confided in her and asked for advice.

That's why it frustrated her that Clay kept his thoughts and feelings under lock and key. It didn't help that Granddad was pretty tight-lipped about his feelings, too.

Yet Rickie seemed to open right up. Clay had expected the two of them to hit it off, but they were getting a little too chummy for his comfort. As they talked about invitations, possible dates and the guest list, Clay stiffened.

As if sensing the tension in the room, Granddad chimed in, as usual, in an attempt to defuse it. "I picked up a DVD of that new Denzel Washington flick while I was out. Anyone else up for a movie?"

"I am," Rickie said. "I love his movies."

"Good. Come on. I'm going to put it on in the den."

As Granddad got to his feet, Rickie began to clear the table of the dessert plates and forks, but Clay stopped her. "Oh, no, you don't. I have cleanup duty tonight."

Once Rickie left the kitchen and was out of hearing range, Clay approached his mother, who stood at the sink.

"Slow down, Mom. You're moving way too fast."

Her brow furrowed. "I'm sorry, honey. I didn't mean to overstep. It's just that..." She paused and blew out a ragged sigh. "I like Rickie. And she's all alone. I only want to help."

"I get that. But it's not your job to mother her. I'm still trying to wrap my brain around all that's happening to me. And I feel…" He paused. Hell, he knew exactly how he felt. Scared. Backed into a corner. But there was no way he'd readily admit it, especially to a woman who'd dedicated her life to fixing things.

His mother placed her hand on his cheek, her gaze loving. "I know it's a little scary for you, especially because you never really knew your father and you didn't grow up with younger brothers and sisters. But believe me when I say this. You're going to love those babies the moment you see them. And you're going to be an amazing dad."

Clay hoped she was right. Because, quite frankly, he had his doubts.

Chapter Ten

Clay drove to Rickie's house in Jeffersville twice the following week. The first time was on Monday morning, after he'd gone to physical therapy. She'd given him her key so he could go inside and paint the nursery. He'd stayed long enough to get the job done, clean up afterward and air things out. Hopefully, she wouldn't have any fumes to contend with when she returned to the house after the end of her workweek.

He'd made that second drive today so that someone would be home when the baby furniture arrived. After the deliverymen left, Clay put both cribs together and set them in the spots Rickie had pointed out when she'd told him of her plans to convert the office into a nursery.

He probably should have locked up the house at that point, but he opened one of the comforter sets so he could get an idea of what the room was going to look like after Rickie made the final touches on the project. Then he'd folded the bedding again and put it back into the plastic pouch.

He had a feeling she was really going to be happy when she saw it. And oddly enough, that made him happy, too.

As it turned out, her doctor's appointment was today. He'd made plans to meet her at the obstetrician's office, which meant he had to hang around in Jeffersville for an hour or so. But he didn't mind. He took the opportunity to explore the area, particularly the main drag, which was within walking distance of Rickie's house.

There he spotted a drugstore, a small post office, a mom-and-pop market and even a fast food restaurant with a drive-through window—Bubba's Burger Barn.

Jeffersville wasn't nearly as big and spread out as Wexler. Nor was it as quaint and touristy as Brighton Valley. But as far as small Texas communities went, it was probably an okay place to live.

The only downside was the distance Clay would have to drive from the Bar M whenever he wanted to visit Rickie and the kids, but he'd get used to it. His truck had a good CD player, so he could listen to his favorite music or to books on tape.

He glanced at the clock on the dash and decided it was time to head over to the doctor's office, but before he could turn off the main drag, his cell phone rang. Poncho's number flashed on the lit display, which was a relief. Clay had called him last Saturday night and had left a voice mail message, but he hadn't heard from the guy in nearly a week.

"Dude," Clay said. "Where the heck have you been? I thought I might have missed seeing a ransom note."

"Sorry about that. I took a week's vacation and spent it fishing at a lake in Canada with a couple of guys from my gym. The cell reception was terrible up there, so I didn't get your message until I got home. What's up?"

"A lot." So much, in fact, that Clay wasn't sure where to start. He began by telling Poncho about Rickie's surprise visit to the ranch and the news of her pregnancy.

"Oh, wow. *Twins?* Are you sure she's telling you the truth?"

Clay'd had his doubts at first, but he'd come to the conclusion that they had to be. There hadn't been any reason for Rickie to lie to him. "Yeah," he said, "I'm sure."

"How do you feel about it?"

"Uneasy. A little scared." Clay didn't open up to just anyone, but Poncho had always been safe—and a good sounding board. "At times, I feel like I'm in over my head, but I'm going to do the right thing."

"You mean you're going to *marry* her?"

"Slow down. I wouldn't go that far. Marriage wouldn't just ground me, it'd probably put me six feet under."

Poncho seemed to chew on that for a moment. "You two hit it off pretty good on the beach."

"That's for sure."

"Has that changed?"

"No, not really." Clay found Rickie just as attractive as ever, just as appealing. But more than that, he'd come to see that she had a good heart. A tender one. And at times he felt compelled to wrap her in his arms. Not just to make love with her, but to protect her. She seemed vulnerable these days, no matter how much she insisted she didn't need any help.

"So why do I sense there's a problem?"

"I guess there isn't one." Other than Clay's fear of

being a hands-on father, of failing his children. But Poncho, of all guys, ought to understand that.

In spite of his reluctance to share his feelings, particularly his lack of confidence, Clay said, "Hell, I pretty much grew up without a dad. So what do I know about being a father?"

"I didn't have one, either," Poncho said. "But you know what it's like to be a kid."

"Yeah, I guess so." But Clay didn't remember being a baby. Nor did he know much about them or their needs—other than the fact that they were fragile and needed lots of love and attention.

They cried a lot, too. And it seemed the only things that made them happy or content were rocking chairs, bottles, and kisses and hugs. Just the thought of getting involved with all of that, of being unable to become emotionally attached to them, was enough to convince Clay to stay out of Rickie's way until the twins were old enough to go to school.

The two men grew silent, and Clay continued the drive to the obstetrician's office, following the directions he'd been given. As he pulled into the parking lot, he added, "For what it's worth, I think Rickie will be a great mother."

"That ought to be a relief."

"Yeah, it's huge." Clay parked in an open space and shut off the ignition, but he remained seated behind the wheel.

"So what *aren't* you telling me?" Poncho asked.

"I don't know. I really like her, but I can't give her what she needs."

"You realize that means another man will probably end up raising your kids someday."

"I realize that. And I'm not sure that I like the idea. Know what I mean?"

"Yeah, I do. I had a stepfather, remember? And it was no secret that he didn't like having me around."

Clay remembered some of the stuff Poncho had told him when they were kids and blew out a sigh.

"There are other options," Poncho said. "You don't have to make a marital commitment. You could live together. Or you could just be lovers."

"I don't think Rickie would go for something like that. Family is really important to her—more than most women, I think. And I'm not a family sort of guy." Rather than delve too deep into the touchy-feely stuff, Clay changed the subject to his reason for calling Poncho in the first place. "Speaking of family, Rickie and her twin sister were separated as kids, and she'd really like to find her. Can you recommend a good private investigator?"

"Actually, I can. Once I get back to the precinct, I'll give you his contact info."

"Thanks. I'd appreciate that."

Poncho paused for a moment. "By the way, I just heard that one of the Life Flight pilots is moving out of state after the first of the year. Any chance you'd be interested in taking his job?"

Hell, yes. In a heartbeat. "I wish I could, but I'm afraid I won't be able to pass the required eye exam."

"That's too bad."

To say the least.

"Listen," Poncho said, "I have to go. I'll give you a call later with the investigator's contact number. In the meantime, check your calendar. It's time for another poker night. If we're lucky and Duck isn't on the rodeo circuit, maybe he'll be able to join us."

"Sounds good. I'll bring the beer."

After the call ended, Clay left his truck in the parking lot and entered the doctor's office. He scanned the waiting room and spotted Rickie sitting in a chair near the window, thumbing through a parenting magazine. She wore a pair of black slacks and a light blue shirt that molded her baby bump. As she stopped turning pages and zeroed in on an article she must have found interesting, her dark curls tumbled over her shoulders.

She looked…cute. And maternal. Yet at the same time, he found her as sexy as hell.

He took a moment longer to admire her then crossed the room and took the seat next to her. "Sorry I'm late."

She looked up and smiled, those honey-brown eyes having a sweet effect on him. "No problem. I thought something might have come up. Or else you changed your mind."

Before he could respond, a brunette dressed in pink scrubs and holding a medical file opened the door and called, "Erica Campbell."

"Come on." Rickie set the magazine aside, got to her feet and reached for her purse. "This is it."

So it was. Clay had flown night ops in dangerous situations without blinking an eye, but he'd never been in a situation like this, one that tickled his nerves to the point of sweaty-palmed apprehension.

His heart was thudding so hard he could feel it in his ears. He imagined those thumps as a warning in Morse code. *Watch out. Do not get sucked in over your head.*

But as he followed the nurse and Rickie into the farthest part of the back office, he wiped his hands on his denim-clad thighs and pushed through it.

* * *

Rickie lay on the exam table, her belly exposed, while Dr. Raquel Gomez applied the gel. Each time she had the opportunity to see the twins on the ultrasound screen, excitement soared. But today, she focused on Clay. He appeared a bit pale and wide-eyed, reminding her of a possum in the headlights.

"This is going to be cool," she told him. "There's nothing to be nervous about."

"I'm not nervous." A twitch in his eyes mocked his words, and she couldn't help but smile.

"Dad," Dr. Gomez said, "you'll get a better view if you step around to the right side of the table."

Rickie wasn't sure Clay actually wanted to get a good look. But he did as he was told.

"Here we go," the doctor said as she moved the probe over Rickie's belly. "There's Baby A."

"That's the girl," Rickie told Clay, whose nervous expression had morphed into one of awe.

Thank goodness. Rickie always found it heartwarming to see her son and daughter moving around inside her womb, but she'd been worried that Clay might find it overwhelming.

"That's amazing," he said. "Just look at her." He leaned forward and studied the screen. "Is she sucking her thumb?"

"She certainly is." Dr. Gomez continued to scan the baby, taking time to make measurements. "And she's growing nicely. She's measuring at twenty-one weeks and three days, which is a little small, but that's to be expected with multiples."

Rickie had known the twins were getting bigger. Her

waistline certainly was. And their movements had gotten stronger.

"Here's Baby B," the doctor said. "And he's right on target, too. He's measuring twenty-two weeks, one day."

The doctor took a few more measurements. When the scan was complete, she wiped the gel from Rickie's belly and gave her a towelette to use to clean up. Then she helped her sit up.

As Rickie adjusted her shirt, the doctor said, "Both babies look good. The placentas are healthy, the heartbeats are strong. And they're growing at a steady rate. Do you have any questions?"

"Not that I can think of." Rickie glanced at Clay. "Do you?"

"No, not really."

"Then I'll see you in three weeks." Dr. Gomez reached out and shook Clay's hand. "It's always nice to have the fathers come in for these appointments." Then she left them alone.

"So what did you think?" Rickie asked Clay.

"I'm stunned. This makes them seem…real."

She'd felt the same way the first time she'd seen them on the ultrasound, their little hearts beating like crazy. And now, when they tumbled around and kicked inside, there was no doubt. Not only were they real, but she'd be holding them in her arms one day soon.

As Rickie got off the exam table and stepped onto the floor, Clay asked, "Have you decided on their names?"

"No, not really. I was going to name the girl after my sister. But now that I have reason to believe Lainie's alive and that I might find her someday, I'd better come up with something else." Maybe Katherine, she thought, after Mama Kate. "I'll think of something."

Clay nodded his agreement. "What about the boy?"

"I'm not sure. I like David."

"Maybe you should consider calling him Goliath instead, since he's so much bigger than his sister?"

Rickie laughed. "Very funny."

He shrugged, then said, "It's up to you. But if I had a say in naming them, I'd call the boy Jonathon—after my dad."

"I like that." She also liked the idea that Clay had laid claim to the twins, which seemed like a sure sign that he'd be involved in their lives. "And just so you know, you do have a say about things."

Hopefully, she wouldn't regret telling him that. Up until two weeks ago, Clay hadn't known anything about her pregnancy. And while there were times, especially in the beginning, when she'd felt all alone, adrift on an uncharted sea, she'd also been able to make all the decisions on her own, without any outside interference.

As they left the exam room, Clay said, "I'm going to drive through Bubba's Burger Barn and pick up dinner. Then I'll meet you at home."

Home. Coming from Clay, in his soft Texas drawl, the word had a nice ring to it, reminding her of the family she'd hoped to create, complete with two children, a mommy *and* a daddy.

While Rickie waited at the reception desk to make her next appointment, Clay headed for the clinic door. She studied the former Black Hawk commander as he walked with assurance, admiring the broad shoulders that suggested he could carry a heavy load—be it physical or emotional—as well as the denim-clad hips and the sexy swagger that reminded her he knew how to treat a woman.

If things continued to progress like they had over the past two weeks, if the two of them grew closer, maybe they'd become lovers again. If so, then her children would not only have a loving father, but she'd have a special man in her life. A friend and helpmate who'd stick by her through thick and thin, who'd love her in sickness and in health. For richer, for poorer.

She'd had plenty of disappointments over the years and suffered more than her share of losses. She didn't want to jinx anything at this stage of the game, but if her intuition proved true, her luck had finally changed.

On the way home from the doctor's office, Rickie stopped to get gas. By the time she'd parked in her drive-way and shut off the ignition, Clay's truck had pulled up along the curb. When he got out, he carried a white paper bag holding their food and a drink carrier with two disposable cups.

She didn't usually eat beef or French fries, but the food would be filling, and the cleanup was going to be a breeze. She would have preferred a more romantic din-ner, but Clay's heart had been in the right place, and his offer to pick up their meal was both thoughtful and sweet.

After unlocking the front door and letting them in-side, Rickie caught a whiff of fresh paint, but the odor wasn't very strong.

Clay set the bag and drinks on the dining room table, then tossed her a boyish grin. "Come on. I can't wait for you to see how the room looks."

She followed him down the hall. When she entered her father's old office, she scanned the green walls, the white cribs, the cute jungle-print bedding, still in the plastic bags and even cuter at home than in the stores.

"This is amazing," she said. "I can't believe the transformation. The nursery looks better than I'd hoped it would."

She turned to Clay, who stood close to her side, watching her reaction to all he'd accomplished. A sense of pride lit his eyes, and her heart took a tumble. "I don't know how to thank you."

Without a conscious thought, she wrapped her arms around him and gave him an appreciative hug. But the moment she felt the warmth of his arms and breathed in his musky, mountain-fresh scent, memories of the slow dance in the sand filled her head, reminding her of the chemistry they had the night they'd made love.

Was he having flashbacks, too?

She drew back just enough to look into his heated gaze. She felt compelled to draw his mouth to hers, but he beat her to it and kissed her as if this evening was just a continuation of that first night.

She relished his taste, his skilled tongue, and leaned into him. But before she could lose herself in him, he drew back and removed his lips from hers.

"I'm sorry," he said. "I didn't mean to overstep."

"You didn't."

He glanced at her baby bump, yet kept his thoughts to himself.

"I'm sorry," she said. "I'm afraid my belly is a lot bigger than it used to be." She hoped it wasn't a turnoff.

"I don't care about that. It's just that I don't want to hurt you."

"You won't. Pregnant women have sex all the time." Her cheeks warmed. "I mean, that's what I read. I haven't actually…" She paused, trying to regroup, and her cheeks warmed. After all, he'd only kissed her. He hadn't said a thing about doing any more than that.

Apparently, he knew what she'd been trying to explain, because he pulled her back into his arms and kissed her again, his tongue seeking hers. As his hands roamed along the curve of her back, passion built to the boiling point, and at the same time, so did her hopes and dreams.

Whatever this was, whatever they'd shared in the past, was more than chemistry, more than sex. At least, it meant a lot more than that to her.

Again, Clay paused and took a half step back. His gaze caressed her, a loving touch she felt as strongly as if he'd done it with his hands. "You're beautiful, Rickie—inside and out."

She was both flattered and skeptical at the same time. As a result, she let out an awkward little chuckle. "I not only look like a blimp, I feel like one, too."

He placed his hand on her swollen womb in a way that seemed almost reverent. "Seeing you like this, with the babies growing inside, makes you all the prettier. And all the more appealing."

His sweet words and his gentle touch stroked something deep in her heart and soul, and she knew at that very moment that she could love this man.

Who was she kidding? She'd already fallen in love with him.

They stood like that for a moment, lost in an unexpected reality. Then she reached for his hand and led him to her bed, where he kissed her again, stirring up a rush of feelings, both physical and emotional.

As they slowly removed their clothing, Rickie knew that this night would be special—and more memorable than the last. They'd reached a turning point to their budding relationship, and it would only get better from here.

She pulled back the coverlet, and they moved to the bed, where they kissed again. Their hands seemed to remember all the right places to touch, to caress. Tongues mated, breaths mingled and hands stroked until she thought she might die if they didn't make love.

Clay hovered over her, and she reached for his erection and guided him right where she wanted him to be, to come. *Home.*

He entered her slowly, taking time to consider the babies, to be gentle. But it was nearly impossible for her to hold back. As her body responded to his, harmonizing in a loving tune only the two of them could hear, she reached a peak, arched her back and let go.

He shuddered, releasing with her in a sexual explosion that would have lit up the night sky if they'd been outside, shattering stars and filling the air with a silent profession of love and forever.

She felt compelled to say it out loud, to tell him exactly how she felt. Instead, she held back, savoring the moment and envisioning their future together. Together, they'd create a perfect home, plan family holidays and spend each night like this, wrapped in each other's arms.

Surely he was having those same thoughts…

Clay lay still, caught up in an amazing afterglow. He hadn't expected to make love with Rickie tonight, although, given their off-the-charts chemistry, he couldn't say that he was surprised. It's just that he had no idea where to go from here. The renewed intimacy between them would make it difficult for him to maintain a safe emotional distance, but did that matter?

He had to admit that their bodies were in tune with each other, and that the sex had been even better tonight than before. But she was probably going to expect some kind of commitment from him, which would be life altering. And his life had changed enough already.

Still, they couldn't go on as if nothing had happened. Could they?

Poncho had suggested that they could become lovers without moving in together or making any serious promises, but Clay couldn't suggest something like that now. Not when he wasn't sure how he felt about all that was happening. Hell, he wasn't sure how he felt about anything.

"Are you hungry?" Rickie asked, pressing a kiss to his shoulder. "We could eat those burgers. They're probably cold, but I can warm them up."

Actually, Clay would prefer to pass on dinner altogether. He needed time to wrap his mind around what they'd just done—and what it might mean.

"I know that I was the one to suggest we eat together, but now that we…" He glanced at her, still wrapped in his arms, and forced a smile. "Well, we got a little sidetracked. Would you mind if I took a burger to go?"

"No, that's fine. What's going on?"

Nothing, actually. He just needed some time alone, time to think and sort things through. But he'd have to come up with a believable excuse, and one that wasn't an out-and-out lie. "My grandfather and I have an early day planned, which means it'll start before dawn. And I have to stop at a neighboring ranch to pick up a few things beforehand, so I really need to go."

"Okay. I understand." She offered up a smile, but it seemed a little…uneasy.

Damn. He didn't mean to stress her out. He just needed some space so he could figure out how he felt about her. About *this*.

He stroked her cheek, then kissed her brow. "I'll see you on Monday evening."

"All right."

He got out of bed, picked up his discarded clothing and got dressed, taking his time so he didn't appear to be eager to escape. The excuse he'd given her seemed to be working, but he didn't feel too good about it.

Rickie stepped out of bed, pulled a robe out of her closet and slipped into it. She tied the sash under her breasts, which emphasized her baby bump.

The sight intrigued him, yet scared him, too.

It might help if he knew he wasn't leaving her high and dry.

"Are you okay with…?" He nodded toward the bed, the sheets rumpled from where they once lay. "With what we just did?"

She smiled. "Yes, but it would be nice if you could stay longer. And spend the night."

"Maybe next time." But would there even be a next time? He wasn't sure.

Rickie followed him out to the living room. The house was quiet, other than the sound coming from the antique clock on the mantel, its second hand clicking a steady cadence. With each tick-tock, Clay's uneasiness rose.

He'd done his best to avoid love and family in the past. He'd always blamed his philosophy on the need to be a man and a war hero like his father. That's also why he'd resisted his mother's attempts to smother him and keep him under her wing. He'd also done his best to keep her at an emotional distance. But now he wasn't so sure about anything.

There was something nice to be said about having Rickie in his life. He had feelings for her.

Could it be love? He wasn't sure. If it was, he had no idea what to do about it.

Once he reached the front door, he gave Rickie a kiss goodbye. Then he headed for his pickup, both glad to be on the road and a bit hesitant about leaving.

It had been an interesting day, to say the least, and as he pulled out onto the highway, he was still reeling from all that had transpired. And that feeling didn't ease until long after he got home.

Even then, when he'd gone to bed for the night, he still hadn't come up with a suitable answer to his dilemma— other than he needed time to sort it out.

More than once, he felt the urge to reach for his cell, to apologize for leaving so quickly. But then what?

That would only lock him into a relationship that scared the crap out of him. For that reason, he decided not to talk to Rickie again until she arrived at the ranch on Monday night.

He just hoped he'd have it all figured out by then.

Chapter Eleven

Rickie wished Clay had spent the night with her, but she understood why he couldn't. He had responsibilities and commitments, and he took them seriously. That was just one more reason why she'd fallen in love with him.

"Maybe next time," he'd said.

She wasn't sure why he'd used the word *maybe*. Probably because it would be up to her to extend the invitation. And, of course, she would. Hopefully, she'd have that opportunity soon, because she couldn't wait until they would be together again.

The next morning, she woke early, glad that it was Saturday and eager to get a few household chores done so she could begin decorating the nursery.

She fixed a bowl of cereal for breakfast and set it on the counter, where she intended to eat. She'd no more than poured a glass of orange juice to go with it when her cell phone dinged, indicating an incoming text.

When she glanced at the screen and spotted Clay's number, her heart swelled. She quickly she clicked on the message box to see what he had to say and read, Poncho sent me the contact info for a PI, so I'm forwarding it. Hopefully he can help you find Lainie. If you mention his name, he knows Poncho as Detective Adam Santiago.

The investigator was with a firm located in Wexler. And his name was Darren Fremont.

Rickie looked at the clock on the microwave. It was probably too early to call, but she decided to do it anyway. Worst case, she'd be able to leave a voice mail message.

As luck would have it, the phone was answered on the second ring. "Langley Investigative Services. This is Darren Fremont."

After introducing herself and telling the man who'd referred her, Rickie explained the reason for her call.

"My sister's name is Elena Montoya. We were both in foster care until we were nine, when she had open-heart surgery. I'd been told she hadn't lived through it, but I've just learned that wasn't the case. As far as I know, she stayed in the system. Either way, I haven't seen her since."

"I'll need as much information as you can give me," the PI said. "For starters, give me the name of the last school she attended and the county where you lived back then. I'll start there and see what I can do."

Rickie told him everything she remembered, going back as far as when their father had custody. "I don't remember the exact date he died, but it happened during a bar fight. I'm sure it made the local news."

"I've got a big case coming up at the end of the week," Darren said, "and that'll keep me pretty busy. But finding your sister shouldn't be too difficult."

Rickie hoped he was right. And that her sister hadn't been adopted in a closed adoption, like she'd been. Not only would it be more difficult to find her, she'd probably have a new last name. They discussed the payment, which included a hundred-dollar-per-hour fee, as well as all expenses.

"That's not a problem." Rickie didn't care about the cost. She'd mortgage the house to the hilt if that's what it took to find her twin.

"I'll be in touch," Darren said.

Rickie thanked him, then ended the call. For the first time in ages, her life was finally coming together and the future looked bright and full of promise.

Hopefully Darren Fremont was as good at finding people as Poncho—or rather, Detective Santiago—said he was. If that were the case and Rickie's luck held out, the sisters could be reunited within days.

On Monday afternoon, Clay drove into town to pick up supplies. Rather than rushing home for dinner, when Rickie would be there, he found himself dragging his feet and looking for various reasons to stay away.

He realized that he and Rickie would eventually talk about Friday night and what it might or might not mean in the future, but he wasn't ready to discuss it yet. Not when he still wasn't sure how he felt about it. A part of him liked the idea of taking their relationship to a deeper level, yet another part was afraid of what she might expect from him.

By the time he arrived home and entered the house

through the mudroom, he heard his mom and Rickie chatting in the kitchen.

"Clay," his mom said. "You're finally home. I put your dinner on the stove to keep it warm."

"Thanks." After washing up in the mudroom sink, he proceeded to the kitchen and found his plate on the table, across from where Rickie sat.

She looked especially nice tonight in a white blouse and dark slacks, and she blessed him with a smile. He did his best to return it, then took a seat. As he began to eat, the women lapsed back into the conversation they'd been having.

"Did the investigator say how long he thought it would take to find Lainie?" his mother asked.

"Not exactly. He said it shouldn't be too hard. I got the feeling I might hear something from him by the end of the week."

"That's great news. I'm so happy for you, Rickie."

Clay continued to eat as the women went on to talk about the importance of family. He couldn't argue with that. But what caused him some concern was the way his mother had warmed up to Rickie. The two of them seemed to have grown awfully close in a very short period of time. But then, his mom had always wanted more children, especially a daughter. And she'd made it pretty clear that she was determined to have a relationship with the twins.

By the time Clay carried his plate to the sink, the two women had moved on to baby talk.

"I'd love to schedule that shower within the next two weeks," his mom said. "I've already bought the invitations, but I think we should wait to set a date until you hear something from the private investigator. That way, we can make sure your sister is able to attend."

"That would be awesome, Sandra."

"I think so, too. Fingers crossed." Mom scooted her chair away from the table and got to her feet. "Let's have a bowl of ice cream to celebrate."

"I'm pretty full after that delicious meal," Rickie said.

"Try to make room." Mom winked. "The calcium will be good for the babies."

Rickie laughed. "Good point."

Clay blew out a sigh. His mother was certainly doting on Rickie. Not that there was anything wrong with that. But it was easy to see that she was going to be a helicopter granny.

Mom pulled three bowls out of the cupboard, then turned to Clay. "I'll dish up a large helping for you, too, son. I know how much you like ice cream."

Damn, Clay thought. He was getting sucked into the female chatter, which made him want to bolt. So on principle alone, he said, "I'll pass on dessert tonight."

"Suit yourself." She dished up two bowls then handed one to Rickie.

Before he could rinse his plate and put it in the dishwasher, his mother brought up Thanksgiving. "I hope you'll join us here on the ranch."

"Thank you, Sandra. I'd love to."

Clay supposed it was only natural to include Rickie. Where else would she go?

"I know it's still three weeks away," Mom added, "but it's not too soon to plan the menu."

"I have my mother's recipe book, so I can bring candied yams. Or maybe a pie."

"That sounds good, but don't bother making it at home. It'll be fun to cook and bake together."

When Rickie's face brightened, Clay's shoulders

tensed. He didn't mind having Rickie spend the holiday with them or helping his mom cook. But it seemed to be a foregone conclusion that he and Rickie had become a couple.

After they'd made love on Friday, Rickie seemed to have made that jump, too. Not that Clay was completely opposed, but he didn't want to be pushed.

Or rushed.

Unlike his mom, he didn't rush heart first into anything. Life was simpler that way. And safer.

Before Clay could excuse himself and escape to his bedroom, Rickie's cell phone rang. She reached for it, glanced at the lighted display and gasped. "Oh my gosh. It's Darren Fremont."

The investigator? Clay decided to stay put, although he doubted the man had uncovered any news yet. He might only have a question or two for Rickie.

Clay couldn't hear what the guy had to say, but he was able to watch Rickie's expression and hear her side of the conversation.

Rickie's eyes grew wide, and she tightened her grip on the phone. "That's amazing. Where is she?"

She listened for a while, then asked, "Where is that?"

A couple of beats later, she said, "Just a minute." Then she looked at Clay's mother. "Sandra, can you please get me a pen and paper?"

His mom jumped right on it. She hurried to open a kitchen drawer, pulled out a pad and pencil then handed them to her. Moments later, Rickie took note of something the investigator said.

Clay continued to listen as Rickie made several oohs and aahs.

"I can't tell you how much I appreciate this, Darren.

How much do I owe you?" Rickie glanced at Clay and grinned. "He did, huh? That was very sweet of him."

Clay shrugged. He'd told Poncho to tell the PI that he'd take care of expenses. At the time, he'd wanted to see Rickie happy. Hell, he still did. But he also had another motive. If her sister came around, that meant she wouldn't need him or his mother to be her support system, right? At least, that's what he'd told himself.

Once Rickie ended the call, she burst into a bubbly laugh, and her eyes glistened with unshed tears. The happy variety, he assumed.

"Lainie is definitely alive and doing well. In fact, she's married now, and her new husband hired a different PI to look for me. But because of the closed adoption, he ran into a dead end."

"So where is your sister now?" Mom asked. "Do you have a phone number?"

"She and her husband are on a Disney cruise with their three little boys. Can you believe it? She has her own family now."

"Goodness," Mom said. "She's been awfully busy. Did she have triplets?"

Rickie laughed. "I don't have too many details, but according to the PI, Lainie and her husband met while she worked at a ranch. The two of them took in three young brothers as foster kids. Then once they got married, they proceeded to adopt them. It was final last week, so they took the kids on that cruise to celebrate."

"She sounds like a wonderful, loving woman," Mom said. "I like her already and can't wait to meet her. When will she get back?"

"I don't know. About a week. So I'll have to wait to talk to her after she gets home."

"Where's home?" Clay asked.

"In Brighton Valley. Can you believe it? She's not too far from here. And neither is the place where she used to live. It's a home for retired cowboys called the Rocking Chair Ranch, and she still spends a lot of time there. Do you know where it is?"

"I've heard of it," Clay said. "My buddy Matt, the guy we call Duck, rides bulls on the circuit. The last time I talked to him, he mentioned that he's going to take part in the Rocking Chair Rodeo, a local event that will promote the ranch, as well as a group home for abused and neglected children."

"This is amazing," Rickie said. "My sister has done pretty well for herself—a husband and a family. That's all she and I ever wanted when we were kids. Well, that and being together."

"I know how you feel." His mother gave Rickie an affectionate hug. "I'm so happy for you."

Actually, so was Clay. And he was glad he'd played a small part in it.

Rickie stepped away from his mom, her eyes sparkling. "You know what? I think I'll drive out to that ranch tomorrow after I finish working at the clinic. My sister won't be there, but at least I can see a place that's important to her. And I can meet some of the people she cares about. That will make me feel close to her."

For some reason, that made sense to Clay. Rickie had believed that her twin sister had died sixteen years ago. And now that she'd learned the truth, she had to be eager to reconnect.

And wasn't that good news for him?

"A home for retired cowboys sounds like a really cool place," Rickie said. "I'm looking forward to seeing it."

Actually, Clay had thought the idea was pretty cool when Duck had mentioned it. "I'll tell you what. I'll meet you at the clinic. Then we can drive together so you don't have to go on your own."

Those glistening, honey-brown eyes and that bright smile damn near turned him inside out.

"You'd do that for me?" she asked.

"Yeah." He'd actually been doing a lot for her in the past two weeks. He wasn't the least bit sorry, but he wished he knew why he felt compelled to keep offering.

Just minutes ago he'd convinced himself to take a step back. But for some crazy reason, he'd done the opposite once again.

He hoped he hadn't unwittingly stepped into a mire of emotional quicksand, but it was too late to backpedal now.

True to his word, Clay showed up at the clinic at twenty minutes after four. Rickie had already asked if she could take off a half hour early, and Glory had agreed.

"Are you ready to go?" he asked.

"Yes, but will you come with me for a minute?"

"Sure."

She led him to the back office so she could introduce him to her boss. Moments later, she found Glory seated at the desk in her office. "Dr. Davidson, this is my... friend Clay Masters."

Clay extended his hand in greeting. "It's nice to meet you, Doctor. Rickie speaks highly of you."

The doctor took Clay's hand and smiled. "Please, call me Glory. I've heard some nice things about you, too."

They made small talk for a moment or two. Then

Rickie said, "If we want to get to the ranch before the dinner hour, we'd better go."

Five minutes later, they'd climbed into Clay's pickup and were on their way.

"I have a question," Rickie said.

"Shoot."

"I know that Poncho is actually Detective Adam Santiago. And you mentioned that Duck's name is Matt. How'd he get that nickname?"

"The cheerleaders used to tell Matt that he had a sexy stride. Poncho and I didn't want him to get too full of himself, so we told him we thought he walked like a duck. And the name stuck."

Rickie laughed. "I would have liked knowing you guys as teenagers."

At that, Clay laughed, too. "I don't know about that. You might not have liked us. We were pretty rowdy back then."

The pickup slowed, and Clay turned into the entrance to the Rocking C. They followed a long driveway to the ranch house, where a couple of elderly men sat in rockers on the big wraparound porch.

As they got out of the car and headed to the house, one of the old guys scrunched his brow and hollered out to Rickie. "I thought you went on a cruise, Lainie. What'd you do with Drew and the kids?"

"I'm not Lainie," she said. "I'm her twin sister, Erica."

"Well, I'll be damned." The balding old man wearing worn jeans and bedroom slippers got to his feet, reached for his cane and made his way toward her. After giving her a closer look, he chuckled. "You look exactly like her."

Before Rickie could respond, an older woman wearing an apron stepped out onto the porch. The moment she spotted Rickie, her lips parted. "Lainie... What happened? You're not supposed to..." She paused and scanned Rickie's length. Apparently, she noted the baby bump, because she laughed and said, "You must be Lainie's twin sister."

"That's right. I'm Erica Campbell."

"I'm so happy to finally meet you." The older woman, whose hair was a pretty shade of red, probably dyed, stepped off the porch and closed the gap between them. "Your sister told me all about you, and I'd been hoping and praying that she'd find you. I'm Joy Darnell, the ranch cook. My husband, Sam, is the foreman."

Rickie again introduced Clay as her friend, hoping he'd correct her, but he didn't.

"Lainie will be so sorry she missed you," Joy said.

"I knew she wouldn't be here. I was just so eager to connect with her that I wanted a chance to see where she used to live and to talk someone who knows her."

"Well, I'm glad you did. We love Lainie here, so it's a special treat to meet you. Would you like to stay for dinner? There's plenty for both of you."

"No, but thank you. We only stopped by for a minute. And to leave my phone number with you. Please let my sister know I was here, and if one of you will call me as soon as she gets home, I'll come back to the ranch to see her."

"Of course I will. It'll be my pleasure."

After saying their goodbyes, Rickie and Clay returned to his pickup and headed back to the clinic, where she'd left her car.

"Did it help you to visit the Rocking C?" Clay asked.

"Yes, it did. Thanks for taking me."

"No problem."

Rickie inhaled softly and slowly let it out, releasing the memories of past hurts and disappointment. Instead, she would focus on her many recent blessings. She seemed to be acquiring a long list of them.

"Now at Thanksgiving," she said, "when we sit around the table eating turkey and stuffing, I'll have one more thing to be thankful for."

Clay merely nodded and continued to drive.

Life was certainly coming together for her, and she had Clay to thank for that. Sandra, too. The woman had been more than kind. She'd welcomed Rickie into her home and her heart with open arms.

"I don't know if your mother told you," Rickie said, "but she invited me to stay at the Bar M after the babies come. That way she can babysit while I work. I told her I'd have to talk to you first."

"Seriously?" he asked.

The surprise in his tone was laced with irritation, which took her aback. "Is there a problem?"

"Not really. It's just that…" He sucked in a deep breath, then blew it out in an exaggerated huff. "My mom should have run that idea past me before talking to you."

Rickie flinched, and her heart crumpled. If Clay was upset that his mother issued the invitation to stay at the ranch, it was because he wouldn't have made the offer on his own. She probably should wait it out and let him explain, but that wasn't necessary.

"Don't worry," she said. "I won't take your mother up on the offer. That's why I told her that I'd talk it over with you first. But you've made it clear, once again, that you want to keep me at arm's distance."

Clay clicked his tongue and shot a glance across the seat at her. "That's not what I meant."

"Oh, no? I keep getting flashbacks of the other times you withdrew from me, starting when I visited you at Tripler. You practically ordered me from your hospital room."

"I was in pain. And I'd just received bad news."

She nodded. "I know. And at the time, I convinced myself that was the reason you were so rude and unfeeling. But now I know differently."

His brow furrowed and he cut another glance her way. "What are you talking about?"

She crossed her arms, resting them on her belly. "It's what you always do, Clay. Remember that day at the ranch, when I came to tell you about the babies? You were a jerk then, too."

"Oh, come on, Rickie. The news blindsided me."

"Yeah, I know. That's what you said when you apologized, and I bought your explanation then."

"It was the truth," he said.

"Only partially. But there's more to it than that. I gave you the benefit of the doubt before, but I'm not going to do that anymore. You don't deal very well with your emotions, and you pull away from anything or anyone who might force you to face what you're really feeling."

He gawked at her as if she'd blindsided him once again. But these days she needed someone who loved her, someone who would stick by her no matter what life threw their way. And a guy who skated around his emotions wasn't going to fit the bill.

Yet while she'd come to that easy conclusion and realized she needed to cut her losses, his harsh reaction, his rejection, still hurt something fierce, making it almost difficult to breathe.

"Like I told you before," she said, "I don't need you and I don't want anything from you. Whatever we had is over."

"Slow down, Rickie. You're getting all riled up. I never suggested ending things. At least, not completely."

There he went again, withdrawing. Building walls between them.

"No, Clay," she said. "It's better this way. I can't take the emotional roller coaster. But for the record, I plan to maintain a friendship with your mom. She'll be the grandmother to my kids, the only one they'll have. So I'm going to nurture a relationship that will benefit my children."

As Clay pulled into the clinic parking lot, he said, "You took my comment the wrong way."

"Did I?" She all but rolled her eyes and slowly shook her head. "I told you before. I can parent the twins on my own—and I can support them, too."

He swore under his breath. "You're letting your hormones get away from you."

"The hell I am. Don't minimize my feelings. At least I can face mine."

Clay parked next to her car and let his engine idle. "Let's talk about this when we get back to the ranch."

As emotion balled up in her throat, and tears filled her eyes, she turned away from him, unwilling to let him see how badly he'd hurt her. Without another word, she reached for her purse, got out and closed the passenger door. He didn't drive away. Instead, he waited for her to slide behind the wheel of her sedan and start the ignition. Only then did he put his truck in gear.

But instead of driving back to the Bar M, as he'd assumed she would, Rickie headed home, tears streaming down her face, her chest aching as if her heart had cracked right down the middle.

She meant what she'd said when she told Clay she could live without him in her life. And she would.

Only trouble was, she'd fallen in love with him. And it hurt something awful to realize her dreams of a loving relationship with her babies' father had been dashed.

Rickie continued to cry and grumble all the way to Jeffersville. When she got within a mile of city limits, a flatbed truck loaded down with hay pulled out in front of her and made a turn to the right. The bales hadn't been tied down properly, so they shifted. Several tumbled onto the street.

Rickie swerved to avoid them, but the car spun out of control, swirling her around like a carnival ride until she slammed into a light pole.

Dazed, she tried to think, to react. But her head hurt. When she reached up and fingered her brow, she felt the sticky flow of blood. She blinked a couple of times, trying to clear her thoughts.

A sharp cramp struck low in her belly, tightening. She adjusted the seat belt, hoping that would help it ease up.

Someone—his face was a blur—opened the driver's door. "Lady, are you okay?"

She nodded, but apparently he didn't believe her. He whipped out his cell phone and called 911.

Minutes later, another pain sliced low in her belly. A contraction? Something was terribly wrong.

Fear gripped her like never before. God help her. If she was going to lose the babies, she needed a hand to hold. Clay probably wouldn't approve, but she didn't give a rip about that. She'd grown close to his mother, who'd become a friend—and the only one she had, it seemed. So she fumbled in her purse and pulled out her cell phone, then called Sandra.

By the time she answered, Rickie heard sirens in the distance. "I've been in a car accident. I'm going to be taken to the hospital in Jeffersville. Will you please come?"

"Oh my God. Are you okay?"

"I…don't know. I think so."

"I'll be right there, sweetie. Does Clay know? If not, I'll call him on his cell."

"Please don't. We had a big fight, and I'd rather he didn't know anything about this."

Sandra paused. "Don't worry. You have enough to worry about, so I won't. I'm just grabbing my keys and leaving now."

"Thank you, Sandra. I don't know what I'd do without you."

"Everything will be fine. I'm sure of it."

Maybe so, but right now, with fear of losing the babies gripping her, she had every reason to doubt that things would ever be okay again.

Chapter Twelve

After ordering a large cup of black coffee and a chocolate éclair at Poncho's favorite doughnut shop, Clay took a seat across the white Formica table from his old high school friend. They sat in silence for a moment or two until Poncho finally asked, "So what was it you wanted to talk about?"

Clay blew out a weary sigh. "Rickie and I got into an argument earlier today. I tried to apologize—or explain—but she didn't want to hear it."

Poncho took a sip of coffee. "So you're looking for a voice of reason?"

"Pretty much." Clay needed to vent to someone he trusted.

"So what upset her?"

"To begin with, my mom and Rickie have become best friends, which doesn't sit well with me."

Poncho eyed Clay the way a highway patrolman assessed the driver of a speeding car. "Why would that bother you? I'd think it would make your life a lot easier."

"Maybe it will." Clay reached for his heat-resistant paper cup, yet he didn't take a drink. "But for some crazy reason, it feels like they're plotting something behind my back."

Poncho leaned forward. "Like what?"

"I don't know. Nothing yet. But it won't take long. They'll team up against me one of these days." Clay raked his hand through his hair. "Now *me*? I can handle whatever comes my way. But what about the twins? Those two women are going to try and put the kibosh on everything those kids want to do."

Poncho sat back, a wry grin tickling his lips. "You managed to rebel and do your own thing."

"Yeah, but it was always an uphill battle." Clay took a bite of his éclair, but the chocolaty treat did little to soften or sweeten his mood. "When Rickie told me that my mother had invited her to live at the ranch after the babies were born, that really sent me over the edge."

"I can see where you'd be upset about her moving in when you're not sure how you feel about her." Poncho took another sip of coffee. When Clay didn't respond, he asked, "How *do* you feel about her?"

"I care about her. A lot. She's sweet and funny. And the sex is out of this world."

"It sounds to me like you're falling for her."

Clay pondered that possibility for a beat. "Maybe so, but I don't want to rush things. And my mom has always tried to force my hand."

"Forgive me for not seeing your mom as the villain in all of this. She's a great lady. And you're lucky to have someone who loves you like that, even if she still tries too hard to keep you on the straight and narrow."

Guilt thumped Clay like a wallop to the chest. "I'm sorry. I shouldn't complain, especially to you."

"I might've had a crappy upbringing," Poncho said, "but I've seen a lot of kids who've had it worse. And you, my friend, had it *good*. If you doubt that, I'll take you on a tour to Kidville, the children's home, and introduce you to some of the little boys I mentor."

Poncho was right. Clay really didn't have anything to complain about. But the flight mishap had sent him into a tailspin, and he'd been trying to recover control of his life ever since. He took a sip of coffee. It was supposed to be a fresh brew, but it had a bitter taste.

As things began to fall into perspective, Clay felt even worse than when he'd walked into the Donut Hole. Instead of his frustration with Rickie, he now had to deal with his guilt.

"Did you tell her you wanted to take things slow?" Poncho asked.

"Sort of." Actually, he'd meant to. "This whole thing has me unbalanced, and I have to admit that I didn't handle it very well."

Poncho laughed. "I hear that love can really throw a man off stride."

Clay grunted. Damn. Not only had he acted like a Neanderthal, he sounded like one, too.

But the more he thought about it, the more he realized Poncho might be right.

"I'm not sure if it's love, but I have some pretty strong feelings for her. I guess I'd better apologize. She must think I'm an ass."

"Probably, but if you tell her how you're really feeling, I think she'll forgive you."

"That's the problem. I was going to try to explain, but she didn't let me. Instead, she flipped out."

"Let me guess," Poncho said. "You went for the just-one-of-the-guys approach. Not a good idea, man. Women are wired differently. They're more in touch with their feelings, and it can really ruffle them when a guy isn't being honest with his emotions or with whatever he has on his mind. And you, my friend, are pretty tight-lipped when it comes to stuff like that."

"Tell me about it." Clay pushed aside the éclair, deciding it had looked a lot more appetizing in the glass display case than it actually tasted. "Believe it or not, I probably would have come to that conclusion on the way to the ranch. And then I could have told her, if she'd followed me there, like I thought she'd do. But she turned right and headed for the interstate. I'm pretty sure she drove back to Jeffersville."

Poncho crossed his arms. "Sounds to me like you ran her off."

"I didn't mean to."

"She'll come around."

Clay wasn't too sure about that. "She made it pretty clear that she didn't need me—now or in the future. And maybe that's true. Hell, she's just reconnected with her sister—at least, she's located her, and soon she'll get to see her for the first time in years. So she won't be alone anymore. She has a real family to rely on now."

"You know what I think?"

Clay had called Poncho so he could blow off some steam. And he'd expected his friend to tell him he was right. Although he was getting the feeling that wasn't what he was going to hear. "Go ahead and tell me."

"You've been running scared of family-type commitments for as long as I've known you. And you're afraid that a solid sense of home and hearth is going to change things. And it will. But in your case, I think it's a good thing."

Clay was going to have to chew on that for a while. He glanced across the table at his friend, who was staring at him like he was a suspect in an interrogation room.

"What do *you* think?" Poncho asked.

"You've got a point." More than one, actually. Clay found himself thinking about Rickie all the time, and whenever he did, a warm feeling filled his chest. He liked being with her. And he wanted to make life easier for her.

As reality dawned, he had to face the truth. And as tough as it might be, he'd have to lay his cards on the table, starting with Poncho.

"Okay," Clay said. "I'll admit it. My feelings for Rickie are too strong for my comfort level. And ignoring them has made it worse."

"So what are you going to do about that?"

"I'm going to let her cool off for a bit. Then I'll drive to her house and apologize."

"Sounds like a wise decision. And I recommend taking some flowers. You owe her, dude."

Clay didn't take time to finish his coffee. Instead, he pushed back his chair and got to his feet. "I'm going home. Thanks for talking me off the ledge."

"Hey. That's what friends are for."

Ten minutes later, Clay arrived at the ranch. He didn't see Rickie's car, indicating he'd been right—she'd gone home to Jeffersville. But that didn't mean he couldn't apologize to his mom first. Over the years, he'd built walls to keep her at a distance, and not always in subtle ways.

He'd start by telling her that he loved her, that he appreciated her unabashed acceptance of Rickie. And that he was going to try to be more understanding of her motherly ways in the future.

But the moment he walked into the kitchen and spotted Granddad warming a can of chili beans on the stove, he realized his mother wasn't home. And that wasn't like her.

"Where's Mom?" he asked.

"She left a note for you on the table."

Clay snatched it and read his mother's handwriting. "Oh, God." His heart sank to the pit of his gut, and his thoughts spun out of control.

He looked at his grandfather, as if the older man could fix this situation, but he couldn't. "Rickie's been in a car accident. She's at the hospital."

He hadn't needed to tell his grandfather. The note had been open and in plain sight. Or else he'd been here when Mom left.

"Why didn't someone call me?" Clay asked.

"Rickie asked your mom not to, and I figured I'd better respect that."

"Dammit. I've gotta go."

"That'd be a good idea, son. She's at Jeffersville Memorial. Your mother should be with her by now."

For once, Clay was grateful for his mother's constant presence—he'd never want Rickie to be alone at a time like this. "Thanks, Granddad. I'm heading there right now."

Clay hurried out of the house, jumped into his pickup and drove as fast as he could without risking a ticket or an accident of his own.

This was all his fault. If he'd kept his mouth shut or chosen his words more carefully, Rickie would have gone home with him as planned. He hoped her injuries weren't serious, that she and the babies had survived the crash. He couldn't stand the thought of losing them—any of them.

Clay pushed down on the gas pedal, determined to get to his new little family as fast as he could.

Paramedics wasted no time in rushing Rickie to the hospital, where the ER doctor diagnosed a concussion then sutured her head wound. Her obstetrician arrived minutes later and examined her, too. Dr. Gomez also checked the babies' heart rates, which were strong and healthy. Then she ordered medication to stop labor, although the contractions had already eased a bit.

After their consultation, both medical professionals decided Rickie should stay overnight for observation.

Rickie wasn't about to argue that decision. She was just glad to know the twins were okay. It had been scary for a while. But from the moment of impact and all during the ambulance ride to the hospital, she'd held her panic at bay.

Yet the minute Clay's mother entered the room, with her brow furrowed and maternal concern splashed on her face, tears filled Rickie's eyes and a lump of emotion balled up in her throat.

"I got here as fast as I could," Sandra said. "Honey, are you okay?"

You. The woman's first thought had been about her, not just the twins. That meant that whatever maternal affection Rickie had sensed from Sandra was real. And not only an attempt to have a relationship with her grand-babies.

"Yes," Rickie said. "I'm all right. And so are the twins."

"Thank God. I prayed all the way here." Sandra, who was now standing beside the hospital bed, took Rickie's hand and gave it a gentle squeeze.

That loving gesture touched Rickie's heart, and in spite of her best efforts to hold herself together, the tears overflowed and spilled down her cheeks. Before she could thank Sandra for coming, for responding so quickly to her distressed phone call, Clay entered the room. He appeared worried and deeply concerned, but she wouldn't let that weaken her resolve.

"What happened?" he asked. "Are you all right, Rickie?"

She swiped at her wet cheeks and lifted her chin. "Yes. I'm fine."

"I know you're angry with me," he said. "And you have every right to be. I was an ass."

"Yes, you were. Apology accepted. So feel free to go on about your day."

The corner of his eye twitched, indicating her curt brush-off had hurt.

"All right," he said. "I'll go. But not until you let me explain."

Rickie glanced first at Sandra, who continued to hold her hand, watching the two of them while clearly biting her tongue. Then she returned her gaze to Clay. "I'm listening, but my response will be the same."

He blew out a ragged sigh. "I did some soul searching and realized a few things. Over the years, I built a wall around my emotions. I considered them a sign of weakness. So the idea of having a wife and kids has always scared the heck out of me. It would make me too vulnerable."

Rickie had figured as much. It was nice that he could admit it, although that didn't make her feel any better about pinning her heart on him. But she let him continue to get things off his chest.

"When you came to town, pregnant with not just one baby, but two, I scrambled to make sense of how I felt—about you, about us, about becoming a family. It's not a good excuse, but it's the only one I have. And the truth is, I love you, Rickie."

She wanted to believe him, but she'd been abandoned before. And Clay had disappointed her several times already. If she didn't have the babies to consider, she might have given him a pass. But she couldn't take a gamble like that. Not when he might harden his heart and hurt the kids someday.

He made his way into the room, although he maintained a respectful distance. "When I heard about the accident, reality slammed into me. I was afraid I'd lose you—and the babies. At that point, I finally felt some of what my mom went through when my dad died. She'd been devastated, and I can see why she'd be afraid to lose me, too. As a kid, I thought she was smothering me. But she only wanted to protect me. I get that now."

Sandra's eyes welled with tears, and she nodded, confirming the conclusion he'd come to.

"I might have gone a little overboard at times," she admitted, "but son, I love you more than life itself."

"I realize that now, Mom. And I'm sorry. I'm going to be a lot more understanding of your feelings from here on out."

Apparently, he thought Rickie should be more understanding, too. But even though she wanted to believe that he'd had some kind of emotional epiphany, she was afraid to. He'd flip-flopped on her one time too many.

Sandra gave her son a warm hug, letting him and Rickie know that she forgave him, that she loved him and always would.

Rickie wasn't going to be as easy to appease as his mother was.

As Clay eased closer to the hospital bed, his mom took a step back, allowing him to take her place at Rickie's side. "If you'll give me another chance, I'll step up and be the man you want me to be."

But could he be the man she *needed* him to be? It all sounded good. He was saying the right words, but she wasn't convinced that he'd follow through. On top of that, her head ached. This wasn't the time to make any emotional decisions.

Rickie glanced at Sandra, who'd taken so many steps back that she'd almost left the room. Then she looked at Clay. "I'll need to think about it."

"That's all I'm asking for, Rickie. Just think about it."

She already had, and she'd made a tentative decision. Actually, it was pretty solid, but the pain meds might be skewing her thoughts. Either way, she thanked Clay for coming, then said, "It's probably best if you go now."

"Okay. I will, but I'll be back. I also want you to keep in mind the babies are going to need a father."

Maybe so. But it would be better for them to never know him than to bond with a guy who might get tired of playing the dad role and leave.

Clay hadn't wanted to leave Rickie's room, but he hadn't wanted to upset her, either. So he'd agreed to give her the time she needed and headed down the hospital corridor, determined to prove to her that he'd been telling the truth. And if that meant he'd have to drive all the way to Jeffersville each day, bearing a bouquet of roses and pouring out his heart, he'd do it.

It was weird, though. He'd been dodging his feelings for years, but facing them actually made him feel better. More focused, more secure.

Rather than stray too far from Rickie's bedside, he went to the hospital cafeteria and bought a large coffee. Then he took it to the main lobby, where he took a seat with several other people who were either reading magazines or watching TV while they waited for word on a loved one's condition.

He'd no more than taken a couple of drinks when his cell phone rang. He glanced at the screen and saw that it was his mom calling.

"I just stepped into the hall so I could call you. I've been talking to Rickie, and it might be a good idea if you came back to the hospital. I think she's having a change of heart."

He'd hoped she would. That's why he hadn't gone far. "What makes you think that?"

"We had a little chat about your father and how, in spite of his imperfections, I loved him. I told her that I'd give anything if he could be here now, if he could meet her. And that he would have been thrilled to know he was going to be a grandfather."

"What did she say to that?"

"That she loved you. And that she thought you'd be a good father."

"Thanks for the heads-up. I'll be there in five minutes."

"In that case, I'll go to the cafeteria so I can give you two some time to talk in private."

Had his mother always been that intuitive, that understanding? That supportive?

By the time Clay returned to Rickie's room, she was alone. Her face was angled toward the window, as if she was gazing outside. When she heard footsteps, she turned to face the doorway, where he stood. She didn't exactly break into a grin when she spotted him, but she didn't send him away, either.

"Is it okay if I come in?" he asked.

She nodded.

He took a slow approach. "I realize things are a little crazy right now."

"Yeah, they are." She offered him a weak, tentative grin. "Part of it might be the pain medication they gave me."

"And another part is because I was a jerk."

"Yeah, that, too." This time a full-on smile crossed her face, and he realized his mother had been right. Rickie had been thinking—and reconsidering.

"I'm really sorry," he told her. "If you give me a second chance, I promise to do better in the future."

"You know," she said, "I spent years believing my sister was dead. Her loss crushed me. The more I thought about it, the more I realized I was about to suffer another loss—the man I love."

"If I'm that man," Clay said, "I'm not going anywhere. And just to set the record straight, I'm glad my mother invited you to stay on the ranch with us. I'd like you and our kids to be close."

"Are you sure?"

He nodded. "Yes, but there's something else I want to tell you, something I've kept to myself, but you should probably know. Part of my moodiness and negativity had to do with the fact that I never wanted to be a rancher in the first place. But that's the way things panned out. I've accepted it, and I'm going to make the best of it."

"But that ranch has been in your family for years. What is it you'd rather do?"

He took a deep, fortifying breath, then let it and the raw truth slip out. "I'd like to do what I was trained to do, what I love."

She nodded knowingly. "And after that flight mishap and your injury, the Army is out."

"Yes, and so is being a pilot for a Life Flight helicopter, a local job that's opening up. It would've been a cool, home-based option."

"Why can't you take it?" she asked.

"The damage to my optic nerve. Remember?"

Her brow furrowed, tightening the stitches on her head wound. She winced, then asked, "When was your last eye exam?"

"When I was at Tripler."

"No kidding? Haven't you had a follow-up?"

"I…uh… No."

She scrunched her brow and winced again. "Why not?"

"I guess I was afraid to hear another repeat of that crappy diagnosis."

"For a guy who's always been Army strong, you're pretty weak when it comes to facing your emotional side."

"You're right. And I'm facing it now. I love you, Rickie. I want to spend the rest of my life with you, raising our children." He paused, waiting a beat before posing the question he'd been thinking about for the past hour or two. "Will you marry me?"

She seemed to ponder that for the longest time, and when he feared she might blow him off, she smiled and said, "Yes, I'll marry you. I love you, too. But I think we'd both be better off if we took our relationship one day at a time."

That's all he'd hoped for, all he'd wanted to hear. He bent over her bed and gave her a kiss. It might've been gentle and a bit hesitant, but it was filled with promise—and commitment.

When he straightened, she said, "So tell me. When are you going to have your vision checked again?"

He hadn't planned on doing that, but with Rickie suggesting it, he figured he ought to face his limitations, too. "I guess that depends on when Dr. Davidson will refer me to an ophthalmologist or neurologist."

Rickie laughed. "The receptionist has quite a bit of pull, so I'm sure she'll have a name and phone number for you first thing tomorrow morning."

Clay kissed this amazing woman again. How had he ever gotten by without her in his life, his arms or his bed?

"I have a question," she said. "I know it was my idea, but maybe we shouldn't take things too slowly. It might be a good idea to get married before the babies come."

"I was hoping you'd come to feel that way, too. I'd marry you tomorrow, but we'll probably need a license."

She laughed once more, then reached for him, drawing his lips to hers. He kissed her again, and his heart as well as his dreams took flight.

For the first time since his accident, he looked forward to the future, one that promised to be happy and bright.

Epilogue

A week after Rickie came home from the hospital, Lainie and her husband, rodeo promoter Drew Madison, and their children arrived home after their Disney cruise. When Lainie heard that her lost twin was looking for her and had left her phone number, she immediately placed the call.

Lainie shrieked with joy and excitement. "You have no idea how much I've missed you."

"Oh, yes I do!" Rickie's voice held the same thrill. "I was told that you died during your surgery. I was devastated to hear that, and I've been grieving for years. Imagine my surprise when I learned you were alive."

There were happy tears shed, and some sad ones, as they tried to play catch up after so many years apart.

Sandra, who'd been standing nearby when the heart-warming phone call took place, listened with a smile and glistening eyes. When she heard the sisters' planning to meet the next day and introduce their new families, she suggested they have a picnic.

"That way," Sandra had said, "we can have a meet and greet during your reunion."

Both sisters liked the idea, especially since the new Brighton Valley Park had an amazing playground the children would enjoy.

And now here they were. Rickie brought her new family, which included Clay, his mother and grandfather. Soon Lainie, Drew and their three sons would be drawn into the fold.

Clay, who'd been helping his mother carry the food and picnic supplies from the car, joined Rickie where she stood in the shade of a magnolia tree, watching the street and waiting for her sister to arrive. He slipped an arm around her waist and gave her an affectionate squeeze. "How are you doing? It's a little chilly. Do you want me to get your sweater?"

"No, I'm fine. In fact, I've never been better." She leaned into him, placed her head against his shoulder and relished his familiar scent.

"My mom is putting out a big spread," he said.

"I know." Rickie couldn't believe the woman's energy. Early this morning, she'd made potato salad, baked beans and a huge fruit bowl, insisting she didn't want help. At least she'd let Rickie bring dessert—cupcakes she and Clay purchased at a local bakery.

Even Roger, who'd asked Rickie to call him Granddad from now on, would be doing his part, cooking hamburgers and hot dogs on a small stationary grill.

"I'd better see if my grandfather needs help," Clay said.

"Have you talked to him yet?" Rickie asked.

"Yes, I did. Right before we left the ranch." Clay had passed the eye exam, although just barely. And he'd accepted the job as a Life Flight pilot.

"How'd he take it?"

"A lot better than I thought he would. He told me that he really hadn't wanted to retire in the first place, but my mom had encouraged it. 'You know how she is,' he said. I would have agreed and rolled my eyes, but for the first time, I found myself saying, 'She means well.'"

"Maybe, on your days off, you can help out on the ranch."

"Yes, I plan to. That is, unless I'm busy being a father." Clay placed his hand on her baby bump. "How are the kids doing?"

"They're a little restless today," she said. "I think they're eager to get out and meet their new cousins."

"Speaking of introductions, have we decided on their names for sure? Are we going to stick with Jonathon and Katherine?"

"Yes, but those are pretty long names for tiny babies. What if we call them John and Katie?"

"That works for me." Clay nodded toward Granddad. "I'd better see if he needs help setting up that grill." Then he brushed a kiss on her brow before walking away.

At the sound of an approaching vehicle, Rickie turned and spotted an SUV entering the parking lot. It looked like a dad, mom and three little boys. That must be Lainie, she thought.

When a brunette climbed out of the front passenger seat, she noted the resemblance and realized she was right.

As Lainie crossed the grass, leaving her husband to help the younger boys get out of their car seats, Rickie hurried to meet her.

"Can you believe it?" Lainie said, her smile beaming. "I never thought this day would come."

Rickie laughed. "Neither did I. You have no idea how much I've missed you. How many times I've thought about you over the years. I'm so glad we finally found each other."

Lainie slipped her arms around Rickie and gave her a hug, one they both were reluctant to end. So they continued to hold each other, their heads touching, their hair the same shade, the length similar. They'd always looked alike, but when Rickie had been the healthier twin, people didn't have any trouble telling them apart. However, that wasn't the case any longer. That is, unless someone looked at their stomachs.

Everyone seemed to be giving them space and time to reunite, but before long, three adorable, dark-haired boys joined them.

"Hey, Mama!" the oldest one said. "There's two of you!"

"You're right," Lainie told her son. "This is my sister—and your aunt."

"I'm so happy to meet you guys," Rickie said, as she stooped to shake each small hand. There'd be plenty of time for hugs and kisses—once they got to know her better. And that wouldn't take long. She planned to be the best aunt ever.

Andre, the oldest had a walking cast on his leg, thanks to a recent orthopedic surgery to correct a bone that hadn't healed properly. But that didn't seem to keep the eight-year-old sidelined.

From what Lainie had said last night, their early years had been rough, but they had a new home and loving parents now. Andre and his younger brothers, Mario and Abel, were as cute as they could be. And they were clearly happy and thriving.

"Can we go play now?" Mario asked.

Lainie caressed her son's head. "Yes, of course."

As the boys dashed off, Rickie glanced across the grass and watched Sandra cover a table with a red-checkered cloth. "You know, I'd better insist upon helping my future mother-in-law."

"And I'd better get the kids' jackets. I don't want them to catch cold. When one gets the sniffles, they all do."

As Lainie strode toward the car, Rickie approached the woman who claimed she was the daughter she'd always wanted. "You're spoiling me, Sandra. Please let me do something to help."

Sandra brightened. "It's nearly done. I love cooking for my family, but I'm really going to enjoy it now that our family has grown. I can't wait for Thanksgiving and Christmas. They're going to be extra-special days from now on."

Rickie agreed. The upcoming holidays promised to be big, happy affairs. She stole a glance at Clay, who'd wandered over to the playground and was pushing little Mario in the swing. Not only was that gorgeous man an amazing lover, but he promised to be a wonderful husband, father and uncle.

She placed her hand on her growing womb and smiled. For the very first time, she could imagine living happily ever after.

* * * * *

Tina Leonard is a *New York Times* bestselling and award-winning author of more than fifty projects, including several popular miniseries for Harlequin. Known for bad-boy heroes and smart, adventurous heroines, her books have made the *USA TODAY*, Waldenbooks, Ingram and Nielsen BookScan bestseller lists. Born on a military base, Tina lived in many states before eventually marrying the boy who did her crayon printing for her in the first grade. You can visit her at tinaleonard.com, and follow her on Facebook and Twitter.

Books by Tina Leonard

Harlequin American Romance

Bridesmaids Creek

The Rebel Cowboy's Quadruplets
The SEAL's Holiday Babies
The Twins' Rodeo Rider

Callahan Cowboys

A Callahan Wedding
The Renegade Cowboy Returns
The Cowboy Soldier's Sons
Christmas in Texas
A Callahan Outlaw's Twins
His Callahan Bride's Baby
Branded by a Callahan
Callahan Cowboy Triplets
A Callahan Christmas Miracle

Visit the Author Profile page at Harlequin.com for more titles.

The Cowboy SEAL's Triplets

TINA LEONARD

For the many wonderful readers who so enthusiastically and kindly supported my work from day one—I thank you from the bottom of my heart.

Chapter One

John Lopez "Squint" Mathison came roaring into town with Daisy Donovan on the back of his motorcycle, making all the good citizens of Bridesmaids Creek, Texas, buzz like bees in a beehive. The five men who were in love with Daisy—her gang, consisting of Carson Dare, Gabriel Conyers, Clint Shanahan, Red Holmes and Dig Bailey—followed behind them in a truck, with Daisy's infamous motorcycle secured in the truck bed.

It was a very strange sight not to see Daisy riding her own bike. No one could remember ever seeing her on the back of someone else's, and the gossip flew fast and thick.

Squint was ready to see the last of Daisy's gang. And maybe even Daisy herself, despite the fact that she'd once possessed his heart and his romantic dreams.

What he'd been thinking, he wasn't certain.

She was completely wild, as everyone in Bridesmaids Creek had always tried to warn him.

The trouble was, he'd made love to Daisy Donovan while they were in Montana, in a weak moment when he shouldn't have let his stupid heart outstrip his good sense.

Making love to Daisy had been even more mind-bending than he could have ever imagined. Then the five Romeos had blown into Montana to retrieve their small-town wild child princess, and Squint had seen that they were—himself included—all dopes dangling after a prize they couldn't win.

At that moment, he'd decided to come back to Brides-maids Creek, check in on his buddies and shift off to the rodeo. After the rodeo, if his heart was still bleeding, he thought maybe he'd get a job teaching ROTC or something, somewhere far away. He'd make those decisions as soon as Valentine's Day was past, although he couldn't have said why Cupid's Big Day was his marker for a quiet exit.

Daisy hopped off the bike as soon as he came to a stop in front of the main house at the Hanging H Ranch. "Thanks for the ride."

"No problem."

"It was great seeing the country from a motorcycle. No windows to block the view." She shook her long, dark locks out of her helmet. "But it's wonderful to be home."

He nodded and headed into the kitchen to find his friends—the men that he could always count on to talk sense into him. Daisy followed, which was a surprise. Wherever Daisy went, so did her love-struck gang, so they came, too.

"I'm so glad to be back in BC," Daisy said, and Squint started. "Montana is beautiful, but after a while, I began craving the comforts of small-town life."

This was news to him. Squint wished he hadn't fallen

head, heels and heart for Daisy, and had put plenty of distance between him and her gang perching at the kitchen island. The gang gathered around the kitchen island, which had over the years become the communal gathering place and feed bag summit. No one ever knocked on the back door of the Hanging H; they just let themselves in.

If you weren't family or friend, you rang the front doorbell—not a good sign in a small town where everyone knew everybody else, and their business. Ringing the front bell meant you were an outsider.

Robert Donovan, Daisy's father, always rang the doorbell. Somehow his daughter had managed it so that she considered herself part of the backdoor squad. Very recently, indeed—and Squint wasn't sure why his poor mushy heart suddenly wished he had his own back door that she could make herself at home through anytime she liked.

But he'd never been one for settling down, never had a "real" home that wasn't on wheels, so he shoved that thought out of his brain, a useless organ that did little to assist him with rational thinking where Daisy was concerned. Out of habit, he shifted the Saint Michael medal he wore, trying to figure out his next move.

"I wonder where Mackenzie and Suz are?" Squint peered into the living room for the house's owners and their husbands, Justin Morant and Cisco Grant—Frog to his friends, though his wife, Suz, had let everyone know that she wasn't kissing a Frog, hence the Cisco. Squint was a nickname, too, given to him for his shooting skills, which were far better than Cupid's as far as he was concerned. Maybe it was time for him, too, to change his moniker back to his real name. Was it more likely that Daisy would fall for "John" rather than "Squint"?

Suz had not been easy for Cisco to catch, but catch

her he had, and they'd celebrated that love for a second time last Christmas Eve. This was February—and who would have thought that only two months after Cisco's wedding, John would have made love to Daisy Donovan, the woman who drove everybody absolutely nuts in Bridesmaids Creek. And he hadn't just done it once—she'd sneaked into his bed many times, all under cover of night.

He had been completely aware she wasn't about to let a sign of their new relationship hit the public domain, especially not since she'd mooned after Cisco for months and months. John was aware that Daisy felt as if she was settling by making love to him, and not as in settling down—just settling. Making do.

He was done with that. He'd tried to "win" her fair and square, by Bridesmaids Creek standards, which meant either running the Best Man's Fork, or swimming the Bridesmaids Creek swim in order to win the love of your life. This was a no-fail charm, according to BC legend. But Daisy'd had three chances at the magic, and no time had he ever won her. Apparently the magic didn't work so well for him. A man had to push forward, even if his dreams were in ruins. He'd learned the hard way when he'd served in Afghanistan with Sam and Cisco that with life you have to keep going.

And he would keep going now. In fact, to make certain there were no more loose moments, he was making sure Daisy was parked here for good—then he was leaving town for the rodeo circuit. It was the only way. The second option would be to just cut out his heart and throw it to the wolves somewhere—that would end the pain of knowing that Daisy was only making time with him, even though she'd admitted that she'd never loved

Cisco in the slightest. She'd only been after him to keep him from Suz.

Which hadn't worked. Suz and Cisco now had darling twin girls, and the magic of Bridesmaids Creek had cast its happy spell on them.

"Ah, cookies," Dig Bailey said. "It's great to be home."

John took that in without comment. The Hanging H had never been Dig's home, and never would be.

I should have taken Daisy to her house, and left her and her gang behind. Then I could start to forget the colossal mistake I made when I fell into her sexy brown eyes the day I met her.

"I missed the cocoa," Carson Dare said, helping himself to some that was staying warm in a heated pitcher.

John could barely think about cocoa. He tried hard not to watch Daisy settle her delicately shaped, feminine assets on a stool at the island. It was terribly difficult to keep his eyes off her.

The first time he'd ever seen Daisy Donovan—at times known as the Diva of Destruction of Bridesmaids Creek—he'd been captivated by her long dark hair spilling from her motorcycle helmet, her heart-shaped lips, big expresso eyes that practically bewitched his soul, never mind the short black leather skirt that swung when she walked. She'd been wearing black combat boots and her shapely legs had transfixed him, making his brain a pile of ham salad.

Life hadn't changed a whole lot since then.

"Chocolate chip cake," Clint Shanahan said, sighing happily as he helped himself to a piece.

Red Holmes joined him and cut a slice for himself. "There's no place like home, just like Dorothy said."

"Listen, you fellows should probably follow the yellow brick road right on out of here," John said sourly. "I didn't see a kitchen's open sign on the back door."

They all stared at him.

"We're from this town," Gabriel Conyers said. "We know when we're welcome. Do you?"

Point well taken. John was the outsider, though employed at the Hanging H for the past three years.

"Besides which, you just want to get Daisy alone," Carson said, "and we've determined amongst ourselves that we're going to make sure that doesn't happen."

"True," Dig agreed. "She may not choose us, but we're not letting you weasel her, either."

Too late, fellows, the weasel's already been to the henhouse. Several times.

"I'm going to the bunkhouse." Since Justin and Cisco weren't here, it was highly likely they were there. Although John was a bit surprised that Suz and Mackenzie weren't around with their plethora of babies. Between them, they had six now at the Hanging H—all girls destined to break young men's hearts.

Something he knew too well about. John shoved his hat on his head, glared at Daisy's gang, and without bothering to look at Daisy, went out the back door. Unable to stop himself, he went around to the front, his boots crunching through the snow piled around the front porch. He wanted just a moment to take in the house, maybe even take a photo on his phone—because he was about to leave forever. There was no point in waiting until V-Day, because Cupid's Arrow Delivery Service wasn't going to bring him an arrow with Daisy's name on it. This was the only real home he'd ever known. Permanent home, to be more precise. When you'd grown up in a beat-up trailer following the rodeo from town to town, home didn't feel as if it had a stationary place. His parents had raised three children that way, and they'd grown up fine.

He supposed he and Daisy, the daughter of the richest man in Bridesmaids Creek, didn't have a whole lot of common ground, anyway—which was why she'd never particularly gone for him, except under cover of darkness. John's father and his grandfather and his father before him had been clowns and barrel men, with the occasional bullfighter gig thrown into the mix. His mother was a cowboy preacher, her three boys sitting in the front pews without fail.

Maybe that was why the Hanging H meant so much to him. It was permanent. Well, it had almost *not* been permanent, thanks to Daisy and her greedy father, Robert. John raised his phone, snapping a photo of the snow-laden house. It was tall and white in Victorian splendor, its heavy gingerbread detail charming and old-world. Four tall turrets stretched to the sky, and the upstairs mullioned windows sparkled in the sunshine. The wide wraparound porch was painted sky blue, and a white wicker sofa with blue cushions beckoned visitors to sit and enjoy the view. A collection of wrought-iron roosters sat nearby in a welcoming clutch, and the bristly doormat with a big burgundy *H* announced the Hawthorne name, which Suz and Mackenzie had been before their marriages. Their parents had built this farm up years ago, as well as the business they'd started here—the Haunted H, a popular carnival and play place for families.

Nothing had changed, which was comforting. And Robert Donovan hadn't managed to take over the Hanging H, though he and Daisy had given it plenty of effort.

Sometimes John felt as if he'd been in lust with the

enemy. He was just so drawn to Daisy, it was as if all that bad-girl-calling vibe shook him down to his knees.

There'd been something of a happy ending, as recently as December, when Suz and Cisco had retied the knot. Robert Donovan had had some kind of epiphany, deciding that he didn't want to be the town bully anymore, and sold the Hanging H back to Suz and Mackenzie for a dollar—though he'd moved heaven and hell to take over the property in the beginning.

Rumor had it that Daisy had turned, deciding she was no longer going to be the Diva of Destruction, and convinced her father—who was already developing a huge soft spot due to his newly acquired desire to be considered a beloved grandfather—that he didn't want to be the town Grinch anymore.

John snapped one last photo, sighed at the memories of the only place that had ever felt like a true home to him, and put his phone away. Then he headed off without another look back, to return to the only other home he'd ever known.

A small trailer he'd recently heard was somewhere just outside of Santa Fe.

He'd be safe there—safe from his heart begging him to make love to Daisy anytime night fell to cover their sin.

"What do you mean, he just left?" Daisy hopped off her stool and ran to the window. Sure enough, there went Squint's truck, hauling down the drive fast enough to make the truck bed lurch. A little concern jumped inside her, but then she calmed it. No doubt he'd just gone to grab a bite at The Wedding Diner. Or gone to see Madame and Monsieur Matchmaker—though now that they were divorced, perhaps it was fair to say that they were no longer Bridesmaids Creek's special matchmakers. Daisy gulped. That split could probably be laid square at her and her father's door, as they'd taken over the establishment where Madame Matchmaker's Premier Matchmaking Services, and Monsieur Unmatchmaker's Services, had once been housed. Now her gang had the space, and they'd put in a hopping cigar bar, sort of a pickup meet-and-get-sweet kind of place that doubled as a dating service and hangout.

There was no going back now.

Somehow she'd have to win the townspeople over, make up for a lot of the wrong she'd done. Daisy went back to sit with her gang, looking around at the five men who professed themselves in love with her.

"Listen, fellows. We've had a long, good run together." Daisy took a deep breath. "But things are going to have to change."

"Change?" Gabriel sat up. "What kind of change?"

There'd have to be lots of change if she was going to convince Bridesmaids Creek that she was a new woman. "Change. As much as possible."

"I don't like it." Red shook his head. "We've got a great thing going, the six of us."

Yes, but they didn't know that she'd been diving under the sheets with Squint. And the lovemaking was fantastic. Mind-blowing. Once she'd gotten through the smoke and haze of trying to keep Suz and Cisco apart—what had she been thinking?—she'd realized the hunky, tall, saddle-brown-eyed Squint was a really sexy guy. Supersexy, to the point of being mouthwatering. And when he kissed her, she melted. Like a puddle of snow in hot sun. "It can't be the six of us anymore."

They looked alarmed. "But we're so good together," Carson said.

She shook her head. "Actually, we're not. We were the misfits and outcasts together. But that's not what I want to be anymore."

"Whoa," Clint said. "It's Squint, isn't it? John Lopez Mathison is getting inside your head."

Daisy jumped. "Of course not!"

"It was Branch Winters," Dig said darkly. "Every time you go to Montana to his retreat, you change. That was when it started, when you went chasing up there after Cisco. You came home different."

"Yeah," Red said. "You came home not mooning after Cisco anymore. And not really wanting to hang out with us, either."

Daisy got up. They were right, of course. Branch's place in Montana was a spiritual retreat where warriors of all kinds went to reboot. She'd gone to throw a few wrenches into Cisco's works—and found a few thrown in hers instead. It was hard to explain Branch. He sort of lived on the metaphysical, and sometimes hippie, edge of life—but he'd helped her see that she was operating out of fear of never belonging in Bridesmaids Creek.

And only she could change that.

"It's going to be okay, for all of us," Daisy said softly, going to the door. "But change is in the wind. It has to be."

She went outside into the cold February chill, knowing this was the right path—if she was ever going to make John Lopez "Squint" Mathison believe that it was *him* with whom she'd been in love all along.

She didn't know if there was enough magic in Bridesmaids Creek to convince him, but she had to try.

Chapter Two

Daisy felt every eye on her as she walked into The Wedding Diner the next morning. She was aware the town didn't have a very high opinion of her, even though she'd managed to convince her father to give up pursuing the Hanging H, and even though she'd talked him into giving up on taking over the land where the Best Man's Fork and Bridesmaids Creek lay in sleepy, small-town fashion. The Hawthorne's Haunted H amusement park for kiddies was now situated on some land near Bridesmaids Creek, because Daisy had convinced the Hawthorne sisters that no one could take over their home and their business all at once if they weren't tied together. Now the year-round haunted house was more of a community venture, which helped everyone in BC, because it was more centrally located, and people were assigned regular hours to run it. It was more lucrative for the town now, and with time, Daisy thought that its popularity would only grow.

But memories were long in BC, and she'd done an awful lot of bad. She smiled at everyone who turned to stare at her, and moved into a white vinyl booth that Jane Chatham, who owned The Wedding Diner, showed her to.

"You're back," Jane said, and Daisy nodded.

"We came back yesterday, Squint, myself and the boys."

Jane's gaze was steady on her. "Squint left town last night."

Daisy blinked. "Left town?"

The older woman hesitated, then sat across from her. Cosette Lafleur—Madame Matchmaker herself—slid in next to Jane, her pink-frosted hair accentuating her all-knowing eyes.

Daisy's heart sank. "He *couldn't* have left." He hadn't said goodbye, hadn't even mentioned he was planning to make like a stiff breeze and blow away.

The women stared at her with interest.

"Did you want him to stay, Daisy?" Jane asked.

"Well—" Daisy began, not knowing how to say that she'd thought she at least rated a "goodbye" considering she'd gotten quite in the habit of enjoying a nocturnal meeting in his arms. "It would have been nice."

"Have you finally realized where your heart belongs, Daisy?" Cosette asked, and Daisy started.

"My heart?" How was it that these women always seemed to read everyone's mind? A girl had to be very careful to keep her secrets tight to her chest. "Squint and I are friends."

Cosette winked at her, and a spark of hope lit inside Daisy that maybe Cosette wasn't horribly angry or holding a grudge with her about the whole taking-over-her-shop mistake she'd made.

"We know all about those kinds of friends," Cosette said, nodding wisely.

"Still," Jane said, "it does seem rather heartless of John to leave without telling you. Had you quarreled?"

Here it came, the well-meaning BC interference of which many suffered, all secretly cherished and she'd never had the benefit of experiencing. She had to say it was like being under a probing yet somehow friendly microscope. "We didn't quarrel."

"But you're in love with him," Cosette said.

"That may be putting it a bit—" Her words trailed off.

"Mildly?" Jane asked.

"Lightly?" Cosette said. "You are in fact head over heels in love with him?"

Daisy felt herself blush under all the scrutiny. Sheriff Dennis McAdams slid into the booth next to her, and the ladies wasted no time filling in the sheriff, who turned his curious gaze to her.

"He left last night," the sheriff said, and Daisy wondered if John Lopez Mathison had stopped by to see every single denizen of this town to say goodbye—except for her.

"Yes, I've heard," Daisy said.

"Not coming back, either," the sheriff continued. "Jane, can I get some of your delicious double-dipped chicken-fried steak and mashed red potatoes with gravy? Maybe chase it with a slice of your four-layer chocolate cake?"

"Gracious," Cosette said, "are you looking to have a four-alarm cardiac event, Dennis?"

"Just hungry, ladies." He pushed back his worn Stetson with a grin. "Sitting up late at night with the fellows, having a good gossip and four-tissue wheeze gives a man an appetite."

Jane eyed him with great curiosity. "A four-tissue wheeze requires a slice of four-layer chocolate cake?"

"Yes, ma'am." Dennis nodded. "Squint was really working on my ear holes. As were Sam, Phillipe and Robert Donovan."

"I don't believe a word of it," Cosette said. "I can't see you five ever getting together for a rooster session."

"It happened," Dennis said cheerfully. "The first order of business was Squint requesting that we call him John from here on. After all, Squint was his military name, and he's gone back to being a cowboy. So, John it is. But the big news of the evening was Robert Donovan announcing he feels greatly that his daughter, our Daisy here," he said, winking at Daisy, "needs a man."

"What?" Daisy shook her head. "My father would never say such a thing. I'm with Cosette. This gathering never took place."

"He wants a man to settle you here in town, far away from the influence of whatever is happening in Montana," Dennis continued, untroubled by the ladies' disbelief. "And I said there was no such man to do the job in this small town."

"And?" Jane demanded, not leaving to put in the sheriff's order, Daisy noticed. When the gossip was flying hot and steamy, food took a backseat. "What was said to Robert's grand pronouncement?"

Dennis shrugged, very much enjoying being the center of the ladies' attention. "John said he agreed with me, and—"

"What?" Daisy stiffened. "How dare he?"

They all looked at her.

"How dare he, what, dear?" Jane asked.

"How dare John agree with my father?" Daisy thought the former Squint Mathison might have reached a new level of annoying.

"Most folks rather agree with Robert," Cosette said, nodding.

"So what happened then?" Jane demanded.

"Could you put my order in before I tell you the rest?" Dennis asked, rubbing his stomach regretfully. "I didn't have breakfast."

"Sing for your supper, Sheriff," Jane shot back.

"Well, I was pretty proud of my two cents, I don't mind saying," Dennis said. "And then Sam said that he didn't think even he had the necessary talent to pull off the job."

"What job?" Daisy asked, her heart beginning an emergency tattoo. It sounded as if all the important men in her life—notwithstanding Sam Barr, otherwise known as Handsome Sam, and understood by all to be a trickster and prankster beyond compare—had clubbed together and cast her to the wind. "Pardon me, but I'm having great trouble seeing my father and my...my—"

"Your what, dear?" Jane Chatham asked, her eyes twinkling with interest.

"My...good friend John," Daisy said, covering herself. "I have trouble seeing the two of them agreeing on anything, but certainly my father wouldn't spend any time discussing my love life with my—"

"With your good friend John," Cosette said. "Yes, yes, yes, we heard all that."

"And yet, it happened," Sheriff Dennis said. "Now may I have that supper for which I sang like a many-feathered bird?"

"Not really," Daisy said as Jane and Cosette nodded

in agreement that the sheriff hadn't quite imparted sufficiently satisfactory details. Daisy's heart rate was still revving as she began to realize that the men had sold her out and the one she'd been spending delicious nights with had slipped out without saying a word to her. "What was the point of this male bonding?"

The sheriff smiled. "You know how it is when we fellows get together. We just hash out life, come to no solutions and feel like we've accomplished something."

"A solution was achieved if John's gone," Daisy said.

"He is gone," Dennis said. "Said something about returning to his home."

"He doesn't have a home," Jane said, "other than the Hanging H, which is his home now."

"Oh, he has a home," Dennis said, "it's just not one you and I would really think of as one. His is on the rodeo circuit."

"All the men say that," Cosette said, huffing out a breath impatiently. "They always claim rodeo is their hearth, heart and home."

"In John's case, it's true." Dennis looked wistfully toward the kitchen. "His family is now heading toward Santa Fe, apparently, hauling along the family domicile. Rather like a circus train, I suppose."

"What in the world are you talking about?" Cosette demanded.

"John's family follows the rodeo. That's how they make their living." Dennis shrugged. "His mom's a cowboy preacher, and his dad and brothers are bullfighters and barrel men, going back generations. They've got a little motor home that they go from town to town in."

"Rather a gypsy-ish lifestyle, isn't it?" Jane asked, and Daisy's heart sank. Just hearing this description of

John's home life made her realize that he might, conceivably, never darken the doors of Bridesmaids Creek again.

"Yep," Dennis said, "and he's not coming back. Not anytime soon, anyway."

There was no way she could let that happen. Not after she'd finally come to her senses, after all the many moons of not realizing what a catch Squint—*John*—really was, hiding under all that brown-eyed, gentle bear exterior. Daisy swallowed hard, realizing the people sitting around the table were studying her, waiting silently for her to speak up.

Maybe it did serve her right to have John desert her for good after the many times he'd tried to win her. But she wasn't the kind of woman who gave up—in fact, there were some who said that adversity only strengthened her will.

"You realize, Daisy, there won't be a race run or a swim swum for you," Jane said gently. "I'm afraid you threw away your three chances."

"She didn't *throw* them away," Cosette said, her eyes softening as she looked at Daisy. Daisy felt this was very sweet of Cosette, especially as much of Cosette's hard luck was Daisy's fault. "She merely misplaced her three chances. Magic is *never* gone forever."

Daisy paused. Of course. She was a Bridesmaids Creek girl, even if she'd come to town late, at the age of three. The magic would still work for her—it *had* to.

Because John made love to her like no man ever could, and it might have taken her way too long to realize it, but she knew in every corner of her heart that she was in love with him.

"I'm going to need help," Daisy said softly. "I could really use some assistance in figuring out the right way to convince John that leaving Bridesmaids Creek wasn't his best decision."

They all took that in.

"We're always here for one of our hometown girls," Dennis said solemnly, and the ladies nodded, and Daisy felt warmed just by being designated a "hometown" girl. Maybe forgiveness was possible after all. She sure hoped so.

Now she just had to convince John that his home was here, and not the place where he'd grown up.

Rodeo.

John found his parents and brothers just outside of Santa Fe. Their small silver mobile home rumbled under turquoise-colored skies, with a truck—his brothers'—following closely behind. If not for cell phone contact, he would have missed them.

Mary and Mack Mathison waved at him as he pulled alongside their white truck, which hauled the silver Airstream mobile home they'd bought too many years ago for John to remember. His brothers Javier and Jackson saluted him, and he fell back into position, trailing behind the white truck lettered *Mathison* on both doors in black. Home sweet home.

This was it. He turned on some tunes, tried not to think about Daisy and told himself he was content to caravan as far away from Texas as possible.

"This could never have been her life," John told the smiling bobblehead dog on his dash. "Daisy grew up with so much wealth, so much of everything, that she couldn't possibly understand this kind of pared-down existence."

The black-and-white bobblehead dog he'd named Joe, because it fit the *J* motif of his and his brothers' names, neither agreed nor disagreed. In fact, Joe didn't seem to be worried about much of anything other than the sunburn he was getting on his furry behind, courtesy of dash sitting. John watched the mountains of New Mexico fade away, thought about how beautiful it would be to see this highway on his motorcycle, with Daisy parked comfortably on the back, her arms around his waist, which she'd done all the way back from Montana. He got a woody just remembering her delicate arms around him, felt a dull hammer begin inside his skull.

"Holy Christmas," John muttered. "I'm going to have to take up serious meditation to get her out of my head."

He'd left his motorcycle in Bridesmaids Creek, under Sam's care, with dire instructions that it was to be in the same beloved condition when he returned. Sam had agreed with a grin, saying smartly that of course it looked even better with Daisy polishing the seat, and would he mind—

"At which point I gave Sam such a glare that he shut clean up," John told Joe, and Joe nodded in approval. Or maybe he didn't nod in approval, but if he wasn't nodding in approval, then what the hell good was a bobblehead dog to a man, anyway?

At the border connecting New Mexico and Colorado, his parents stopped the caravan at a roadside rest stop. He hadn't expected them to stop so soon, as life on the road was about putting the miles between destinations. But they were more than happy to halt the train soon after he'd joined them, to welcome him back to the fold.

"What the hell, son?" Mack demanded, giving him a tight hug. "You took a year off my life showing up like that. I thought I'd seen a ghost."

"Might as well be a ghost," Mary said. "He hasn't been around in four years."

His brothers banged him on the back with enthusiasm. "We missed the hell out of you," Javier said.

"We've been keeping Mack and Mary on the circuit," Jackson said. "It'll be good to have you back. You can help us keep them focused. They keep wanting to run off to New Zealand."

"New Zealand?" John looked at his parents as they began checking over the ancient trailer. There was never much time for idle conversation. Everyone had their chores and responsibilities at each stop, where duties were parceled out and executed with a minimum of discussion. It was all business: check the equipment, use the facilities, stretch the legs and get back in the trucks.

As a child, John had carried along a soccer ball to kick with his brothers at the stops. He'd always wished they could stop long enough to have a real picnic at one of the shaded tables that usually graced a rest stop. On their birthdays, they did—but as a rule, the road was a demanding mistress, and must be gotten back to immediately.

"It's my birthday," he said suddenly, wanting his parents and brothers to cease their ant-like scurrying, and act as if him showing up in their midst after four years away was actually a big deal.

"Your birthday?" Mary frowned, thinking. "Is it?"

John nodded. "Yes."

"Good heavens," Mack said. "I think he's telling the truth."

"I'm a Navy SEAL," John said. "I lean toward honesty."

They stared at him, perplexed. "It's just that we stay in our groove," Mary said. "We don't mean to seem uncaring."

"I know." John shrugged. "No big deal. Let's sit down and have a water bottle or something. Talk."

His parents took that in.

"All right, son," Mack said after a long moment. "Javier, do we have any birthday cake in the trailer freezer?"

John sighed, remembering this well. Birthday cakes, of course, were kept in the freezer, for birthdays occurring on the road. No muss, no fuss. And nothing home baked. The boys had been homeschooled, too, which meant a rolling education. But Mary was smart, and they'd learned everything they needed to know to do very well on the standardized tests. At one point, young Javier had even decided he might want to attend college and had applied to Florida State, finding himself a very desirable candidate before he'd ultimately decided he preferred to stay with the family.

That was what happened: you spent your life on the road, and nothing else seemed as exciting.

They sat under one of the awnings at a concrete table. A couple of birds hopped near, wondering if the humans might drop any crumbs. *Pity the bird that thinks it is getting crumbs from the Mathisons*, John thought—feeling bad when Javier came out from the trailer triumphantly bearing five slices of cake, one of them anointed with a lit candle. Javier put this one in front of John, grinning. He whistled a long note, and his family all burst into the "Happy Birthday" song.

"Make a wish!" they exclaimed, so John blew out his candle—totally annoyed with himself when he realized that the image that flickered across his mind the instant he tried to think of what he'd wish for was Daisy's beautiful face.

Before he'd had a chance to stop his brain, he'd wished she were here with him right now.

What a stupid wish.

Chapter Three

John couldn't have been more stunned when Sam's truck pulled up beside the family trailer, but his brain seemed to separate into two parts when Daisy's long-legged sexiness got out of the passenger side.

He shoved his cake with the birthday candle still smoking far away from him—clearly Bridesmaids Creek didn't have the only claim to mystical mayhem—and got up to greet his friend. And the woman who drove him mad even in his sleep.

"What the hell, buddy?" John said to Sam, slapping the bearlike man on the back by way of embrace. Over Sam's shoulder, John's gaze was locked onto Daisy. She smiled, looking a trifle unsure of herself, which was unusual for Daisy. "What brings you two here?"

"Following you," Sam said, then went to say hello to Mr. and Mrs. Mathison, and Javier and Jackson.

That left John staring at Daisy, drowning in her dark eyes. "Hi."

She smiled. "Hello."

"So, is somebody going to tell me what's going on?" John asked.

"You left without saying goodbye."

"How did you find me?"

"It wasn't hard. You told the fellows exactly where you were headed. Sam said we'd just get in the truck and follow the smoke of your truck as you burned rubber out of BC." She frowned. "How could you leave without saying goodbye? After…after we rode on your motorcycle all the way home from Montana?"

That was a nice way of saying *How could you just leave like that after we'd made love like crazy?* John sighed. "I'm sorry. I was probably a heel. Didn't think it through."

"I'd say you didn't." Daisy's frown deepened, and he could tell she was really hurt.

"Daisy, look," he began, "we just don't suit. You know that."

She stared at him silently.

"I mean, we suit *sexually*," he said, lowering his voice, then pulled her farther from the group. His parents would be concerned about getting off schedule, but for the moment, they seemed happy to visit with Sam. Sam, of course, had helped himself to John's slice of cake, casually flinging the candle in the trash. "What happened in Montana is best left in Montana."

Daisy shook her head. "I don't believe that's really what you want."

"Do you see my family, Daze?" He pointed to the trailer. "This is my life, and it's as far away from Bridesmaids Creek and all that crazy magic as it could be. This is real life, this is the real John Lopez 'Squint' Mathison. I ain't no Prince Charming, sweetheart."

"I understand that you're—that you've misunderstood what I need from a man after I chased Cisco, stupidly, of course," Daisy began, but he shook his head.

"I don't even think about that. I knew what was going on all along. I understood that you were just trying to fit in, and to find your own place in BC. But, Daisy, beautiful as you are, as desirable as you are, I'm not the man for you. I'm sorry." He took a deep breath. "I'm really sorry that you came all this way having to listen to Sam's hot air, too."

"John," Daisy began.

"I'm not going to turn into a handsome, secret prince like Cisco did."

"Cisco's from some kind of minor, minor royal lineage. And that's not why I'm here!"

"But at the time, the idea of a title was dazzling to you, and this," he said, gesturing to the beat-up trailer, "isn't dazzling. It didn't dazzle you then, and it's not going to dazzle you now, but this is my family. This is our way of life." He touched one of her long dark locks ruefully. "And I don't think you're exactly cut out for the migrant sort of life, princess."

She moved his hand. "Thank you for your opinion, but I'm capable of figuring out what I want."

"Because you knew what you wanted last year?" he asked, hating to be an ass but needing to make her see.

She stepped closer. "John, I *know* you care about me."

"Always have, and part of me always will." He moved away from her. "Trust me, Daisy, this would be an even bigger mistake than you and Cisco would have been."

"I was never in love with Cisco. I never cared about him, not the way you think I did." Daisy looked like tears might sprout any second, which was also a very unusual thing for the town's ex-bad girl. "You and I belong together, John Mathison."

He had to give her credit, being a daddy's girl had taught her to go after what she wanted. Or thought she wanted. But John understood human nature, and in this case, Daisy had just turned her gotta-have-it shopping list from one man to another. "Next year, it'll be someone else, beautiful, I promise."

She reached out, lightly touching the Saint Michael medal under his denim shirt. "You and I both know about this medal. You got it from a peddler you met when you and your family were following the rodeo. He told you it would always protect you. All of you SEALs have one, but you and Cisco got yours switched overseas one day at training, and Suz thinks that tangled up something. She said it misplaced the Bridesmaids Creek magic, so that I thought Cisco was the man for me." Daisy took a deep breath. "I'm not sure it happened that way. You've always been the only man for me. In fact, I *know* it in my heart. It just took me too long to see it. But I'm not going to beg you, John." She smacked his chest, right over his heart, and his breath flew from him, his brain shot into outer space and that red corpuscle-driving organ that was trying to deny how much it cared for Daisy seemed to stop beating for just the space of a second. Peace and tranquillity descended upon John just as Daisy walked away from him to go introduce herself to his family— only to be replaced by red-hot lust and fiery passion engulfing his entire soul as he watched her walk away from him. It felt as if he were drowning in desire, as if his impulses were threatening to overtake his good sense. Aching to take back every word he'd said, he rubbed his chest where she'd lightly smacked his heart, willing himself to come back inside his body and be rational, damn it—but he had never really been rational where Daisy Donovan was concerned, and today was probably not going to be the day he started.

Bridesmaids Creek's reach appeared to be long-ranging.

"I'm fine," Daisy said as she and Sam got back into his truck. "Thanks for driving me out here to find John's knuckleheaded self."

Sam laughed as he pulled onto the highway. "I told you he'd have his *cabeza* pretty well stuffed up his butt."

"It's a lot of my own fault." Daisy sighed, resisting the urge to glance over her shoulder in the vain hope that John might have had second thoughts about sending her away and was even now charging after Sam's truck. "I chased something I didn't even want too long, and ignored the man who is right for me. I don't blame him for not being entirely convinced that my heart belongs to him."

"So now what?"

"Now," Daisy said on a long breath, "hopefully, I enjoy a healthy pregnancy—"

"What?" Sam slammed on the brakes.

"Don't you *dare* even *think* about turning around and going back."

"But you didn't tell him that! I know you didn't! John would never have let you go if he knew you were pregnant! Are you really expecting a baby?"

"Keep driving," Daisy said in a toneless command. "Yes, I'm expecting a baby."

"Holy crap!" Sam turned the air conditioner on full blast, though the day was chilly and overcast. "Listen, you're going to get me in a whole lot of caca with one John Lopez Mathison. If he finds out that I knew—"

"It's all right, Sam. John's made his choice. I'm not using a baby to change his mind. Absolutely not. And if you tell him," Daisy said, staring at him, "I'll set the matchmakers in town on you."

The gentle bear of a man literally developed a peaked cast under his skin. "You wouldn't!"

"I *would*."

"I don't want a woman! I don't want a bride. Everyone has long known that I came along with John and Cisco just for the ride. Just to cause trouble, really."

"I'm aware." Daisy nodded. "But troublemakers sometimes find trouble."

He pulled off a ramp and parked in a deserted parking lot that appeared to once have housed shops, but was now long abandoned. "Daisy, listen. When Ty Spurlock invited us to BC to find brides, I made it clear that was for everyone but me. I made a deal, in fact, with Cosette that she leave me out of any sprinklings from her magic wand." He mopped his brow with a blue bandanna. "I'm everybody's friend and nobody's fellow, you see what I mean?"

She shrugged. "All you have to do is keep your lips sealed very tightly, Sam. If I'm going to catch John, I don't need you bringing him back home when he thinks he needs to be free."

He gulped, his brown eyes rolling nervously. "I don't want to agree to this, but I've seen the BC magic at work, and it's *potent* stuff."

"When applied correctly, yes, it is. Don't think for one

minute that I couldn't convince Cosette that you're just talking big, Sam Barr, and like every other man claiming you don't want a woman. It wouldn't be hard to convince Cosette that settling the mischief-maker of BC down would be a pièce de résistance for her magic wand."

He took a deep, shuddering breath. "Excuse me," he said, and got out of the truck. Reached into the double cab to pull a handful of ice from the cooler, wrapped it inside his blue bandanna and stuck it against his forehead. "He's going to know, Daisy. Someone will tell him."

"I'll cross that bridge when I come to it. But he can't know, not yet. He will know eventually," Daisy said. "You're going to have to give me time."

He nodded. "I know. I get it. I totally understand. You don't know John like I do, and he's superstitious as hell. You learn these things about a man in a war zone."

"Superstitious?"

"Yeah. He really bought into all that BC charm and nonsense."

"Nonsense!" Daisy sat up. "BC makes its living on that nonsense, and though I may be late to understanding it, I certainly endorse anything that fiscally benefits our town!"

Sam got back in the front seat, handing her a water bottle and cracking one open for himself. "Whatever happened up in Montana really changed you, Daisy. I don't know what potion Branch Winters poured over you, but it's a humdinger."

Daisy shook her head. "I fell in love," she said softly. "Branch helped me see the path, but the fact is, I've been in love with John for a long time. I was much too invested in my own pride to see it. And now I'm going to have to earn his, and the town's, trust. I'm willing to do that, but it's going to take time, which I won't have if you go bumping your gums all over BC."

"They'll know as soon as you start showing." He cast an aggrieved glance at her tummy.

"I have time." At least she hoped so.

Sam shook his head, glanced up at the roof of the truck. "Daisy Donovan, I'm only going to say this once because my whole body is going to go into shock, but there's only one way to bring my buddy back home, and to his senses, even."

"I'll happily take any advice you can give me." She meant every word, too. Earning John's trust wasn't going to be easy—she'd made quite a mess of things, and Daisy didn't need Sam, or Cosette or anybody else in town to spell that out for her.

"You're going to have to let me put a ring on your finger," Sam said, before passing out and falling over like a giant bear with its cotton stuffing pulled out.

She patted his face urgently. "Sam! Don't be a schmuck, I'm not marrying you!" Grabbing the cold bandanna, she wiped it over his face, shrieking when John knocked on the driver's-side window.

"John!"

He pulled open the door. "What the hell is going on?"

"Sam fainted!" She patted his face some more, willing color back into the dark skin. "He proposed to me, and then he—"

"What?" John helped her lay Sam across the seat and Daisy got out of the truck to make room. She worked on Sam at one end of the cab, and John worked on Sam from the driver's side. "You're gone five minutes and work a proposal out of Handsome Sam? Wake up, buddy," he said, touching cold water to Sam's face, "so I can knock you back out again!"

* * *

Sam came to—finally!—and John breathed a sigh of relief. "Helluva a beauty nap you took there, buddy."

"What can I say? I need my forty winks." Sam sat up, glanced over at Daisy, whose face looked tragically concerned for Sam. "But I'm doing fine. This sexy, amazing woman has just agreed to—"

"Yeah, yeah." John helped his friend none too gently to sit up. "You big faker."

"Faker!" Sam looked outraged, any trace of the fallout he'd had gone for good. "I'm not faking anything!"

"Oh, you're a faker all right." John glared at the man whose back he'd had in Afghanistan, and vice versa. "Yelling at the top of your lungs that you want nothing to do with marriage, and the second I turn my back, you go and get—"

"What does your back have to do with anything?" Sam demanded.

"I'd like to know that myself." Daisy's concern turned to annoyance. "And what are you doing here, anyway? Last I saw you, you were heading north."

"I am heading north." He could barely meet Daisy's gaze. The truth was, his good sense had evaporated once he'd realized he was an epic dunce for letting her get away. He'd hopped into his truck and followed, not sure why, his heart driving him like a mad man. "You shouldn't have to drive all the way back to Bridesmaids Creek with Handsome Sam here. The least I can do is offer to fly you back. However, I had no idea that you and Sam—"

"Yep," Sam said, coming out of his coma ever more strongly by the second. He thumped his chest with pride. "Offer me the cup of congratulations, old buddy, old pal, I'm getting married."

"So you claimed."

John glanced at Daisy, but she didn't deny Sam's astonishing brag. Everyone knew that Sam was the last man on earth—the very last of any tribe, clan, or nationality—who would ever marry. Daisy gazed at him steadily, not appearing to be preparing to open her sumptuous, delightful lips for any sort of rebuttal, and John's heart fell to the ground, rolled around in the dust of the parking lot, then gave up the ghost.

"In fact, I'm having a baby," Sam said cheerfully, and the ghost of John's heart not only gave up, it poofed into nothingness. He felt cold all over, then hot, then drained. "*We're* having a baby."

"A baby?"

"It appears I'm going to be a father." Sam shook his head. "An astonishing thing, no?"

"Very." John raised a brow. "Let me get this straight. Daisy came after me, but you wanted her for yourself, and so you offered to drive her—"

"Just so." Sam nodded. John glanced to Daisy, who merely shrugged.

He stepped back from his friend, trying to piece all this together. Everyone knew Sam was a trickster beyond compare—if Shakespeare had still been alive, he could have written plays about this wizard of wackiness—but marriage? A baby?

John shook his head. "You two are fibbing through your teeth, but I'm darned if I know why."

Daisy didn't say anything, and Sam kept very still, like he was one breath short of hyperventilating again. John sighed. "Are you really this fickle? Or are you trying to make a point? Because I wouldn't put it past either one of you."

"What difference does it make to you?" Daisy asked.

"None." It meant every difference. He'd waited years for Daisy to come to her senses and realize he was the man of her dreams. Then, when she had come to her senses, he'd lost every one of his, apparently. Maybe lust had fried his brain. "Anyway, if you're content to ride home with my loose-marbled friend here, that's fine. I just wanted you to know that you could go by plane, too."

"You couldn't call to make your generous offer?" Daisy looked at him, and he thought she wasn't buying his cover story.

"I could have, but it seemed best to inquire in person." He looked at Sam. "My friend here means a lot to me. I know he was trying to do me a favor by bringing you after me."

"Really?" Daisy put a hand on a slim hip. "A favor? Does Sam truck women after you often, then?"

"Not at all. Which is why I felt the occasion merited the personal treatment."

"Well, thank you *so* much."

Daisy didn't sound very grateful. In fact, he thought he'd detected a tiny undertone of snark. He looked at her. "A baby? You two expect me to buy that you're having a baby?" He cast a gaze at her very flat stomach, with which he was intimately familiar, having spent hours kissing that very toned, very delectable flesh. "Something's off about this whole story."

It was indeed off. He'd used condoms with Daisy. She'd been very fine with that, in fact, one might even have said helpful, a foreplay which had stretched his manly capabilities to the max. John practically got stiff thinking about it. "A baby," he repeated. "I just don't think you have it in you, old man."

"What?" Sam squawked, sitting straight up with indignation. "I think I can handle parenthood just fine, thanks."

John shook his head. There was an alternate reality in here, he knew there was, but these two were thick as thieves about something. He looked at both of them, and then it hit him: his buddy was attempting to paint a bull's-eye on him with one of his infamous pranks.

Yes, Handsome Sam Barr was trying to pull a fast one.

And the only way to neutralize having a bull's-eye painted on one's hindquarters was to pull a faster one.

"You know," John said, "as I recall, Vegas is only a couple hours from here. Probably quite doable as a wedding destination in one day, considering how you like to apply your boot to the pedal."

Sam nodded vigorously. "We should be able to make it by nightfall for a romantic destination."

John looked at Daisy. "I wish you two well."

Daisy nodded, but she seemed uncertain. "Thank you."

"All right, then." Taking a deep breath, John got into the double cab, seating himself behind Sam and Daisy, and belted himself in with a grin.

Chapter Four

"What are you doing?" Daisy turned to meet John's mischievous gaze.

"I'm riding with you to Vegas." He put his hands behind his head, looking very comfortable and even pleased with himself.

Daisy frowned. "Why?"

He clapped Sam on the shoulder. "I can't let my buddy get married without a best man. And I *am* the best man. You may not know this about Sam and me, but we've seen some very dark days. Together, we survived."

Daisy glanced at Sam. He shrugged, and she thought she saw a little *what-can-we-do?* in his expressive eyes.

"We *are* best friends," Sam said.

Daisy turned to stare out the window. "I don't care."

"You don't mind if he tags along?" Sam asked.

"Hey! I prefer to think of myself less as a tagalonger and more as part of the wedding party."

Daisy didn't turn to look at John to sanction this silly statement. She was well aware he was taking Sam's role of being a trickster, but she wasn't going to be the one to cry "uncle." If these two wanted to play chicken, it was probably a game they'd played before. "I don't care one bit."

Sam turned to glare at John. "You can't cause any trouble."

"Me?" John feigned surprise and innocence. "I never cause trouble."

"Never cause trouble," Sam muttered under his breath, starting the truck, and Daisy wondered how this situation was going to end up by nightfall. John appeared determined to call Sam's bluff, so there was a great possibility that Sam might find himself at the altar saying "I do," something he'd always proclaimed he would never do.

Until today.

This was terrible. With John sitting in the backseat goading his friend on, Sam might not feel as if he could bow out. Sam had just been trying to bring John to his senses—but like other plans in Bridesmaids Creek had been known to go, this one appeared to have taken a turn for the worse.

I don't even need anyone to marry me.

With the two men dug in for the long haul, apparently, Daisy decided she might as well take a nap. Pretend to take one, anyway—as if she could ignore John's long, lean body in the backseat. She could feel his gaze on her, studying her. Waiting to see if she'd crack.

The man really believed she was so hung up on him that he could haul out of town without saying goodbye—

then show back up in her life and throw the equivalent of a cold, wet water balloon to explode her plans.

Ass.

"I'm sorry, pumpkin, did you say something?" Sam asked, clearly intending to play the *This Is Chicken and I'm Not Gonna Lose* scenario to its incongruous end. "It sounded like you said *ass.*"

Daisy shook her head, kept her eyes closed. "I didn't say ass."

"I thought I heard her say ass," John said, putting his two cents in from the backseat.

"Guys, leave me out of the rooster-like posturing, please," she said, and they had the nerve to guffaw.

"Daisy, lady, you're far too much for my gentle friend to handle," John said.

"And yet he's handling me just fine," Daisy said, and that shut John up for the space of five blissful minutes.

Of course, John had to start fielding calls on his cell phone. From the backseat, she could hear him gossiping about today's wedding plans. He told everyone who called that she and Sam were running off—which of course brought on a flurry of phone calls, all of which John seemed pleased to discuss in laborious detail. Daisy's nerves were stretched tight, and Sam looked positively unlike himself.

Handsome Sam had turned into a shadow of his former devil-may-care self.

Daisy was relieved when Sam finally pulled up in Vegas. He'd found a quaint little chapel, a white incongruous place that didn't shout Elvis.

"I'll take the groom in and tidy him up," John said jovially, and Daisy snapped, "Fine."

"Ooh, bridal nerves," John whispered to Sam, but he made sure his whisper carried. "I think she's got 'em bad!"

She was going to clock John Lopez Mathison a good one if he didn't take his annoying self far from her. A delicate, elderly woman approached. "You must be the bride."

"Not today," Daisy said. "I'll give you five hundred dollars if you sneak me out of here and keep those two hunky cowboys I came in with busy long enough for me to get to the nearest airport."

Knowing the first place Sam and John would look for her was Bridesmaids Creek or Branch Winters's place in Montana, Daisy took herself somewhere she knew she was totally safe. She went to New York, waited a day for her father to overnight her passport, and flew out to Australia, where Robert Donovan had recently purchased properties. It was a great excuse to check out the real estate, which made her father happy, but most of all, it gave Daisy time to think through her situation.

For a girl who loved riding fast on her motorcycle, her life had become way too fast-paced. She was going to be a mother. It was time to sit and think, figure out what she was going to do. Here she was completely safe from the game-playing duo of John and Sam.

She put a hand on her stomach as she looked out over the Sydney skyline. John had never suspected the baby was his—which had annoyed the heck out of her, but they'd been completely faithful about using condoms, so she guessed she could understand why he might assume the baby was Sam's.

Then again, he was still an ass. She might have been wild, but she'd never been promiscuous, and John knew that. Part of her wondered if Sam would tell him the truth—but one never knew with Sam. He marched to the beat of his own unseen drummer, one that played a tune no one could predict.

It would all work out. She had to believe that. To think otherwise would mean giving up on the BC magic—something she would never do. Her father owned buildings around the world; she could live anywhere she liked. But Bridesmaids Creek was home.

And that's where her baby would be born.

She just needed to let the smoke clear. Once John and Sam cooled their jets, she'd return.

It was time to make up for her part in the problems in BC—and she'd never been a girl to back down from what she knew had to be done.

She couldn't wait to get started.

"That's the funniest story I ever heard!" Sheriff Dennis slapped his thigh, causing the biggest frown he could muster to crease John's face. Cosette Lafleur and Jane Chatham didn't appear to be any less amused by the tale of Daisy ditching both him and Sam at the altar, so this was just one more BC legend John was going to have to live down.

He didn't mind admitting that he didn't understand Daisy. He prided himself on being able to catch anything that moved on the planet—anything. He'd been an excellent sniper—hence Squint, short for Squint-Eye—he'd been proud to protect his fellow countrymen. He had no trouble bagging any kind of game, and horseshoes and hand grenades were right up his tree of fun.

But the sexy brunette with the key to his soul—she confounded him. Eluded him, and stunned him. He'd had every intention of making her go all the way up to the altar with Sam, for the sheer pleasure of watching her back out at the last second.

Oh, she'd backed out big-time. They were lucky she hadn't taken the truck and stranded them in Sin City.

One day he'd have to thank her for not doing that. He couldn't really have blamed her if she had.

The worst part was nobody knew where she'd gone— or if they did, they sure as heck weren't telling. John sent a sour look to his booth mates at The Wedding Diner.

"One of you has to know something. She couldn't have just disappeared."

The three haphazard matchmakers shook their collective heads in the negative.

"You won't find her, wherever she went," Cosette said. "Robert's got ventures all around the world. Last I heard, he'd bought up something in Shanghai." She frowned. "Or maybe it was Bangkok."

John tipped his hat back. "It's all my fault, anyway. If she wants peace and quiet, she should get all she wants."

"Your fault?" Dennis asked.

"Yeah. I pushed her." He sighed. "Sam's mad as the dickens at me, too. He said I was being a louse, and that he was doing his very best to get me moving."

"To be fair, Daisy never gave you a whole lot of encouragement until lately."

"I wish I could use that as an excuse, but I can't." Since she'd seduced him in Montana—or had he seduced her?—it had all happened so fast and seemed so beneficially organic.

"It's funny how we used to call her the Diva of Destruction." Sheriff Dennis laughed. "That seems a long time ago now."

Daisy was still a diva to him—the Diva of Delights.

They couldn't understand how mad he was about her, had been from the moment he'd laid eyes on her zooming around on her motorcycle.

"Patience has never been a virtue of mine."

They laughed. "Nor ours," Cosette said.

"In the meantime," Jane said, "you can be our fall guy. Just until Daisy gets back. She will come back one day, you know."

"Fall guy?" He perked up. This sounded distinctly dangerous. One didn't sign up to be a fall guy in Bridesmaids Creek willy-nilly. This crew could think up some wingdingers.

Jane nodded. "We need you to find out whose baby Daisy is having. We must be prepared."

The blood left John's head. "Whose baby?" He couldn't bear thinking about it. "I thought they were just making up that tale."

The ladies looked at him, concerned. "Daisy's really expecting," Jane said.

He sat dumbfounded, shell-shocked.

After a moment, Jane sighed and went on. "Well, it's clear Daisy thinks she's going to do this all on her own. She's just that kind of independent woman. Goodness knows she doesn't need a man for financial reasons." Jane shook her head. "If that's not your baby—"

"I'm afraid not." His ears were ringing, to go with the light-headedness assailing him. He couldn't bear to think of Daisy even kissing another man, much less having a baby! "Do you have anything stronger than tea, Jane?"

The three gentle folk looked at him with grave concern.

"I keep some whiskey in the back for after hours," Jane whispered. "On occasion, our close-knit group likes to sit in one of the circular booths and enjoy a small tipple."

"I could use a small tipple." John couldn't imagine Daisy being held in another man's arms. Oh, Sam had tried to make him jealous, but no one was jealous of Handsome Sam.

But he hadn't thought through the fact that Daisy might be with child by another man.

"We're wondering if Branch Winters did more than reroute Daisy's brain," Dennis said, and cold and hot swamped John in nauseating waves. "Something happened up there, something big."

"He changed her," Cosette said. "We're wondering if perhaps Daisy might have fallen for—"

"I can't," John said. He leaned back in the booth, and when Jane put the "tipple" in front of him in a sweetly painted tea cup to disguise its contents from the other patrons, John knocked it back without hesitation.

"Easy there, sailor," Dennis said. "It'll be closing time soon. I'll take you to my place and we'll cauterize your brain for a bit. Or maybe Phillipe's place for some yoga. I'm really getting into that yoga crap Phillipe's got going on, Cosette. Do you do it?"

"I do, and I'm getting so flexible! Who would have ever thought my husband would become a yogi of sorts?" Cosette looked pleased, and John noticed that she didn't refer to Phillipe as her ex-husband. Maybe matters were looking up for them. He sure hoped so.

"I'll pass on the yoga." After their divorce, Phillipe had moved into a small house, and outfitted it with hanging beads and floor cushions for the yoga practice he'd started. It looked like a regular hangout for hippies, which had caught them all off guard because Phillipe and Cosette were anything but the hippie type.

Cosette picked up the delicate floral teapot and poured some more amber liquid into his cup. "You look like you could use another smidge of whiskey."

"And all this time I thought you sat in this booth and drank tea." John shook his head.

"We do!" Jane glanced at her friends. "But on occasion, like right now, something with a little oomph is required. Now, if you're feeling fortified, let's get back to the topic at hand, which is Daisy."

He froze up again. "I can't be the fall guy. I can't even think about it." He swallowed hard. "Anyway, isn't it her business who the father of her child might be?"

"Maybe," Dennis said, "unless the father lives in Montana or something."

Crap. He could see where they were going with this. Daisy Donovan might just have allowed herself, in a moment of heartbreak and confusion, to be seduced. The cold chills he'd suffered a moment ago came back with a vengeance, despite the whiskey he'd quaffed out of the eggshell-thin teacup.

She might not ever return to Bridesmaids Creek.

"I suppose you're absolutely certain, one hundred percent sure that the baby couldn't possibly be yours...not that we're trying to pry?" Jane asked gently.

He read between those lines. "Oh, you're dying to pry, but I know you mean well." He took a long, deep breath. "I suppose the way things work in BC, I can't entirely count out the remote, infinitesimal poss—"

"I knew it!" Cosette clapped her hands.

Jane beamed. She made another pour out of the teapot

for the entire table, making sure John's went clean to the rim of his cup. "This calls for a celebration!"

"Now wait," John said. "I was going to say that Daisy's baby being mine would be something on the order of a miraculous—"

They all looked at him, their faces gleaming as his words drifted away. Each of them looked so pleased he couldn't bear to let them down.

"You have to understand, you'd be better off looking for another bachelor," John said. "I'm not your man."

"He may be right," Jane said thoughtfully. "I don't know that I'm feeling it."

Dennis wore the same suddenly thoughtful look. "And then there's the matter of Sam. I still can't figure out how he got into this."

John didn't want to hear about Handsome Sam. "Trust me, my buddy was just trying to help me get to the altar. It was all an elaborate sham to coax me there."

"Most men don't offer to marry a woman who's having a child that isn't theirs." Cosette grew pensive now, too. "I mean, *you're* not."

His throat got a bit tight. "I haven't really thought about—"

"The thing about Sam," Dennis said, "is that he really is an ultimate bachelor with a golden heart. Someone should hook him."

John shook his head. "You'll never catch Sam."

"But he was taking her to Vegas," Jane said. "That gives me pause about this bachelor song he sings."

A little doubt crept into John. "Sam's just up to his usual tricks. We all suffer from it. And love him for it, too," he said truthfully.

"Well," Cosette said brightly, "I suppose it doesn't

matter whether you're in love with Daisy. She's not here, and who knows when she'll come home after the shock she's suffered."

"Wait a minute." John's brain whirred like a pinwheel. Which fallacy should he start with—that he was in love with Daisy, or that she might never return? This was BC: she *had* to return. "I'm not in love with Daisy."

The second the words left his mouth, causing glints of mirth and knowing to shine in his friends' eyes, John knew—just as they knew—that he was head over heels, gone-and-not-coming-back, certifiably in love with Daisy Donovan.

"Oh, crap," he said, and they high-fived each other, and then him, for good measure.

This was a problem. He was now squarely in BC's sights, and the worst part was, he had no clue where Daisy was, and if that was his child she was carrying.

Holy smoke.

Chapter Five

"And that's that," John told Daisy's gang. "You lot are going to help me make this right. And if that's not high irony, I don't know what is."

Daisy's gang of five, seated in their new man cave, shook their lunkheads. "We can't help you," Dig said.

"No aid to the enemy," Red said.

"She's our girl," Clint said, "even if she didn't choose one of us."

"We don't see what a great girl like her would see in a squid like you," Carson said.

"And we haven't given up hope," Gabriel said. "We're not helping any Handsome Sams, Squints or Frogs. Where do you guys get these names, anyway?"

So he was sitting square in enemy camp, with conspirators unwilling to be his wingmen in his hunt to find

Daisy. "Listen, Daisy's having a baby, and she's going to need our help."

"*Our* help," Red said. "Not necessarily *your* help."

"Unless you're the father," Carson said, "and we don't see that being the case."

John shrugged. "Of course I'm the father. Who else do you think it would be?" Here he was fibbing just a bit because he didn't know for sure, but in the night, he'd ruminated over what his friends had said to him at The Wedding Diner and realized it really didn't matter who the father of Daisy's baby was. He was in love with her, and he'd be a good father, a dad to her child.

As far as John was concerned, that made it case closed for his suit.

They glared at him, not believing him.

"Daisy would have told us," Clint said. "We've got our money on it being that fellow up in Montana. The airy-fairy one who lives in the wild and communes with nature and all that crapola."

John laughed. "Branch would get a real charge out of hearing himself described that way."

"So?" Carson demanded. "How do you know Daisy's not with him?"

"Because she's not. And we need to find her, fellows."

"Again," Dig said, "*we* need to find her. There's no you and us in this situation. *We've* known her since she was three years old, and *we* don't need any outside help rescuing her from what was clearly an unfortunate decision on her part."

"That's too bad." John leaned back in one of the leather chairs, glanced around the man cave. "It'd be good for your new business to showcase your first success as date makers."

"You're not one of our clients," Red said.

"Because you don't have any yet," John said, pointing out the obvious. "If you're going to be the premier dating service and cigar bar," he said, glancing with doubt toward the leather-wrapped cigar bar and wooden walls that shouted man cave, in complete opposition to the idea of being a dating service, "you need a high-profile client to highlight what you can do. And that's me."

They gawked at him. John could hear the wheels turning.

"He's right," Clint said reluctantly.

"Never say that an out-of-towner is right," Carson said, his words hushed.

"Nevertheless, he has a point," Dig said, his voice stunned.

"At least it's not Handsome Sam," Gabriel said. "I think I can stand anything but giving our girl up to a man with a handle like that!"

The six men got out of the two trucks, warily eyeing the Donovan compound.

"Well," Dig said to John as they stared at the massive two-story gray edifice, "here's the yellow brick road. And while you might want us to play your Cowardly Lion, Tin Man, Scarecrow, Toto and—"

"I'm not playing Dorothy," Red said, "no cracks about my hair or anything."

They gazed at his long red mop for a second. John didn't think there was a man on earth he'd rather deem Dorothy less than Red. The man had arm muscles that looked like a bear's.

"Cowardly Lion, Tin Man, Scarecrow, Toto and a flying monkey," Dig said, his tone impatient with his friend.

"Okay, I can go with a flying monkey. They were kind of cool," Red said, but they ignored him and went back to staring at the house where Daisy lived, and thus, her warlock of a father.

John shook his head. "I really don't know if this is the right plan, fellows."

"Well, you came to us for help, need I remind you?" Carson said. "And this is how we suggest you help yourself. You're going to have to man up and ask for his daughter's hand in marriage."

"What?" John said, and Daisy's gang favored him with narrow gazes.

"That's what we're here for, isn't it?" Gabriel demanded.

"I was going to start small," John said, "like maybe let Robert Donovan know that I'd like to find his daughter."

They shook their heads.

"Here's the problem," Clint said. "We have it on good authority that Donovan doesn't know his little angel is expecting his grandchild."

"That can't be possible. This is BC," John said. "Everybody knows everything about everybody, and if they don't, it's because they've buried themselves deep under a rock."

"And just who do you think would tell Mr. Donovan that his daughter is in the family way?" Dig asked, staring at him. "Don't you think he'd have had a word or two with the man he thought had knocked up his daughter and left her high and dry?"

"You being that fellow and all," Red said, "now that the truth has come out."

"No truth has come out!" John said, but he was beginning to wonder himself. He'd asked Sam, but Sam had denied knowing who the father of Daisy's baby was. Swore up and down that he didn't care, either. If Daisy needed a husband, then Sam Barr was more than happy to be that husband.

Jealousy had practically eaten a hole in John's cool, calm persona—and Sam knew it. Enjoyed it, even.

"But admit it, you're beginning to think you're going to be shopping for blue or pink in the very near future," Clint said, and John's breath hitched.

"It's actually a pretty appealing idea," he said, and they clapped him on the back in the nearest sign of camaraderie he'd experienced from them. "Hey! You're trying to get me to go up there, spill the beans—which are Daisy's beans to spill, by the way—and get my head pounded down my neck!"

They guffawed, just a bunch of knuckleheads having a great day, more than happy to add him to their group for the moment because it made them a whole half-dozen cars on the crazy train for a change.

"Aw, Donovan's not going to pound your head," Dig said. "Nobody's afraid of Daddy Warbucks anymore. But you *are* going to get the speech about how you're not worthy of his adorable daughter, and how he ought to bury you under Best Man's Fork where no one can find your remains for knocking up his baby girl, and that if you think you're going to get one penny of his dough you're crazier than a bedbug."

"Well, when you put it that way, how can I resist?" John asked, not that worried about Donovan, anyway. A security truck pulled up, with Donovan riding shotgun to see who was trespassing on his holy land, and the five dummkopfs scattered in their truck.

"What brings you to my humble abode, Squint?" Donovan demanded as the dust plume rose from John's new-found friends' hauling asses.

"It's John now, Robert. And I'd like a moment of your time," John said, and the man narrowed his eyes at him.

It wasn't a stare most people would like to receive, but John had seen a lot worse. He shrugged. "If you have time, that is. Sir."

Just like his military days, he knew when to apply the courtesy treatment. Robert perked up.

"I might spare you five minutes. Start talking."

"Actually, what I've come to say is private." John glanced at the armed guards and the driver, who was no doubt packing as well, with a shrug. "Regarding family business."

Robert grumbled a bit. "I suppose you want to be invited in."

John shrugged again.

"Those five wienies who just hit the road have never darkened the doors of my house. Why would I let you in?"

"I can talk out in the fresh air just as well as inside four walls, Robert. I'm just asking for you to hear me out in private."

After a moment, Robert got out. His men drove away. "So, you've come to find out where my daughter is. She said you would."

"I'm glad she knows me so well."

"Harrumph!"

"Look, Robert, I happen to think an awful lot of your daughter, and—"

"Son, let me stop you." Robert drew himself up to his full six feet four and glared. "I know where you come from, I know about your family. What do you imagine you can possibly offer my daughter?"

John ignored that, took a deep breath and then the plunge. "There's a very good chance Daisy may be having my baby. I need to find her."

Robert shook his head gravely. "My daughter isn't expecting a child. Not yours, or anybody else's. Someone's been blowing smoke in your face, in order to get you to make this ill-advised journey. And it *was* ill-advised."

John shrugged. "Regardless, I need to find Daisy. I'd like to talk to her."

"My daughter has asked me not to reveal her whereabouts. Says she'll come home when she's ready." Robert shook his head at John. "I'll honor Daisy's wishes."

Robert turned to leave.

"One more thing, sir."

Robert turned again. "I appreciate that Daisy needs some time to herself." He met Robert's eyes with determination. "Just know that when she does return to BC, I will be asking for her hand in marriage."

"You'll never get a penny of mine," Robert warned.

"I don't recall asking for any of your money," John said. He eyed the great gray house behind them. "Honestly, your way of life wouldn't suit me at all. I'm used to something far different. And just know that Daisy, should she accept my suit, would always be taken care of in every way."

"Your parents are itinerant rodeo workers!" Robert sputtered.

John nodded. "That's right. Good people, too. Daisy and I would do just fine on my earnings as a rodeo worker. Don't count your daughter out, Robert. She's tougher than you think she is."

He got into his truck and departed, feeling really good about the way the conversation had gone.

Daisy's gang was waiting for him at the end of the drive, around the corner and well out of eyeshot of the main house. John pulled over, and got out to join them.

They stared at him, agog.

"It was brave of you to hang around, but I told you everything would be fine." John waited for the onslaught of questions, which began almost as soon as his words left his mouth.

"Are you getting married?"

"Did he know Daisy's pregnant?"

"Where's our Daisy?"

"Fellows, fellows." He held up a hand to stem the cacophony. "I said everything was fine. I didn't say that Robert had given away any information. I know nothing more than when you last saw me. However, Donovan now knows of my intent to marry his daughter, so that puts a new wrinkle in the dynamic of everybody's favorite busybodying small town."

He tipped his hat to them, and got back into his truck. With a jaunty wave, he drove away, not giving away that he had no idea what he was going to do next.

John settled into bed at the bunkhouse, placing himself on his back, one arm behind his head so he could lie still and stare at the ceiling. Not that he could see the ceiling in the dark, but stare he did, deep in thought.

His mind was turned inside out; he hardly knew what to believe. BC claimed Daisy was having a baby; no one knew whose.

Robert Donovan said she wasn't, and that his daughter merely needed to be left alone.

Someone wasn't telling the truth, and if John had to guess, he'd say none of them was telling the unvarnished truth. Oh, there were probably bits and pieces of truth scattered in and out of all the stories—but he was being steered, there was no question of that.

It was the way BC operated. Besides which, the only person who had all the information was Daisy—and she clearly intended to remain a silent party.

Very unusual for her, too.

The door opened. Someone came in, closed it behind them.

"Hello?" John waited, holding back a yawn. More than likely Sam or one of the hands didn't realize he'd gotten back. Listening carefully, he knew he wasn't in danger.

Two people, both women.

"John!" Cosette's delicate French accent hissed in the darkness.

"You can turn a light on." He sat up, swung his legs over the bed, reached for his jeans, pulled them up.

"Are you decent?" Cosette asked.

"I am now." He waited, decided to flip the lamp on the bedside table to put his visitors out of their misery. "Hello, Jane, Cosette."

They solemnly nodded. He studied their clothes. Both women wore black, from their little feet to their necks, including long sleeves. They each had on a black hat. "Are we getting out our cauldron tonight, ladies?" he asked.

"Very funny." Jane waved an imperative hand at him. "Please dress yourself. We dare not linger. Someone will surely notice that you have visitors in your room."

"Surely they would notice, since I haven't had any female companionship in my room in, oh, since I've been employed at the Hanging H." Sighing, he stood, reach-

ing for a white T-shirt with a Hanging H advertisement
on the front. He happened to glance at the ladies, noted
their raised eyebrows, tossed the white shirt away. "I take
it you prefer more of the look of the cloak and dagger?"

Cosette gave him a narrow look. "A little less laughter,
a little more action. I thought SEALs could get dressed
in under sixty seconds or something? That they even
sleep in their clothes?"

"Our SEAL appears to be more of the relaxed variety.
And remember, he did come in dead last in the Bridesmaids Creek swim." Jane said this with a perfectly innocent face.

"I had a leg cramp!" John said for the hundredth time
that story had been brought up. He pulled on a black T-
shirt. "Shall I camouflage my face and get my night vision glasses?"

"Sarcasm," Jane whispered to Cosette. "Some men
employ sarcasm when they feel nervous or inadequate."

John grunted, recognizing he was being needled.
"I assure you, I am neither. However, I am wondering
why you've crept into my bedroom in the middle of the
night dressed like munchkin witches escaped from the
Haunted H."

"A laugh a minute," Cosette said.

"A regular riot," Jane agreed. "Let's go."

They sneaked him out the back, making certain not
to alert any of the other bunkhouse inhabitants to their
presence. Once outside, they shooed him into a waiting
truck, driven by Sheriff Dennis.

"Really? You let them talk you into this kind of
midnight debauchery?" John demanded, getting into
the back.

"Just settle in, son. We have a lot of work to do."

John buckled up. The ladies piled in the front next to their getaway driver, and the truck disappeared into the night. "I guess you realize that if something happens to me, if you're planning to hide my body in a secret location, no one will know it was you who talked me out of my comfy bed. You'll be free and clear from public suspicion."

"Again, he's just stocked with knee-slappers," Jane said.

"Your audience is rolling in the aisles," Cosette chimed in.

John decided to sit quietly and just wait for his friends to get their practical joke out of their systems. They were so serious, completely unlike their normally lighthearted selves, that he caught the mood and settled back for the ride.

Fifteen minutes later, he judged they were near the creek. He refrained from inquiring whether they were planning to drown him, which would go over like a lead balloon with them in their current disposition. They got out, and he noted Dennis had hidden the truck behind a stand of trees.

He had a very strange feeling about these late-night fun and games, but he followed the trio obediently.

"Did I tell you I had a chat with Robert Donovan?" he asked, and they automatically shushed him.

That was the biggest piece of news he had, and if they weren't interested in that, he was literally just a fourth wheel on their nocturnal excursion. Cosette and Jane went behind some trees, and suddenly, they disappeared. John stopped, waiting, glancing at Dennis, who pointed to a rock wall.

"Go," the sheriff said.

John didn't move. "What about you?"

"I'm the lookout. In case you don't come out."

"That makes me feel better," John said drily, but suddenly, a small feminine hand grabbed his, jerking him behind the rock and down a long incline that seemed to go on and on forever. John had new respect for Cosette's and Jane's ability to power walk, allowing himself to be dragged deeper into the cavern. Clearly this was a secret kept from the general public, and probably known only to these three stalwarts of Bridesmaids Creek. He figured they were a good bit under the creek now, far deeper than he cared to be subterranean with only the ladies' flashlights to light the way.

Suddenly a room appeared, grand in scope and design. He stayed very still as the ladies lit torches on the walls, revealing a place so hauntingly beautiful it might have been spun by prehistoric fairies. "Holy Christmas."

"Indeed." Cosette gazed at the room. "You are now in the presence of the secret of Bridesmaids Creek."

Chapter Six

"Well, this is *one* of the secrets of Bridesmaids Creek," Jane clarified. "This cave was discovered by my great-great-great-grandmother, Eliza Chatham, who was the original founder of our town. This secret has been passed down in my family, and I've shared it with only the people here tonight."

"I'm honored."

"You should be." Cosette looked around the room. "This place has withstood every kind of weather condition imaginable. Never flooded, never cracked from a tremor. It's clearly a marvel of engineering."

"Who built it?" John looked at the medieval decor with some fascination.

"We're not sure. There were Native Americans in this area at the time, but some of the carvings appear more French or Spanish in nature." The ladies seated themselves at a carved rock table, pulled a box from a hiding place in the center of it.

"Why are you showing this to me? I'm not a son of BC."

"No," Jane said, "but would we trust this knowledge to Daisy's gang?"

"Why trust it to anyone?"

They gazed at him, their faces sincere in the lamplight. "It's time to pass the knowledge on. We chose you," Cosette said, "to be the guardian."

"Why?" He found this hard to believe. He wasn't a true son of BC, not the way Ty Spurlock was. "Why not Mackenzie or Suz or Jade?"

They considered him, as if he were slow on the uptake.

"The magic is here," Jane said. "And you need the magic more than most."

That was probably an understatement. "You're feeling sorry for me because I never got the girl. In fact, the girl in question barely looked my way for years." He shrugged. "Thanks, ladies, but I'm not sure there's enough magic in BC to get that one to the altar. At least not with me."

"What did you and Robert discuss?" Cosette asked.

"Daisy." Just saying her name made him happy, then gave him a sense of despair. "He wouldn't tell me where she is. Says she doesn't want to be found."

"All right. Focus," Jane said, placing the box in the middle of the table. "We're going to figure out the best way to get Daisy back."

"How are we going to do that?"

"We're going to talk about it," Cosette said, her tone perplexed. "Did you think we have a crystal ball?"

John laughed. "I wouldn't put it past you."

They stared at him in bemusement.

"Sometimes I wonder about this younger generation," Jane said. "No seriousness at all."

He forbore to say that, at times, both these ladies had been known to have their humorous and maybe even irreverent moments.

"We put a private eye on Daisy," Cosette said. "Not to spy on her, just to locate her, you understand."

He leaned back. "I don't think that's quite the way I want to locate Daisy. It might be creeper-like, if you ask me."

Jane sniffed. "Okay, we have one handsome prince who doesn't care to travel to Australia."

"Australia! Are you serious?"

They peered at him, their faces concerned.

"Okay, okay," he said. "I get it. This is a serious night. Poor choice of words."

"Yes," Cosette said sourly. "Now, then, what are you going to do about it?"

"Look, why don't I just do the simple thing and call her?" John thought that sounded reasonable.

"How do you know she'd answer?" Jane asked.

"Why wouldn't she? She's not angry with me. She's just—" John told himself to slow down, not let the ladies stir him up. "Daisy's on an important mission to find herself."

"With a baby," Cosette said.

"Maybe *your* baby," Jane said. "Does that add up to you?"

He felt a cold splash of reality hit him. "Why are you two so positive she's having my baby?"

Jane looked reluctant to spill, but then the dam burst. "Because Daisy was taking the same medication Suz and Mackenzie and Jade Harper were taking, to boost their chances of pregnancy. We know you spent time together in Montana. Before you, Daisy had never had a—"

He looked at them. "Never had a what?"

"A real man," Cosette said, and he coughed.

"*Any* man," Jane said. "She's never, ever had a boyfriend, even. Robert was far too protective for silly boys hanging around his princess, you may be sure. In fact, we always thought Daisy's gang were handpicked plants. Robert knew every one of those five guys were no threat to his princess, his baby girl. Or his kingdom. They didn't have the firepower nor the candlepower to warm Daisy's heart."

The cold splash turned positively glacial, chilling him. It wasn't possible. Daisy Donovan couldn't have been a virgin. He would have known—wouldn't he?

He thought back, realizing that she had seemed a bit more heated the second and following times they'd made love. He'd put it down to the fact that she'd been shy the first time they'd made love. Not shy—a virgin.

The chill intensified. She'd been on the secret, super-duper ovary-booster of which Mackenzie, Suz and Jade had spoken of. All of those women had given birth to multiples. He wondered why Daisy would have needed—or wanted—to take a drug like that, couldn't focus on that for more than a second before he realized the implications: he could wind up a father of multiples—if Daisy was, as Cosette and Jane seemed to believe, pregnant from their very sexy interlude in Montana. "How do you know Daisy was on that medication?" John demanded.

"Suz told me. Daisy was hoping to have a baby one day, figured it would take a long time for the medicine to start working. I believe she started the medication right before she went to Montana." Cosette shrugged. "You could be in for a big shocker, John Lopez Mathison. You may not want to go to Australia, but you'd better figure out a way to get our hometown girl back home where she belongs!"

Five hours later, after coffee-klatching with the ladies until the crack of dawn, John rolled into the kitchen at the Hanging H with a new sense of purpose.

"Whoa," Justin Morant said, pouring fresh coffee into a mug, and adding another mug when he saw John's face. "Who pounded steel into your spine this morning?"

"I've had a revelation." John hesitated. "Hey, remember when you first came to Bridesmaids Creek?"

"I do, thanks to Ty Spurlock, it's burned in my mind forever." Justin laughed. "Best thing that ever happened to me."

"You love being a father to those four girls."

Justin nodded, grinning. "Those little ladies make my every day a reason for happiness. And, good news, just between you and me, Mackenzie is expecting another baby." His grin grew more huge. "Thankfully, this time it's a single."

"Congratulations." John high-fived Justin, raised his coffee cup. "If I can do as good a job as you are of being a father, I'll consider myself a success."

Justin looked at him, dug out a couple of slices of homemade cinnamon cake for both of them and slid a plate over to John. "So, Daisy's having your baby. You ready for fatherhood?"

"I wasn't yesterday." John shrugged. "But I figure you stepped up for Mackenzie and her four. I can handle one little baby." He sipped his coffee. "I hope."

Justin raised his mug. "I have faith. It's easier than it looks."

"Becoming a father to four doesn't look easy at all."

"You'd be surprised how much fun it is." Justin forked up a bite of his cake, chewed thoughtfully. "Those little ladies just wrap you around your finger, and the next thing you know, you're hooked like a prize fish."

John felt hooked, reeled in, and tossed into the boat freezer. "Hey, I'm thinking about taking a sabbatical."

Justin raised a brow. "To Australia?"

"How'd you know?"

Justin laughed. "It's all over the town grapevine. You're going to bring the hometown girl home."

"Yeah." John shook his head. "I'm not sure it's a good idea, but the sweet busybodies seem to think I should give it a shot. Personally, I feel I should give the lady in question some space."

"Too long apart can make her forget you ever made her happy."

"I don't want to think about that."

"And a little morning sickness can actually make her hate your guts, especially since she's suffering on her own." Justin laughed at the expression on John's face. "Well, it's just an idea. What do I know about love?"

John polished off his cake and headed out the door. It would take him two days' travel to get to Australia—and every second counted.

He was astonished to find Daisy Donovan sitting on her motorcycle, just like old times, wrapped in black moto wear and looking hotter than summer. "Hello," he said, too shocked to say more.

She gazed at him for a long moment. "Do you have a minute? There's something we should talk about."

The cold chill that had cast itself over him ever since his nocturnal kidnap by Cosette and Co. completely evaporated, to be replaced by a raging inferno of sexual desire. And a lot of other emotions, none of which he had time to dissect. "Sure. I'm good for a chat."

"Hop on." She jerked her head to indicate the portion of seat behind her, and John had never grabbed a helmet so fast in his life. He was on the bike in record time, carefully wrapping his hands around her waist, noticing a couple of inches that hadn't been there before. Actually, without letting his fingers wander, he very much detected quite a bit of a rounding tummy, maybe four inches worth.

John grinned to himself. He was going to be a father.

At least he hoped so.

Daisy took him to The Wedding Diner, which wasn't open yet due to the early morning hour, but Jane seemed to be expecting them. She ushered them in through the back door—apparently as expected. She seated them in a corner, away from prying eyes and ears, which seemed odd to John as there was no one there but Jane and a couple of kitchen helpers. Still, he wasn't going to complain about the location of the white vinyl booth since it meant he was almost virtually alone with the woman with whom he wanted to speak badly.

Jane set a teapot of hot water with its accompanying tea basket and a blue-checked cloth-lined basket of zucchini and pumpkin mini muffins in front of them, and then went to seat another group. Daisy poured hot water into both their cups, they selected some teas from the basket, and John waited with his heart hammering in his throat.

"When did you get back?" he asked, by way of icebreaker. It seemed like a safe topic, but then again, there was really no such thing in BC.

"Last night. My father said you wanted to see me."

"I didn't figure he'd tell you I went to rattle his cage a bit."

"Actually, he claimed you asked for my hand in marriage."

Now this seemed promising. John perked up. "In fact, I did."

Daisy gazed at him, no smile on her face, but a steady look that didn't speak of revulsion, either. He took that as a good sign and swiped a pumpkin muffin just to look like he was casual about the whole going-by-to-see-your-dad-and-asking-for-your-hand thing—which he most certainly was not.

"So?" Daisy said.

"So nothing. We had a bit of back and forth, and that was it." He saw no reason to go into more detail. "I felt it was a good conversation, with points of view presented on both sides."

Daisy sipped delicately from her teacup, her gaze locked on him over the rim. "Dad says he told you he'd rather have a village idiot for a son-in-law."

John laughed. "Your father talks big. And yet here you are, clearly open to my suit."

"You're pretty sure of yourself."

He grinned. "You're having my baby, aren't you?"

It wasn't a question; it was a bald statement of fact—the little ladies had convinced him that it could be no other way. Daisy was finally going to be his. He could hardly wait to shout it from the rooftops.

"I'm having your triplets," Daisy said, and the smile blew off John's face. His head spun. All he could do was stare at her in stunned silence.

Daisy put her cup down. "I didn't mean for that to happen, honestly."

"I think someone's telling a wee fib," John said. "Our dear friends tell me that you were on some kind of miracle ovary juice. That isn't the mark of a woman who doesn't want a man's child."

"I meant," Daisy said calmly, "that I didn't mean to have *your* child."

He raised a brow. "We did use condoms every time."

Condoms being plural, of course, which spoke to the truth, which was that each and every time he'd gotten his hands on this deliciously wild woman, he'd made the most of it.

There could have been some slippage. A misfire of eagerness, perhaps, with a condom not being appropriately placed. The thing was, Daisy's hands were so small, so feminine, so deft, that when she stroked him, helping with the condom, it was all he could do not to—

"The thing is," Daisy said, and John forced himself to focus on her lips and not the sweetest times, "it wasn't my intention to rope you into a wedding. And I'm afraid that's what you think, judging by the fact that you bearded the lion in his den."

"Your father's not much of a lion these days," John said absently. "Why did he tell you all this? And why didn't you tell me you were expecting in the first place, Daisy? Why'd you leave?"

"I left because it was crazy-town around here. I wasn't sure what I wanted to do."

"It's always crazy-town. You didn't expect BC to change, Daisy?"

"I didn't want you to feel compelled to marry me. I don't need a husband."

"And yet, you're going to have a husband." He frowned at her. "Daisy Donovan, you're going to marry me, next weekend as a matter of fact. Enough lollygagging and floating around. I've pursued you for years, and whether you want to admit it or not, you've enjoyed being the princess of my passion."

She raised a brow. "I'm not getting married."

"Yeah, you are." He sipped his tea, stuffing more pumpkin muffin into his mouth. "Eat up. If you're eating for four, you're going to need your strength."

His blood got weird, sort of wobbly, when he voiced aloud the idea that he was going to be a father to triplets. A triple whammy. Still, he'd seen three of his friends adapt quite nicely to the father role, and the good news was, between the four of them, they could now field a decent-sized girls' soccer team. He pondered that. Heck, counting Justin's new one, if it was a girl, they were well on their way to having enough to justify buying their own bus for the Hanging H.

"John, I'm not marrying you," Daisy said softly.

He looked up at her. "Those little girls need me. They need their father. I'm going to be a helluva lacrosse coach, you wait and see. I'm not so much for ballet and hair buns and the girlier stuff, but I'll suck it up and work on it."

"We're having boys," Daisy said, and John's head started swimming again.

"Boys?" He gulped. "Three *boys*?"

She solemnly nodded.

"I thought everyone in Bridesmaids Creek had girls. That's why there's, like, five thousand women to every man here. There's something in the creek water that does it." He slipped off his Stetson, wiped his brow, realized he was still light-headed, and was babbling like a baby. The muffins weren't helping his sudden brain fog.

She'd blown his mind. Again.

"Strangely, we're having boys." Daisy reached for a muffin. "And as I know your family raised you on the circuit, I hope you'll appreciate that I want something more stable for my sons."

He blinked, came back to earth. So that was what this sudden meeting was about. *Her* sons. She was staking out territory, letting him know that she didn't want an itinerant lifestyle for their family—in which she didn't appear to be including him.

Yet in his heart, he believed that she was meant to be his. He didn't know how, he just knew it in his gut.

Plus, he didn't think the wise elderly troublemakers— er, pillars—of Bridesmaids Creek would have revealed one of its major secrets to him unless they considered him a favored son, and even an important part of this town and this woman's life. Cosette, after all, had never given up her matchmaker's crown, even though she'd lost her shop.

No, they'd revealed secrets to him because they didn't want him to give up hope. He was the guardian of the magic.

John dived into the wellspring of hope they'd gifted him. "Daisy, listen. Whatever you want is fine with me." He swallowed, his throat dry, completely aware for the first time that the sexy woman across from him regarded him as an obstacle of sorts, maybe even an enemy.

Oh, hell, who was he kidding? She'd never given him an ounce of encouragement. He didn't even know why she'd made love to him, unless she'd only wanted a child.

She'd been on that funky medication. But she claimed she hadn't wanted *his* child. Which would really dent his ego massively, except Cosette and Jane claimed she'd been a virgin. Still, how the hell would they know? Daisy was a grown woman, she wasn't going to share her exploits—

He shut down that train of thought. He knew he was her first.

"Daisy, you were a virgin. I know you were."

She eyed him steadily. "So?"

He grinned, the whole matter going crystal clear for him. "So, either you're not being honest because you're trying to get the upper hand here—very Robert Donovan of you—or you're not letting your subconscious tell you the truth." He reached across, took that delicate little hand of hers that had always wrapped around him so sweetly in his. "You were taking medication to get pregnant. You chose to seduce me, little lady. That means either you wanted me or you wanted my baby or both, but it's time for you to start telling both of us the truth."

The problem with John was that he was annoyingly macho, Daisy thought, feeling his big paw engulf her hand. He had no idea how sexy he was, and by all rights, she shouldn't have fallen for a man who'd lived out of a trailer most of his life. It didn't make sense. But the thing was, she was in love with him, and that love had made her do stupid things.

Like hop in the sack with him every chance she got.

In fact, she'd like to hop in a sack with him right now—her whole body seemed to miss his, miss him—but she was going to fight it with everything she had.

"How far along are you?"

She hesitated. "You should know. Six months."

He grinned, so happy, and so handsome because he was that happy, that she tugged her hand out of his grasp. "Don't look so thrilled."

"I am thrilled. I'm over the moon. Hey, Jane!"

"Don't!" she hissed, but when had John ever listened to anything?

"Daisy and I are having triplets!" he told Jane, his voice carrying to the diners who'd begun pouring in for breakfast once the doors had opened.

Daisy felt her face turn red, her neck burning with embarrassment. "John!"

Jane grinned at Daisy. "Well, what do you know? That medication our resident quack gives out strikes again! Hey, everybody, muffins on the house to celebrate Daisy and John's new triplets!"

A roar went up, and applause, and the diner burst into chatter. She glared at John, who was glancing around at everyone, waving hello to this person and that, and generally enjoying his moment as the big man of Bridesmaids Creek.

"Was that necessary?" Daisy demanded.

"To share our good news with our friends? Indeed it was." He winked at her. "I don't mind public opinion helping me to shanghai you to the altar, beautiful."

She sniffed. "I've never bowed to public pressure."

He laughed. "I'm going to marry you, Daisy Donovan. And you're going to ask me nicely to do so."

She rolled her eyes, but couldn't deny his claim as well-wishers began crowding their booth. She didn't think she'd ever seen John look happier than he was at this moment.

It was endearing, and it was sexy. Daisy felt a bit of the glow steal over her, finally living one of the big BC moments that had always seemed to escape her.

But it couldn't last. And no one knew that better than her.

Chapter Seven

"Into bed you go." John took her home, placing her tenderly in his bed in the bunkhouse. "A little nap is good for the soul, they say. I'm sure you're jet-lagged, and you really should be resting up for my three sons. They're going to keep you very busy in a few months."

Daisy told her heart this wasn't exactly where it wanted to be, eyeing him as he tucked her into the covers. "I'm not much of a napper."

He looked at her. "You look a bit pale. I'll get you some water. Air travel is dehydrating."

"I don't want to be smothered during this pregnancy." She tried not to notice how manly and lean he looked in his worn jeans. "It'll be a long few more months if you mother-hen me."

"You rest. Then we'll proceed." He tucked a strand of her hair behind her ear, and Daisy basked in the feeling of being revered. It was certainly a novelty for her—but John had always treated her this way, she realized.

Her heart warmed even more.

"Proceed with what?"

"We have a lot of planning to do." He landed next to her in the bed but didn't touch her, practically hung on the edge, creating distance. "I have to close my eyes now. My brain's on overload."

She didn't know if she could rest with him so close to her. Surely he should be trying to kiss her.

Of course he should be trying to kiss her. She *wanted* him to kiss her.

He began to snore instead. Daisy sucked in an outraged breath. In Montana, all she'd had to do was think *bed* and John had seemed to appear to tumble her into one. If not a bed, then a hallway, a blanket near a wooded stream—even once on a cliff top gazing up at the stars. Parts of her that shouldn't get warm not only warmed but wished for John—who was resting his "overloaded" brain with enthusiasm, judging from the expulsion of jet-like snores coming from his handsome frame—to wake up and focus on the way they'd created these children she was now carrying.

Daisy reached over, gave him a tap.

"Mmm?" he asked, the snores coming to a full stop.

"The doctor says it won't be much longer before I lose my, er, sexy—"

"I'm on it. No worries." He patted her hand, rolled onto his side facing the wall.

Okay, that hadn't worked.

"Also, I'll be on bed rest, probably in a few weeks."

"Sounds good to me. We can start now, if you like."

She didn't reply, and soft snores began to emit from

him again. "John Lopez Mathison, I think you're playing hard to get."

"I am. It's working, too." He rolled over, scooped her
against him, kissing the back of her neck, shooting tin-
gles all over her. "If you sleep off some jet leg, I promise
to buy you an ice-cream cone at the Haunted H tonight.
You'll be surprised how much that place has changed
now that you got it moved to the creek."

His arm tucked solidly around her, holding her to him
in the most intimate way. He was being dense, as dense
as a thick, night-shrouded forest, but this felt good, too—
and he *had* received a shock. Rest was probably a restor-
ative for his bachelor system—so Daisy relaxed into his
warmth and fell asleep.

"Sorry," John said, waking he wasn't sure how much
later. But clearly he'd napped for hours, as the sun was
beaming high outside. "I didn't mean to pass out on you."
He had a delicious brunette in his arms, his dream come
true—and he'd sacked out like a large bag of potatoes.

"I'm sure the news was hard for you."

He released Daisy and sat up, trying to remember what
chores he was on the list for this afternoon that he might
be late for. "No, I'm happy about the babies. I appreciate
you coming home to tell me in person. The old ladies
dragged me out of bed last night and I missed about six
of my eight typical, desired sleep hours."

"The old ladies?"

John tugged on his boots. "Cosette and Jane. That was
probably disrespectful. I should have said, the time-en-
hanced matchmakers of BC."

Daisy giggled. "They kidnapped you?"

"They encouraged me to join them for some late-night

high jinks." He leaned over and dropped a fast kiss on her lips. "That's to keep you happy until later."

"Later when you plan to ravish me?"

He laughed. "Later when I get you that ice-cream cone I promised you. Make yourself at home, if you want. I've got to get to my chores. I'll be done in about eight hours."

She swung her legs over the side of the bed, and John thought he'd never seen a more sexy woman. "I still need to see Dad."

He felt a tremor of unease. "Okay, so I'll get you for dinner, then take you down to the new and improved Haunted H."

"Sounds good." She smiled at him. "Remember what I told you."

"Remember what I told *you*."

She raised a brow. "That you're going to get me a cone tonight?"

"That I'm going to marry you, and you're going to ask me nicely to do it." He grinned. "And if your doctor's right and you're going to be couch-bound very soon, you'd better hurry, beautiful, if you want some of what you were trying to get from me a little while ago."

"You think highly of yourself, don't you?"

"I think highly of you."

"Here's the thing, John," Daisy said, taking a deep breath, and he heard it—the I-can't-marry-you-because—so he cut her off as fast as he could. Whatever it was, they'd deal with it. If it was Robert, they'd deal with him and so on. Nothing was going to keep him from Daisy and his sons—not anymore.

"I've got to run," he interrupted, before she could get to the juicy part that was sure to make him cry. "You save that thought for later."

"All right."

She actually looked a little relieved. John dropped his hat on his head, decided against stealing one more fast kiss, and headed out the door. She followed, hopping onto her motorcycle.

He frowned. "Daisy, I'd like you to give up the bike while you're pregnant."

She shrugged. "I'd like you to give up letting Cosette and Jane drag you around in the middle of the night."

"Why?"

"Because they'll eventually get you into trouble. They're very sweet and very darling, and I love them dearly, but I feel like anything that's done in the dark in BC might be dangerous."

He grinned. "You just remember that tonight when you tap on my back again. Interrupting a man's REMs for a little sexy playtime. Whatever were you thinking?" Now he did kiss her—he could no longer resist it—especially as she'd let out a demure little gasp at his comment, her lips parting too prettily to pass up. She clung to him, surprising him a little.

"Tonight I'm all yours," he told her.

"I flew two days to be with you. Be ready to do more than talk."

John laughed, tipped his hat and headed for the barn, thinking there had never been a saucier, sassier lady. And the way things were going, she was soon going to be all his. Mrs. Daisy Mathison.

It had a very nice ring to it.

Which reminded him, he needed a ring to do an honorable proposal—when she finally got up the courage to ask him. And he *was* going to make her ask him—she'd waited far too long to cast her dark eyes his way.

Daisy Donovan was going to have to jump off the spot and fight for *him* for a change. He whistled, everything in his life looking up, skyward, even. He was going to be a father, he was about to have a wife.

That BC charm stuff *really* had some kick to it.

"I can't fix this for you." Robert Donovan gazed at his only daughter, his eyes sorrowful. "I wish I could. I'd spend all my fortune to see you happy, Daisy."

"I know." Daisy sat in the garden room with her father, gazing pensively at the beautiful statues and blooming flowers outside.

"When are you going to tell him?"

"Soon. Tonight." Daisy took a deep breath. "I tried to today, but he cut me off. Almost like he knew I was going to drop some bad news on him."

"He's no dummy." Robert leaned back in his favorite chair and sighed. "I actually have a lot of respect for John Mathison, as I told you when I called you in Australia to tell you of his visit. He was a little opinionated, but that didn't trouble me. I rather appreciated him stating his case for my little girl with such enthusiasm."

Daisy managed a smile, but the man who walked into the room next made her hesitate. "Ty, what are you doing here?"

"I invited him," Robert said. "Welcome home, son."

He got up to hug the son he'd discovered two years ago. Daisy didn't know what to do, so she remained seated. As much work as she had to do to make it up to people in Bridesmaids Creek, she wasn't sure what to do with a new half brother. Ty Spurlock was a good man and a SEAL, obviously on leave from the Navy, home to see Jade and their new twins.

"Daisy," Ty said, nodding in her direction, and Daisy nodded back, feeling very out of her element now that she and her half brother had been called home at the same time so the father they shared could speak to them. "Congratulations on the triplets." He grinned, completely comfortable, a happily married man and favored town son.

"This is all your fault," Daisy said. "You brought a bunch of bachelors to town to find brides."

"And you fell right into the trap?" Ty laughed and took the seat Robert gestured him to. "Don't feel bad. I fell into my own trap before you did."

"Speaking of traps," Robert said, "Daisy doesn't want to get married."

Ty grinned at her. "She will when the time is right."

Daisy was shocked by this show of support. She looked at her father to see how he was taking Ty's comment. As she suspected, her father looked none too pleased.

"I asked you here today for a couple of reasons, one of which was to help me convince your sister that she has to marry this John." He mused silently for a moment. "Believe me, that's not an easy thing for me to say. I never thought I'd be talking about marrying my little girl to a man formerly named Squint." He brightened. "However, he has convinced me that he has my daughter's best interests at heart, and that he loves you, Daisy. Trust me, you don't want to pass up love."

"You can pass it up," Ty said. "If you don't love my buddy, just tell him you don't love him. He'll be devastated, he'll follow you around like a puppy for the rest of your life because you're having his children, and you'll always have all the support and backup you ever needed because he's that kind of guy. He'll never ask you a second time, because he's got too much pride, so it'll never be awkward or weird for you."

"It's already awkward," Daisy said. "I'm pregnant with triplets. And we were as careful as could be."

"Then it was meant to be." Ty seemed quite amused by this. "You got hit by the BC magic. Isn't that what you always wanted?"

"Tell your brother why you don't want to marry the father of your children," Robert urged.

"When I met his family, I met his two brothers. Who, by the way, are very nice. But Javier happened to mention that John has never been in a relationship for very long. They never *stuck*, was the word he used."

"So?" Ty shrugged. "Most of us hadn't. It's no reason not to give the man a chance."

"But that's the thing," Daisy said. "I've never been in a relationship at all!"

Her father and brother stared at her.

"Oh," Ty said, "I forgot about that. I guess I always assumed with that gaggle of boys hanging around you that one of them—"

"No," Daisy said. "I never dated any of my friends."

"They were in love with you," Robert said.

"So they claim." She sighed. "And that's how I'm going to renew Bridesmaids Creek. It's going to be my ultimate act to ingratiate myself into a town I want desperately to accept me."

"How?" Ty asked.

"Get married," Robert said. "If you throw a wedding party, you'll be forgiven. Around here, forgiveness comes with a couple slices of wedding cake real easily. Haven't you noticed?"

Daisy frowned at her father. "Dad, I don't think John and I have what it takes to be parents together. According to his brother, John's never stayed in the same place more than a few years, as a consequence of the way they were raised. Not that Javier and Jackson were complaining. They just noted that their way of life isn't for everyone."

"Let me get this straight." Ty leaned back in his chair, smiling his thanks when the butler put a tray on the table in front of them. It had a whiskey decanter, some glasses, some soda and small edibles. "You guys live differently here, don't you?"

"Thank you, Barclay," Daisy said to the butler as he mixed them up some whiskey and sodas. "Just some sparkling water for me, please."

"Anyway," Ty continued, "if I understand you correctly, you're afraid."

"Not exactly," Daisy shot back.

"You don't want to raise your children on the road. In a trailer, going from rodeo to rodeo."

"We're having boys," Daisy said. "Eventually John's going to remember how he grew up."

"Maybe he didn't like it," Robert said.

"I'm going to ask him," Ty said thoughtfully. "I'll just say, 'Hey, John, old buddy, are you planning on raising your boys in rodeo?'"

"Would you mind?" Daisy asked. "I don't want to ask him."

"Why? The man isn't quiet about his opinions," Robert said. "He'd tell you."

"It's a hard life. And he has restless feet."

"Says the woman who ran off to Montana after another man." Ty grinned at her, holding up a hand when she began to protest. "I know, I know, that's when you fell for my pal. But you can't put all this on him."

Daisy shook her head. "Eventually he'd regret marrying me."

"Why? Because you're such a good person?" Ty looked at her curiously. "Because you're going to be an awesome mother?"

Daisy felt tears well in her eyes. "I don't know how."

The men stared at her.

"Ah," Ty said slowly. "Now we're getting down to the truth. You don't feel like you deserve John Mathison. You think you're going to let him down. You're afraid you're not going to be a good mother."

Robert looked misty. "That's not going to happen. You're going to be a wonderful mother."

"Why? How?" She wiped at her nose. "I haven't been a particularly good anything in my life."

They sat quietly, sipping their whiskeys. Daisy put a hand on her stomach as she looked out into the beautiful garden. Occasionally she could feel the babies move inside her. In time, they'd get even more active.

Very soon she'd be bed bound.

"Daisy, listen."

She glanced up at Ty, waiting.

"We'll all be here for you. If you don't want to marry the man, you don't have to," he said softly. He reached out, touched her hand. "We've given you a bit of rough road over the years, sure. But the thing is, we're going to take care of you, because that's what Bridesmaids Creek does. We take care of each other."

Daisy felt giant tears leap to her eyes and threaten to slide down her cheeks. "Thank you," she murmured.

"There now," Robert said. "It'll all work out eventually. It always does."

Daisy shook her head, the words sounding a trifle incongruous from the man who had once been the most hated in the town. She felt a huge burden from that, too. Her parents—and Ty's—hadn't even had a happy marriage. How would she know how to make a happy marriage? And it wasn't totally the way Ty said it was; they had given her a lot of rough road, but she'd deserved a lot of it, too.

She'd feel better when she'd had time to make amends.

She'd feel better when she had a better sense of who she was.

Barclay reentered the room, and Daisy thought he was coming to refresh the tray. But then she realized there was a man joining their family gathering, and to her astonishment, she saw that it was John.

What was even more astonishing was the giant leap her heart made inside her, as if it recognized the man of her dreams, and the only man for her.

Chapter Eight

"Sit down, sit down," Robert said genially, pointing to a seat near him. He eyed Daisy's gang who had followed John into the room. "Barclay, if we could have some more whiskeys and snacks, please."

They all seated themselves, her gang gazing at John like slightly uncomfortable combatants. He seemed immune to their displeasure.

"It's good to see you, man." John reached over and slapped Ty on the back. "When did you return to BC?"

"This morning. Went to see my wife and little girls, then came straight here. Have yet to pay a call to the Hanging H, but I hear you've been keeping everything in good shape."

"Not to cut the happy reunion short, fellows," Daisy said, "but I'm glad you're all here. I have something to say."

Her father and their guests turned to her in surprise.

"Wedding plans?" John said.

"No." Daisy shook her head.

"Ah. I thought maybe these gentlemen were going to offer to be my ushers or something." John gave them a grin that said he was more than aware of their disapprobation with him, and really didn't care.

"John, we're not discussing anything relating to a wedding," Daisy said.

John smiled at Daisy, and her heart jumped. The gleam in his eyes told her that he wasn't about to give up on the idea of marrying her. In spite of everything she'd told her father and brother, didn't she want to marry him?

I'm just so scared. Marriage wasn't a good thing for my father and mother. I've heard the stories, and they weren't the stuff of dreams and fairy tales.

"Anyway," Daisy said, "I have a lot to do in a small amount of time, so I have to be really organized. I hope you won't mind me springing this on you all at once, but I'm hoping that you'll consider giving up your lease so that Cosette and Phillipe can have that space again for their shops. Madame and Monsieur Matchmaker need to be back where they belong. They're an important part of the magic of BC."

Dig, Clint, Gabriel, Red and Carson stared at her, as did John and her father. "I'll help you find another place for your dating service and business."

"We were just about to think about franchising," Red said, unhappy.

"Franchising?" Daisy stared at her "gang," stunned. "Are you even profitable yet?"

"You'd be surprised. Cigar sales are booming," Gabriel said.

"I thought your core business is a dating service," John said.

"It is," Clint said. "But we're finding that cigars are where it's at. Especially high-end cigars."

Daisy and John glanced at each other. He shrugged, clearly not sure what to make of the new "business" in town. Daisy looked at her father, who also shrugged.

"Would you consider moving your cigar bar?" Daisy asked. "So that we can get some equilibrium back in BC?"

Red shook his head. "That's a primo location. Easy for out-of-towners to find."

Daisy considered that. "So your customers are mostly from surrounding towns?"

"Yes, that's right," Dig said. "But honestly, we've got a whopping mail-order business, too. And sometimes folks come in from the big city."

Daisy shook her head. "I had no idea."

"You haven't been here," Gabriel said gently. "You've been in Montana and other places."

"And when you *are* here, your attention is divided." Clint slid a glance at John. "You haven't been hanging with us like you used to, Daze."

She sighed. "This is all my fault. I got Phillipe and Cosette out of their comfortable space, because I was being selfish. But I didn't understand what I was taking from them, what I was taking from BC."

She was really, really sad about that. And now there was no way to fix it, which was not good for the older couple. Their marriage had suffered because of the financial distress she'd helped cause.

"But you've done a lot of good, too," Carson pointed

out. "You've changed so much, Daze, we hardly recognize you anymore."

The lights flickered. Daisy glanced out toward the garden, realizing it had gotten very dark outside. The sky was steel gray. She looked at John, and he smiled at her. She felt instantly better.

"I agree with your friends. You've done good things lately, Daisy." John glanced at Robert. "And you're not the only one who's turned into a productive and upstanding citizen."

Robert raised his glass to the gathering. Ty and everyone raised their glasses back.

"Here's to remaking BC," Robert said. "I would like to say that Daisy's idea of moving the Haunted H to the creek was brilliant."

"Remember when the Haunted H was a liability?" Ty grinned at Robert. "We were convinced you were deliberately trying to kill people out there to run off business."

The lights flickered again and Daisy looked to the window. "I'd better make this quick so you guys can hit the road."

"Take your time." Carson held up his glass. "We've got no place better to be than right here with our nearest and dearest."

She said with a little apprehension, "Those days of taking over businesses aren't over, Carson."

"What do you mean?" Her gang gazed at her from their comfortable chairs, lulled into complacency by her father's good whiskey. Carson shot her a quizzical look.

"I'd like to buy out your dating service." She looked at all of them in turn.

"But we haven't gotten it off the ground yet," Dig said. "We've been so busy with the cigar bar."

Daisy went to sit by John. "Name your price. We're in the market for a dating business."

John caught her hand in his. "I like it when you wheel and deal. But not so much that you don't get enough rest for my boys."

Every eye in the room bounced to her stomach and then over to John.

"Heck, we'd let you have it for free, Daisy," Gabriel said. His friends nodded. "Friends don't charge friends. We'll incorporate you into our business."

"I'll take you up on that." Daisy glanced at John. "You're now the proud owner of a dating service."

"Which will become Madame Matchmaker's Premier Matchmaking Services once again?" He grinned at her.

"We'll see how it works out." The lights flickered again, and then went out altogether. Five lighter flames instantly sparked to life in the room.

Daisy looked at her gang, their faces glowing in the dim light. "Really? I feel like I'm at a concert."

"Can't have a cigar business without fire. Where's your candles, Robert?" Red asked.

"There are some decorative ones on the table there you can use," her father replied. "The generator will be on in a moment. And Barclay will no doubt be in with news."

John's phone buzzed. Daisy turned to him as he pulled it out, scanned it.

"The sheriff says a tornado has touched down in town," he said, reading further. "He wants everyone to stay inside in safe locations." He looked at Daisy. "There's no warning siren out here, I take it?"

"None this far out. In fact, there's really not anything like that in town, is there, Dad?"

He shook his head. "Not to my knowledge. Even if

there was, it wouldn't reach us or the Hanging H. We should probably have one put in."

"Hang on," John said, looking at his phone again. "Dennis says…" He stopped. She saw his face tighten with concern. "There was a direct hit on the creek. The Haunted H is gone."

Daisy gasped. The whole room went still. It was a strange tableau with everyone staring at each other by lighter and candlelight. Barclay strolled in with a huge flashlight to set on the table. It threw a wide beam on the ceiling, relieving the darkness.

"The generator will come on any minute," Barclay told Robert. "The foreman and the groundskeeper are checking it over now."

"Thank you." Barclay left and Robert looked at John. "My phone isn't working. Do you still have cell service?"

"It's weak, but I have it," John said. "Of course, out here in the county cell service can be spotty at the best of times."

"My phone's working." Daisy turned to John. "Dennis's text says nobody was hurt. But I feel like we ought to go see what we can do to help out at the Haunted H."

"No," her father said. "My advice is you stay right here."

"Your father's right." The lights came on, and John stood. "The sheriff said he wanted everyone to stay put, in case of another tornado. To relieve your mind, I'll drive to the creek and see what needs to be done immediately."

"I'll ride shotgun," Ty said, rising.

"Bring anyone here who needs shelter," Daisy said, and Robert nodded.

"Absolutely. It's safer here than anywhere in town," he said. "We have plenty of room."

Barclay came in with another tray of food and drinks. Daisy looked at him. "Barclay, would you mind packing up some food and first-aid items for John to take to town with him?"

"I'm coming with you." Daisy rose, and every man in the room said, "No!"

"All right!" She sank back down. "It's going to be a long pregnancy for all of us."

Her gang rose. "We'll follow him. We'll keep a close eye on John, and make sure he gets back to you in one piece."

"Watch out," she told John. "Once they appoint themselves your good friends and protectors, you'll always have your own squad looking out for you."

John looked at the five men doubtfully. "I'm used to traveling alone."

"Not anymore, you're not. If I can't go, you can't go alone," Daisy said.

"Fair's fair, I guess." He looked at Robert. "I don't have to ask if you'll make sure she rests."

"We have it under control." Robert waved them on. "Let us know what we can do to help."

As soon as the seven men left, Daisy turned to her father. "Are you sure this isn't going to be too much for you?"

"I'm not doing anything, except maybe giving a few people shelter."

"I just don't want you taking on too much. One of the reasons I came back was that I was worried about you.

You're still not exercising." She gazed at her father. "It wasn't that long ago that you gave us all a scare."

He hmmphed. "I'm fine. Barclay makes sure I get all kinds of vegetables. Very little red meat, no cakes or treats after every meal. Special occasions only. It's giving him the chance to boss me around, which he enjoys."

Daisy stood. "I'm going to call Cosette and Jane. Make sure they're all right."

"Those two will outlive us all."

Daisy laughed. "Probably. I'll be right back."

She went up to her room for some privacy. "Cosette? It's Daisy. Are you all right?"

"I'm fine. Phillipe's fine." Cosette sighed. "Did you hear? The Haunted H is gone!"

"I heard. It's terrible. But as long as no one was hurt, it can be rebuilt." She looked out the window at the dark skies, still too gray and bruised-looking for her comfort. The faster John came home, the better she'd feel.

Home? When did you start thinking of this as his home?

It wasn't. John would be more comfortable on the road than here. This would never be home for the father of her children.

She would never be home on the road. She wasn't like Mrs. Mathison, who could raise three boys in a trailer, following the rodeo circuit.

I'm having three boys. He's going to want them to be rodeo people. Why wouldn't he? It's what he knows. And there's nothing wrong with that at all.

"Are you there, Daisy?" Cosette asked. "I asked how you're feeling."

"Oh. I feel fine." Daisy sank onto her bed. "I'm just worried about Mackenzie and Suz and you guys. I feel terrible about the Haunted H. It was my idea to move it to Bridesmaids Creek." And now it was gone.

"Daisy, you couldn't have known. You were trying to help. Frankly, the creek was a very successful location for the Haunted H. Visitors really liked it being in a wooded area, too. Especially a place where we have often held our charmed swims."

"I'm in shock that it's gone." She felt almost adrift by how her idea had affected Suz and Mackenzie's business, and the town itself, now leveled, almost extinguished.

"Every town has to grow or it dies. Daisy, don't blame this on yourself. You didn't cause the tornado." Cosette was silent for a moment. "Did you hear that mine and Phillipe's old shops, and the jail, are gone, too?"

"Gone?" Daisy was horrified.

"Every last stick and twig." Cosette sighed. "Check your phone when we get off. I'm sure you got the text, too."

Tears jumped into Daisy's eyes. "We'll rebuild Bridesmaids Creek, Cosette. We'll put our town back together."

"I know." Cosette sniffed. "We have a lot to be grateful for. No one got hurt. As far as I know, not even a cow was injured."

"Okay. That's the best news of all. I've got to get back to Dad. I'll check on you and Jane and Mackenzie and everybody in a little bit."

"Be sure to rest. The best thing to do is keep yourself healthy. We'll all get through this. Together."

They hung up and Daisy went back to her father.

"The jail is gone, and the fellows aren't going to be too happy to learn that their new cigar bar has been lost." Daisy sat near her father. "All these years nothing so much as a tornado sighting, and then suddenly the town takes a direct hit." She burst into tears, finally overcome by what she'd been trying so hard to hold back. "If I hadn't insisted that Suz and Mackenzie move their business to the creek, it would still be operating. I'm too embarrassed to call." She took a deep breath, wiped her eyes. "Of course I will, just as soon as I have a grip on myself."

Robert shook his head. "You can't blame this on yourself. And no one else will, either, Daisy."

"I wish I hadn't always been such a negative spirit in BC."

He sighed heavily. "They say the sins of the fathers visit on the children. To be honest, I started us off on the wrong foot here. I didn't take care of your mother, and I've always regretted that. I wanted to be king of all I surveyed, but in the end, it never made me as happy as my family does. It's a lesson that came late, I'm afraid, and that it's affected you, too."

"I don't know, Dad." She reached over to touch his hand. "We can do our best going forward to build the town up, and help people."

"It's really all we can do. But it's a plan I like."

They sat looking out at the garden, the dark skies seeming to bring night on even faster than usual. "The sheriff isn't going to know what to do without his jail."

Robert laughed softly. "We'll start there. We have to have law and order in Bridesmaids Creek."

For some reason, that made both of them smile. Daisy didn't know if there'd ever been anyone in the lonely jail cells. But it was Dennis's place, and it stood as a solid center of BC. "Okay. We'll help with the Haunted H, and the center of town."

He nodded. "I think I'll sell a few buildings I've got in other countries."

She looked at her father. "Why?"

"I don't need the biggest kingdom. What I need is right here in BC." He reached out, took her hand in his. "I've got you, and Ty and my grandchildren. That's really all the kingdom I want these days."

She smiled. "So you're planning to really step up for Bridesmaids Creek?"

"If there's something we can do to help, it wouldn't do any good to leave cash sitting around in our bank accounts."

"No, it wouldn't." Daisy grinned. "And I'm sitting on a little plan of my own concerning BC. I'm taking over the dating service, and I'm going to take lessons from our resident matchmaker."

Robert whistled. "That'll be an education of a different stripe."

"Exactly." She nodded. "And I have my first victims in my sights."

Chapter Nine

Daisy looked at the text when it came in two hours later. Done what we can do here, for now.

She hesitated, then replied, Are you coming back here?

Her breath was trapped in her lungs as she waited. It was the first time she'd ever invited John to her home, and surely he'd get that he was being invited to spend the night.

If that's what you want.

I want, she wrote back.

I'm on the front porch.

She shot out of bed and hurried down the stairs, pulling open the front door. John was, in fact, standing right there, grinning.

"Thanks for coming back."

"My family's here. My lady, and my three sons. Where else would I go?"

"No place." She smiled and pulled him inside and up the stairs to her room.

"What about your father? Barclay? The pillars of Bridesmaids Creek?" John asked.

She kissed him. "My father is a few thousand feet away, and would be worried if you weren't here. Nobody in town needed to come back here for shelter?"

"No. The damage is extensive, but most everybody was at home when the worst hit."

She was delighted when he kissed her, too, drawing her to him. "I was glad you were safe in this fortress," John said. "But I missed you."

"I missed you, too." He kissed her fingertips, making Daisy shiver.

"Is it really horrible?"

"We'll be rebuilding for a while."

They sank onto the bed, and he put a hand on her stomach. "But I don't want you worrying. I don't want you starting a committee to fund-raise or do anything like that. Resting is all I want you to do."

"Too late," she said. "You knew better than that."

"Yeah, I just wanted to see how much I could get away with."

"Not much." She kissed him again. "Thanks for coming back. I was afraid you wouldn't."

He raised a brow. "It's going to be hard for you to get rid of me now that you're having my children."

"Is that the only reason?"

John kissed her gently, lingering over her lips. "Yes."

Daisy laughed. "That's mean."

"It's important to keep you guessing."

"I suppose that's fair."

He kissed her belly. "I knew you'd figure out that I was the best catch around eventually. I just waited for you to come to your senses."

She was so glad he was back—and safe—that she didn't want to pepper him with questions. "Do you want to shower? I'll go get you some coffee and food. You have to be starving."

"That sounds great." He suddenly sounded tired as he tossed his belt onto a nearby chair. "Are you sure Robert's going to be okay with me being here?"

"Haven't you noticed a distinct thawing in his manner lately?" Daisy glanced at him as she hung in the doorway.

"Yeah, what's that all about?"

She smiled. "We'll discuss that later. You shower. But yes, Dad will be glad you're here. And glad for anyone else that needs a place to stay."

Daisy went downstairs, dialed the Hanging H. Suz answered. "Suz, it's Daisy."

"Hi," Suz said, and she sounded sad.

"Listen, Suz, I should come by to tell you this, but John isn't keen on me being out at the moment."

"And he's right! You don't go anywhere! There's downed trees everywhere and all kinds of debris scattered around."

"I know." Daisy swallowed. "Suz, I'm sorry, more sorry than I can say, about the Haunted H. I wish I'd never suggested you move it there."

"Daisy, you didn't plan the path of the tornado. You couldn't have known. We'll rebuild bigger and better than ever and be ready for another Bridesmaids Creek swim or Best Man's Fork race."

But when would that be? "We should do that soon."

"We need a new influx of bachelors for that to happen," Suz reminded her. "We have no shortage of bride-worthy material."

"It'll be a long time before BC gets cleaned up enough to handle large crowds."

"Well," Suz said on a deep sigh, "we've rebuilt before. Sometimes it feels like it's a snakebit project, but then I see all the happy kids coming with their families, and I realize the Haunted H was a dream my parents had that needs to stay alive."

"I agree. Good night, Suz," Daisy said.

"You listen to John," Suz said. "Those babies of yours need all the rest they can get, because when they come out, you're going to be busy! You're having one more than I did, and trust me, life is crazy these days!"

Daisy hung up, gathered some hot coffee, tea, a small bit of whiskey in case John wanted it, and warmed up some pot roast and veggies from dinner. Barclay came in, took a glance at her tray and added a cloth napkin, some fresh cookies and utensils.

"Thank you, Barclay."

"I'll carry it. Up you go, Miss Daisy."

"I can—"

"In another few months you can," he said, very respectfully, and that was that. Daisy followed him up the stairs and to her room, amazed that John was already out of the shower, with a towel slung on his waist, barking orders on his cell phone.

"There's hot cocoa in the pot for you, Miss Daisy," Barclay said, and filtered out.

John hung up and looked at the assortment of food. "Thanks. I'm starved."

She nodded. "I know. I figured you would be—" she began, realizing his eyes were locked on her. Heat shot through her, and she managed a slight smile. "You have to eat first," she said softly. "Barclay will get his feelings hurt."

John went to the tray, fixed himself a whiskey, watching her as she made a space at a small table near her window for him to sit.

"I like this side of you."

"Domestic?"

"Caring."

"I suppose I haven't given you that much opportunity to see that I do have a soft side." She sat in the flowered, skirted chair across from him. "I just talked to Suz."

"I know. Cisco called me, playing the part of the concerned husband." He dug into the pot roast and vegetables with obvious pleasure.

"Concerned about what?"

"Oh, I think they don't want anyone to know that the Hanging H sustained a little bit of a wind shear at the ranch."

"What?" Daisy's heart skipped a beat. "Is there a lot of damage?"

"A little bit of damage to their roof, apparently. They don't want to make a fuss about it, though, because they're afraid people will rush over there to help them. There's a lot of folks in town who need help, and they want all resources going to the people who really need it."

"What are they going to do?"

"Right now, they've got some guys on the roof covering it with a tarp. This is great food."

"Thanks," she murmured. "What about Suz and the babies?"

"Well, remember Suz and Cisco live in a house they built on the property. I think Cisco's more worried about Mackenzie and her crowd of four, and since she's pregnant again—"

"She needs to come here," Daisy said quickly. "With the babies. They can't be there with all that banging going on. The children will never be able to rest."

"Are you sure you have enough space?"

She looked at him. "There's a spare bedroom or two," she said, not wanting to share that there were ten rooms that could be used for bedrooms alone.

"Robert wouldn't mind? Barclay won't give notice if four little girls start running around his perfectly kept domain?"

She slowly shook her head. "Barclay would love to have more people here to take care of. Years ago, Dad hired him away from several families who shared his services. Barclay is used to busy, and around here, it's just Dad, and sometimes me."

He dragged her onto the bed with him. She wanted desperately to pull off his towel, hang on to him, make love to him. But sadness hung over both of them, and she could tell he was tired, and that he was holding back everything he'd done at the creek. No doubt he'd hauled, towed and helped the sheriff digest the loss of his jail, too. It was a devastating blow to everyone. She sensed his mood, felt the tension and tiredness in his muscles.

So the towel stayed, but she remained in his arms, held tightly, securely. And there was no place she would rather be.

Something woke Daisy, and she lay in bed for a few seconds, disoriented, wondering if she'd merely heard a branch tapping on a windowpane. Then she realized what had awakened her was that John wasn't in bed with her. The place beside her was cool, as if he'd been gone awhile.

She hopped out of bed, dressed and went looking for him.

"Barclay, did John say where he was going?" She went into the kitchen, took the hot tea the butler offered her but didn't sit. She wouldn't be here long.

"I believe Mr. Mathison mentioned he was needed in town, Miss Daisy."

Barclay usually didn't hold back details from her, and she sensed he was now. "Why are you up at this hour, Barclay?"

He fixed a tray of fresh vegetables with a side of yummy-looking hummus. "Mr. Mathison asked me to prepare you a nutritious meal, organic, when you awakened."

"Yes, but I'm not usually up at three in the morning, and neither are you." She looked narrowly at him. "So, why are you pretending that you're awake to give me carrots and dip?"

Barclay shook his head. "It's not my place to note the comings and goings of our guests, Miss Daisy."

This was a new side of Barclay. "Okay. Thank you. Could you put this nutritious snack in a bag for me? I'm going into town." And when she found John, she was going to explain to him that he didn't need to oversee her diet.

What she needed was for him to make love to her.

He hadn't been lukewarm about doing so in Montana.

"Mr. Mathison said he would prefer if you didn't go

out, Miss Daisy. He says the roads are dangerous because of fallen tree limbs."

"I'm going out."

"Have the security detail drive you."

She shook her head. "I'll be fine. I promise to stay away from tree limbs." Rain was falling gently outside, but there'd been no notification of more storms on the radio. The power had been restored, at least to their house. She wondered about people farther out in the county than her house.

"Miss Daisy, I fear your father and Mr. Mathison will be very angry with me—"

She grabbed a flashlight. "I'll tell them I sneaked out. Go to bed, Barclay. You deserve the rest."

He followed her to the door. "I haven't rested since you were a little girl, Miss Daisy. Many a night I've stayed up waiting on you."

She smiled at him. "I know," she said softly. "I'll be back soon." Wherever John had gone, she wanted to be with him. She was part of BC, and she wanted to be there for whomever it was that needed help. He wouldn't have left if someone hadn't called for backup. Getting into her truck, she dialed his phone.

No answer. Which was weird, because he always picked up immediately when she called.

She could drive toward town and see if he'd gone to the main area of damage. Maybe cell service still wasn't available there. Light rain began falling again, splattering on the windshield. Daisy made sure her lights were on low and started into town.

To her surprise, she saw John's truck turning onto the main road leading to the creek. Possibly downed trees had damaged something, and he and the sheriff had decided the situation required immediate attention.

"Plus I have the snacks Barclay packed, and the lady with the snacks is always welcome," she said under her breath, following close behind his truck.

He parked and got out in an area with which she wasn't entirely familiar. She parked beside him, not surprised annoyance was clear on his face when he came to her window. She rolled it down.

"Daisy, go home."

She shook her head. "I want to be part of whatever is going on."

"No." He looked completely put out with her. "Daisy, there is no reason for you to be here, and it's not safe. It's raining, for heaven's sake, and you're pregnant. With triplets."

She'd just so wanted to be with him! "I'll sit in the truck. I promise. I'd feel better if I was here in case—" She glanced around, deciding not to say *in case something happens to you.* "Where's the sheriff?"

"Why would Dennis be here? It's the early hours of the morning."

She looked at him, surprised. "Then why are you here?"

"I can't tell you."

She drew back, annoyed now herself. "You want me to marry you, but you can't tell me what you're doing?"

"It's not that simple." His hair was getting damp, and his shirt was starting to stick to his broad chest and big shoulders, yet he still looked incredibly hot to her. Daisy wondered why it had taken her so darn long to realize just how sexy this man was.

She wished he'd get in the truck and kiss her senseless, maybe even make love to her the way he had in Montana. But something was wrong.

"It is that simple. You got out of my bed and skulked off to the creek without telling me."

He sighed. "I'm sorry. But please go home, babe."

"I'd really like to stay. Especially if the sheriff isn't here to help you with whatever you're going to do." She frowned. "What are you going to do?"

"I'm just making sure everything's safe."

She shivered. "Come back home and get in bed with me."

He smiled. "I'll take you up on that offer. You go warm the bed, and I'll be right there."

"I don't mind waiting."

A tree branch cracked loudly overhead, a sharp sound that made her jump.

"Nothing's safe here." John gave her the sternest look she'd ever seen him wear. "Go home."

She stared at this dark and dangerous man who was suddenly giving her orders. Daisy didn't recall anyone in her life ever giving her an order, and certainly not in that tone. She looked at him, worried.

"I'll be home soon."

"Fine."

"Thank you," he said, his tone softening. "I just want you and the babies to be safe." He made sure her seat belt was secure. "You know I'm crazy about you."

Did she? Of course she did. "I've been spoiled all my life."

He laughed. "I know. It's something I love about you."

"You do?"

"Of course I do. Would I want to marry such a princess if I didn't think I could handle it?"

She frowned. "I'm not a princess."

He laughed again, kissed her through the open window. "Okay."

She turned on the engine. "I don't remember you being so domineering in Montana."

"I wasn't. I didn't have to be. You weren't wandering around in an area where a tornado has recently hit."

"I'll warm up some cocoa for you."

"I'll be there soon."

She pulled away, not liking this at all. Didn't like leaving him here without the sheriff, didn't feel good about him roaming around where tree branches had been weakened by the storm. Rain came down harder even now.

She drove home slowly, carefully minding the roads. Going inside, she put her wrap away and went into the kitchen. Barclay sat there with her father, and a tray of gingerbread.

"It wasn't Barclay's fault," Daisy said with a sigh, and her father nodded.

"I know. Believe me, I know you quite well."

Barclay cut her a slice of gingerbread, warmed it, smoothed a small bit of creamy butter on the top. Daisy breathed in the scent thankfully.

"I've been craving gingerbread, Barclay. Thank you."

"You always liked it when you were a little girl." He poured them all some hot tea.

"So where was your fiancé headed?" her father asked.

"My fiancé?" Daisy thought about that as she took a bite of gingerbread. "I don't think we ever established that."

Robert waved a hand. "He established it when he came over here and gave me what-for about marrying you."

"Did he? Give you what-for?"

Robert raised a brow. "He didn't sound like he much cared what my opinion on the matter was, and that it was a foregone conclusion. As far as I'm concerned, we'll probably hear wedding bells before those babies are born."

Daisy put a hand over her stomach, feeling the babies shift and move inside. Sometimes it felt like they had an elaborate dance routine going on in there that only they understood. Every time she felt them move, she caught her breath with the wonder of it all.

Sometimes she couldn't believe she was actually having triplets. For a girl who'd always wished her dreams would come true, this time they had. "Anyway, I don't know where John was going. He was being very mysterious. But he'd gone to the creek, and I guess he was going to check on what's left of the Haunted H."

"Not much but twigs, I heard." Robert scowled into his teacup. "Damn shame. But we'll make it bigger next time."

"You old softy." Daisy grinned at her father, then jumped as the doorbell rang. "Who would be here at this hour?"

Barclay went to the door at a pace less formal than usual. Somewhere there had to be an unwritten code that the well-trained butler never hurried.

But Barclay just had. Daisy and her father waited.

Sheriff Dennis made his way into the kitchen, shaking his head at Barclay who offered him tea and gingerbread. Barclay made up a plate, anyway, and Dennis seemed hardly to realize Barclay had steered him into a chair and served him. Dennis picked up a fork absently. "Jane Chatham's gone missing."

"What?" Daisy glanced at her father. "She wasn't at home with Ralph when the storm hit?"

"I guess she was down at The Wedding Diner. I'm not sure. That's the last place Ralph said he knew she was. Doing inventory, he said."

"But if your jail got hit, and it's across the street from the diner," Robert began.

Dennis sipped his tea, hardly noticing Barclay hovering at his elbow. "The diner didn't get so much as a scratch."

"That's wonderful news!" Daisy felt a strange cramp hit her stomach, ignored it for the moment. Sipped some more tea, told herself it would pass.

"Anyway, she's not in the diner. I checked. So I came here because, frankly, Robert, I'm going to need to borrow your security detail to help us search."

"Fine. Barclay, give the boys a ring, will you? Have them come in to go with the sheriff."

Daisy looked at Dennis, worried. "I'm sure everyone has tried her cell phone, but of course some phone service is still out."

"That's what's making it tricky." Dennis shrugged. "If Jane was supposed to be in the diner doing inventory, and the building didn't get hit, I can't imagine why she's not there now."

"I don't know, but I'll take my truck and help search, too," Daisy said, and Dennis, her father and Barclay all said, "No!"

"Pardon me," Barclay said. "It's not like me to insert an opinion—"

"Never mind," Robert said. "Daisy, sweetheart, you're not leaving the house again. If I have to sit up all night playing chess and gin rummy with you to make sure you don't leave again, that's what I'll do."

The strange cramp slithered over her stomach again. Daisy put a hand on her tummy. "More hands on deck means we find her faster."

"If I have the ranch crew, that'll be enough." Dennis stood. "Thanks, Robert."

"No problem. Take what you need. The hitch, the hauler, whatever."

"Just the manpower for now. Daisy, get your gang up, too. Tell 'em to meet me at the creek."

"Why the creek? What's going on at the creek all of a sudden?" She looked at Dennis. "I thought you said Jane was at the diner?" She felt another cramp. "John's down at the creek now."

"He is?" Dennis seemed stunned. "Why?"

"I have no idea. I didn't want to leave him there, but he insisted."

"Since when has someone insisted on something that you listened to?" Dennis demanded.

"I don't know. Motherhood must be softening me up."

"I'll say." Dennis whistled. "Or being a married woman has done it."

"I'm not married yet."

"Rumor on the grapevine is that it'll happen before frost hits the pumpkins." Dennis lifted his hat, and he disappeared down the hall. The front door opened, and they could hear the sounds of trucks revving up. She texted her gang to let them know the sheriff wanted them at the creek, then looked up to see her father smiling at her fondly.

"It does my heart good to see you so happy, Daisy girl."

"Happy about what?"

"Motherhood. Becoming a wife. It's what you always wanted more than anything."

It was true, not that she would admit that to anyone, not even her father. She was crazy in love with John, absolutely head over heels for him.

"I wish I'd been better to my wife." Robert sighed heavily, and Daisy started. Her father rarely talked about her mother, but Daisy remembered her mother as a soft, gentle, quiet soul. Very set apart from Robert, their marriage more formal than loving.

"Thing was, I got married early. We were young. I was full of hotheaded big plans for the world, everything I wanted to do. Put my marriage second. Last, really." He shook his head. "Should have been first, damn it."

"Oh, Dad." Daisy reached over, patted his arm. "Don't think about things like that."

"I just want you to have everything you want. Everyone always said you were a wild child, that I should rein you in. But I knew what your heart was, and that you dreamed of a home, a husband, children and to belong in this small, opinionated town." He laughed ruefully. "I wasn't much help with any of those goals, but now they're all within your reach. I think you've found the man for you."

She'd feel better when John returned, that was for sure. "I can't imagine where Jane is. I talked to Cosette earlier and I thought everything was fine."

Barclay hovered at her elbow. "I notice you keep rubbing your stomach, Miss Daisy. Are you feeling well? I could make you some warm milk—"

"I'm fine. I think I'll go to bed. Thank you, Barclay." Maybe if she went to her room, Barclay and her father would retire. There was no point in keeping them up just because she was worried about John. And Jane. And everything. Even the idea of a wedding was gnawing on her mind. The sheriff had said there'd be a wedding before frost was on the pumpkins, but that wasn't possible. She rubbed her stomach as she walked upstairs slowly. Each stair seemed to take longer than the last, with more effort needed, effort that seemed to drain her.

And then, just as she reached the landing, Daisy realized she was going to faint. She grabbed on to the balustrade and pulled herself up over the final stair, letting herself gently sink onto the floor safely before she gave in to the blackness.

Chapter Ten

"High-risk pregnancies are not uncommon with triplets," Dr. Costa said. "But you're young and healthy, so fortunately, I think there's a good chance you can carry the babies longer."

She'd been taken into Austin by ambulance. She was embarrassed for taking up all the manpower and resources when help was needed in Bridesmaids Creek. On the other hand, it'd been so scary when she'd realized she was blacking out and falling that she was glad she was here and getting medical assistance.

"What happened?" she asked, her voice sounding weak even to her. John glanced at her, concerned, her hand held tightly in his.

"Three babies are a lot on your system, basically. We're running tests to find out more, but I suspect low blood sugar, maybe some anemia."

"I've always been extremely healthy," Daisy protested. "And I'd been eating gingerbread and drinking tea. I don't think I could have had low blood sugar, Dr. Costa, I really don't."

"We'll see. It's just my initial guess. Now that we have you stabilized, we'll just let you lie here and rest for a while."

"How long?"

"Maybe a week." He didn't glance up from his chart. "We're going to run tests on the babies, as well, to make certain there isn't anything wrong with the pregnancy—"

She felt the blood turn cold in her face and arms. Hopefully there was nothing wrong with her precious babies.

"Did anyone find Jane?"

"I did." John rubbed her hand. "Don't worry about anything. BC's still going to be there when you get back. Right now, you just need to rest."

Daisy felt herself getting sleepy against her will. "Where'd you find her?"

"Don't worry. Everything will be fine."

Her eyes snapped open. "That's why you went to the creek, wasn't it?" she asked groggily. "You were looking for Jane."

"Go to sleep, babe."

"But we never made love," she said, whispering because it was so extremely difficult to speak. "I wanted to make love to you."

"Shh, babe," he whispered. "Everything's going to be fine."

She closed her eyes, letting her cowboy soothe her, wishing she could stay awake and tell him how much he meant to her. How sorry she was that she'd made him chase her like crazy for so long. She'd known all along that John adored her, and foolishly, she'd ignored what he was offering.

Like her father, she completely understood what it meant to have regrets.

Sam walked in looking concerned, his arms full of a big white teddy bear. "No worries, the cavalry has arrived."

"Cavalry?" John raised a brow.

"Indeed." Sam kissed Daisy on the cheek, shook John's hand. "When I heard Daisy would be laid up for a while, I knew you needed my presence."

"How so?" John asked.

Sam set the bear down and grinned. "Because I've never let a brother down yet. And while you weren't looking, I became ordained to perform weddings. Ordained via the internet, but that suffices here in Texas." He seemed really happy to report his new standing. "It's the least I can do, considering that I once offered to marry Daisy myself. And if I don't do it, you're going to end up with children and no wife, John."

"Daisy and I will get married soon enough," John said, but he sounded hesitant.

He glanced toward her, as did Sam.

"Don't look at me. I can't even think about a wedding right now." Daisy was adamant.

"Hmm." John seemed to consider Sam's words. "You *have* given me the slip once before."

"Yes, but—"

"Actually, if you think about it, she's given you the slip several times." Sam flung himself in a chair, delighted to be stoking trouble. "Let's see, first there was—"

"Never mind. Let me see this license of yours." John

waited for him to produce it. "I'm assuming that if you're here, it's because you think your services are required."

Daisy felt like she'd been tossed into a whirlwind. "Hang on a minute. There's too much going on to even think about a wedding!"

"What's going on?" John asked, and she thought he sounded a bit wary.

"Well, Bridesmaids Creek for one." Daisy swallowed. "How could we even think about getting married when Jane is missing—"

"I found her and took her home last night," John reminded her.

"Okay, but the jail is gone and the Haunted H, too. And there's damage to a lot of homes. It seems selfish to get married when our friends are suffering," Daisy said, floundering. How could she explain that she didn't want to get married while she was bed bound? Was that vain? She wanted what the other brides in Bridesmaids Creek had gotten: the full hometown wedding with family and friends.

"Actually it's not selfish at all. It's being very considerate," Sam said, throwing in his two cents like the trickster he was. "After all, you need to be married for the sake of the babies, I should think. And there's so much turmoil in town that your marrying out of town, sort of like an elopement, in fact, exactly like an elopement, would keep everyone from feeling compelled to drop everything and do their wedding duties."

"That's true…" Daisy saw the good sense in what Sam was saying. It was a guaranteed fact that as soon as everyone heard that there was going to be a wedding, everyone would cease everything they were doing to help her out. Weddings weren't done small in Bridesmaids Creek.

It was something she'd always wanted, though. The big wedding for Daisy Donovan, once the town's bad girl, making good, finally. Acceptance was a dream very near to her heart.

"How legal is this stupid internet ordination you've gotten?" John sounded like he was almost growling, probably not pleased that Sam was ramrodding this new twist.

Yet Sam's plan had a lot of merit—this time.

"Oh, it's all very legal," he said cheerfully. "I worked real hard to obtain my certification, because I figured you two might mess around long enough that you might need some kind of emergency bell-ringing."

"That's just not really funny." John definitely sounded like he was growling now. Daisy glanced at him, surprised.

"Why do you act like you want to gnaw his head off?" she asked the man who suddenly didn't sound very much as if he wanted to become a husband.

"Never mind." John shrugged. "It's up to Daisy."

She stared at him. "That's it? It's up to me?"

He shrugged again. "Of course. As Sam said, you've left me at the altar before. And I recall telling you that you'd have to ask me to marry you, since you've been notably reluctant to race to the altar with me."

Drat. She'd forgotten that he'd wanted a clear green light from her this time.

Daisy swallowed, suddenly aware that she'd been expecting John to make all the sacrifices in their relationship. "Here's the thing. I don't really want to get married like this, John."

"Like what?" His brown eyes hooded a bit, the muscles of his broad chest stiffening with tension, preparing himself for bad news.

"In the hospital, for starters. By Sam, no offense," she said quickly to Sam. "But not with an internet-earned diploma of some kind." She looked at her maybe-soon-to-be husband. "You know very well we have no reason to expect that it's valid."

"It is," Sam said.

"Excuse me," Daisy said quickly, "but I have some experience with men with an agenda. My father for starters, my gang for further illustration of my point. And you're definitely a typical guy who likes to move people around like puzzle pieces. You've been doing it since you came to Bridesmaids Creek."

"Hey!" Sam yelped. "I resemble that remark!"

"Yes, you do." Daisy frowned at him. "What I've noticed is that you manipulate people into doing what you want them to do—"

"I *help* them," Sam emphasized. "The spirit is pure."

"And what you usually want someone to do is get married," Daisy went on, "yet I notice you never, ever date anyone yourself. Why is that?"

"Yeah, Sam, why is that?" John laughed. "Daisy's made several good points."

Sam sighed, pulled the big white bear into his lap. "Is it wrong for a fellow to want his friends to be happy? The same friends that came here looking for brides? Looking for love?"

"I'll let you officiate a ceremony for us, Sam, when you've gone out on a real date. So you better make it snappy. These babies may not be content to stay put until the end of time. Which is exactly how long I suspect you were planning on going without dating a living, breathing woman."

Sam shook his head. "Greatness can't be rushed."

"Neither can mediocrity. Laziness." Daisy settled back against the pillow.

"You've figured me out, then. When it comes to love, I'm lazy. I admit it. Relationships are too damn much work. And I don't think I'm cut out for henpeckery."

Daisy laughed. "I don't henpeck John."

"Yeah." Sam glowered at his buddy. "But only because you respect a man who can shoot the head off a nail. Who's going to respect me?"

"Handsome Sam?" John grinned. "Everyone respects Handsome Sam."

"No, they don't." His face was woebegone. "If they respected me, they wouldn't be talking about my looks. They'd be talking about my deeds."

"That's the most pathetic, pitiful bit of sorry-for-myself I've ever heard," Daisy said. "You're trying to make me feel bad about not letting you use your piece of paper that's so new the ink is still wet on it to officiate our ceremony."

"Yeah, I am. Is it working?" Sam peered at her.

"No. I'm not getting married here. I'm not getting married in a hurry, by a man who printed a fake license from his computer so he could claim he was certified to get John and me to say we do!"

"Damn shame, that." Sam leaned back in the chair, closed his eyes. "Then again, I'll take a nap and let you lovebirds talk it over. I'm sure there'll be plenty of backchat to be said over the matter."

"There's not going to be any backchat!" Daisy wished she could get out of the bed and go home where she didn't feel so powerless. Here she was connected to tubes and monitors. She'd been rushed here without her typical clothes, didn't even have a hairbrush. John had done his best to pack for her, but what man knew what a woman needed in her overnight bag? Barclay had tried to help, apparently, but John had waved him off in his great hurry to follow the ambulance to Austin.

She'd been charmed by John's desire to take care of her himself. She smiled as Sam began to snore lightly. "It's him, not you."

John winked. "I know, beautiful. Trust me, I know. A little of my buddy goes a long way."

"He is right, though." She hadn't expected to find herself off her feet so soon. "But I can't think about getting married when I'm worried about the babies. I don't think I've ever been so scared as when I woke up and found myself being carted off into an ambulance."

"I completely understand." He came over to sit on the bed next to her, leaned her head against his shoulder. "It's all going to work out."

"I hope so."

"It is." His voice was strong with determination. "You know what we should do?"

"Let Sam perform the ceremony his way, and do it our way later? Just to cover all the bases?"

"I was going to say get a cup of warm water and put his hand in it to see if we can make him pee himself," John said, "but yeah, your plan works, too."

"The warm water idea is definitely intriguing." Daisy looked up at him. "He drove all the way here to see us, he bought the babies a bear, he claims he somehow got himself ordained just for us, and we want to put his hand in a cup of warm water. Is that wrong?"

John laughed. "It's so right that it's hard to believe I'm not going to do it."

"Softy."

"Me! You're the one who wants to let him use his faux piece of paper so he can brag about being the one who got us married."

"Yeah." Daisy slowly nodded. "When you put it like that, it doesn't sound so silly."

"No, it doesn't."

They sat quietly for a few minutes, and John kissed her hand. Brushed her knuckles with his lips. Daisy looked at their sleeping lump of a friend, who was good-hearted in spite of his prankster ways, remembered that this man had served overseas with her husband.

"I just wonder if it might be good for your friendship to allow Sam to have his moment in the sun," Daisy said.

"I don't want you to do anything you'll regret later. And it might be just as exciting to do the warm water trick. At least from your perspective."

Daisy looked at Sam. "It was sweet of him to try to play Madame Matchmaker's role."

"Those two are in cahoots, along with Jane. Don't feel too sentimental for him."

Daisy looked at John. "Are you sure?"

"Sure as I'm breathing."

She smiled. "All of you who came here for Ty are no stranger to trying to finagle your way to what you want. You, Sam, Cisco, Justin, even Ty. You're brothers in schemes."

"I'll tell you a secret. We didn't really come here to find brides. I know that's the line in BC, but honestly, that was sort of window dressing."

Daisy was astonished. "But that's all any of you have

done, try to march each other to the altar. You've competed in the Bridesmaids Creek swim and the Best Man's Fork run, egging each other out of bachelor status!"

"I know." He grinned. "We were okay with that rumor going around. After a while, it sort of became rural legend, and we were okay with that, too. But the truth is, we only came here to support Ty Spurlock because we could tell he needed help."

Daisy thought back. Justin Morant had come to Bridesmaids Creek first, meeting Mackenzie Hawthorne and her four little baby girls, falling head over boots in love with all of them. Then Ty had gotten caught in his own trap and fallen for Jade Harper, which still amused all of BC, because he was supposedly shepherding his brothers-in-arms to the altar. Cisco Grant went down hard for Suz Hawthorne—and that had left John and Handsome Sam as the last bachelors standing among the group Ty had brought to town with the intention of growing Bridesmaids Creek. "What kind of help?"

"We could tell he was worried about how stuff was going around here. Frankly, at the time, your father wasn't doing a whole lot to help out."

"That's true," Daisy murmured, feeling horribly guilty about the part she'd played in all that, too.

He tightened his arms around her as if he could tell what was she thinking, absolutely wouldn't let her have any regrets.

"So Ty felt like we could help out around the town. At the time, he talked about odd jobs and stuff. Working around both the Hanging H Ranch and the Haunted H year-round Halloween attraction. We liked the thought of being outdoors, and the town sounded cool. The idea of living in a family oriented kind of place was appealing to all of us. So, Sam, Cisco and I decided to head here, at least for a couple of months. BC grows on you, though, and now it's been a few years."

Where might John have gone otherwise? He clearly had no desire to live the same way his parents and brothers did, even though their lifestyle certainly suited them. "I'm glad you came to BC."

"It goes without saying that I am, too."

She looked at Sam, who was snoring like crazy. "So what about Sam? Has he ever dated anyone?"

"Not that we know of. Not since we've known him, anyway."

"Poor Sam!"

"Don't feel sorry for him. He says he's too busy. I don't know with what, but he says he is."

"So he just works at the Hanging H, and becomes a doting uncle to all the babies his SEAL brothers have?"

"I guess."

Daisy took a deep breath. "We're going to have to do it."

"Put his hand in warm water while he's snoring?"

"No. We're going to have to let him officiate our wedding."

John pulled away slightly to look at her. "Are you sure you don't want to do the water trick instead?"

"I'm sure." She gazed at Sam, the big bear of a man collapsed in the chair like a tired doll. "He put a lot of thought into this. We can't let him down."

"So you're asking me to marry you?"

She turned to face him, stared deep into his eyes. "Yes. I am asking you to marry me. When our snoring friend awakens, would you, John Lopez 'Squint' Mathison, do me the great honor of becoming my sexy, handsome husband?"

Chapter Eleven

"I accept," John stated in a hurry, before she could take her sudden proposal back. "Sam, get up off your duff! You've got a job to do."

Sam blinked his eyes sleepily, then jackknifed to a sitting position. "Is there a raid? What's happening?" He looked around wildly. John realized he was probably searching for his firearm and primed to hit the ground running.

"Easy, brother. We're in Austin," John said softly, and Sam relaxed as if someone had pulled the air out of him. His brown hair was stood on end, but John could almost hear his blood pressure calming. "Didn't mean to scare the hell out of you."

"Man, I don't know. Guess I was dreaming." Sam looked at Daisy, who wore the cutest expression of alarm. "Sorry, Daisy."

"It's fine. John should be more delicate when he disturbs you."

Sam rose, his face returning to the teasing expression they all knew so well. Cagily, he said, "So now that I'm awake, am I performing ministerial duties?"

"Is that really all you came here for?" John demanded.

"I came to see Daisy, and to bring the impending bundles of joy their first present from Uncle Handsome Sam."

Daisy laughed, but John scowled. "Daisy's asked me to marry her." He said it with pride.

"That's awesome!" Sam laughed. "I hope you don't regret it, beautiful. I swear I'm the better man," he teased, going to kiss Daisy's cheek. John pulled him back when he deemed Sam was being just a bit too attentive.

"That's enough. Easy, Romeo."

Sam looked at Daisy. "You don't have to marry him, you know. I'd do the honors in a heartbeat."

John sighed. "You don't even want to get married."

"No, but I can make an exception in this case."

"That's enough. You have a wedding to perform, and it's not your own."

"And perform it I will!" Sam rubbed his hands together. "We don't have a second to spare."

"Well, actually," Daisy said, "we need to spare a few moments."

John put up his hands. "You asked, I accepted, we have a willing pastor to officiate. Don't slow us down, Daisy. We're over the hump here."

"And it wasn't easy getting over that hump," Daisy agreed. "But we can do a lot of good with our marriage, if we play our cards right."

John sank into a chair, stared at the woman he couldn't

quite seem to catch. "Let's skip playing cards and just get married already."

"The thing is, we need to do this right. To do it right, we need Madame Matchmaker."

"We're already matched. She's had her hands in our relationship up to her elbows. Maybe not as much as she would have liked, but enough." John was eager to get the "I do's" said.

"Not necessarily," Sam said, and John frowned.

"Whose side are you on? You do realize this woman has eluded me for years? Do you really want to give her a reason to get away from me again?" John demanded.

"Here's the thing," Daisy said, ignoring the good-natured ribbing between the men. Sometimes it didn't sound good-natured, but she knew they had a relationship that went deeper than any silly argument. That was the thing about Daisy, the more time went on, the more comfortable he felt around her. Not too comfortable, of course—he still wanted to make love to her wildly day and night, as they had in Montana. But he felt comfortable with her.

She made him smile in a way he'd once wondered if he'd ever smile again.

"Cosette, our illustrious matchmaker, believes her magic has deserted her." Daisy looked at the men. "This is a golden opportunity to help her get her mojo back."

"Oh, no." John shook his head. "I'm not waiting for Cosette's magic. I've got three little babies who are going to wear my name from the second their eyes open in this world. Plus, if you recall, she had your gang tie me to a tree during the last race. No, I'm not waiting on Cosette."

"I see where you're going with this," Sam said to Daisy, and John wondered if telling his buddy to butt out would be a foolhardy thing to do. It was Sam and his new freestyle ordination who just about had Daisy to "I do," so John contented himself with gazing at his lovely bride-to-be-as-soon-as-he-could-manage-it and waited for Sam's epiphany to reveal itself.

"If Cosette believes you two are together and getting married because of her matchmaking skills, then she'll feel like her magic hasn't deserted her." Sam looked pleased. "It's two for the price of one."

John didn't like the sound of that. There was already one more attending this marriage proposal than necessary. Again, he reminded himself that his buddy had his back, so he kept silent.

"We get Cosette's magic to recharge her belief in herself, and Bridesmaids Creek comes back to life." Sam nodded wisely at Daisy. "People don't always see your good side, Daisy Donovan, but you definitely have some angel running strong in you. Sexy angel, too," he said with a flourish, and John said, "Hey!" as sternly as he could manage it, secretly grateful that Sam was saying nice things about Daisy because she deserved it.

"Thank you." Daisy sounded happy, and John forgave his buddy all his interruptions and interferences on the spot. Just to hear someone else acknowledge what he himself had always seen in the brunette stunner made him realize all over again why he'd allowed Sam into his tight-knit circle of brothers in the first place.

"Thanks," John said softly.

"No thanks needed." Sam began scrolling through his phone. "Now, we need a bouquet, and maybe a veil?" He looked at Daisy. "Do you want to call Cosette or shall I?"

"But we haven't decided how to do this, have we?" Daisy was so adorable as she sat in the hospital bed, looking worried about Cosette, that John fell in love with her all over again.

"One of us is going to tell Cosette that you and John can't get married because he believes your marriage won't last since the Bridesmaids Creek charms have failed for you. If you recall, none of your three chances at the magic ever pointed to John being the man of your dreams. The prince of your heart, as it were." Sam looked quite pleased with his plan.

"Hell, no, we're not telling Cosette that! Don't stir up that BC magic nonsense," John said.

Daisy gasped, and Sam looked chagrined. John realized he'd stepped in it big-time. "Oh, come on. It's just superstition. You know that, right?"

"And you've always been superstitious as hell," Sam said. "You know *that*, right?"

Daisy's expression was still steeped in anxiety. John tried to look like a man who'd just been proposed to. "In the real world, the world outside of BC, not everybody jumps around to the tune of busybodies. Cute little busybodies, but busybodies with an agenda just the same."

Daisy looked like she might cry.

"May I just remind you, brother, that Madame Matchmaker said, and I repeat, 'there will be no wedding in BC for you?', as a result of your unsuccessful attempts in the Bridesmaids Creek swim and the Best Man's Fork run?" Sam looked disgusted. "What SEAL gets a leg cramp during arguably the most important swim of his life?"

"First of all," John said, "going back to my original point, those were not the most important missions in my life. I can think of a few swims we did in very dire parts of the world, my friend, and you can, too, wherein my leg did not cramp up, nor did my shooting skills."

Daisy's eyes filled with tears. Sam cleared his throat.

"Oh, hell. I'm not being very romantic, am I?" John crumpled into his chair. "Daisy, I'm sorry. Sorry as heck." He pushed his hat back, shook his head. Pointed at Sam. "You are causing trouble, buddy."

Sam looked innocent. "Your lack of romance is not my fault!"

He snorted. "One day, Sam Barr, some little lady is going to decide she wants to pin you down, and all of us are going to eat popcorn and watch with smiles on our faces."

Sam's face contorted from astonished to concerned. "Dude, that's a horrible curse to lay on a brother! It's bad, really bad. Friends don't put that on friends."

"Anyway," Daisy said, "getting back to Cosette, if you don't want to go with the local customs, that's a decision I leave up to you." She looked at John, her dark eyes a little sad, and his heart felt as if it sank to his boots.

"Absolutely not. I let my pigheaded mouth get the best of me." He manned up big-time, determined to make Daisy happy. "I'll call Cosette myself."

Daisy looked pleased, and Sam appeared relieved.

"Thank you," Daisy said, and John felt better.

"I knew you'd want to do this right. Any man would want to redeem himself after the leg cramp episode," Sam said.

"You know, I wish we had put your hand in a glass of warm water while you napped," John groused, and Daisy laughed, and Sam postured as if he wasn't worried but he knew very well anything was possible.

John grinned at Daisy and pulled out his phone. "Let's get this party started. What do I tell our illustrious matchmaker?"

* * *

"I'm afraid I don't know," Cosette said when John called her a half hour later with a well-prepared script he'd been given by Daisy.

He hoped he could pull off the magic.

"*You* don't know what to do?" John said, when Cosette paused.

"It's not a matter of you and Daisy getting married," Cosette told him. "But as far as the magic goes, I'm afraid I don't have any pull."

"You don't have any pull?" Beside him, Daisy's face went a little pale. He had to fix this—and fast. "How can you not have any pull? You pull everyone's strings in BC!"

"Yes, but you see, I'm divorced now. I'm on my own. If I can't make my own match work, how can I make a match for anyone else?"

John swallowed hard. "Cosette, you know that you and Phillipe are meant to be together like salt and pepper. Marriage isn't the only bond between you."

"Maybe not. But to be honest, I started losing a bit of faith when Mackenzie Hawthorne's first marriage hit the skids. Though, to be sure, her first husband was a weasel. She should never have married him."

"So you're saying that the magic makes mistakes?" John was trying very hard to see through the fog of superstition BC layered over itself.

"I made a mistake." Cosette took a moment to compose her thoughts. "The magic never does. But my confidence really ebbed a little. Up until then, I had a perfect record, and Phillipe was Monsieur Unmatchmaker in name only. He had no job, except for tutoring, of course.

But no matches to unmake. We never needed that service."

John's head swam. "It's okay, Cosette. Ty Spurlock said that Mackenzie's first marriage really hadn't been prodded along by you but by him."

"Oh, what does Ty know?" she asked huffily, but he thought he heard hope in her voice. "Anyway, what do you possibly think I can do for Daisy? No one gets more than three chances at the magic. It's just not possible."

"So what would happen if we get married without assistance from Bridesmaids Creek magic?"

Daisy's eyes went huge. She'd been listening attentively this whole time, but now she looked positively stunned. John decided right then and there that nothing was going to keep him from giving her the thing she'd been dreaming of all her life.

"You'd just get married," Cosette said. "Nothing happens at all."

He hesitated. That didn't sound right. Something had to happen—this was Bridesmaids Creek. Everyone was always in a stew about the magic.

"So do I take that to mean that you and Daisy have agreed to get married?" Cosette asked.

"We certainly would like to. But as you know, our getting to the altar has been—"

"Difficult. Strewn with rocks. I know," Cosette said, and he glanced at Daisy again. She looked as if her heart was in her eyes and in danger of melting away. "And you want it to work out between the two of you, anyway."

"More than anything."

Cosette was quiet for a minute. Then she said, "Do you remember the night we took you to the cavern?"

"Yes. I do. I found Jane Chatham there that night after the storm."

"Then that's all you need to know. Give Daisy my love. She's such a sweet girl, you know. Always has been. Although I'm putting good money on the fact that those three boys of hers are going to be rootin' tootin' rascals."

She hung up, leaving John wondering what the hell had just happened.

"What did she say?" Daisy asked eagerly. Sam remained motionless in his chair, his gaze hooded, waiting for the big pronouncement.

John couldn't talk about the cave. It was secret, sacrosanct. There was nothing to tell, anyway, because he didn't know what he was supposed to have seen that night. It had been a wonderful underground place, nothing more. A hidden part of BC no one knew about. When Jane had misplaced herself after the blowout storm that had hit BC, he'd had a hunch and gone looking for her there. Sure enough, he'd located her at the mouth of the cave, but he hadn't gone in it a second time. He hadn't asked her what she'd been up to, and she hadn't offered any information. With the town devastated the way it had been that night, he'd been only too happy to grab her, then call around to let everyone know he'd found Jane.

The cave wasn't his secret to share. He had no idea why Cosette brought it up now. He looked at Daisy, the woman he hungered for, the woman who'd driven him mad with desire and love and all the wonderful emotions a man needed to feel about a woman.

He wasn't letting her get away. Not if he could help it.

"It's okay if we get married," John said.

"Okay?"

He nodded. "Cosette said nothing will happen if we get married."

"That's the point. Nothing will happen." Daisy looked worried. "The magic won't happen."

His heart curled up a little as some concern sank in, but he couldn't deny Daisy's words. "I had a funny feeling that's where Cosette was going with that."

"So basically you have to fix this on your own," Sam stated. "Wouldn't it have been better if you hadn't gotten a leg cramp in the first place?" He laughed, and John told himself he was going to turn his buddy into a pretzel if he didn't hush up and quit stirring up trouble.

"It's not all his fault," Daisy said.

"It's not?" Sam asked.

"No. It's not." She looked at John. "I deliberately didn't win him in the second race. When I saw him on the banks instead of Cisco, I slowed down. Probably in the last fifty, I definitely wasn't swimming faster than Suz."

"You slowed down on purpose?" So this was heartbreak. He'd always suspected—everyone had always suspected—Daisy hadn't swum lights-out once she'd realized he was the prize, but it was still hard to hear coming from the only woman he'd ever wanted to win.

"And then Cisco nullified the third race by winning and declaring himself already married," Sam said. "That was a day that really set BC on its ear. The big dummy." He sounded vastly amused by that.

"I don't need the magic, John. I don't think it exists for me, or ever will, no matter what we do."

He studied Daisy. He could hear the despair in her voice. "Cosette didn't seem all that hopeful."

"That's that, then." Daisy's shoulders slumped. "Sam, you might as well go ahead and marry us. This way, at least it's done. The babies will have their father's name at birth, and I'll—"

John held his breath. "You'll what?"

"I'll be married." Daisy looked at him, and she smiled, but it didn't look like a smile. More like a determination. A vow, to do the right thing.

He didn't want to be the right thing. Hell, he never had been in his life. Why should he start now?

"Nope," John said. "There'll be no wedding today."

"What?" Sam demanded. "Listen, buddy, I don't know if you heard, but your bride actually said she'd accept your dumb ass. If I was you, I'd hop on that offer."

John grinned, suddenly feeling on top of the world again. "Can't do it." He leaned down, dropped a kiss on Daisy that turned sexy in a heartbeat. Oh, his girl liked him fine. She wanted to marry him.

She just wanted the magic, too.

He was fine with that.

After all, there wasn't a prince in fairy-tale land that had ever stumbled upon his princess without having to go on an enchanted win-your-lady grail first.

And if there was one thing he'd always been good at, it was life on the move.

Chapter Twelve

John got Daisy home under strict instructions from the doctor, who said she wasn't to move. She had to stay on medication to keep the babies "in as long as possible," which nearly gave John heart failure. Any man would be frightened by that kind of talk.

And they still weren't married. He didn't know how he was going to manage that trick.

"You lie right here and don't move. Not a muscle," John said, ensconcing her in a downstairs bedroom in the main house at the Donovan compound.

Daisy looked up at him. "I can't stand being away from all the action. I'll go mad in here."

Barclay cleared his throat, and Robert shuffled from foot to foot nervously. Daisy's gang had all crowded into the room, too, trying to be part of the welcome-home committee.

"We could make a place for her in the den, which is closer to the kitchen and living room," Barclay suggested. "Miss Daisy has always needed to be close by the action."

"And it would be easier to keep an eye on her," Robert added.

John decided he needed to give in gracefully. "But no excitement. I leave you in charge," he told Barclay.

"I'll see that she doesn't leave the sofa bed."

John felt that Barclay's word was probably as close to gold as anyone's could be. And Robert looked as if he was probably going to turn out to be quite a hoverer. "Okay, den it is. But the doctor scared the bejesus out of me, babe. You and I are going on autopilot until my sons are born."

"We'll all help," Carson Dare said.

John thought that for once he was probably grateful for Daisy's band of rowdies. If nothing else, they were loyal, and he valued loyalty and brotherhood. "We'll take all the help we can get. You have to arrange all of that with Barclay, though," he said, belatedly realizing he might be stepping on the butler's domain. And Robert's, too, for that matter.

"I'm going to head out for a bit. I need to check in at the Hanging H. Are you going to be okay, babe?" he asked Daisy.

"Do I look like these guys would let me be anything but?" Daisy asked, smiling.

She was the center of attention, which she loved more than anything. John grinned. "Call me if you need anything."

"Take your time," she said sweetly, and later on John would remember that his best girl had said that.

He should have taken heed.

* * *

Daisy got on the phone with Cosette as soon as John departed. She'd shooed everyone else away, too, claiming she needed a nap.

But she had way too much to do.

"Cosette, I'm ready," she said when her friend picked up the phone.

"Ready for what?"

"Ready to start training as your apprentice."

Cosette didn't laugh. "Are you sure?"

If there was anything Cosette needed to get her groove back, it was someone to mentor—at least that was the conclusion Daisy had come to.

She was pretty sure she'd hit on a winning idea. If she was right, she'd get everything she'd ever dreamed of.

"Of course I'm sure. If you don't accept me as an apprentice, how am I ever going to learn?"

"I do need help," Cosette said, her voice quavering a bit. "However, I'm not sure I'll make all that good of a teacher. My magic wand no longer has any spark."

"We'll worry about the wand later. We have to get cracking on this project. Otherwise, Bridesmaids Creek is going to really lack for marriage matches. Think about that for a minute."

"It's too horrible to contemplate!"

"I know. The guys meant well with their dating service idea. Whoever heard of a cigar bar in a matchmaking establishment?"

"Not me," Cosette said, her voice a little unsteady.

Daisy took a deep breath. If it was the last thing she did, she was going to get Cosette and Phillipe back in their old establishment. She should never have sided with her father on taking over those spaces. "Okay, then. The doctor has me on bed rest, so I can't move. You're going to have to teach me by phone."

"I can do that. But I may drop by, just to make sure everything's sticking."

"Even better. If you have time, that is."

"My dear, I always have time to take on an apprentice. My first! This is a happy day!"

"I'll try not to let you down."

"Impossible! Who's our first victim?"

"I'll tell you when you get here."

She hung up, smiled when her father came in the room.

"How are you feeling?" Robert asked.

"Like a million bucks. I'm going to be Cosette's new matchmaking apprentice."

Robert hesitated, then grinned. "Who are you practicing on first?"

"What if I said it was you?"

He shook his head vehemently. "Absolutely not. I was a terrible husband."

Daisy took that in. "Then we'll start with Carson Dare."

"He's been in love with you forever. Won't he be a tough nut to crack?"

"It'll be a good test of my skills. If I can get Carson matched, the rest should fall in line."

"I don't know," Robert said, sounding worried. "This could backfire."

"It could," Daisy said, "but it won't."

When John returned, he was surprised to find Cosette and Daisy peering at some kind of flowchart and what looked like pieces of paper they'd tossed in a frilly pink hat with a huge red feather on it.

"Hello, Cosette. Daisy, darling, shouldn't you be resting, beautiful?" He realized they were paying him little attention beyond a cursory greeting. "So I'll just go find your father, okay?"

"Dad would love that." Daisy favored him with a huge smile, and John felt a warm glow run all over him. Okay, he was good and smitten, and she wasn't going to listen to him about relaxing, anyway.

Even he'd known that was going to be the impossible dream. Daisy'd always had too much energy to just sit on a sofa and nest like a bird. He was going to have to ease off a little.

He went and found Robert hanging out in the kitchen. "Evening."

Robert nodded. "How is everything in town?"

"Slowly getting put back together." He glanced back toward the garden room. "How long has Cosette been here?"

"Thirty minutes." He shrugged. "I think they're planning the nursery."

With a hat with a huge feather on it straight out of Cosette's eccentric closet? "I don't think that's what the girls have up their sleeves."

Robert poured him a whiskey. "Well, then, it's probably nothing we need to be involved in."

"That's it? You're going to cave that easily?" John was dying to know what the ladies were up to. He had a feeling his wife-to-be was getting into something more exciting than she should be for a woman who was supposed to be on strict bed rest. "Cheers," he said, lifting his glass to Robert. "I'm going to head back and check on them for a second."

"You do that. I'll be here." Robert stared moodily at a map of the town, but John decided he'd worry about that later. Back in the garden room, the ladies gave him a quick glance and went back to their flowchart, which appeared to be filling out nicely.

He had an uneasy feeling about what was going on here.

"Daisy, babe, is there something I can help you ladies with?"

"I don't think so, darling. Unless you want to become an apprentice to Monsieur Unmatchmaker, in which case we would have a lot to do together! Wouldn't that be fun?"

He hesitated, caught by Daisy's bright smile. God, he loved it when she smiled like that. "I'm sorry, sweetheart. Become a what kind of apprentice?"

"I'm working with Cosette now."

He sank into a chair. "You're going to become a matchmaker?"

"Yes, I am." She smiled so proudly he felt himself get hard, which caught him by surprise. It was Daisy, everything about her, that made his heart fire up in his chest and burn like red-hot coals. He adored her, he loved her and he had absolutely zero desire to become Monsieur Unmatchmaker the Second, learning the ropes of BC from Phillipe. And then one day ending up chanting and practicing yoga with strings of beads hanging from every doorway and incense permeating his domicile.

"Don't worry. I can do this and rest, too," Daisy told him. "Cosette and I think you're the perfect man to become Phillipe's apprentice."

He swallowed hard. Stared at that bright smile. Told himself that sometimes a man just did what he had to do to win the fair damsel.

"I'm really better with rodeo. Stuff like that," he said. "I'm a traveling man. I don't think I know much about marriages. Or un-marriages. I've got enough trouble trying to figure out how to get my own bride to the altar."

"It's just a different kind of race." Cosette smiled at him. "You see what I mean?"

He held his breath, not wanting Daisy's smile to disappear. They were hardly asking him to sit in the desert and pray he didn't get nailed by enemy sniper fire. "Not really, but I guess I could give it a shot. I mean, what the hell, right?"

Daisy beamed. "We'll make a great team."

He loved the sound of that. "Sure. Of course we will."

"So I'll tell Phillipe it's all set." Cosette rose. "In the meantime, you work on those matches, Daisy. It'll be your first test. I just know you're going to do wonderfully!"

Daisy's smile could have lit the sun. "Thanks, Cosette. It means a lot to me."

He got it suddenly: this was the pinnacle of Daisy's dreams. Far from being the town bad girl, she'd be the woman to whom Cosette passed the mythical magic wand.

Damn, it was a lot to live up to. He was proud of her, and scared as hell for himself.

He knew nothing, and wanted to know nothing, about what an Unmatchmaker did. All he wanted was to be a different kind of family from the one he'd grown up in, set in reality and grounded in practicality, in one place, one home, or at least only moving when they wanted to, not when the rodeo circuit moved on. Not when the military said it was time to move.

"I'll walk Cosette to the door, doll face."

"Thank you. Good night, Cosette."

Cosette flopped a hand Daisy's way. "I'll be back tomorrow to check your progress."

"Cosette," he said, his voice low as they walked to the front door, "I'm not sure about this."

"You'll be fine. Phillipe specifically mentioned you by name."

"Me? Why me?" John couldn't have been more astounded. "I don't even know what he does."

Cosette patted his shoulder as she went out the door. "Did you find what you were looking for tonight?"

"You mean when I went to the cave? No, I didn't. I'm not sure what I'm looking for. You keep hinting that that's where I'll find answers, but I don't think so somehow."

"Where do you think the answers are?" She gazed up at him curiously.

He stared down at the pink-frosted-haired woman watching him patiently. Like a benevolent grandmother but with a spicy and unpredictable twist. "All I know is that I'm in love with Daisy, I have been forever, she's having my children and I want to marry her. You're supposed to be the keeper of the magic flame on that topic."

"I'm teaching everything I know to Daisy. Much good may an old matchmaker's wand do her." Cosette sighed, downcast.

This wasn't good. John and Daisy needed a matchmaker with spark. Wasn't that why they were going through the charade of Daisy becoming a matchmaker's apprentice, and he apparently now would become an unmatchmaker's apprentice? To put the mystical spark back into Cosette, make her believe in herself again?

Once a long time ago, he'd taken a helluva fall from a bull. His head had hurt for ages, and he'd felt as if his brain wanted to come unglued from his cranium. The doctor had said he had a concussion, but it felt more like a devil's rock band playing in his skull. Time had been the healer, but time couldn't be rushed. Worse, he'd lost his faith in his skills, and the confidence that a man needed to face the depth of his worst fears and challenge himself.

After he'd recovered he'd gone into the military and learned quickly that a concussion was better than getting one's body parts blown off. He'd learned to hang on, stay focused, develop extra senses.

That was the place Cosette had to reach. Back in the saddle, back on her horse, dispensing fairy tales and magic with grandmotherly dynamism.

"I'm going to marry Daisy."

"I know you are." Cosette looked surprised. "I told you before, you don't need me for that."

"But Daisy wants a wedding that you've dredged up from the mysteries of your eccentric little BC-beating heart."

She pursed her lips, disgusted. "Is that any way to talk to a matchmaker?"

"I'm too desperate to mind the niceties. Cosette, you've got to fire up your skills one last time. Daisy needs you. *I* need you."

She looked doubtful. "It has to come from you." She tapped his chest, and John felt light-headed. Then stronger. Cosette gazed at him closely. "Everything you need is right here. It always was. Even when your parents took you from town to town, you were learning the things you needed to know. What did living on the road teach you?"

"To appreciate constancy. And variety. And people. Most of all, people. Everywhere we went, I met the most amazing people. I've met jugglers, puppeteers, ventriloquists, men who could fiddle like mad and women who could raise hell and a family at the same time."

"So, everything you see in Daisy."

"I hadn't thought of that, but yeah. She's amazing."

"So the answer will come to you. You can't rush the answer. Inspiration is the magic."

She floated out the door and John escorted her to her car. "Thanks for coming by. I know it means a lot to Daisy. And me."

"I know. It will all work out." She drove off, and John went to find Daisy.

Daisy waved him over. "See—my first victim is Carson. I've got just the woman for him."

John eyed the hat, which still contained several slips of paper. "Are those victim names on those papers?"

"Don't ask. Matchmaking secrets." Daisy pointed to her list again. "Once I get Carson married, I move on to Gabriel."

He cleared his throat. "As much as I'd like to see your gang settled, I thought you'd be busy planning a nursery? Picking out baby names?"

"We'll do that together. Where'd you go earlier today, anyway?"

There was no reason to tell. He didn't know exactly what he was looking for. Cosette had him worried, though. "I just checked on some things."

"You seem bothered about something."

"I'm not. I'm fine." He sat on the edge of the sofa,

picked up her hand. "That's not exactly true. I'm worried about you. I wish you'd rest."

"I have plenty of time to rest."

"But this project," he said, pointing to all the materials on the table.

"Is nothing for you to concern yourself with." She blew him a kiss. "If you don't stop worrying and get close enough for me to really kiss, that's all you're going to get, I'm afraid."

That was an invitation he wasn't about to pass up. He got as close to Daisy as he could, loving the feel of her lips against his as she smooched him a good one. "I love you, Daisy. I hope you know how much."

"I love you, too."

He smiled, then realized she wasn't smiling back. "What?"

"I'm just worried that you're going to be bored here after a while. That you'll miss the lure of the open road."

"What about you? I don't imagine your motorcycle stays parked forever."

She laughed. "Have you thought about how we're going to handle getting the children around?"

He looked at her. "Side cars?"

"No." She laughed again.

"Not their own motorcycles." The thought was pretty dazzling with its own worrying consequences. He could see the next generation of Daisy's gang growing up, his sons on their own tiny motorbikes, following their mother into town. John gulped. "I can't think about that."

"I meant a van," Daisy said. "We're going to need to think about buying a van."

"Oh." He relaxed a little. "I hadn't thought that far ahead."

"We could have Dad send the limo to get us home from the hospital after the babies are born, but—"

"I'll get a van." John looked at her. "Daisy, that's a bigger issue we need to discuss. Eventually, we have to move you out of the family compound."

"Dad owns property everywhere. We'll find something."

"No." He kissed her hand. "I mean, we'll need to move into something that *I* own."

"Would you want to own a home?"

"What do you mean?" She didn't reply, and it hit him what she was asking. "You think I'm going to pack the boys up and hit the road with them? Buy a family trailer and travel Mathison style?"

"It's not a wholly unappealing life," Daisy said.

"But not for you."

"Not for me," she said carefully. "I hope you understand."

"It's not for me, either." John hesitated. "Of course every young boy wants to rodeo, Daze."

"What if these don't?"

He shrugged. "They at least have to learn how to ride horses."

She nodded. "So we're getting our own place?"

"I think we have to."

"Is that a completely horrible thought?"

He shook his head. "Has it ever occurred to you that, of the two of us, you're much more likely to miss life on the road than I am?"

"I want you to be happy. Not stuck."

"With you, you mean." He gazed at her. "Daisy, I don't feel stuck at all. Do you?"

"Stuck? My parents were sort of stuck with each other.

Strangely, I don't feel stuck. I feel like I should have swum faster in that second race and beaten Suz Hawthorne. I could have, you know."

He perked up. "Yeah. You could have. And I was a helluva prize."

"I just didn't see that like I should have."

"It's okay." He touched the Saint Michael medallion at his neck. Suddenly, he felt a sense of destiny wash over him. "Everything always works out for the best."

Even in a small town with its own mystical secrets.

Chapter Thirteen

The first chance he could get to sneak off from Daisy's watchful gaze, John headed back to the cave. He'd missed something there, he was sure of that. And Cosette's hints weren't making him feel any better about it.

His fiancée was being altogether too easygoing, even going so far as to claim she didn't mind moving out of the enormous Donovan compound. It seemed the only thing John had to do was find them their own home, and buy a van, and life would be good for him and Daisy and their children—once they convinced Cosette that she still had her hot streak. Which wasn't proving simple. But the answer supposedly was here, in this secret cavern.

He glanced around, amazed by the shiny, sparkling crystals in the walls, and the beautiful iron sconces to hold candles. There was rough seating, and even a table in the center, where Jane and Cosette had once shown him some of the BC secrets.

Jane appeared like a ghost, almost as soon as he thought about her. "Why are you here again? I thought when I rescued you here the other night, we agreed you wouldn't come down here again alone."

Her mouth turned down. "Young man, I've been coming to this cave longer than you've been alive. I only agreed to that silly proposition of yours to make you relax. You've been quite tense lately. New fatherhood appears to be taking its toll."

"Not new fatherhood." He pondered that for a moment. "I can't get my girl to the altar. That's got me tense."

"It'll work out. I have faith in you." Jane beetled off to the table. "I might ask why *you're* here."

"I don't know why." He looked around. "Something keeps drawing me here. But it's just a cave, isn't it? And I suppose you three held your secret meetings here, you and Cosette and the sheriff, and created some kind of BC lore to keep the locals all stirred up."

Jane laughed. "Maybe. Maybe not."

Sometimes he wondered if this whole BC thing was just an elaborate gag to keep everybody in line. He wouldn't put it past the sheriff and these two ladies, and even Phillipe, to pull the town pillars routine just to keep matters serene. To keep the town in its time warp of harmony and fund-raising efforts, which the Bridesmaids Creek swim and the Best Man's Fork were: elaborate fund-raising efforts.

He sat on a rock carved out to make a nice chair, and watched Jane messing around in the box she'd pulled from the center of the table. Jane didn't look like she was in the grip of trying to orchestrate a huge ruse on the town. Her face was set in serious lines, her movements efficient. He watched her more closely, the way he'd once watched for enemy combatants.

Whatever was in that box had her complete attention.

"The town would go broke without the Bridesmaids Creek swim and the Best Man's Fork run, wouldn't it?" he asked, suddenly struck by intuition.

"Most assuredly. Haven't you noticed how small towns are dying off in this economy? And if not the economy, then time marches on. Large land parcels get eaten up by big conglomerates. We barely dodged Robert's plans for this town. But we managed to pull the pin out of his grenade."

This grabbed his curiosity. "How did you manage that?"

Jane smiled. "Daisy, of course. We always knew she was the key to our success. You have to understand Daisy is a daddy's girl. All Robert needed was to understand how much it would mean to his daughter to have the right kind of man in her life. That man was you. And everything changed."

John wondered if he'd ever heard more malarkey in his life. "You didn't know I'd be in the picture."

"That's right. But when you came into the picture, and you were crazy about Daisy, we saw that with a little time, everything would work out for our wonderful, quaint town."

"There was no way to know that she would ever agree to marry me."

"Cosette said you were the dark horse to bet on." Jane extracted a small ledger from inside the box. She leafed through some pages. "Yes. Exactly three years ago, Cosette wrote that the man who would rescue Bridesmaids Creek had arrived."

John came to look at the ledger, peering over her shoulder. "You're not making this up. It's right there," he said, eyeing Cosette's small, neat handwriting.

"Indeed I'm not!" She glared at him. "What in the world would make you think I'd fabricate a yarn like that?"

"I don't know. I thought you and Cosette and the sheriff, and even Phillipe, made everything up to keep people in line. Make them hop when you want them to hop."

Jane gasped. "Are you saying that you think we're fantastic storytellers? Just making this up as we go along?"

"Aren't you?"

She gave him a light whap with the ledger. "Ye of little faith. You're sitting in a secret cave that we've allowed no one else to learn of, and you have to ask?"

"You let me into the club because I'm the—"

"Yes, yes," Jane said impatiently, "you're the man who's going to save Bridesmaids Creek."

He liked the sound of that, especially if it meant he'd finally get Daisy to an altar, but something was off in the story. "Save it from what, exactly?"

Her eyes went wide. "Why, save it from itself, of course. Extinction."

"I thought Robert Donovan was the enemy, once upon a time."

"Does he act like an enemy now?"

"No. He'd like to help as much as anyone."

"All right, then. Now you know."

He wasn't sure what he knew. "I know that BC is a wonderful place to raise a family."

"Yes." She put the ledger back in its box and slid it into the table. "What else do you know, Einstein?"

He looked into her eyes. "That you're handing the wands over to Daisy and me. That we, and our friends you've recently dispatched to the altar, are the future."

"Now you're getting somewhere."

That was the key. The town had to stay young, in order to grow. Stay vibrant. Daisy and he would take over important roles, and their children would grow up steeped in the lore. "But how do I get her to finally say I do? She's all worried about Cosette getting her magic back. So worried she won't get married until Cosette feels like she's had a hand in running it."

"Do you expect Daisy not to want the magic for herself?" Jane looked at him steadily.

"No. She wants everything BC that every other bride has had."

"Can you blame her?"

He shook his head.

"Then my suggestion is you give her that very thing. And then you'll have Daisy Donovan, and everything will be all right."

Jane marched to the front of the cave. He followed, thinking to walk her to her vehicle, but she was nowhere to be seen. She'd just vanished, like some kind of spirit.

A delicate spirit with plenty of sass.

He thought for a moment, then walked back inside the cave and pulled out the ledger to look at it for himself.

It is early morning here in Bridesmaids Creek. There isn't much but dusty, barren fields. We rode here by wagon, and my family back home said they can't see why we'd choose this place to settle.
—Eliza Chatham

John flipped to the front of the ledger to look at the hand-drawn family tree. Eliza Chatham's name was at the top, the first resident of Bridesmaids Creek, and Jane's great-great-great-grandmother. John saw that there had been a Hiram Chatham, but whatever had happened to him had been rubbed out. Or had faded. Hiram wasn't on the same line with Eliza; she was accorded the top spot. Beside her name was written Founder of Bridesmaids Creek.

John flipped through some deeds that had been filed, all in Eliza's name. There were pages and pages of notations, each filled out in neat handwriting. He took the ledger over to the light to settle in for a good read. Then the ledger shut tight, snapping closed with a click. He tried to open it again, but it was sealed, somehow stuck fast.

He went back to the table, to the seat where Jane had been sitting, taking the closed ledger with him. It stayed clam-like and stubborn, and though John would have once thought that was impossible, now he knew that Bridesmaids Creek simply wasn't ready to give up all its secrets to an outsider.

Not yet. He wasn't one of them, even if he'd been handpicked to become an unmatchmaker, whatever that was. A newer version of dusty, history-loving Phillipe.

Maybe he wasn't cut out for this type of steadfast responsibility. Taking on this role would mean he'd be forever tied to one place, a keeper of a town flame.

The worry passed as fast as it had come, extinguished by the sudden vision of Daisy and his future children that popped into his head. He smiled, loving the picture. Maybe Daisy was right: maybe he hadn't seen himself spending his life exactly tied to one location, one way of life.

But he could see himself bound to Daisy, and the binding would feel wonderful every day of his life.

First he had to get the magic to accept him. Allow him to take Phillipe's place.

"No doubt the only way to do that is to marry Daisy, since this is a wedding-happy town."

The ledger stayed locked in his hands, resisting him. John realized he'd been expecting it to fall open, once he uttered the magic verbal key. There was something else he was missing, but whatever that was, it seemed determined to elude him.

Daisy was eluding him, too.

He put the ledger securely back into its hiding place and went to find the most beautiful, motorcycle-riding mother of his children a man could ever hope to have.

And he did hope to have her. Soon.

If there was something magic about Bridesmaids Creek, it appeared that John wasn't going to experience it. He spent the next two months assisting the town with rebuilding the jail, and helping put Cosette's shop—actually Daisy's gang's dating-service cigar-bar thing—back together, and still John didn't have the epiphany he knew he needed. Daisy was much bigger now, staying very still when he was around, though he knew that was largely for his benefit. When he wasn't with her, he could guess that she kept the mansion pretty active, like a beehive. She hadn't changed a bit from the woman he'd chased up to Montana, and that was one of the things he loved most about her.

She had her gang coming by, and Cosette, and sometimes the sheriff. Cosette had found time to knit baby booties, three pairs of blue ones that were so small they could probably only fit on a doll. Reality smacked John in the face as he realized his boys were going to start out very tiny, and he went a bit weak in the knees.

He went home to see Daisy, tell her that magic or no, it was time.

"Marry me," he said as she lay on the sofa.

She smiled at him. "I thought you'd never ask."

He stopped. "Just like that?"

"Of course just like that. If you've finally made up your mind—"

"Hey!" He went to sit next to her, looking at the burgeoning mound that was his fiancée's stomach. "My mind has been made up for years. *Years.*"

They sat together for a few minutes, and he stroked her hair. "How are you feeling?"

"The nurse came by today to check my contractions. Tomorrow I go on some kind of drip."

He sat straight up. "Is there a problem?"

"No. Not really. The drip will help the babies stay inside a little while longer. Longer is better."

He took that under advisement. "I guess you shouldn't have a whole lot of excitement."

She giggled. "What did you have in mind? Dad and Barclay are out looking over a property, and I could—"

Her small hand stroked dangerously close, an obvious invitation to please him. John picked up her hand, kissed it. "I don't think I can concentrate."

"I bet I could get you to concentrate," she teased.

He felt like a thousand wires were short-circuiting his brain. "Daisy, I could be a father any day now. You and I could be parents. Literally any second."

"Does that scare you?"

"Hell, yes!" He thought about that for a second. "And no. But mostly yes. There's so much to do!"

"And speaking of doing things, you'll never guess what I've got scheduled for next week." Daisy looked proud of herself. "You are looking at a woman who has the first phase of matchmaking apprenticeship well in hand." She took a deep breath. "I've set up a Bridesmaids Creek swim for next week!"

"Wait a minute, Daze," John began, then reminded himself he needed to be supportive. This was a big step for her. Besides which, their marriage would start off on a good footing if Daisy felt that she had made up for past transgressions in BC. "I mean, that's great, babe. Really awesome. It's not too much excitement for you? Considering the IV you're getting tomorrow?"

"Well, obviously I didn't know about the IV when I set this up. But it's going to be fabulous!" She pretty much glowed as she sat up, getting more excited as she relayed her big news. "I've got all *five* of my gang swimming!"

"Swimming for brides?" He wondered if any of Daisy's gang had truly given up the idea of catching her for themselves.

"I have wonderful local girls participating. There was more interest than I thought there'd be."

"You didn't expect your gang to be a draw for the ladies?"

She smiled at him. "I wasn't sure. They haven't done a whole lot of dating over the years."

He kissed her hand, enjoying the closeness. "But you think that now you're off the market, they may be more open to looking around for wives."

She nodded. "And the local beauties are definitely excited!"

Nothing could go wrong with this plan, could it? He had a funny feeling there was a hook in here somewhere, a hook with his name on it. "So, back to our own special vows, Daisy."

"Yes?" She smiled, and he took a deep breath.

"How about if I give Sam a shout to come over and do his thing?"

Her expression turned serious. "It's so sudden."

"Tomorrow you'll have an IV," he reminded her.

"That's true." She swallowed hard. "I don't have a veil. Or anything."

"We could have a more elaborate wedding ceremony in the summer."

"True." She carefully considered that, nodding. "All right. See if Sam can come over."

Her face caught his attention, stopping him in mid-dial. "You don't want to do this, do you?"

"No, it's fine." Daisy nodded. "I'm ready, I really am."

She didn't sound ready. In fact, she might have sounded reluctant.

Of course it was no woman's idea of a big day. But he had to get her to say *I do*, before his babies were born.

He'd fix everything else later.

Chapter Fourteen

Daisy and John were married the day before the big race was set to happen. John could tell his bride was nervous about the huge event she'd organized—more nervous than getting married, more nervous than the nurse coming to give her the new medication.

But they were married now, thanks to Sam, with Barclay as a witness, and Robert giving his daughter away. John felt he was the luckiest man in the world.

"Thank you," he told Daisy, because that was the first thing that popped out of his mouth, and because it was truly how he felt now that she was his bride. *Grateful* was the first word that came to mind, as well as *relieved*.

She smiled. "Thank you?"

"Yes, thank you very much, Mrs. Mathison, for becoming my wife and making me the happiest man on the planet."

"I still say you could have done better," Sam said woefully to Daisy, "like me."

They all laughed because the last person to ever say *I do* would be Sam Barr. Sam was many things but a marrying man wasn't one of them.

"Welcome to the family, son," Robert said, shaking John's hand. "For a wedding gift, I hope you'll accept half ownership of this house, and an office building in Australia."

John coughed, finding himself suddenly out of breath.

"Thank you, Daddy," Daisy said, hugging her father from her perch on the sofa.

John couldn't believe what he was hearing. "Hang on a second, Daze, babe," he began, but Sam grabbed his arm, steering him toward the punch bowl Barclay had set up in the den.

"Careful, buddy," Sam said, his voice low. "I know you've been caught off guard, but you'll want to take a few deep breaths in order to start your married life off on the right foot."

John felt as if all the air was being sucked out of him. "I don't want half this house, or a building in Australia!"

"Easy, hoss." Sam pulled out a flask and dumped a bit of extra party fun into the glass of punch he handed to John. "It's not about what you want, it's about what Daisy expects and what she knows is to be hers. Don't get in the middle of family wrangling, is my advice. You're family now, but Daisy and Ty are Robert's flesh and blood. He's going to do for them what he wants to, and you'll sound ungrateful if you try to back out now. It's Daisy's share, if you see what I'm saying."

"I can take care of my own wife!"

"I know you can," Sam soothed. "But you knew what

you were marrying into, buddy. This isn't a woman who grew up in a trailer following the rodeo circuit."

John tried to follow Sam's rationale through the crazy, panicked haze enveloping him. "I don't want any of that stuff."

"You might not, but she will. Take my advice, zip your lips, dude. Smile and say thank-you."

"He's going to think I married his daughter for money! He all but accused me of it in the beginning!"

"Words spoken in haste continue to live on," Sam said sternly. "Listen to your pastoral counsel, because it's all you've got at the moment."

"Helluva pastor you are," John grumbled. He swigged some more punch, delighted to see Cosette and Jane rush into the room for the small wedding party they'd planned for after the vows. They handed Daisy gifts and hugged her, and made a big deal out of her, as if she truly was the revered daughter of the town she'd always wanted to be.

He felt a warm glow start inside him. It was all going to work out. The Bridesmaids Creek charm had been wrong: he had found a bride, and he had married her in Bridesmaids Creek, and it was great.

Phillipe and Sheriff McAdams came in, followed by Daisy's gang. John didn't think he'd ever get past calling them *the meatheads* in his own mind. They greeted him, disappointment etched pretty deeply in their faces.

Still, they were trying to man up. John nodded at them. "Thanks for the congratulations. I know I'm a lucky guy."

"The best girl in Bridesmaids Creek," Carson said, "and you got her."

"I know," John said, "I realize how fortunate I am."

"Some might say it was just luck," Red said.

John laughed. "I don't think so."

"Could have been." Gabriel shrugged. "Not that we're not happy for you."

But they weren't jumping up and down like excited Christmas elves. "It's all right. I get it. You guys have known her all her life. She's special. Trust me, I'll take great care of Daisy."

In fact he couldn't wait to do just that. Sometimes it was hard to believe that she was having his sons—three sons!—and now she was actually his.

"It'll never stick," Dig said.

John's happy thoughts did a nosedive. "It's going to stick. Let me get you guys a beer. You're awfully hot under the collars."

Their beefy lunkheads looked like they might be about to start smoking. John realized the whole room was staring at him and the gang, listening intently.

"Barclay," John said, "I think these guys may need a beer. Or six," he said under his breath. "Maybe with a sleeping potion in it."

Barclay went to retrieve the beer, and John went back to join the gang. It was time to make nice.

Daisy deserved this, at least.

"So we hear you're now the owner of half this place," Carson said, glancing around.

"And commercial real estate in Australia," Red said.

John wanted terribly to refute that. It sounded awful, the way they'd said it, as if he was some kind of gold-digging cowboy. And that was the way they meant it. He hadn't won Daisy in a Bridesmaids Creek swim, the way things were done here, and yet he'd fallen into a fortune.

"Sitting in pretty tall cotton, I'd say, for a Navy SEAL who just works a farm," Gabriel said.

"I'm not a part owner—" John began.

"Yes, that was very generous of Robert," Sam inserted smoothly, coming to join them. "Completely unexpected gesture, but Robert has shown his generosity to the town quite a bit lately."

There was no arguing with that. Daisy's gang stood around for a moment like floor ornaments, and John decided it was now time to make his escape. "My bride—"

"Thing is," Dig said, "it's a shame the best girl in the town didn't get what she deserved."

"Ah, well," Clint said. "We'll all be in our own races tomorrow. Daisy's brought in some great gals for us, though she won't tell us who. It's going to be a total adventure."

John wondered if one could poke a guest in the nose at their own wedding party. Several noses, in fact, distinctly needed a poking.

"I never did quite understand how a Navy SEAL could come up with a leg cramp." Carson's face wore an expression of confusion. "Isn't that what SEALs do? Swim? Stay in shape?"

"Swim, as they say, like a SEAL?" Red gibed, turning up the torture on John a notch.

"Listen—" John began.

"He swims fine, fellows," Sam said. "Lay off the guy, huh? It's his big night. He'll never get married again."

"No, but he'll probably get divorced," Red said, sounding happy about the possibility. "You'll see."

"That's silly. I don't believe in juju and the tales from the crypt you people spin around here," John said, overriding Sam, who was trying to shush him.

"Tales from the crypt might be a bit harsh," Sam said. "Come on, buddy, let's get you some wedding cake."

"We don't have any wedding cake." John stopped, catching sight of Daisy. She was staring at him, her eyes huge. Belatedly he realized she'd overheard everything—as had everyone else in the room. Suz and Mackenzie Hawthorne had come in while he wasn't paying attention, along with their husbands Cisco and Justin. Jade and Ty Spurlock had arrived, and Jade's mother, Betty. Everyone had witnessed his unfortunate remark. It also came to him that Daisy had no veil, and no bouquet. She'd simply worn a white caftan as her wedding gown.

He gulped. At least he'd gotten her a ring, although her hands were so swollen she'd put the ring on her pinky and said it would be lovely when it fit, after she had the babies and maybe a few months after that.

Maybe the meatheads were right. A horrible gnawing sensation settled into his stomach. What if Daisy woke up one day and realized their relationship was totally uneven? That he'd never be able to provide her with real estate around the world, that he would never be wealthy like her father. He could certainly afford a house in town, and it wouldn't be one on wheels, but it would definitely require a thirty-year mortgage.

"Don't let them get to you!" Sam said. "Come on, let's get you a congratulatory cigar. Outside. Where we can get some good, bracing fresh air into you."

"I don't want a cigar." He watched Daisy as she chatted with their friends, enjoying her big moment.

But it wasn't the big moment of which she'd dreamed.

"I can hear you thinking, buddy. You need to let it all go." Sam dragged him to a corner, poured a little more whiskey into his glass. "Listen, you and Daisy share equal blame here. She avoided you winning her."

Perhaps that was true, and Sam had his back for saying so, but it didn't matter. "I just don't want Daisy to have any regrets."

"She'll regret you standing around looking like you've lost your best friend if you don't pull up. Get a grip on yourself, man! Don't let those dumb asses rile you. They're trying to. Don't let them win."

He was already riled. In fact, he was worried.

"So it's a swim tomorrow, is it?" John asked Daisy's ex-gang.

"It is," Clint said. "Lots of ladies to be won, I hear."

"Not that you'd know what to do with one if you caught her," John said, "but I think I'll join you fellows."

"Join us?" Gabriel asked, and the five men perked up, staring at him with sudden interest.

"Buddy, slow down a bit, think what you're doing here," Sam said, low, the way they used to talk to each other in dangerous locations. Low and encouraging—and warning.

"Yeah. I think I'll join you." John drew himself up. "I think I'll win Daisy all over again."

"No!" Daisy exclaimed, her voice in a chorus with Sheriff McAdams's, Cosette's and Jane's.

"No?" John looked at them. "I want to win my wife, fair and square."

"No, John—" Daisy began, but Dig grabbed his hand, shaking it.

"We'll save a spot for you," Dig said. "Right up at the starting splash."

"Yeah. See if you can live down that leg cramp problem, okay?" Red asked.

"The only cramping there'll be tomorrow is a cramp in your miniscule brains when you realize that I've outswum you by a mile."

No one in the room was smiling, except for Daisy's gang, and they looked like their typical jack-o'-lantern-headed selves.

"Can I see you outside a moment, buddy?" Sam dragged him away and gestured him to follow him several yards from the house, where no one could overhear. "Dude, what the hell are you doing?"

"Showing my wife that we were always meant to be together. Nothing's ever going to separate us. There's no BC charm that I wouldn't buy into to win Daisy. No weird BC backfire's going to...backfire on us."

"That's what you don't get. It's a trap, John."

"A trap?"

"Yes! And you walked right into it." Sam looked despondent. "You dummy. Why do you always leap before you look?"

"Me?" John laughed. "I think that's your calling card, Sam. Leaping before looking."

"No, I'm a strategist and you're a grab-the-ring guy." Sam sighed. "You realize that if you don't win tomorrow, you make everything worse?"

"How?"

"Because everyone in this town knows that the races are all-important. Daisy isn't supposed to get another one. Three's the charm."

"Says who?" John growled.

"Says the legend."

Sam seemed pretty adamant. A little more worry crept into John. "I've lived all across the USA and there was never any town as lost in its mind games as this one. You have to admit that, Sam."

"It's too late to back out and claim you don't believe."

"Why? What will happen if I lose?"

Sam took a deep breath. "You lose Daisy. Maybe not tomorrow, maybe not the next day, but eventually."

"Bull." He loved Daisy. They were meant to be together. No goofy town crystal ball wackiness was going to change that.

"It will happen, because she'll know," Sam warned. "It's not juju, it's who Daisy is. She's a daughter of Bridesmaids Creek. And she *believes*. Think, John, all her life she's seen the magic work. She believes it, wants it desperately for herself. But she's not going to get it. And you weren't even supposed to have a marriage in BC, Cosette said so. You blew it. Only somehow, because you're crazy, I guess, you figured out a way to make it happen, anyway."

"No, I didn't," John said slowly, realization dawning on him. "*You* did."

Sam was silently watching him. A chill crept over John's scalp. The thing about Sam that very few people knew was that, beneath the banter, beneath the fun and games, Sam was a helluva thinker. He was Mensa-gifted, with a brain that was always working, two gears ahead of the next guy. They'd relied on him for those gears—Ty and Cisco and John were probably alive because of Sam and his ways.

"You got yourself certified to perform weddings because you knew something would keep getting in the way for Daisy and me here in Bridesmaids Creek. So you decided to perform it outside of BC, with an online class or something that would vest you with the power. You went around BC, in effect. You countermanded the charm," John said.

"I figured it might be something like getting married at sea. You know how if you're so many miles out, you're bound by different laws than when you're on solid ground?" Sam nodded with satisfaction. "That's what I did. I decided to perform your wedding with powers vested in me that were not of the solid ground of BC."

"That's a helluva thing to do for a friend."

"A fellow SEAL," Sam said. "You'd have done it for me. So don't go blowing it now. I've put a lot of effort into this plan. I don't need you lighting it on fire."

"I have to do the race." John knew this as sure as he knew his name was John Lopez Mathison. "The only way I'll ever really have Daisy's heart is to win it. The same way the other brides in this town were won." He thought about the cave and the ledger, knew how long and deep the traditions were here. "The charms are important, more important than I ever realized."

"All right, then. Now that you know that truth, that's half the battle." Sam snapped his fingers. "All you have to do now is march yourself inside, tell them you took leave of your senses, and that there's no way in hell you're going to horn in on the big day that Daisy planned and worked so hard on."

Easier said than done.

Chapter Fifteen

"What?" John stared at Sam. "I'm not going to do that!"

"You have no idea how hard Daisy has worked on her conversion. Her rebirth in this town," Sam said sternly. "Don't be selfish, dude."

"Selfish?" John was agog. "I'm trying to give her her big day!"

"*Tomorrow* is her big day. She planned it, she set it in motion. She's taking on the crown of Madame Matchmaker. This isn't about you. This is about *her*."

There was some twisted logic going on, and John wasn't sure what his buddy was trying to do to him. Taking a deep breath, he reminded himself that Sam always, always had another level in his game, sometimes just to watch people spin themselves into knots.

"I'm not going to be talked out of this," John said quietly.

"That's your pride talking. You only want to race because those five troublemakers razzed you about it. You're still embarrassed about that cramp. Let it go, is my advice."

He couldn't. He couldn't let Daisy go. Sure, he had her—they were married—but every woman deserved to have her heart won. Every man wanted to know that his woman's heart belonged to him totally until the end of time. And Daisy was a daughter of Bridesmaids Creek. The magic that flowed here—or even if it was just superstition—flowed in her, too.

He thought about the ledger sealing itself shut when he'd tried to read further. Despite Cosette and Jane letting him into the secrets of BC, BC itself hadn't yet accepted him as one of its own. He had to win Bridesmaids Creek's daughter's heart—Daisy's—if he ever truly wanted to belong in Bridesmaids Creek, so that Daisy would know he'd given every last inch of everything he had to win her.

That was how fairy tales worked.

"What is this, a secret SEAL gathering?" Cosette and Jane appeared in their midst. "If you're done saying your piece, Sam, I'll take a turn at fricasseeing him."

"I'm not sure anything I'm saying is getting through his thick skull."

"It is thicker than normal," Jane observed. "John, what are you thinking?" She held up a hand. "Never mind. I know what you're thinking. You're outrunning ghosts."

"It's not possible to outrun ghosts, Jane, if there were such a thing as ghosts." John regretted that statement the moment it came out of his mouth. Both the women gasped and Sam shook his head at him.

"I mean, I know there are ghosts and spirits and

things," he said, trying to dig himself out. "What I'm trying to say is that this isn't a ghost issue."

"Because you're not trying to outrun yours or anything." Cosette stood on tiptoe to peer into his eyes for a second, then settled back on her feet.

"Were you trying to look into my soul?" John demanded.

"I was checking to see if the secret sauce Sam's been pouring you is addling your brain," Cosette shot back.

"For someone who doesn't think they're affected by ghosts, you sure do seem antsy," Sam observed. "Good grief."

John sighed. "If you came out here to talk me out of competing tomorrow, you're wasting your time and might as well be back inside eating cake."

"You didn't buy any wedding cake," Jane observed. "Lucky for you, I brought a beauty. Betty Harper and Cosette helped me with it, and it's my finest masterpiece. In fact, Daisy told us to tell you to get a move on and help her cut it. She wants to stuff some cake into your face—er, your piehole."

"She's unhappy with me," John said.

"What do you think? You're horning in on her big day," Sam said, scoffing. "It's supposed to be about her, her big moment the only way she can have it. You're turning it into a day that's all about you."

"Nuts," John said. "When you say it like that, I actually hear the voice of reason. Lucky for you, I'm pretty deaf."

"So stubborn," Cosette whispered to Jane, loud enough for John to hear. "Listen, as head matchmaker in this one-stoplight town—"

"Two. I think we're getting another one," Jane said, "although one never knows how these rumors get started."

"As head matchmaker," Cosette continued, "I'm going to make an educated guess and tell you that you're only doing this because Robert's generous gift freaked you out."

"I don't want his money," John said. "Put your mind at ease on that. I'm well aware that he's doing everything for Daisy."

"You don't have to deserve it," Jane said, "or live up to Robert's success in any way."

"Not that you could," Sam said helpfully. "It makes me laugh just to imagine you living in this heap."

Daisy's home was hardly a heap. John wondered if his friends were deliberately trying to bounce on his nerves and get a rise out of him. "I'm not trying to prove myself to anyone. Except Daisy. Which is why I'm participating tomorrow, and nothing you can say will change my mind. But thanks for caring." He hugged the ladies, gave Sam a swat on the shoulder. "I'm off to help my bride cut the cake."

"Be careful," Sam called after him. "Daisy's got great aim."

She did at that. John grinned, and walked faster. If his bride wanted to feed him cake from her dainty fingertips, he couldn't get there soon enough.

And tomorrow, after he'd won her by all measurements that mattered in Bridesmaids Creek, she was going to experience the magic she'd always wanted.

He understood about needing to fit in. He really did.

"John," Daisy said that night when he crawled up next to her on a divan he aligned by her chaise, "I'm going to give you some sleeping pills tonight so you can't race tomorrow."

He laughed, wrapped his arms carefully around her.

She was big as a moose, and felt like it, too, but some-how, John always made her feel delicate, desirable. "Even sleeping pills wouldn't keep me from my goal, gorgeous."

She rolled to look at him, moving like a floundering hippopotamus. "I don't want you to do this."

He seemed to decide he was more interested in her lips than in what they were saying. The kisses he sud-denly stroked across her mouth made her brain scatter its thoughts.

"John!" She gave him a tiny push backward so she could gaze up into his eyes, even though all she really wanted was him kissing her. But this was important. "Don't let my gang goad you into this."

"I should have done it a long time ago." He picked up her hand, kissing it as if she was some kind of princess. He made her feel like a princess. "You deserve all the magic in the world, Daze."

Her breath caught. "You know I love you, don't you?"

"Yes, I do." He grinned. "How could you not love a rascal like me?"

"I do love you, and you don't have to win me. Or what-ever it is you think you're doing tomorrow."

"I'm winning you. There's no thinking about it." John gazed down at her with eyes that said he found her very sexy. "And, Mrs. Mathison, you're going to like being won."

Her breath caught again, and Daisy told herself to breathe, to tell John why him going on the creek swim was such a bad idea. He didn't understand the ways of BC.

But it was oh, so tempting. What woman didn't want to be won by a handsome, god-bodied hunk of a man? "The thing is, I'm already yours."

"That's bothering me a bit. I'm not sure I trust Sam's certificate of authenticity."

"What do you mean?"

"He says he got this online power of marriage thingy, but it's Sam we're talking about. Do we know for sure?"

Daisy hesitated. "That's a terrible thing to say about your brother. He wouldn't let us go around thinking we were legally married. I'm having children soon. He'll be a godfather." She looked at him, ran a hand over his strong chest. "Go back to kissing me. You need to get your mind off of crazy stuff."

"It's not crazy if we're talking about Sam."

"Okay, well, then, this need you have to justify your racing tomorrow…" She looked up at him, stroked his lip with her finger. "I don't care about that stupid leg cramp."

He caught her hands in his. "You don't think I can win, do you, buttercup?"

"I'm telling you that I don't care if you do."

"Oh, you care. This is Bridesmaids Creek, so you most definitely care. Besides which, women with fathers who pass out real estate in dream locations think highly of themselves. They want to be won." He kissed her nose. "In your case, you deserve to be wooed and won." He worked his way from the tip of her nose to her lips, giving her a kiss that made her heart race. "Besides which, beautiful, you can't tell me BC doesn't care about this. Jane and Cosette said that once word got out that the SEAL who cramped up before was having another shot at it, ticket sales went crazy."

Daisy sighed. Pulled back a little. "This is all about your ego."

"No, this is about my beautiful wife." He kissed her shoulder, and Daisy fought the urge to wriggle closer to his wonderfully roving mouth. "I want you, Daisy Donovan Mathison. I intend to have you forever."

He certainly didn't seem to notice that her belly was shaped like three basketballs were rolling around inside her. "It will all be nothing," she said airily. "I won't be there to see."

"You're not supposed to leave this bed, anyway. Unless I carry you out into the garden room." He kissed her again, stealing her breath.

"Oh, John, would you mind? Could you?"

He laughed. "Of course I can. You're light as a feather."

She was not light as a feather, unless the feather was glued to a two hundred pound weight. "You're trying to romance me into giving in. But I really don't want you to compete against my guys."

He carefully picked her up, carried her to the garden room she loved so much. "Their tiny little egos will still be fine after I spank them soundly. I have no idea what women you'd find to be the prizes, but I'm sure you found some real honeys."

Daisy looked out the window, marveling at each change in the fall-blooming landscape. "It's so beautiful. This is my favorite room in the house."

"I know. If you look out in the garden near that awesome statue of the naked lady—"

"John," Daisy said, laughing.

"Can you see it?"

She leaned forward, peering outside eagerly. "I don't see anything."

"That's right. Because there's nothing there. Yet." He grinned, and her heart did a funny little flip.

"Yet?"

"That's right." He pulled out a long white scroll with a gold bow wrapped around it, handing it to her with a flourish. "But there will be something in the garden very soon, if you accept my wedding gift."

"Do I unwrap this?" She could hardly wait to see what he was up to.

"Go. Just remember it's only a gift, it's not set in stone. It's something I'm hoping we can do together."

"I can't wait to see." She ripped off the bow and unwrapped the scroll. "Oh, John! A waterfall!"

He leaned close. "Obviously these are just some initial plans. Your father thought we might take out the statue out there, despite her lovely nakedness, and put the waterfall there." He grinned, pleased with his surprise. "You see I stayed within the keeping of the Bridesmaids Creek theme with the water element. And I thought we could christen the waterfall with some creek water for the effects only Bridesmaids Creek seems to have."

She laughed. "I love it. Thank you so much. It's a wonderful wedding gift."

He kissed her. "You're the wonderful wedding gift, Daisy. I waited a long time to have you, and it was definitely worth the wait."

"So you're okay with Dad's present?" She looked at him, trying to read his expression.

"At first I was startled. Any man would be," he said. "But then I realized I didn't care what came with the package, because all I wanted was the package, anyway." He kissed her shoulder again, just the way she longed for him to do.

She smiled. "I'm the happiest woman on the planet. I really believe I am."

"Good." He stood. "I have to carry you back into the other room now. I was under strict orders from your nurse to bring you in here, give you your gift and get you back to your command center."

"Oh." Her face fell a bit. She glanced back toward the beautiful garden. She'd missed getting to see this during the time she'd been bed bound. "Thank you, John. It means so much to me that you brought me out here."

"I know, babe." He scooped her up as if she was no heavier than a bag of marshmallows. "You like looking at that naked lady out there, don't lie."

She laughed. "That naked lady happens to be a lovely rendering of the goddess Diana."

"I'd rather have a lovely rendering of you in my garden, but then I'd never get any work done." He laid her carefully on the sofa bed again. "However, I get to have you in my bed every night, so that's even better."

She smiled up at him. "Me and three little babies very soon."

"Not too soon. Let's not be jumping the gun, little lady. Whew, one of us needs to bulk up a bit." He flexed the muscles in his arms, winking. "These big strong guns you see before you are going to get me to the finish line tomorrow way ahead of the other combatants."

"John," Daisy said, "sit down here a moment."

He sat next to her. "One day, babe, you're going to invite me to your bed for a whole other reason besides idle chitchat."

"This isn't idle chitchat." She tried not to think about how much she'd enjoyed the many times she'd been in a bed, or anywhere for that matter, with John. "This is absolutely serious. You can't race tomorrow."

"Don't you worry, beautiful." He leaned back against the sofa, his grin confident. "You're going to have your big day."

Daisy took a deep breath. "It already is my big day, because I set everything up. Not to underappreciate what you're trying to do for me—it's very sweet and romantic— but you really shouldn't. And saying that Sam probably didn't legally marry us is just you trying too hard to give me what you think I want. What I want I already have." She put a hand on her stomach. "I have you, and my babies. What else is there? That's magic enough for me, darling."

He put his hand over hers as it rested on her belly. "Once the babies are born, I want a wedding where you and I are married in front of our friends, your father gives you away, and my family rolls into town to throw birdseed at us."

Who would have ever thought John would be such a traditional guy? She loved him all the more for it. "Even if you win tomorrow—"

"*When* I win tomorrow."

"Nothing changes, John," she continued, desperate to make him see. "You and I are already married."

"Yeah, but Cisco raced for Suz after they were already married. You have to admit that was well-played. Did wonders for their marriage."

Suz and Cisco were two of the happiest people she knew. "But it's different this time. If you don't win, every- one will always question whether we were meant to be."

"I won't. I know we are."

She had to love a man who had so much confidence it seemed to rub off on her, too. Daisy reminded herself to keep to her mission, and not focus on his long, lean body. "John, as a matchmaker's apprentice, my reputa- tion as a matchmaker must be absolute."

"Meaning?"

She thought his eyelids were starting to drift lower

now that he'd gotten comfy on her bed. His hunky body had relaxed into languid, sexy lines that had her gulping a little. "Meaning that if you don't win, I'll look like a matchmaker who can't handle her own match. You saw what's happened to Cosette and Phillipe now that they've gotten divorced."

His eyes popped open. "The ol' magic wand emptied out?"

She nodded.

"Still swimming, Daze. The way I see it, when I win, your magic will be red-hot. Blazing. That wand of yours will be shooting sparks. The ladies and fellows will come from miles around to get a dose of your spellbound ways."

He wasn't listening. He wasn't going to change his mind. It was maddening, but it was also quite endearing. Daisy felt herself fall just a little bit more in love with her husband. "You could actually undo our magic if you don't win," she said, finally stating the real reason he absolutely couldn't race.

"No, I won't. Cisco didn't." He sat up. "In fact, Suz didn't even tell Cisco he shouldn't race for her."

"Because they were keeping their marriage a secret. From me. From everyone. Cisco had to race."

"Didn't matter, doll face. They're perfectly happy."

"Because Cisco won."

"And I'm going to win."

She looked at him, and he looked at her, and the seconds stretched by.

"You don't think I can."

She smiled. "We've had three chances. None of them really panned out."

"So? It's just a race. Just a fund-raiser."

"There's no such thing as 'just' anything in BC. Which you should know by now." Daisy took a deep breath. "The thing is, if you don't win, John, I'll never have any magic at all."

"Why? What does that mean?"

"It means that no one tempts BC's charms. I don't have more than three chances at the magic. No one gets a fourth, it just doesn't work that way."

"There you have it. No one gets a fourth, no one's ever tried. It'll be fine, because all that legend crap is just a bunch of hokum, anyway."

He didn't look as if he quite believed what he was saying. Daisy knew that John was plenty aware of the enchanted ways of Bridesmaids Creek; he was just being stubborn as an ornery old mule. "We don't do hokum in BC. It's all very well established, and the magic is recorded in a ledger somewhere. Cosette and Jane keep records of all these things. It's quite serious."

"I know," he grumbled. "I'm an outsider. I come from a family of people who don't believe in magic. I'm the most superstitious person in my family, and they think I'm a little weird about it. My mother does cowboy preaching. She never thinks about anything to do with enchantment." He took a deep breath. "The only thing my family believes in is hard work. It doesn't earn us much money, we don't own office buildings in faraway lands and we don't have a mansion. Our house rolls on wheels 365 days a year, even birthdays and Christmas. My brothers and I were all born in different towns. What I'm trying to say, Daze, is that I've got my reasons for competing tomorrow, and I'm comfortable with that."

Chapter Sixteen

"He's so pigheaded he's impossible," Daisy told her father the next day when he came in to visit. Her IV had been inserted, and she was lying here, trying to be still, when all she really wanted to do was hop out of bed and ride her motorcycle to the creek to see what was happening on the biggest day of her newly formed magic wand.

"I think you like that about John," Robert said with a grin. "He's quite won me over with his determination to pursue you."

"He doesn't need to pursue me. We're married." Daisy shook her head. "I'm surrounded by lovingly obtuse, romantic-to-their-core males who can't see the big picture for the trees!"

"It's not altogether a bad thing." Robert seemed quite tickled to be lumped in with his son-in-law. "You know, life seems awfully good from where I'm sitting. I've got a new son-in-law, a new daughter-in-law, a son I didn't know I had and a bunch of grandbabies. I say if the man wants to run or race or fly a kite, let him take a crack at it."

"If he doesn't win this time, it's going to be disastrous."

"Life's about chances," Robert said philosophically.

Why was she talking about this to her father? He of all people believed in rolling the dice, taking big risks. "Dad, John isn't like us. He's sensitive. He doesn't take things in stride."

"Some would say we've come a long way ourselves."

"Yes, but deep inside, I always knew I was going to be all right. We had to work harder to be together, so we'd appreciate it more. So when John got that leg cramp and came in last that day, it was actually the magic on our side. He can't go and mess it up now by losing again!"

"Who says he will?"

"Have you seen my gang lately? They're ripped like ridges on a mountain. This is their big moment, their chance at the brass ring. All the new guys to town are out of the game. Justin, John, Cisco and even Ty himself are matched up and married."

"Not Sam."

"Sam doesn't count. He won't race. The only time he ever even threatened to race was just to get his buddies goosed up to the starting line." Daisy laughed. "Sam isn't the marrying kind."

"It's a rare man who isn't."

Daisy looked at her father. "Of course there's you. You're not married."

He held up a hand. "Yes, but I have been, and I'm not looking to do it at my age. In fact, now that I've given this house to you and Ty, I think I'm going to move."

Daisy gasped. "Why?"

"Because you lovebirds need your own nest. Besides," Robert said, getting all excited, "I think I'll buy that ghost house."

"Dad! Not the abandoned Martin place! Those love-struck bank robbers lived there and ran cattle, but couldn't turn a profit. Why would you want to do that?" Daisy couldn't imagine anyplace she'd rather live less, and she sure didn't want her father out there. "It's been empty forever, Dad. It's going to have all kinds of rats and roaches and things. You'll stay here with us."

"Don't forget the ghosts. I'm really looking forward to those." Robert rubbed his hands gleefully. "Of course you know there's no such things as ghosts. Those bank robbers aren't still hanging around in paranormal form."

"Dad, there's no reason for you to leave."

"There can only be one king in a castle. This place belongs to your brother and you now. And your fami-lies." He looked pleased. "For an old man, I'd say I've done pretty well. I'm looking forward to a new project."

"If you're looking for a new project, start Betty Harper up in a business selling her Christmas cookies. They're works of art. Or get my guys out of the space where Co-sette and Phillipe belong. We don't need a cigar bar in this town." Daisy sat up a little. "That space belongs to Cosette and Phillipe, anyway."

"I don't know," Robert said. "The guys like that lo-cation pretty well. They claim they're getting all kinds of calls."

"For cigars, and hookers."

"Hookers?" Robert raised a brow. "That doesn't sound right."

"Well, how many men go to a cigar bar looking for a bride? None that I know of."

"You have a point. We certainly can't get that kind of reputation in BC."

"No, we can't. So there's two really important projects that could use your input," Daisy wheedled.

"All right. But I'm still buying the Martin place. I really like the location."

"Dad!" She couldn't bear to think of her father out there alone. "This house is big enough for all of us, even if Ty and Jade decided to move in with us."

"Nope. I've made up my mind. I love real estate, and the Martin place needs my attention."

"I don't like it. The babies need their grandfather." Family was so important. But today was clearly the day for the men in her life to be stubborn mules. "Will you at least go try to talk some sense into my husband?"

He shook his head. "My days of meddling are over. I leave that up to the younger crew. I'm going to be happy as a local real estate fixer-upper. Once that storm came through town, I realized I had a new mission. Putting this town back together," Robert said happily.

"Dad, if John doesn't win, I'm not sure what will happen."

"Yes, but that's what makes life interesting." Robert rose, kissed her on the forehead. "You worry too much, daughter. Let your fellow be your handsome prince on his holy grail if that's what he wants. You have to admire a man with that much getalong in his hindquarters. Wish I'd had it when I was married to your mother," he said, retreating from the room. She heard him and Barclay chatting up a storm in the kitchen—as much as Barclay chatted—which turned into a discussion of a noon libation and a good lunch for her father. Daisy shook her head. It didn't even sound like her father was going down to the race.

"And I'm here, like Sleeping Beauty, consigned to resting and waiting for my prince. Argh!" She lay back, putting a hand on her tummy. The boys were doing gymnastics inside her, and Daisy smiled.

These little guys were going to be just like their father: busy, strong and opinionated.

And no doubt daredevils who couldn't resist a challenge.

John loved a challenge. And just for once, she was the prize at the end of it.

She lay back, resting, her smile huge.

Yet so many things could go wrong.

She picked up her phone and dialed Cosette.

"We all tried to talk him out of it," Cosette said, when Daisy told her that she didn't need a big day, she didn't need anything. She just wanted John, and her babies. Nothing mattered to her but them. Of course her father and the townspeople and Bridesmaids Creek mattered to her, but for once in her life she had exactly what she'd always dreamed of—and her Prince Charming was off to the races.

"You have to do something, Cosette. Please!"

"Not me. I interfered last time, remember? Had him tied to a tree?" She giggled with delight. "Your gang of gentlemen loved that assignment, I can tell you!"

"You can't tie him this time, he'll be ready for tricks." Daisy thought quickly. "What if we waylay all five members of my gang?"

"I think John would suspect that you're trying to let

him win, honey," Cosette said gently. "You're just going to have to let this play out."

"Cosette, from a matchmaker's apprentice to a matchmaker, you know better than anyone that the art to matchmaking is making sure that things go a certain way. This time, I really need your help."

"Yes, but you're the matchmaker now," Cosette said with a happy sigh. "I've officially turned over my wand."

"I haven't even made a match yet."

"I have great faith in the five ladies you picked out for your gang. They'll be delighted. And I heard you sent the ladies to the salon and had them beautified and transformed for their big day, courtesy of a certain secret benefactor, who I happen to know is Daisy Donovan." Cosette giggled gleefully. "The girls were thrilled. I peeked in, and they looked smashing. The fellows are going to swim their hearts out."

"You appreciate that I caught myself in my own game?"

"Oh, yes. That's what makes it so delicious! That SEAL husband of yours is going to have real competition this time, once your gang gets a look at the lovely prizes they're swimming for!" Cosette's laugh was merry.

Daisy grimaced. "They won't be able to outswim John."

"You hope. Otherwise—"

"About that otherwise," Daisy said. "What exactly happens if a man is married, swims and doesn't win? Cisco won when he was married to Suz, so do we even have precedent in BC for this?"

"No, we don't, which makes it very exciting!"

"Not if you're the one who wants to keep your husband! You realize I can't get off this sofa. I won't know a thing about what's happening!"

"That's the way it should be, I think. You don't want to be there if John gets another, er, ah—"

"Don't even say it." Daisy wasn't sure what would happen if John lost. Maybe nothing.

Maybe everything.

"In the olden days they said the charm was what built this town," Cosette said. "There was magic in the water, in the very earth of Bridesmaids Creek. Of course, Jane's great-great-great-grandmother settled this town, as you know, and she was the one who knew the secrets. Discovered them, you might say."

"Or maybe Eliza Chatham was just a great story-teller," Daisy reasoned.

"I wouldn't bet on it. Rumor has it that Eliza wanted a match of her own, but it was years before one came along for her." Cosette let out a gentle sigh. "By the time her prince came along, Eliza had two gentlemen vying for her hand."

"What happened?" Daisy asked breathlessly.

"Well, they swam for her, of course."

"And she married the winner."

"Right there on the banks of Bridesmaids Creek. That was the deal. That was how they solved the problem of which man would win her hand."

"But didn't she like one man more than the other?"

"It was a different day and time, Daisy. Back then a woman just needed to be married by a certain age, or she was considered a liability to the family. Or odd. A leftover. And as you know, our town has never been full of men." Cosette giggled again. "Personally, I think the race goes back to the days of yore when men fought over a woman. We just have a more gentle way of going about it. Plus all that survival of the fittest stuff plays into it, too. Natural selection and all that. Obviously a woman wanted the strongest, most intelligent mate to father her children."

"I can't imagine not making up my own mind."

"Well, you didn't really," Cosette said. "If you think about it, you thought you wanted another man. John happened to be the fittest mate for you. And today, he's going to prove it once and for all!"

"I hope you're right." Daisy didn't want to think about what might happen if he didn't win.

"How are you feeling, anyway, my dear?"

"Like I'm full of babies."

"Which you are!" Cosette sounded delighted. "You lie there and rest, and I'll bring you some of my fresh gingerbread cake after the race!"

"Cosette, I expect you to text me every single event that transpires! Don't you dare leave me hanging without any news!"

"This is more fun than we've had in years in BC," Cosette said. "Don't you worry, Daisy. Your reputation as a matchmaker will be secure after today, I just know it! Ta-ta!"

Cosette rang off. Daisy put her phone away and leaned back. It wasn't about the matchmaking, it was about her marriage. Maybe there was no such thing as a charm. Maybe Bridesmaids Creek wasn't charmed at all.

She knew better.

All she'd ever wanted was to belong to Bridesmaids Creek. She'd wanted the magic that the other brides had known—it was impossible to miss their happiness and joy on the day each of them had been "won" by their suitor. More than that, even, she'd wanted to be a true daughter of Bridesmaids Creek, accepted and loved. The only reason she'd ever acted out, acted differently from the other girls, was that she'd always known she was an outsider.

After today, if John lost, she'd still be an outsider.

Maybe she wasn't meant to belong.

She hoped that wasn't the case. She had a lot of friends she wanted to make, a lot of good things she wanted to do for Bridesmaids Creek. It was her home. She loved it here.

Her heart was here, and now even more so with John and her babies.

Suz walked in the room, followed by her sister, Mackenzie.

"Hi!" Daisy said, surprised. She sat up. "Why aren't you at the big race?"

Suz put a platter of cookies on the table. Mackenzie smiled. "We already have our men," she said. "We thought we'd come and keep you company while you wait for yours to return."

Daisy's heart glowed inside her like a Christmas star. "I'm so glad you're here."

"I've been in the same position you're in now. Bet you're ready to get off that sofa."

"I am." Daisy looked up as Jade Harper and her mother, Betty, walked into the room.

"We come bearing gifts," Jade said, setting down a large hamper topped with a big blue bow.

Daisy felt tears start to swim in her eyes. "Thank you. Thank you all so much."

"We thought we'd have an impromptu baby shower while the men are amusing themselves being competitive," Betty said. "We haven't had a baby shower in a long time!"

"But, then," Suz said as Barclay came in carrying a large box full of white-and-silver wrapped gifts, "we realized we hadn't had a bachelorette shower for you yet, either. So we had the idea that we'd have a double shower!"

Barclay had retreated after putting the basket down, but now he returned with a silver platter with a pitcher of tea and several crystal glasses.

"This is wonderful," Daisy said. "This is... You're the best," she told them, looking around at her friends—and then it hit her.

They really were her friends.

At some point, Suz and Mackenzie, though they'd once deemed her too wild for their circle, had accepted her. Liked her, even. And so had Jade Harper, and her mother, Betty. Jane Chatham and Cosette, too—they were her friends.

She was no longer an outsider.

She truly was a daughter of Bridesmaids Creek. By the genuine smiles on their faces, Daisy knew that she would never, ever be on the outside again. No matter what happened today with the race, everything, absolutely everything, was going to be magical, from this day forward.

And that was the real gift.

The starting line seemed full of meatheads, or at least that was John's opinion. He had this—he had it in the bag. Today was his day, he was golden, and he was going to give Daisy the day she deserved, and all the magic that went along with it.

He could beat these guys. He was a SEAL, he was in top condition.

And he was in love. He could run all day.

Just thinking about Daisy and his boys made him want to run to New York and back. Montana, California, he could just keep going.

Only he didn't have to anymore. Home was right here, in Bridesmaids Creek, with Daisy.

He looked over at Dig, Carson, Clint, Red and Gabriel.

"You realize you're going down," Carson said.

"You just keep thinking that," John shot back.

"Might as well just stand right there and save your strength," Red said.

"Keep talking," John told Daisy's gang. "It's all over but the crying."

"Hope you drank your special anti-leg-cramp juice this morning," Dig said.

John laughed. "You fellows. I'm going to throw confetti at all your weddings after today."

"Today we're going to prove that Daisy made a mistake. She shouldn't have married you," Gabriel said. "Any of us would have been a better choice."

"That's okay, boys. I know I got the best girl in town. You just swim your little hearts out and try not to let the waves I send back on you blow you out of the creek." John felt pretty good about his chances. All the smack-talking felt great, too. He enjoyed the brotherhood and camaraderie of small-town rivalry.

And it was all for Daisy. He wouldn't have had it any other way. Spectators lined the banks of the creek, waving posters with the combatants' names on them, cheering occasionally. The Haunted H might be gone from these banks thanks to the storm, but they'd rebuild it here, bigger and better. Everyone loved coming to Bridesmaids Creek, for the community and the happy endings, and yes, the fairy tales. There was a lot of fairy tale in BC, and it charmed him just as much as anyone else.

To his astonishment, he spotted his mother, father and brothers on the banks, too, waving a banner with his name on it. John grinned. Oh, this had Daisy's fingerprints all over it. She was all about family, and it warmed his heart in the best way that she wanted to be a part of his family, too.

"On your mark!" Sheriff McAdams called. John took a deep breath. "Get set!"

The pistol fired, and John took off like a Navy SEAL on a mission. He could hear the guys next to him churning up the water, flailing away, but he never had a doubt that there would only be one winner today.

This race, this day, was for Daisy, the most beautiful bride a man could ever have.

He felt great, swimming along like a salmon in a hurry. A roar went up from the banks, but he didn't stop, he kept on going.

At the finish line, he touched, came to the surface with a huge gasp for air. Sam pulled him out of the water.

"Congrats, old son! You did it!" Sam told him, trying to hand him a towel.

"Damn right I did," John said, and took off running down the road.

Behind him he could hear the roars growing louder. He heard car engines and a general melee breaking out. But he kept going, until he reached Best Man's Fork. Up ahead he could see Sheriff McAdams in his truck, keeping an eye on the proceedings. Cosette and Jane were in the truck with him, and he thought he saw Jane videotaping him as he jogged down Best Man's Fork.

He ran the entire length of the race, if it had been a running race today, making sure everyone knew when they told this story over the years that this was the SEAL, this was the groom, who not only swam to win his bride, but ran to win her, too.

Daisy's gang had given up long ago, presumably taking the time to eye the lovely women Daisy'd had at the finish line that they hadn't won today. They would have had to beat him to win their special ladies, but they hadn't, so their stories would have to wait.

Today was all about Daisy.

He crossed the finish line, puffing for breath. The sheriff pulled up alongside him, with Sam in the back. Sam handed him a water bottle, which John grabbed gratefully.

"Remind you of the old days?" Sam asked. "Training until you dropped?"

"Not yet," John said, and took off jogging for home.

He had no intention of stopping until he ran right into Daisy Donovan Mathison's welcoming arms.

And that was his happy ending.

Chapter Seventeen

Daisy let out a yelp when her husband roared into the den where she was having a lovely tea and bridal/baby shower with the ladies. John looked wild, his hair askew, sweaty as all get-out—and he'd never looked better to her.

"Excuse me, ladies, I have to kiss my bride," John said, and Daisy flung her arms around his neck as he came to get a winner's smooch.

"That was something else," Jane said, following John in with Cosette and Sheriff McAdams on her heels. "I wish you'd seen this bowlegged cowboy run, Daisy. He sure can get a move on."

"Really?" Daisy grinned at her husband. "I thought it was a swim I organized for today."

"I swam, I ran, I lived up to any charm Bridesmaids Creek cares to throw at me," he bragged. "I'm all about the magic, beautiful."

"And now you're stuck with him," Sheriff Dennis said, and Suz handed everyone a glass of tea so they could toast the newlyweds.

"It was really special," Cosette said. "We have it all on video, so you can show your sons exactly what their father did for love."

Daisy beamed, feeling so much joy pour into her. She didn't think she'd ever been happier. "Thank you, John."

"It was nothing," he said, and everyone in the room laughed, because it was more than something.

It was everything.

"Wow, look at all these booties and teddy bears." John was amazed by all the wonderful gifts stacked around. He held up a teddy of a different sort, filmy and white and lacy. Daisy blushed a bit. "This isn't for my sons," John said.

Everyone laughed again, but Daisy saw a spark of something she remembered very well jump into her husband's eyes.

"It won't be too long before I fit into that," Daisy said. "Just a few months."

John laid the sexy teddy back down. "Clearly someone in this room wants me to have a heart attack. And I'm going to enjoy every second of it."

They dug into the cookies and tea, and sat around sharing stories and enjoying each other's company. John went to shower, and when he returned, his parents had arrived for the party.

Daisy held her breath, but John went right to his family, wrapping them in big hugs. Robert milled around, introducing himself.

Her big, sexy husband loved her enough to make sure she had her own magical day.

He plopped down next to her, leaning over to give her a smooch that curled her toes and left her breathless.

"So, Mrs. Mathison, you're certainly full of surprises."

"Yes. And I plan to keep on surprising you." She looked at him. "You had a few surprises yourself. What inspired you to run the Fork, too?"

"You, beautiful." He kissed her full on the lips. "And the sheer joy of beating your gang all over again. Setting up a record so big they'll never be able to touch it." He grinned. "And I outdid even my SEAL brothers."

"Yes, you did." She laughed. "You're part of BC history, now."

He sat up. "I am. I'm part of BC history now!"

She smiled. "I'm glad that makes you happy."

"You have *no* idea."

He had a funny little smile on his face, and Daisy wasn't sure what it meant—but the smile left in a hurry when she kissed him long and slow and sweet. Their guests applauded, and Daisy knew that, even if she'd never thought she'd have her big day, the magic had woven its spell for her just the way she'd always dreamed.

And it was absolutely, completely Bridesmaids Creek–perfect.

Of course the babies were in just as much of a hurry as their father had been, and John found himself the recipient of three bundles of joy a week later. He could hardly believe it, but he had three—three!—sons of his own to hold.

It was a miracle. In fact, it was magical.

"Daisy, look at their toes!" John couldn't believe anything could have toes so tiny. And their fingers were so small he couldn't believe they would ever hold a baseball, rope a steer, play a guitar or touch a woman.

But they'd grow.

He looked at his beautiful wife. "You're the most amazing woman on the planet. I swear I'm the luckiest guy around."

"You are." Daisy glowed at the praise. "I'm pretty lucky myself."

He couldn't stop staring at the babies. The nurses had to convince him to let them take them to the neonatal nursery, and finally they shooed him out of the OR so they could finish whatever it was they were doing to Daisy. Delivery by C-section was supposed to have been the best choice, considering they'd suddenly decided the babies needed to be born. There'd been a question of heartbeats and distress, and John had known a few moments of terror, but it had all worked out. Now he had three healthy boys. They'd stay in the hospital for a few weeks while their lungs became more developed, but even so, John thought his sons were perfect.

So was his wife. He followed the nurse down the hall to wait in the room where Daisy would be, pacing until they finally wheeled her in.

"I love you," he told her. "The best thing that ever happened in my life is you. Hands down."

A luminous smile brightened her face, though he could tell she was tired. "I hope you've picked out names."

"Names!" John straightened. "You're the matchmaker, you do the picking. But please do it quickly. I didn't realize we had no names for our boys!"

The nurse, overhearing all this, laughed. "You can take a few days if you need to."

"That's all right," Daisy said. "I was thinking John,

Cisco and Sam for first names. We could choose Robert, Justin and Tyson for second names. We want to include your father, as well," she continued, but John waved a hand.

"Why is Sam part of this?"

"Don't you know?" she asked curiously.

"Know what?"

"Sam helped Cosette set everything up for all you guys. Laid the traps, he called it. You, Cisco and Ty—"

"Were like lambs being led to their shepherd," Sam said, walking in, his arms full of teddy bears.

"Hey, buddy," John said, slapping his friend on the back. "You already brought us one bear. In Austin, remember?"

"What's an uncle without a bear?" Sam grinned. "Besides, these are monogrammed with each baby's name on them."

Squint lifted a brow. "We just chose names. How can they be monogrammed?"

"Cosette told me their names." Sam held up a cute brown bear with a blue T-shirt. "This one's named Sam. But I call him Handsome."

"Oh, brother." John shook his head. "Don't tell me. The other two are named Cisco and John."

"How'd you know?" Sam went to kiss Daisy's cheek. "I just stopped by to see the little cowboys. They've already roped the nurses like true wranglers."

Daisy took a bear from Sam. "I wish you weren't leaving, Sam."

"Leaving?" John perked up, his heart dropping a bit. "Leaving for what?"

"Hitting the road, buddy. My job here is done."

"You can't go. We haven't paid you back for what you did to us," John said. "I mean, for us."

"I'm going." Sam's grin went huge. "I'm not the marrying kind, like I've always said."

"I really wish you wouldn't, Sam," Daisy said. "But I understand, too. Everyone has to find their dream."

"I guess." John frowned. "But we're a team. The three of us stick together."

"I'll be around." Sam kissed Daisy on the cheek, thumped him on the back and went down the hall, whistling.

He looked at Daisy. "You knew he was leaving?"

She nodded. "He'll be back one day. Bridesmaids Creek doesn't leave anyone untouched."

"I hope so." John was a little dumbfounded that his friend had hung around just long enough to see his babies born. "It's not fair that he gets away without getting dragged to the altar."

Daisy laughed. "Yeah, like you were dragged."

"We're getting married again this summer. I hope you know that. With full regalia. Wedding dress, lots of guests, huge cake. The works. Just like we said we would." John considered that for a moment. "You know, I never asked Sam if he really is certified to perform weddings. You can't trust him, you know."

"Oh, you can trust him. You always have."

It was true. No one had your back like Sam. Now that he looked back over their time in Bridesmaids Creek, he realized Sam had been doing the same thing he had when they'd been serving: keeping everybody in line, moving forward, spirits light, eyes on the prize.

"He needs a wife," John grumbled. "It's the least we could do for him. Ask Ty and Cisco if they don't agree."

She took a long drink of water, lay back against the pillow. "So, did you know that my dad bought the Martin place?"

"The ghost house?" He shuddered. "I'd be a little superstitious about that."

"You're superstitious about everything." Daisy's eyes drooped. "Dad's got big plans for that place."

"Your father always has a big plan working."

"And he's put Betty Harper in business selling her frosted Christmas cookies through mail order. She and Jade are going to be growing as fast as she can bake and design."

"You know, I live in this town. I live with you. I should know something that's going on," John said.

"You've been busy. I think you slept for a week after the big races."

"I could do it again tomorrow," he bragged. "But I feel like Rip van Winkle. I woke up, and everything had changed."

"It's Dad. He says that now that he has all these grandchildren, he's got a lot to do."

He shook his head. "We'd better put him to work babysitting as soon as we can, before he decides to buy another town or something."

Daisy's eyes were starting to flutter closed. "I'm going to sleep now, my sexy husband."

He touched her skin, needing to connect with her. "When you wake up, beautiful, I'll still be your sexy husband. Just like the prince in the fairy tale. See how that works?"

Daisy rolled her eyes, her lips curved in a gentle smile, and the next thing he knew, a deep, sweet snoring came from his beautiful bride.

This was bliss. This was heaven. John sank down

into the chair next to her and held her hand for a moment. He was a father. She'd made him a dad. And he had three sons.

How great was that? For as long as he could remember, he'd wanted a home, a place that was solid, one hearth to call his own. And he had that and more now.

John pulled off his boots to ease the blisters he'd developed the day he'd run all over Bridesmaids Creek to win his bride, and realized Sam had left one last gift behind, pinned to one of the teddy bear's ears.

He reached for the small envelope and opened the note.

John, ol' son, when I first met you, I thought you were the most hammerheaded dunce I'd ever met. Then you saved my life with that squint eye of yours. I can still hear the shots you squeezed off, and how you hit those marks I'll never know. No one shoots like you do, that's for sure. I guess you're still shooting good, or you wouldn't have those three bundles of joy. That's the thing about you, John, you're steadfast, you hang in there until the end, after everyone else has quit and gone home. You're a friend, a good man and you'll be a helluva father. Be happy, stay sane and always remember home is where the heart is. It was the only thing you were missing. And now you've got it. Congratulations. Three little boys to follow your footsteps and learn from you, and become men like their dad. I call that a happy-as-hell ending. Sam

John closed his eyes. Shoved the note into his pocket. And picked up Daisy's hand again, placing it over his heart.

Sam was right: it was a happy-as-hell ending.

* * *

"So I never did figure out exactly what an unmatchmaker does," John said, a month later, after they'd brought the boys home from the hospital and began settling them into the castle where his princess lived. John was getting used to living in the Donovan mansion, though some days he felt as if he needed a compass and a treasure map just to find the kitchen.

"An unmatchmaker unmakes matches." Daisy looked at him as she finished diapering little John.

He sat down, popping the bottle into John's mouth right before he let out the squall of the century. "But there aren't any matches in BC that were unmade, except for Mackenzie's—"

"Which wasn't Cosette's fault."

"And Cosette's own match."

Daisy nodded. "I know. It's hard to feel like we've had a happy ending without Cosette and Phillipe being together. So much of that feels like it was my fault."

John didn't think so. "I ran for them, too, you know. I thought that if we could get the magic back in Cosette's wand, get her belief in herself back, she and Phillipe might find their way back together. Which would be good for Bridesmaids Creek."

Daisy went to lay her head against his shoulder. "You did your best. And everyone knows it. You're a huge part of BC because of it." She leaned up to kiss him. "And I love you for it."

Life didn't get better than a wife kissing you until you could feel your insides practically melting from love, desire, anticipation—everything that was Daisy.

He sneaked his hands into the waistband of her skirt, the promise of "later" revving his heart rate further.

"Daze, I'm going out to Phillipe's for a while. He wants me to help him look over an area of his yard for some chicken coops. He's decided he wants to raise his own organic chicken. Really going granola, is Phillipe."

"We'll all be eating farm-fresh eggs soon. Go ahead and go. Your family's coming over to dote on the babies for a bit."

"They've stayed in BC a little longer than I thought they would." John looked at Daisy. "Did you notice?"

"I did." She had a big smile on her face. "I think they want to talk to you about staying on here."

John raised a brow. "Staying on?"

She nodded, her eyes twinkling. "Putting down stakes in BC, is how they put it."

"My parents, who have never owned a house that didn't move, want to put down stakes." He was stunned. "I didn't see that coming."

"They really like it here. Your brothers, too. They want to help with the rebuilding of the Haunted H down on the creek, and I think Justin's been hiring them to do some stuff at the Hanging H, especially helping with the roof repairs."

"My brothers can do anything." When you lived on the road, you learned a lot of do-it-yourself handyman skills. "That's awesome. I'm glad to hear it."

"Are you?"

"Yeah. Thrilled, actually. It's great news."

Daisy wore a pleased expression. "There's another draw to BC for your family, apparently."

"Oh?" He could tell his bride was holding back the big news.

"Yes. They're a bit fascinated with the matchmaking lore in our small town."

He grinned. "Looking to settle down, are they?"

"It seems that the idea of families of their own appeals to Javier and Jackson. And your parents love the idea of settling where there's a lot of grandchildren."

"I can't believe it. Who would have ever thought all it would take to get my family off the road was a bunch of babies?"

Daisy laughed. "Our babies settled us down."

He loved her, that was all there was to it. She was so happy to call herself settled, to be a mother and a wife. "I love you."

"I know." She smiled. "And lucky for you, your entire family is staying here tonight to babysit."

He raised a brow. "Why is that lucky for me?"

She got up, came to slide her arms around his neck. "Because tonight we're going to have our honeymoon night, husband. I've got that lacy teddy you liked so much packed and ready to go."

His heart started beating real hard. "You're sure?"

"I'm sure, the doctor's sure. Everyone's sure."

He sucked in a breath, felt his whole body responding to her. "Daisy, you drive me wild, beautiful."

He kissed her, drinking in the moment. Daisy and he, well, it had been worth the wait. She'd tried real hard to outrun him, but somehow he'd always known that this woman was the only woman for him.

His heart always beat faster when she was around. Like right now, beating like crazy. Felt like a motorcycle in a fast lane, going hard to its destination. And the funny thing was how good it felt, as if everything in his life was exactly perfect now.

John Lopez "Squint" Mathison had made it home, for good.

* * *

Several hours later, John made it back to the underground cave. There was one thing he had to know, and this was where he'd find the answer.

The cave was completely deserted, although he wouldn't have been surprised to find Jane here. She appeared to be the keeper of the ledger, and Cosette was the keeper of the legend. Eventually, he'd figure out what his role in all this was to be, but for now, he wanted to know if the magic finally accepted him.

He approached the table, pulled the ledger out of its hiding place. It fell open easily, surprising him.

He sat down, turned a page, and started reading where he'd left off when the book had sealed itself before.

Somehow I knew when I first arrived here that this place was my new home. We were hot and dusty from travel on the wagon, but most of the people decided to push on. I felt my heart beating harder here, racing with excitement, the moment I stepped down from the wagon and my feet touched the soil.

    I decided to stay, and so did Thomas.

John looked up. There'd been no mention of a Thomas previously. He checked the tree in the front of the book quickly—no Thomas. He went back to Eliza's fine, spare handwriting.

We might not have made it past a few days if Hiram hadn't come to see what the newcomers to the area were doing. How he must have laughed at our efforts. Thomas being from New York was hardly versed in how to survive on a prairie, and though I had nursing skills and knowledge of vegetation and cooking, settling was daunting.

At first we were a bit unsure about this tall, dark-skinned man with the darkly electric eyes, but it was clear Hiram was educated and meant us no harm. Hiram said later that he'd only come to help us because I wore a pretty blue dress, unlike any blue he'd ever seen outside of the creek, which he later led us to so we could get fresh water.

I think secretly Thomas hoped I'd give up on my adventure and return home, once the Texas heat and estrangement from my family wore me down. I can only say that, for my part, every day I grew more excited about my new home. And Hiram's assistance made our settling go that much easier.

Soon we had a shelter built, a very small house, with a room partitioned for me and one for Thomas. He very much hoped I'd accept his suit, but without any family here, it didn't seem as important to me as it once had. Marriage was a lifetime commitment, and for the moment, I was committed to this new world that fascinated me.

To my surprise, once people passing through on their way to farther off destinations saw our small house and the land we were clearing, a few more decided to stay. Within six months, we had neighbors of a sort.

Thomas, however, had grown impatient. I realized he very much hoped to be back home for Christmas. I had no intention of leaving Texas. We were at an impasse—and then Hiram offered a suggestion, surprising me.

He challenged Thomas to a race, to win my hand.

Thomas did not accept that challenge outright, as he believed I would not be interested in the suit of a man from a tribe, an Indian whose way of life was so different from what the two of us had known.

But in my heart, I felt a strong, strange connection to Hiram—even though I wasn't sure his name was actually Hiram, or if that was just a name he gave us to sound civilized. He'd been tutored by some priests who had passed through their grounds over the years, and so he was quite comfortable with our language and our customs. If not for the fact that he was obviously a native, one would not have known by his manners and refinement.

He was tall and strong, and well built, his face honest with its dark eyes and the clear intelligence he'd shown. I knew he liked to laugh—while Thomas was of a more serious bent.

I accepted Hiram's offer. Reluctantly, Thomas did, as well.

They agreed to swim the creek for my hand. Some of our new neighbors came to watch. It was a close race, as Thomas was fit, but Hiram knew the waters better, and I believe swam with more purpose. To be honest, I think Thomas had begun to realize over time that I was not the bride he sought; I would never be happy in a refined drawing-room setting. Already I was eager to visit the village where the natives were and use my nursing skills to help, and learn from their style of preparing food. Thomas had no interest in the community, and I believe he didn't compete with the same fervor as he once might have.

I don't know that for a fact, of course. It's only a suspicion.

Secretly, I was terribly glad Hiram won that day. I have been, ever since. He's a good man, and he treats me well. His tribe let me know I was welcome. We settled not far from the creek, and it's so beautiful here that some nights I just sit and stare at the stars and wonder what my life would have been like if I hadn't come here.

As far as I am concerned, it's magic.

John stopped reading, surprised by the story and yet somehow not surprised. All the women in Bridesmaids Creek were strong and independent; the founder had certainly set the precedent for courage and steady determination. He leafed back to the tree, seeing that Eliza had several children, three girls, one boy.

Even back then, BC was destined to be a woman's town.

He read that she'd named Bridesmaids Creek and then Best Man's Fork, after she and Hiram were married. It seemed romantic, and besides, the creek was how she'd come to have a husband. John learned that back home Eliza had been in several weddings, and folks had teased her that she might be destined to "always be a bridesmaid and never a bride." But they'd been wrong.

The footpath of the Fork became a very special spot for her and her beloved husband. They walked it often, gazing up at the stars and listening to the crickets and cicadas.

"Hi," he heard suddenly, and John looked up to see Daisy standing in the cave entrance. She looked like an angel, and his heart skipped a beat.

"Hello, wife." Closing the ledger, he stood, walked straight to Daisy. "Fancy meeting you in this place."

"Cosette said I might find you here," Daisy said, her face a little awed as she glanced around. "This is amazing. How did you ever find it?"

John grinned. "The same way you did. Cosette and Jane."

"So this is where you were going the night the tornado hit. You were coming here to check on it."

John wrapped her in his arms. "Once the ladies and the sheriff admitted me to their secret club, I felt a duty to make sure it stayed safe."

Daisy looked up at him. "It's what you do best. Keep things safe."

He loved the sound of that. He loved her holding him in her arms. "You realize we're the new Madame Matchmaker and Monsieur Unmatchmaker? I don't think there's any way of getting away from it, now that we've been shown the secrets of Bridesmaids Creek."

Daisy tucked her head against his shoulder, close to his heart. "I think that's exactly what we were always meant to be. It just took us a while to figure it out." She looked up at him. "By the way, Cosette and Phillipe got back together. They're getting married next weekend, and they've invited Sam back to do the honors."

"That seems appropriate. Sam's going to figure out eventually that Bridesmaids Creek has no intention of letting him go. That's just not what our town does. Once you're here, you belong."

"And I'm so glad."

They walked to the cave entrance together, holding each other. This was heaven. He could have kept living everywhere and anywhere, but with Daisy and his children, he'd found home.

They looked up as a shower of stars fell from the sky. Daisy laughed with delight, and John held his matchmaking bride close. It was magical here, and Daisy was magical, and John Lopez "Squint" Mathison might have been superstitious as hell, as his friends always said, but he'd always believed in magic.

And in Bridesmaids Creek, love was the magic.

Which made for a happy ending, every time.

Epilogue

Sam found himself performing another wedding ceremony, this time for John and Daisy on a beautiful July day, when cicadas sang in the trees and crickets chirped at dusk by the creek. It was the perfect music to accompany Daisy on Robert's arm, as he walked her toward John, who stood waiting for his wife under a canopy of oak trees that had probably been around for the past two hundred years. Maybe as long ago as when Bridesmaids Creek had been settled and named by Eliza Chatham.

Daisy was always beautiful, a stunner, but today she was a vision in a long white gown, her chocolate locks caressed by a veil flowing down her back. She carried a beautiful bouquet of white roses and greenery, and as she came to stand at his side, John caught his breath, falling in love with his wife all over again.

Every day he loved her more. And his babies had

sucked him into their busy worlds, drawing his heart further in with every breath they took.

Their families and friends grouped around to watch the wedding, and John felt the blessing of their presence. Since the big storm, the town had become closer. Working together, they'd rebuilt the Hanging H, and the Haunted H had come back bigger and better than ever along the creek, drawing more visitors than ever. The sheriff's jail had been completed, so "fancy," as Dennis said, that it was more of a hotel than a jail—not that anyone ever spent any time there except to visit him.

Cosette and Phillipe had their original shops back. Phillipe was teaching yoga in his shop, and Cosette taught deportment classes, which she called cotillion, on her side, and reopened the tearoom. Though she'd definitely gotten her matchmaking groove back, she left the matchmaking business up to Daisy, and that gave John plenty of time to watch his wife finagle unsuspecting victims up to the wedding altar. She'd already had two very successful matches so far: the first, her father, Robert, to Betty Harper. John had never seen that one coming, but Daisy wisely had, right about the time she mentioned to her father that Betty's frosted Christmas cookies would be awesome in a mail-order business. His entrepreneurial-minded wife had been right—and the cookies proved an easy way to get Robert and Betty to see each other in a new light, which was something, considering the row they'd once had long ago.

The meatheads—Daisy's gang, John reminded himself—had talked Robert into selling them the Martin place. A ghost-riddled house was the perfect place to set up their cigar bar establishment, they claimed, so Robert sold it to them and stayed on at the Donovan compound. That was fine with John. He was comfortable with lots of people around. His parents had bought Phillipe's house once he moved in with Cosette, and Javier and Jackson were staying at the Hanging H bunkhouse, with Justin finding that they were more than handy and welcome on the team. It was great having his family around, and they spent every second with the babies that they could, which brought them all closer together as a family, something John treasured.

He didn't shed a single tear when the old silver family trailer found its way to a buyer, and rolled off for the last time. For his family, he bought a van, and told Daisy it would never be used for distances greater than visiting family and friends.

Mackenzie and Justin had once thought they'd never need additional hands at the Hanging H, but now business was booming, thanks to the Haunted H going so well. People came from miles around to look at the beautiful Hanging H, which had become something of a monument to the town. The Hawthornes would have been proud and awed by how their daughters had kept the family business going, and supporting Bridesmaids Creek.

Daisy's second match had been to fix Jackson up with one of the local girls, a sweet librarian who was compiling all the family's road adventures into a book and a video. Though he'd never thought their family life was all that interesting, it turned out that people were fascinated by how a family could be raised on the road. There were already offers on the project to publish the book and do something with the video, much to John's astonishment.

But he was more interested in life in Bridesmaids Creek.

John loved taking his babies on jogs, staying in shape the way a SEAL needed to do. He'd developed a stroller that would accommodate three babies safely, and every Saturday, he took them for a run down Best Man's Fork.

It was the most peaceful, serene time of his week, and the babies loved it. To his surprise, his jog had caught on with the town. First his SEAL brothers started out joining him with their broods, and that had made for a nice-sized group. Then the wives decided to join in, and that led to their friends coming out, too. Soon they had so many people coming out on the weekends to run the Best Man's Fork that they decided to turn it into an annual charity marathon, because if there was one thing Bridesmaids Creek did really well, it was take care of each other, and anyone who might have a need of a helping hand. The charity was hugely successful, keeping John busy.

But not too busy to be a great husband and father. He smiled at his darling wife as Sam began the wedding ceremony. Daisy smiled back up at him, her eyes full of love, and John knew he was the luckiest man in the whole world.

"I love you," he whispered.

"Excuse me," Sam said, grinning. "I'm trying to conduct a wedding."

Daisy smiled. "I love you, too, my big hunky husband." She stood on her toes to kiss him, and John breathed her in, held her tight, his heart expanding with joy. He heard Sam laugh and the guests applaud, but he didn't let go of Daisy. *This* was the magic he'd always wanted.

And he was never, ever letting her go.

Because this was Bridesmaids Creek. The magic had always been here, right where he and Daisy had hoped to find it.

They were finally home.

Together, forever.

* * * * *

He stuck his head around the corner of the fasteners
aisle just in time to see a tall brunette stagger into the
revolving seed display. Some of the packets went flying,
but she managed to steady the display before the whole
thing toppled. He took in what probably had been a very
nice silk blouse and tailored trouser suit before she was
drenched in the storm raging outside. The heel on one of
the ridiculously high heels she was wearing had snapped
off, explaining why she was stumbling around.

"Having a bad morning?"

The woman looked up in annoyance, strands of dark,
wet hair falling across her face.

"You could say that. I don't suppose you have a shoe
repair place in this town?" She looked at the bright red
heel in her hand.

Nate shook his head as he approached her. "Nope. But hand it over. I'll see what I can do."

A perfectly shaped brow arched high. "Why? Are you going to cobble them back together with—" she gestured around widely "—maybe some staples or screws?"

"Technically, what you just described is the definition of cobbling, so yeah. I've got some glue that'll do the trick." He met her gaze calmly. "It'd be a lot easier to do if you'd take the shoe off. Unless you also think I'm a blacksmith?"

He was teasing her. Something about this soaking-wet woman still having so much…regal bearing…amused Nate. He wasn't usually a fan of the pearl-clutching country club set who strutted through Gallant Lake on the weekends and referred to his family's hardware store as "adorable." But he couldn't help admiring this woman's ability to hold on to her superiority while looking like she accidentally went to a water park instead of the business meeting she was dressed for. To be honest, he also admired the figure that expensive red suit was clinging to as it dripped water on his floor.

He held out his hand. "I'm Nate Thomas. This is my store."

She let out an irritated sigh. "Brittany Doyle." She slid her long, slender hand into his and gripped with surprising strength. He held it for just a half second longer than necessary before shaking off the odd current of interest she invoked in him.

Don't miss
Changing His Plans *by Jo McNally,*
available September 2020 wherever
Harlequin Special Edition books and ebooks are sold.

Harlequin.com